ACKNOWLEDGMENTS

I WOULD ESPECIALLY like to thank Ilsa Sharp, who took me for a tour of Raffles in her excellent book, *There Is Only One Raffles: The Story of a Grand Hotel.* Also Eric Hansen, who let me walk along on his fascinating jaunt in *Stranger in the Forest: On Foot Across Borneo.*

For the
estimable
Gloria

Providence conducted me along a beach,
in full view of five miles of shipping—
five solid miles of masts and funnels—
to a place called Raffles Hotel where the
food is as excellent as the rooms are bad.

—Rudyard Kipling, 1889

Show me a hero and I will write you a
tragedy.

—F. Scott Fitzgerald

BORNEO

Fall · 1990

MIRI KNOWS NOW the Tantu are going to kill her, take her head. Tugged, pushed, stumbling along, jerked up from falling every few yards she accepts it. Overhead, fragments of moon pierce the roof of rain forest, vertical columns beaming down to illuminate the eyes of giant owlet moths. They flutter up and brush the dust of iridescent wings against her face so that it takes on their eerie glow. Ahead the twist of giant trees are like the illustrations of evil forests in fairy tales. God! This is it! If anyone was on the way to the kingdom of the wicked witch, she was. Why? Two weeks ago she was in downtown, swanky Singapore having lunch, laughing over fashion failures.

They slog to the top of a rise and an amazing sight comes into view. Empty space. Spread before them is a natural clearing in the suffocating weave of jungle, a scoop of a bowl formed by the outcropping of an ancient lava bed: a layering of slick stone. Washed clean by the torrential rains, only stubborn shoots thrust between fissures, a tracing of green lines: cracks in a skull. In the blue light of moon it is a place mysterious and unsettling. As Miri is led up on its hard surface, hearing the slap of prehensile feet, feeling the feral heat off their bodies, she has a terrifying sense of the primeval. Then, her heart skips a beat.

A helicopter!

The outline of fuselage, overhead rotors; silhouette of a pilot at the controls. *Hooray!* It sits backed up to the wet wall of jungle poised to take off. *She was wrong about these two!* How embarrassing: Well, so much for snap judgments about headhunters. They have brought her to some kind of government station. Oh, God! She could be flown out of here and shopping on Tanglin Road in hours! She jumps up and down pointing, "Whirlybird! Whirlybird!" The two Tantu laugh with her, making circular motions with their arms. They follow as she trots across the clearing, puffing up the slope toward the machine. Closer now, and with the angle of the moonlight, she clearly makes out the figure of a pilot in the cockpit, the shape of his helmet. *But . . .* she waves, shouting, "Hey there! Hello!" Silence.

Continuing on, the two behind her, covering their mouths, holding back. Still closer, she slows . . . what? . . . stops dead—stepping back with a little gasp. *There is no head in the helmet:* black empty space. The helicopter is burned out, a shell. The Tantu break up at this, pounding their chalky knees, mouths open in silent laughter. What a joke!

Stunned, Miri squats down with them near the ashes of many dead fires. There are bones scattered everywhere, piles of them: thigh bones, cages of ribs, hundreds, half buried in the ash, picked clean, some polished by the wind and rain, gleaming in the moonlight. The Tantu dig in the plastic sack and take out cans of Yoo-Hoo. They explode when the tabs are pulled and the two are delighted, turning the spray on each other. As they sip, watching Miri, they must know she is thirsty, but it would never occur to them to offer her a drink. Why bother?

Terrified, Miri tries to make sense of it. How could she be here? How did it happen? It doesn't matter. She is. It did. Wait . . . think . . . She can control it, turn things her way. All her life she has dealt with men. It's what she's good at. From the time she was a kid she'd been able to manipulate those who found her attractive—and there were few who didn't. These two are men. Are they different than any others? Do they want the same things? She looks at them, smiles, and they smile back, eyes lost in the dark overhang of eyebrow: faces are shiny black, hair rough and matted with grease, lips narrow slits. One has large ears and both bodies are hard, angular with scarred shins and smooth gray spots at elbows and knees. They look incomplete, she thinks, like a primitive model not quite finished for lack of new parts. They squat with their legs apart and the uncomfortable splints hold the penis in an erect position. This is bizarre, but given man's preoccupation with erections, a straight-forward solution.

Are these two any more repulsive than some of the men she's slept with for fun or profit? It's a draw. The difference is, Miri knows they are going to kill her, she can feel it in the air. She must do something to convince them she is more valuable alive. She starts by reaching up and taking off the scarf tightly binding her hair, shaking it out, fluffing up the great blond mop. They react by stopping mid-sip, cans poised at lips, riveted. Next, the zipper is tugged down on the jumpsuit, past the wet separation of breasts. A line of perspiration follows the curve of belly in the zipper's track, zipped to its farthest travel. A flag of blond hair, a signal.

She stands, shucks off the jumpsuit, kicking it aside and just for an instant poses, legs cocked, hands on hips, the tumble of hair falling forward. Gilda? *Well, what can I do for you now, boys?* But they stare at the hair. Dropping down, she sits facing the two, legs together. They continue to squat where they are, immobile, still holding the cans of soft drink, but not drinking, eyes on that hair. She sees now that the splints are unnecessary. Then very slowly she opens her legs . . .

A flare explodes overhead. A flat slap of reverberation turning everything an astonishing pomegranate shade, showering down burning pieces of magnesium. In its terrible light the trees are distorted and appear to burn. For those caught under it, the sky seems on fire and descending directly on their heads. The Tantu instantly jump up. Dragging Miri along, they run for the edge of the jungle.

"Wait! My clothes . . .!" But they pay no attention, racing across the slick lava bed carrying parangs, blowguns and the plastic sack of soda. "Stop! Please . . ." And she begins to cry, "Bastards! Pygmies! Cocksuckers!" As they reach the edge of trees and change gait, she tears free, stumbles and turns. But before she takes the second step the Tantu with the big ears has her by the hair and yanks her back.

When she continues to fight, he throws the loop of hair over the low branch of a tree in an easy motion and jerks her off her feet. Then, with the other hand, he brings the blade of the parang around.

They arrive two hours later. The Iban stand aside as Arrowjoy and Slinng climb up on the outcropping of lava, boots clacking on its hard surface. "What is this place?" Slinng asks in nearly a whisper. The angle of the moon has shifted and its light leaves part of the clearing in the dark, as though a line has been drawn across the middle, a bowl half filled with shadows.

"I have no idea," Arrowjoy answers, but lowering his own voice.

Look! They both see it at the same time. A helicopter bisected by the shadow line, striped with darkness; paint blistered, plastic parts melted—a tangle of entrails: Wire and cables hang down burned black— still giving off a foul electrical stink. When they reach it they find the figure of a pilot sitting in place, helmet facing forward. The two men stare at it for a long minute. Then, with great reluctance, Arrowjoy reaches through the shattered canopy and gingerly takes the helmet off.

It is propped on a stick inside a moldy jumpsuit filled out with leaves.

Stenciled on the helmet is *Murray* and under it a COD Air Force insignia. Australian. They look at each other, asking the same question: *What happened?* But each man now thinks he knows.

Arrowjoy turns and strides in the half dark among the ashes of old fires, kicking at bones, angry. "Do you know what these are?" Slinng follows, saying nothing. Arrowjoy squats and picks up a large femur. "Male, five-six perhaps, prime of life . . ." Slinng is annoyed. *The bastard thinks he's preparing me.* "There must be hundreds here—old ones from past feasts, others . . ." He picks up a rib cage, bending it before it cracks. ". . . more recent. You will also notice there are no skulls, heads. They took them along as trophies."

The Iban tentatively venture up on the clearing, scouting, and minutes later find Miri's jumpsuit, the scarf that bound her hair. Slinng holds them in his hands but refuses to accept what they could mean.

He looks up at a shout.

Salt stands at the border of jungle with the other Iban. Between them is the twist of a dead tree bleached white in the light of moon. A low branch points like an arm and their eyes are fixed on that branch. When Slinng and Arrowjoy reach them, they see it very clearly; long skeins of tangled hair stuck to the limb with dried blood. In the light they are very blond.

"I'm sorry . . . ," Arrowjoy says quietly. "They've killed her."

Slinng reaches for the hair, taking it gently down, examining it. "Oh, no, I don't think so—where's the body?"

Where? Arrowjoy can't believe the man could be that obtuse.

Slinng keeps shaking his head. "No, I can't accept that—we don't know—maybe she was hurt—a scrape. No. I'm going after her. I won't believe . . . anything until I find her body." And he moves toward the jungle, pushing into its dark pocket.

"*Enough!*" Arrowjoy shouts behind him. Slinng stops. "You damned stubborn one-way bastard! They've chopped her head off! Whacko! Believe it! They're going to eat the rest of her!" His chest is heaving with the exertion of shouting at this altitude, his breathing a pulse between them. He continues, voice lowered, trembling. "We've pushed these people beyond their endurance. Look at their faces! Are you going to ask them to go into the country of the *bali saleng,* those they fear the most? Do you want us all to lose our heads and be eaten like those back there?

No. We've done enough, all we could do. If you want to go—go alone."
And he turns with the Iban back down the mountain.

There are two dreams, one remembered, one imagined.

In the first a man paddles up a dark river, a tunnel of jungle so remote
that even the birds are silent. He bends to his effort, squat and brown-
colored with the blended blue of many tattoos: a fierce Tantu, one of the
last of the working headhunters, the original of the Wild Men of Borneo.

Fighting the force of current, bank and river blur by—then he sees
something that so frightens him, he drops the paddle.

Passing the longboat is a body. It sweeps gracefully downstream on its
back near the surface, clearly seen as through a transparent veil. The
body is white, very beautiful and without a head. It passes in a serpentine
movement, disappearing in the roil of water.

When he turns back, the head speaks to him from the bow of the
longboat. Mounds of yellow hair frame it and green eyes look into his as
the red mouth says, *"I was a descendant of the White Raj and you killed me."*

Lawrence Slinng wakes from the dream and realizes *he* was the pad-
dler, the accused. Pushing up from his wet sleeping mat, he crosses the
longhouse and, stepping over Iban and dogs, goes down the pole ladder.
The smell is damp—rotting vegetation, fecund. He hears the slap and
snort of pigs nosing out droppings under the floor. Cooking fires,
banked and gray, send a wisp of smoke on the breeze. He follows this
track toward the river, bare feet imprinting on the sandy clearing. There
at the edge of treeline is the shine of river, current whipping past, eddies
white-tufted, the race to the sea.

Always the soothing sea. Growing up on an island, Singapore, trained
up on another, Britain, he has been cradled by its movement. Now, eyes
following the rush of river, he tries to push Miri and the dream out of
his head but instead another enters, the beginning.

Slinng sees them, two young people checking in the great hotel and
shown to a room high in its tower. Alone, they embrace with a fervor
that carries them to bed. Later, they lie back, telling each other the things
they want to hear, making promises. The girl cries softly, he soothes her,
and they make love, this time slowly and with detail.

In the morning they order breakfast in bed and scribble postcards and one long letter to their families. Then, dressing carefully in expensive clothes bought just for this occasion, the two go out on the balcony. The view is marvelous, the weather balmy, wind at this height bringing a caress. They mount the railing and, without looking at each other, jump, hand in hand.

SINGAPORE

Summer · 1990

2

BLOWING IN off the South China Sea, the wind sends out a last gasp, a pitiful puff that climbs the wall of summer heat rising from the city. Air-conditioning hum is audible miles at sea, and along the coast where chehai-ch'uan ice junks once brought the only relief there is a crosshatching of masts: pleasure boats squeezed into miles of artificial coves, squared off and called, in trendy English, Marina Bay. The shore edge is built up, dumped, grassed over and looped with parkways as if it were Long Island or Los Angeles, and the traffic is nearly as daunting. The crash of metal and howl of siren are heard where once only the call of monkey and parrot competed. Each night the police make a harvest of the day's auto carcasses.

The city itself rises in a stack of towers, slick new shapes, squares and angles—the sharp edge of the future. In the morning sun they shine with modern promise. Approaching the shimmering city from the perspective of the sea, one can imagine it as a barge, towed from the West to be anchored at the entrance of the East.

Closer there are fan-shaped traveler's palms and through heat waves the Padang, a green sward fronting yesterday's colonial buildings. But the thrust of poured concrete towers and bronze windows shoulder up and stand facing today—feet planted on bulldozed Malay kampongs. As the sun shifts, their windows wink at the circle of jets stacked up over Changi Airport, backsides presented to Keppel Harbor and the ancient *entrepôts* that made it a great port.

"There they are," he said, giggling and sucking his teeth.

This particularly annoyed Webbshaw but he took the glasses and saw what he meant. A small motor sailer with a nasty list and only a ragged spinnaker presented. On deck were three women, one on the helm black as a yard up the chimney and the others burned to a crisp by the sun and wearing little if anything.

They had received a signal from an RSN Orion on an overflight to Bintan and detoured from North Pier in the customs launch. Actually his job as senior in the Customs Harbour Division did not require him to bounce about the harbor with these nitwits but he liked to show the flag of his skin. Being the only remaining white man in the service, he was nearly ready to retire from the Singapore service and leave it to his little brown brothers.

As usual Keppel Harbor was chock-a-block with shipping. Every possible kind of vessel was in the roads with the pilot boats running like taxis. It was one of the largest shipping ports in the world, some two hundred new arrivals a day, including the wreck they were about to intercept. Chang throttled down and they came abeam as the deck men gawked. It was a British motor sailer built in the way of 50-50's: half sail and half power. But there was no power now and very little sail. The deckhouse shelter had been carried away along with a good deal of the rest of her.

Keeled over to the deck line on the port side, she was shipping water even in the calm sea. Forward, two young women, bare feet braced against the gunwale, worked a hand pump, arms moving like metronomes. A line snaked below deck and another discharged a small stream of water over the side. Their expressions were stony with exhaustion while the black girl at the helm stared straight ahead ignoring the customs launch.

Webbshaw felt foolish even having to ask, but he shouted over, "May we assist you?"

"Fuck off," the black answered in a hoarse voice.

He wasn't sure he had heard her right and in any case the question was rhetorical. Hooks went out and he jumped aboard with the easy grace of a small-boat man.

"Permission to come aboard." The women at the pump looked up and he was rather surprised to see they were not particularly attractive: one with an aggressive chin, the other too thin for his taste. Both had been fried in the sun and were smeared with grease. He nodded and continued on, adjusting to the steep angle of the deck and catching hold of the stub of deckhouse shelter. There was no sign of a radio or even minimal electronic navigation devices. Approaching the woman on the helm at this range, he was knocked back by the power of her—blue-black with wild electric hair that could never be untangled short of sheep shears. She wore, or almost wore, a string bikini.

"With your permission we'll put a line aboard and give you a tow." He tried a smile.

"Not bloody likely."

"Madam . . ."

"Do you think we sailed this thing four thousand miles to be towed the last five?"

"Are you in command here?"

She looked at him for the first time, nodding her head toward an open hatch leading below. The hose from the pump showed the way. "Down there."

He turned, got a grip on the transom and went down several steps of a ladder to a dim cabin. The foul smell hit him at once and he paused on the lower rungs adjusting to the light. Below showed a good two feet of seawater sloshing about, carrying with it cabin trash. There was a single oil lamp (unlit), all very primitive. To his left a narrow bunk and on it a man: filthy with a tangled beard and long hair. From Webbshaw's position behind him it was not possible to see his face, turned as it was to the bulkhead. His left leg was splinted straight out with an aluminum tube and wrapped with dirty bandages. He wore only cutoff shorts pulled in with a heavy belt and hung with a seaman's knife.

"Sir!" But there was no response. He was unconscious or perhaps even dead. Webbshaw was not going to step off into that putrid water. Stretching forward, he leaned in as far as he could. "Sir!" The face was perfectly still and he noticed a pale blue star tattooed on his left ear. Hanging on to the ladder rung with one hand, he reached out with his other hand and felt for a pulse in the fellow's neck. He was still alive.

The whole messy business left him angry and, going topside, he was short with the black. "What happened?"

"He broke his leg."

"I can see that. How?"

"A storm two days ago. A bloody big one. He hasn't been good for anything since. We've had to take all the watches."

"Now you're going to take a line on for a tow," Webbshaw said, and meant it. No more nonsense.

An ambulance was waiting at Sheers Wharf and the injured man was taken off to the Keppel Road Hospital. Webbshaw interviewed the women in his office at Maritime Customs. The three sat there like bizarre bathers, clutching the chair arms, still rolling with the movement of the sea. They were fit after their experience and all possessed proper papers.

The man (they said), was the boat's owner and captain. They had answered his ad in the London *Daily Telegraph* asking for "Adventurous young women to share expenses and crew on a glorious voyage to the Far East." After a shakedown week crewing The Solent they set off. He was an excellent seaman, a licensed master they thought.

Webbshaw found that hard to believe and shook his head at the gullibility of young females. They had been unable to discover any papers or the ship's log, although the women remembered seeing him write in one. "Well, never mind," he said "he's not going anywhere," and advised them to find proper clothing. Despite popular fiction, Singapore was a very moral place.

The emergency room at Keppel Road Hospital was jammed as usual with motorbike accidents and tourist complaints, and the seaman's trolley was parked in the corridor. Nurse Alice Changi checked his vital signs and found them strong. He had gained consciousness and managed a weak smile. Smiling back, she told him to be patient, they would be with him in a minute. When she returned an hour later he was gone.

3

OVER THE ELGIN BRIDGE that crosses the Singapore River the road turns to the left and at the corner of Philip Street is another of the large luxury apartment houses that define the skyline. This one rises a slick monolith, showing bright cookie-cutter grilles of windows that reflect the stab of sunlight downward, causing those below to avoid looking up. On the next corner is the Ue Hai Qing Temple, all green roof tile and seasoned teak, exuding an aura of what Singapore must have been like once. Beyond are the convoluted beginnings of Chinatown.

On the fifteenth floor of the apartment building, Mr. A. L. Ling does his exercises. Standing over a painter's table he flashes the bold strokes of calligraphy across the paper, brush dipping to connect the ideographs in a running style, as if the hand were walking fast while writing. Like the ballet or power lifting it's a thing that must be practiced each day. Mr. Ling is that individual rare even among the *literati:* the artist-connoisseur who was a poet with probably the finest private collection of Chinese paintings anywhere. But he lives modestly enough, his only vanity invested in the conceit that he is a legitimate descendant of a lineage that had its feet planted in the Sung dynasty eight hundred years ago. His way, he likes to think, was inspired by the high art of the Tang masters of the eighth century. He is an old man now and lives only for great expectation—the discovery of rare work.

The doorman buzzed and announced Captain W. Lawrence Slinng. There was a moment's hesitation and then Mr. Ling remembered a letter he'd received some months earlier. He asked that Captain Slinng be shown up and, laying aside his brush, went into the foyer of the apartment to receive him. As usual he wore a long, black traditional Chinese gown. His white hair provided a nice contrast, capping a small face, with the shine of button eyes behind tinted glasses.

Captain Slinng proved to be impeccably turned out, silk suit and carrying a grade of Panama Mr. Ling hadn't seen in years. His greeting was fluent Chinese and they talked for a minute of mutual contacts at Sotheby's and Burlington House. His was a strong face that had been shoved against the elements: a seaman no doubt. The eyes bothered him, not that pale blue of so many Anglo-Saxons—windowpanes showing nothing—but a black that snapped with wit and challenge, suggesting that a game was in progress—what game?

Mr. Ling bowed him into the studio and the Captain commented knowledgeably on the large Ming painting, using the Chinese word *wei-tao,* meaning flavor. Mr. Ling liked that. Besides his painting table and brushes, the room contained Tang ceramics, bronze and stone figures, and on the opposite wall, a bold Sephardic script. Mr. Ling was caught up not only in Chinese calligraphy but in medieval Hebrew and Jacobite ideographs as well. At last they switched to English and business began.

"I've carried these out from Britain," Captain Slinng said, indicating a stout aluminum tube. "I didn't want them drawered in a museum and I was certainly not going to put them on the block for some speculator. I considered who would want to live with them, pull them on, so to speak. You were my first choice." Another nice smile. Mr. Ling bowed and didn't believe a word of it. The tube was uncapped and a thick roll of silk scrolls drawn out and laid on the long table. The Captain bowed. "Please."

Taking a forked wand, Mr. Ling gently lifted the silk scroll to suspend it from special wall hooks where it might be viewed from the correct perspective. Then, stepping back, he entered "landscapes of the mind." He was stunned, recognizing at once the brush work of the elusive Ch'ü Ting, a pupil of Yen Wen-kuei in the early Sung dynasty. Only one painting was extant, none others thought to exist. A sepia landscape unfolded: riverbank, cascades of white water like the clutch of fingers, dark swirls of rocks and a pavilion on stork legs, the single figure of a man in profile, watching. At the left was a poem and the avatar's seal. The name of the painting was *Summer Waiting*.

He sighed. "If the brush work is the song, then we are presented with great music." A favorite simile.

"Ch'ü Ting."

"Remarkable." Mr. Ling had of course considered forgery. The world of Chinese painting was full of it. Authentication and attribution were tricky. The late Chang Ta-ch'ien, another great artist and twentieth-century *literatus*, was also a notorious forger and had painted in this style. But he knew better, because he knew where these missing paintings came from: the Imperial Palace Collection. In 1926, Ts'ai Yuan-p'ei, chancellor of Peking University and then chairman of the Imperial Palace Museum, had been his mentor. Ling had helped inventory the collection. In the late thirties, when Generalissimo Chiang Kai-shek "evacuated" the Palace Museum, his crony Curio Chang was put in charge of the move. Curio was a banker, stockbroker and, yes, an international dealer in rare Chinese antiquities. For twenty years his agents hauled the art works around the Chinese countryside in thousands of crates to keep them out of the hands of the Japanese, then the Communists—or so they said. When the war was over no one knew what was missing. Ling knew. A lot. Curio Chang took himself to Europe and opened galleries in Paris, London and Geneva. He died in New York on September 3, 1950, the grand old crook of Chinese art.

"How many are there?"

"Five scrolls in all."

"That many." What were they worth? One million? Two? Nothing? The minute they became public they would be claimed by the Chinese Communists. The scrolls had surfaced briefly in Hong Kong in the fifties, then once again vanished. They were elusive, priceless and stolen. "These are works to be enjoyed in private," Mr. Ling said, sighing again. "There are some things spoiled by sharing."

"My thought exactly."

In the end he paid a little over a hundred thousand pounds. It was an investment for his old age—a travel ticket. He would sit on the riverbanks and mountains of his precious landscapes and travel toward a horizon of brush strokes . . . ah . . .

There was one black cloud on that horizon. During the negotiation he had identified the seller, had actually known his father and—worse—thought he now knew what the game was.

It was very sentimental and silly. In the end, of course, they all tumbled in bed.

It began in a private dining room at the Golden Million. The sailors sat at a table with Daphne at the head, her dreadlocks clipped to a half inch and wearing a blond "Princess Di" wig. Her dress was paper-on-the-wall Lurex cut to expose cleavage that had the appearance of hammered steel. The other two, Viv and Beth, were done up in eyelid sparkle, lip gloss and dangle earrings that gave off hundred-watt blinks. Three separate perfumes were locked in combat and conversation overlapped like bird caws in a pet store.

"You two bitches look like a road company of the 'Tart's Review,' " Daphne said, laughing and blowing her champagne out in a spray.

"Well, you can be the pimp," Viv answered. "You got the dick for it," and they all burst into laughter, scaring the Malay waiter who scampered to cover, goosed by Daphne.

"Gotcha!"

Slinng came in carrying more champagne. He had insisted on supervising the preparation of "Nonya" cuisine, a specialty of the Peranakans: half Straits-born and half Malay. "You are going to love the poh piah."

"I'm going to love this," Daphne said, grabbing his crotch.

"A little bit to the left," he instructed, pouring the champagne.

"Horny bitch," Viv said, "you'd grope a baboon."

"Show me a baboon and I'll show you a grope."

"Rotten."

"I've been on that fucking boat for six weeks."

"There is nothing worse than a sex-crazed, drunken sailor on leave."

"I'll drink to that."

"All right." He stood and offered a toast. "Here's to the gallant sailors of the *Slippery Roger.*"

"Hear! Hear!"

"A dreadful little boat."

"Poor thing. It is true we abused her."

"Gave her bottom for the cause."

"Like Princess Di here."

"How'd you like to kiss mine, mate?"

"Can I find a clean spot, do you think?"

Slinng rattled his glass. "Now for the shares." Standing and waving envelopes. "Fitting reward for those stout things who brought us safely across the bounding main."

"Bloody right!"

He walked around the table laying a fat envelope at each place, leaning over to kiss each sailor. "Viv, there was nobody more intrepid at trim."

"Shit, I'm going to cry."

"Beth, you made that pump sing."

"Yours, too, I hope." She blinked back a tear.

"And Daphne, what would we have done without you on the helm?"

"Probably got here two weeks earlier," Viv said, but it was in good fun and she was quicker than the shrimp roll that sang past her head.

The eating went on, fiery prata dishes, rojak mee goreng—thick yellow noodles fried with bean curd, potato, egg and pea. And drinking, knocking back the champagne, then stingers, screaming with laughter and pounding the table until glasses and bottles hopped. The management was intimidated. A young assistant manager who had gone in to ask politely if the broken glass could be swept up had the zipper jerked down on his fly and retreated in disarray.

At last, near dawn they rolled out of the room and went through the restaurant bar, arm in arm. A sleek Nissan dealer sat with a paid escort in a kimono, and as the sailors came past, he whispered something in his companion's ear and they both laughed. Daphne hit him up alongside the ear, knocking him off the stool, and then punched the escort in her obi. Viv and Beth broke the necks off beer bottles as they'd seen barroom combatants do in films and prepared to take on all comers.

Slinng managed to drag them outside and flag down a cab before the police arrived. They piled in and Daphne immediately climbed aboard his lap and stuck her tongue in his ear while the others laid on hands. The driver, watching in the rearview mirror, went up on the sidewalk and ran over a chestnut seller's foot, regaining the street only when Slinng kicked the back of his seat, knocking off his porkpie hat.

At the hotel they staggered through the lobby singing "Rule Britannia" and once in the empty elevator began shucking their clothes. Getting off at the tenth floor, they ran up the hall naked, yodeling Tarzan yells, and burst into their room, dived on the giant bed.

Nobody would remember later who did what to who. There was a tangle of limbs in a variety of shades, some hairy, some not, a foot in the eye, an elbow in the ribs: Daphne on top at one point, posting English style; convoluted positions, wet sounds, smacking of flesh and finally utter exhaustion, a dropping off until only the indefatigable Daphne was left, nursing, she thought, a wet noodle.

"Say that last bit again," Swee asked.

"A tattooed star, sir." It was in the customs report on the missing seaman.

Inspector Swee thought about it. "I've seen that description before." The Singapore police force was the very model of modernity. Six thousand regulars and nine thousand of the Special Constabulary for 210 square miles of City State island. And thanks to the paternal grip of the People's Action Party on its inhabitants (led by Prime Minister Lee Kuan Yew) there was a paucity of decent crime, outside the triads, of course.

A tattooed star. "Get me the *R*'s." Swee was an anomaly, a native-born Malaysian from the colonial period who had risen to head his department after Singapore became an independent state in 1965. If the British had remained in control he would still be a sergeant today. At sixty, he had survived the move from the old buildings on St. Andrew's Road opposite the Padang to glass-curtain walls and interfacing computers.

His assistant returned with a folder from the stack of cardboard transfer files behind his desk. These were a department joke, but the Inspector would not let go of them. He found the newspaper clipping under RAFFLES.

Mr. Neville L. Slinng, manager of the famous Raffles Hotel from 1940 to 1967 and since retired, died at that hotel on the 25th of this past month.

Inspector Swee knew both Neville and his son. "Get me the S's." They were produced:

SLINNG, W.L. (b. April 10, 1949—Republic of Singapore) Ship's Master, *Singapore Exile* (27 tons deadweight). Common cargo carrier, *Far East.* West Wind Ltd.

And there it was in part of the description:

. . . Iden. Marks as follows: *five-pointed star tattooed left earlobe.* 6-inch scar r. shoulder, vert. 10-inch scar r. leg (com. frac.), ice pick perf. right lower abdom. shotgun pellets upper chest, gaff indent left palm, missing l. small toe, burn inside right arm, semicircular (human) teeth marks l. buttock.

This was part of ASEAN, an Asian Interpol report. A cargo hauler had been intercepted by a Sri Lanka corvette on the night of 2/7/86 running guns to rebels in the Palk Strait. The ship had been damaged but escaped and was identified as the *Singapore Exile.* In a subsequent action, the captain, W. Lawrence Slinng, was sentenced in absentia. The name of the cargo company told the story: West Wind Ltd. This was a subsidiary of the infamous Ah Kong triad–United Bamboo—with roots in Singapore and Hong Kong.

As one of the nation members of ASEAN, it was Inspector Swee's obligation to report back any information on listed fugitives. Well, he knew exactly where he could find him. Black sheep returned.

4

THEIR PLANE was to leave late afternoon, but even then it was a struggle to batter them into shape: steamy showers, face slaps; half cock-eyed, thick tongues, breath like fermented palm wine. But Slinng was an old hand at sailor-town liberties and straightened them out with stiff jolts of Fernet-Branca, a bitter stimulant that contained, among other things, bryonia, gentian, cinehona, galangal, myrrh and 39 percent alcohol by volume.

Dressed, they now appeared as what they were: secretaries and a travel agent. "God," Viv said, "back to the computers." And it was true.

He kissed them all at the airport, tenderly this time, and there were more tears and reluctant farewells. Then, with last good-bye waves, he got in the cab and gave the address.

As you come up Beach Road it is impossible to see because of the skyline. Then, a glimpse through palm rows; the solid shape of a white building: three stories and angled toward the roadstead, squatted down for the correct nineteenth-century view. A survivor. Next to it a vast hotel-shop-office complex, a block of seventy-two-story towers and connecting arcades: architecture that has been touched by the wand of Mr. I. M. Pei and has the nerve to call itself "Raffles City." Shame. But in the afternoon light it is the small building that throws the larger shadow. Once the bay was at its front door and the jungle crowded in on verandahs. The last tiger in Singapore was shot under one of its pool tables and Kipling, Maugham and Coward sat in the palm court sipping stenghas and chatting up its fabulous guests. It is a place that is immediately connected with Singapore and "Britishness," the very symbol of the old Raj—a monument to a vanished way of life: expected luxury, high-calorie cuisine and fawning service, by God, the one, original Raffles.

It hits him as childhood memories confront reality: seeming smaller, angles and perspective wrong, things altered, missing, the restoration as disturbing as a familiar face lifted.

He pays the cab and threads through somnolent trishaw drivers and their bicycle mounts, drawn up to milk the lucrative tourist pitch outside the Beach Road entrance. Smoking, sucking in the last millimeter of butt, eyes flat, not giving an inch: arrogant, peddling union men: fuck-you transportation. Once, the front of the building was on the opposite side, but the Japanese had changed the main entrance during the occupation and it remained so—like Pearl Harbor and the notorious Changi prison camp, yesterday's history.

The entrance is now in one of the corner towers carried out in the not-quite-French-Renaissance style, framed by trademark traveler's palms and a brief curly lawn.

An old doorman in solar topee and pukka sahib coat salutes and reaches for the door, smiling but detached.

"Lee?"

He pauses, expression shifting, puzzled, then, "Who knows me?"

"Lawrence Slinng—Neville's son."

"God damn me! It *is* you! The kid who sawed old Raffles' head off!" They shake in a seesaw of motion and Lee shoves the door open, still holding his hand, propelling him along, calling to another old bellman and startling a young desk clerk. "Look who I've got! A Colonel! Oh, I cannot believe it, no! That damn bad kid!"

The news goes up the tiled lobby, is relayed to the open second and third corridors and minutes later the staff slips down and gathers around him, elderly waiters and maids, Hainan Chinese whose families have worked at Raffles forever, many of them for his father. Among these old ladies are former nannies, a wet nurse. They had raised him. Now they shyly touch his arm and admire his stretching out as they call it, saying he has grown up so handsome, yes, such a blondie with wavy hair and a profile like Prince Charley on the stamps. They know quality and are impressed by the clothes, the cordovan shoes with black cherry polish. They tell each other that he had been a crazy little boy, walking the third-floor roof railings at midnight and yes, putting shit in the shoe of a guest who insulted one of the maids. They shriek at this, cutting their eyes over to see who he favors. They notice the star tattooed on his ear but frown and say nothing, sure it means a bad thing.

For Slinng old faces are overlaid with the young he remembers and there is the shock of *déjà vu*—Raffles has always had an eerie sense of time standing still. If you blinked it was 1960 or even 1940. Twenty years ago he had grown up playing in these halls and courtyards and early on could pick through Malay, Mandarin and Tamil. The staff was his real family and their children his companions. Together they had explored the great hotel, spent their days and secret nights shadowing the guests, watching them dance, make love—learned the amazing anatomical connection called sex—ran their errands, changing money, bringing back liquor and passing them on to other shadowy places who could supply girls and drugs. All this before he was ten. A fast-talking kid con man.

Roberto Triestino came out of his cluttered office attracted by the excitement. He was the fourth Italian manager at Raffles, a busy man with a deceptive easy way, coatless, expansive, possessing a personal style that allowed him to double at public relations. "Larry!" They embraced in a rapid exchange of back slaps and extravagant hand gestures, swerving into Singlish. "You will stay with us of course!"

"I don't think that's wise for either of us, Roberto."

"You are family." He lowered his voice. "Take your father's old rooms—please—it's the least I can do for him. And don't worry, there will be complete security."

They walked through the Tiffin Room, busy now with tourists drilled in accelerated dining. The rattle of dishes and conversation rose in the three-story central airwell supported by elegant columns and squared by balcony railings of open corridors. Floors were paved in geometric tiles that fooled the eye and seemed to march on toward infinity. Far above, the glass roof let in filtered lights; below, ceiling fans hummed.

"I put in the ceiling fans," Roberto explained. "People don't think it's the Far East without them, and although we have air-conditioning we really don't need it, but nobody will believe that."

Raffles had been renovated in 1899 to combat heat and tropical glare. The architects, Swan and Maclaren, cooled it with space, thick walls and punkah wallahs. These individuals once sat in the public rooms and verandahs with a cord tied to a toe, working a white sheet attached to the ceiling.

The hotel was the first in Singapore to be lit entirely by electricity—which was strenuously resisted by the entrenched colonials. A columnist in the *Straits Times* wrote for the conservative view: ". . . *electric light is still the toy of civilization. What do we want with toys? Did we sail through the gate of Suez bent on pleasure? Did we come to Asia to spend our time in clamouring for a miserable mimicry of metropolitan luxury?*"

It was an odd reversal: The Sarkie brothers, who had built the hotel, were regarded as go-ahead, forward-looking businessmen who pushed Raffles into the twentieth century. Now, a hundred years later, the current management was just as aggressively pushing it back into the nineteenth. The only thing that had saved it from the developers was this retreat into the past.

"We have ballroom dancing again on weekends and violins in the Palm Court—oh, and caged songbirds for breakfast. Guests are crazy for anything old." They stopped at the entrance of the Long Bar. It had been redone in decorator colonial. "Yes, I know, it was never really like this—but guests would be disappointed if they saw the real thing. I've got pictures of it years ago—looking like a *wagon-lit* stop on a provincial rail line. Everyone's idea of Raffles and Singapore comes from the films."

Slinng recognized the barman.

The Ngiam family had been behind Raffles' bar from the beginning, tending the most famous watering hole in the Orient, passing it down the generations. Only the Slinngs preceded them at the hotel, and it had been Ngiam Tong Boon, the first barman, who concocted the famous drink in their honor in 1915. It had originally been called after them: Singapore Slinng. But over the years one "n" had been worn away by sloppy spelling, finally disappearing altogether, much to his father's relief; he said he hated the vulgar connection. Now one thousand of the cocktails were served each day and in 1977 a record had been set by five drinkers who poured down 131 within two hours.

Slinng watched his old friend at the bar and tried to make a connection. Once they had been close, hotel kids moving beyond Raffles to the streets and alleys of the city. It was a time of political foment when the Malay word "merderka"—freedom—was on the wind. They had formed the "Raff Gang" and joined the agitators—adolescents, experts at rock throwing and window breaking, dirtying the town with graffiti, accelerating to sabotage, then committing the act that forever changed his life, got him arrested and exiled.

When the barman raised his eyes Slinng smiled at him, but there was no response. What had once been a bond now separated them. Moving from the violent politics of the street to support of Prime Minister Lee Kuan Yew and "Twenty-five Years of Nation-Building," his old friend could no longer afford troublemakers.

Roberto led on to the main stairway, Tigran Sarkie's pride, centered between private dining rooms. It swept up to the floors above in a show of rubbed wood and handsome moldings. At the bottom, flanking newel posts provided plinths for bronze statues. He caressed the bronzes as they passed. "These were stolen during the war, and then returned mysteriously." As they climbed Roberto ran his hand along the buffed railing reciting Raffles history, legends Slinng had heard from his father, passed down to each manager, told in the first person as if it happened in their time: talking of the hotel as if it were a respected if slightly raffish relative, someone who had gone on to become famous; a living thing with a sense of humor and a soul.

They arrived at the top floor and followed tile patterns to the heavily varnished door of a corner suite. Roberto pressed the key in his hand. "Please—stay as long as you want."

"Roberto, this could be difficult for you . . ."

Roberto held his finger to his lips. Then his eyes dropped, finding the next speech difficult. "We . . . were all desperately shocked at your father's death . . . It was . . . so hard—and to have it happen here . . ." Slinng could see there were tears in his eyes, as if somehow it was his fault—no, *he's offering condolences from the hotel, Raffles is speaking.* He wiped his eyes, switching to the living. "I hope your mother is well?"

"Yes . . . yes, living in Hong Kong—remarried."

"That's right, to a scholar, I believe."

"Dr. A. N. Kung, curator of the Kuchin Yao Library."

"Right, well, I'll be on my way." Brightening, he added "We'll have dinner one night." He turned. "Oh, there are two of your father's trunks stored here—shall I have them brought up?"

Slinng was prepared to say no, but instead agreed. "Yes, thank you, Roberto—for everything." He gave that particular Italian shrug and was gone when it hit Slinng that like everything else connected with Raffles, he and his father had been collected—added into the legends of the hotel.

He paused in front of the door, then unlocked it carefully, handling the familiar shape of the knob. He felt poised on the threshold of a time machine, the Twilight Zone. He crossed over.

Does time stand still? Is it the same?

No.

Wall-to-wall carpet, a serpentine sectional couch in metallic thread, oversized porcelain lamps, hotel art. Pastel blurs. Nothing is the same. *Did he really expect it to be?* Wait . . . a tall antique desk is familiar. He remembers the long doors and above, a broken pediment holding carved urns, a shell cut in the spandrel. His father had always kept it locked. Inaccessible. As a child he believed it filled with family treasure, secret things. He finds the brass key in the lock and opens it. A Sony television set presents itself rooming with a VCR and music center. Of course.

The view is the same, although framed with the wrong drapes. Still, the original half shutters are on the outside of balcony doors and through their slats the sun contrives to set at this very moment, as though brought on stage for dramatic effect. It drops rapidly in those latitudes and he is crossed with shadows from the slats, the room tinted an unreal bloom of pink.

He turns toward the bedroom, relieved that everything so far *has* changed. Thank God. Ghosts exorcised by new decorating. Opening the door, he stops cold, facing the same bed *they* slept in. His stomach drops. There is the carved headboard: a flight of cranes done in the Chinese way picked out in mother-of-pearl, the lap of scalloped waves against pillow tops. He has lain on that bed, head back, eyes upside down, and those birds have flown for him, lifted off. Soared. He can see himself on the rare mornings his mother allowed him to share breakfast; can hear her read aloud from the *Straits* social page, her laugh and bite of wit . . . and what else? *The sound of water for his father's bath running.* He looks to the left, toward the closed bathroom door, hearing it now drawn by Benny Chin, his father's personal servant. Then sees the old man himself, robed, toweled, bath cap in place, striding by, followed by Benny, back-scrubber, giggler. Hears his mother say to be sure and wash possible. Both laughing at a joke he never understood.

Is the water running? He moves toward the closed bathroom door, twists the knob, reaches in, switches on the light.

Nothing here has changed. Glazed wall tile in black and white running bond; marble-top pedestal sink, foot bath, ornate turns of chrome pipe. And the tub—a boat, huge, putting down lion's-claw feet for the ages. At the head a stand of massive controls, capped by fat porcelain handles, the long curve of a poised tap. Finally a soap dish punched out in a fleur-de-lis pattern. And at the very top, the bud of knob. At its twist the tub would empty. *Why didn't he use it?* He steps over, resting his hand on the tub's smooth rim. As a child he could barely see over the top.

How many gallons of scalding water would it hold? How long did it take to fill? *How long did he take to die?* Was he held down by a party or parties unknown? Or . . . and this takes his breath away, causes him to actually burst out laughing, sending a boom of echo along the tile.

Had the hotel taken its own revenge? After all, his father had once grievously wounded it—turned it over to the Japanese, made it a collaborator.

Had Raffles killed him?

5

L AWRENCE SLINNG opens the window of his rooms facing the
Strait. It is morning and the sun rising from the East hits him square on.
He has survived the night in his father's bed. The mother-of-pearl cranes
did not fly, the carved waves remained calm, and no ghost lay next to
him to whisper in his ear. Still, he feels enfolded, drawn into the old
man's life, remembering his nearly unintelligible honk of a British accent
as he carried the banner of colonialism forward into the twentieth century. There is an annoying continuity about it—all those generations of
Slinngs stretching back into Singapore's history—and here he is, returned after swearing never to set foot in the damn place again.

He steps out onto the narrow balcony on this third, top, floor directly
above the "R" in the Raffles sign. Below, the sound of traffic comes up
followed by its exhalation: the sweet smell of Singapore success. His view
dead ahead is past the white spike of War Memorial (which war?) and
beyond the Nicoll Highway and the East Coast Parkway: two multilane
blacktops humming now with morning commuter traffic (Radio SING
counting down the Asiatic Top Ten and current weather report: continuing hot). Looking past still another marina, the Strait can be seen
shimmering through a thicket of small boat masts. It's hard to grasp that
once the sea actually lapped at Raffles' front door.

To his right is the uncomfortable pile of its namesake, Raffles City—
two circular towers of hotels that contrive to resemble seventy-two stories
of unwashed saucers and a third, even taller office complex angled to
examine the padang of the old Singapore Recreation Club. With its
pleasant cricket field and connection to Merlion Park, it provides the
only green relief in the pour of concrete.

As he turns toward the towers, eyes squinting against glare, there is
a flash of color against the neutral gray, a streak dropping past windows.
He sees them very clearly, two young people jumping hand in hand. For
that nanosecond they stare across at him and he believes he can read
their expressions; mouths framed to ask one last question, one he can't

conceive—and it occurs to him his face is the last they will ever see. They fall in perfect order, hair streaming, the flutter of a bright cheongsam, toes pointed toward the ground. Then they are gone, disappearing behind the hotel, an awful thud—as their bodies hit a sightseeing bus on Bras Basah Road. The bus continues on for a few yards, its garbled tour message sputtering then squelched by the screams of passengers.

When he pushed out Raffles' entrance on Bras Basah Road, Slinng found the doorman, another Chinese "uncle," comforting the tour bus passengers. They had disembarked and stood huddled on the sidewalk.

"Most disgraceful! Such very bad manners for young people to risk lives of others and dent bus! There are better places for these things!"

Slinng wondered where. Apparently, for these two at least, the new towers of Singapore had provided a launching place into the next world. It would have been a difficult trick to manage from a palm tree.

"Why would they do it?" the tourists wanted to know, shaken, their day spoiled; no one had even snapped a picture.

The doorman shrugged. "No apartment space, family disapproves, lovers can't get married—common thing." His face brightened with a joke. "Then, too, falling is to be expected in a place of tall buildings, heh, heh, heh!" They didn't get it.

The bus had stalled in the middle of the road with traffic backed up and bleating. The constabulary was yet to arrive, the whooping wail of siren approaching. Meanwhile a plague of motorbikes snaked through every opening, office boys and secretaries, helmeted, double-up, using feet to push off between blocked cars, skinny legs and trendy shoes. A great deal of shouting went on about these footprints from drivers and when one of the bikes detoured up on the sidewalk in front of Raffles, his genial doorman "uncle" aimed a kick at it that kissed the taillight. A crowd had gathered and tourists and locals discussed the event, pointing out the bodies of the jumpers embedded in the top of the tour bus, legs protruding, a high heel still in place on a bent foot.

Slinng looked at his watch and, dodging traffic, started across the street when a remarkable motorcar appeared. A Van Den Plas Princess. Without the need of its horn it nosed ahead as lesser vehicles gave way. Big, in a country where the meanest small car cost $20,000 and a medium-size Mercedes went for $190,000, it was treated with respect. An elegant long-wheelbase limo done in the marvelous British razor-edge style last seen in the fifties. It stopped opposite the tour bus, and from his position he paused and watched.

A mirrored window winds silently down and an extraordinary face appears. A young woman so fair she seems perhaps albino. But no, there are shadowed blue eyes and a hint of pale amber to the hair. It is a small face, with arresting features: expression at once intelligent and witty. But it is the hair that is astounding, a great tumble of natural curls lit now by the morning sun and luminous—disquieting. Placed as it is against the dark interior of the car, the head appears disembodied.

For just a minute Slinng believes she is looking at him and starts to smile, but she is staring past into the side windows of the bus. He turns and is sorry. The head of the woman jumper has punched its way through the top and her eyes, upside down, stare back.

When he turns to the car, the window is rising and he catches the image of a man behind the beautiful girl. He is laughing, saying something. But it is the face that stops Slinng, breath catchingly ugly. She laughs and leans forward to kiss a nose as erose as a cauliflower. Then the arc of the window completes and he is left to stare at his own reflection in the mirrored window as the great, smooth car continues, sliding by.

At Lloyd's Singapore, Colonel Pynge-Gilbert was listed as senior underwriter. Arranged around him were dozens of lesser "names" as they were called: brokers, junior underwriters and secretaries, all Chinese. Lloyd's had once been a British preserve but these days there were overseas members of all persuasions formed up in syndicates. What was required were substantial assets and unlimited liability to meet a claim— liability down to your last shirt button.

Like the London original, all the names were in one large room operating from cramped boxes divided as offices. Lloyd's shipping intelligence was unrivaled and although dispatches were still posted on bulletin boards in the old way, modern communications, via satellite, fax and telexes brought Lloyd's List and Shipping Index in the new way. It was necessary to keep track of the worldwide movement of 21,000 merchant vessels. Over two hundred of those ships moved out of its thirty-three miles of Singapore Harbor every day.

Slinng came into the big room and was hit by a wall of noise. A mob of Chinese in business suits doing business on their feet, hands and arms moving, underwriters yammering at brokers who were their contact with the insuring public. Others scribbling in the open boxes, territory defined by a narrow slat of a desk, topped by ledgers containing handwritten records of the syndicate's underwriting transactions.

He was rescued by Colonel Pynge-Gilbert. "My dear Larry, how very nice to see you after all this time."

"Thank you, sir."

"Looks an explosion in a Chinese laundry, don't it?" Using twenties upper-class-British slang, he nodded the way. "Come on." He led off, an aloof figure above the bob of heads.

His office might have been lifted from the original Lloyd's on Lime Street: mahogany and leather, bound books and centered above a faux fireplace, a dense oil of John J. Angerstein, "Father of Lloyd's." "This calls for malt, I'd say." He crossed over to a plump Biedermeier cabinet set with lead-crystal decanters. It was a trip often made. The Colonel was seldom without a paper cup filled with vodka and orange juice. But he did not consider that drinking. Vodka was not to be taken seriously. It was for ladies and faddists. Gin was serious, Scotch whiskey was serious. He poured off two stout shots of malt Scotch in proper crystal glasses and handed one over. "Here's to you, old son." As they drank, the Colonel saw that the wrist under the shirt was thick as a drainpipe. "Been to sea then?"

"Yes, sir."

"How long now?"

"At sixteen."

"Well, that's in the tradition, isn't it." He lowered himself into a chair at the partner's desk and nodded at Slinng to take another. Behind them, the view through fake mullioned windows was across Raffles Square, centered by the bronze monument of the man himself. "As I remember, you went to Gordonstoun."

"Yes, that's correct."

"Damn fine school."

"Well, it prepares you for the prison system—although I believe it more severe." A smile.

The Colonel wasn't sure he should smile over that; after all, Prince Charles had gone there.

"A joke, sir, of course."

A pause. Then, "Damn hard news about Neville, I hated that."
Did he? Slinng wondered.

Leslie Pynge-Gilbert was tall and imposing with wild eyebrows and a mustache camped under an elegant nose that sniffed out malcontents like sewer gas. The staff called him God, because despite his hovering presence he could never be found when you needed him. He had been a subaltern in the British army when the Japanese captured Singapore in 1942 and had spent the war years at their labor camp in Seletar. As he grew older he felt the rank didn't fit his image and advanced himself step by step until, at sixty-seven, he was a full colonel. On his seventieth birthday he planned to make himself brigadier.

"You've come back to stay?"

"Nothing like that. To see to my father's death."

"Oh."

"Gladys doesn't believe it was an accident."

"Is that right? Really—she's married again though."

"Yes . . ."

"Chinese, ain't he?"

"Dr. A. N. Kung."

"By God, that would have screwed old Nev in the ground like an auger." Laughing. A pause; then: "I was best man at your parents' wedding, you know?" *Of course he knew.* "I tell you, it knocked us over, I mean the fellow was near fifty—and his first time, too." *Not counting the hotel "wives," Malay mistresses and odd tourist bedding.* "And to an American at that. You know how he went on about foreigners." *Yes, indeed.* "None of us could understand why he'd marry one."

It wasn't difficult. Gladys McCormick Whitten, who described herself as an Illinois farm girl, was a descendant of Cyrus Hall McCormick, inventor of the reaper, and that "farm" was several acres of downtown Chicago real estate.

"Lovely girl, never took herself seriously, which went down hard with the locals. Now that I think of it, I'll be damned if I know why she married Neville, for that matter."

She had written Slinng at sea not that long ago, talking about the years at Raffles and his father. ". . . *I married him for those piano-perfect teeth—rare in an Englishman—I have always been a fool for teeth as some others are for musician's hair or a penis that matches a twelve triple E shoe size . . .*"

"I miss them both," the Colonel said, getting up to refill his glass. "Nobody was more amusing at bridge."

"You didn't resent it that he was allowed to stay on as manager at Raffles by the Japanese during the war while the rest of you were hauled off to the camps?"

The Colonel treated this carefully; it was a damn rude question. "If they'd asked me I'd have taken the job straight away." He smiled. "It was his good fortune."

After the war people thought the Colonel had won the Victoria Cross for his exploits because he wore its distinctive maroon ribbon on his lapel. He was bitter. After the horrors of Seletar he wore it because he believed he *should* have won it. If anyone had the gall to ask, he told them it was for best in shows for burgundy noses.

"And after all, old Nev saved the roast beef trolley—he might have been knighted for that." The magnificent silver server, famous at Raffles, had been buried by the staff in the Palm Court to save it from the Nips.

He sat down and examined the malt in his glass. "Some believe they can taste the peat in this. I suspect it may just be dirt—the housekeeping is a char here."

Slinng had no idea what char was—he hadn't heard anyone talk this British since Terry Thomas films. Looking at him, he wondered if *he* could have killed his father. The image of one old man deliberately drowning another in a bathtub was nearly comedy.

"You're still in the mercantile then after that Sri Lanka business?"

"Oh, yes, these days I contract as an independent—voyage charter out of Port Moresby, New Guinea."

"What about the Sris?"

"They'll have to catch me—won't they?"

"Yes, well, they're damn stiff at the moment but my guess is the government will swap ends again and you'll be a bloody hero."

"I'm counting on it."

"Hell, I remember when it was called Ceylon—one more place those people have mucked up." He finished his drink. "Your ship's in port?"

"No, Singapore is still out of bounds. I've come out from England on the quiet—given myself leave to do a bit of business and look into this thing about my father."

There was a pause while the Colonel mulled it over. "Y'know, maybe you can do me some good while you're here."

"Of course, sir."

"Have any time in on yachts and the like?"

"Well, I worked for Sun-Med Charter when I was coming up. They had a two-hundred-and-twenty-six-foot diesel Benetti"

"Yes, that's the thing." The Colonel spun the chair and got up to fill his glass again. "We've got a vessel here, just put in—fifteen hundred tons, a singular yacht, the *Sulu,* built by Supercraft in Hong Kong—you may know them."

"David Lieu—IOR race boats."

"Right. An Australian owns this toy, rich as Croesus. Wants to go cruising the North Borneo coast, Sarawak and around the tip of Sabah and through the Sibutu Passage to Tawau in the Celebes Sea." Glass full, he sat down. "Although why a man would want to holiday among headhunters and Bajaus pirates is beyond me.

"The fellow wants to jump insurance for the voyage into the strato. These toys are not cheap today, y'know. If the vessel goes down the pan so will my arse in a left-hand swirl."

"You must have done a go-over—bottomry?"

"Oh, yes, she's sound, and armed. Our people have been hard at her, it's just that I'd like an . . . outside . . ."—he almost said white—". . . man to look at her. Give me a private opinion. This policy is on my say-so."

"All right—when?"

"Let me get to it. Are you at Raffles?"

"On the QT."

"Of course. Actually, you might enjoy this yacht chap—quite a character. Before he made it big he was a labor boss on the docks here in Singapore—the Japanese interred him also."

"You knew him then?"

"Not at Seletar, he was at Changi."

"You've kept in touch?"

"Part of the old-boy network. I suspect that's why he's sending the business my way." He walked Lawrence to the door. "If there's anything I may do for you while you're here . . ."

"Thank you, sir. I won't be here long. I just want to be able to reassure Gladys that the old man's death was an accident—I'm sure there's nothing to it."

"No . . .," the Colonel said slowly. "No, I wouldn't say that."

. . .

Off the Pan-Island Expressway in Tampines is a factory district with a smog density rivaling London or Los Angeles. But unlike the embattled ecologists of the West, locked in a struggle with polluters and supported by troubled citizens, the East, Singapore, had gotten off to a late start ruining the environment and was racing to catch up. Belching stacks and unpleasant odors were still looked on as a sign of modern progress.

Standing in front of a raw factory building pumping out a particularly vile effluvium is the lovely Van Den Plas Princess. A chauffeur is braced at the parade-rest position by the right rear door. And if he seems small to guard the great car and its owner, then few would recognize him out of his military kit as a Gurkha.

Inside, the ugly man is escorted through the ground floor of the plastics factory by its manager. The space is broken up by complicated shapes of machinery; insistent noise, and the heat from hot presses rises in visible waves. As the two continue toward the office they are followed by the beautiful girl. The workers at injection molds and brewing vats watch her passage in awe; the flow of blond-white hair floats through the filth of the shop like a mysterious light. For them she is the fabulous girl who reaches out from their television sets offering the romance of oral hygiene or feminine deodorants while nuzzled by a handsome gentleman. They have seen that kind of face on giant billboards, lips poised at a Pepsi, and have been instructed that this is the ideal—this is what women aspire to in the modern world—and they despair. The manager and the ugly man enter the office followed by the beauty. The door is shut and the workers wait.

The office is filled with product samples: a line of plastic dolls, masks of rock stars and famous politicians. They are looped around the room, painted in vivid colors and fitted with Dynel hair.

The beautiful girl puts on a mask of a Zulu warrior, startling against the pale skin and halo of blond hair. *"Uggauggga boo boo!"*

Her companion ignores her, studying a mask of Princess Margaret. "I danced with her once," he says. "Moved like an anvil."

The manager returns from an adjoining storeroom carrying a cardboard box. The desk is piled with dirty paper cups and remains of lunch. Shoving them aside, he places the box at its center. Then, lifting its top, he carefully takes out a highly polished teak hat box. Its corners are bound in silver and an elaborate handle has been fashioned for the top.

It is a superior item made in the old way and nothing to do with plastic. He squares it and, removing the cardboard box, steps back. "I hope you will be pleased, sir."

The ugly man and his companion contemplate it. A key is fitted and framed by a scrolled escutcheon. He turns it, opens the lid, and hoots in an explosion of laugher. *"Bloody damn lovely! Whooeee! Would you look at that!"*

The girl leans over and peers into the box but says nothing. Only pale eyes are visible behind the Zulu mask, and they are impossible to read.

Outside the workers hear the boom of laughter and look at each other uneasily.

6

AT DUSK LAWRENCE SLINNG crosses Raffles Square on his way to a confrontation. He has come to settle with the man whose head he sawed off. He finds him waiting on his pedestal. Bronze arms crossed, leg cocked, gazing over his right shoulder toward the city he founded. Behind him a flutter of birds rise from the clock tower of Victoria Memorial Hall as it strikes 6:00 P.M. The square is empty and they are alone.

"Well, sir, I'm back and glad to see they got your head on straight. I've come to apologize."

This was a man whose wide-screen life was the stuff of a miniseries: born at sea; at fourteen the sole support of his mother and four sisters; at twenty-three assistant secretary to the governor of Penang; at thirty lieutenant-governor of Java, ruling an archipelagic empire of seven million.

At once a fellow of the Royal Society and awarded a knighthood. Orientalist, founder and first president of the London Zoo:

Sir Thomas Stamford Raffles.

What else?

As in all great miniseries there were gobs of romantic tragedy: the shattering death of a wife; failure and demotion to the miserable pepper port of Bengkulu on the west coast of Sumatra. Buried alive while the Dutch regained possession of *his* archipelago. Enough! He acted, persuading pussy-footing authority to establish a fortified post eastward of the Strait of Malacca, a wedge to open the gateway to the China seas.

After a near shipwreck (a miniseries staple), he landed the morning of January 29, 1819, on a steamy, jungle-covered island on the southern tip of Malaya. It was small (twenty-six miles by fourteen—the size of the Bronx), a mess of mangrove swamps and shallows, populated by fierce Malay fishermen, tigers and pythons. Ahh . . . but it sat astride the merchant routes. Risking war with the Dutch, Raffles leased the island from the Sultan of Johore and established the treaty port of Singapore—from the old name, Singapura, "City of the Lion."

It was unique not having been fought over, wrenched away like other British colonies. No, like Manhattan it had been purchased from the natives at nearly the same bargain price.

He was a man who might have conceived the modern buildings, the traffic. Standing here on his pedestal, he would have forgiven the exhaust fumes that ate away at the molecular structure of his bronze statue. He had the vision to see Singapore as it would become.

Why had he attacked the great man? Slinng explains:

We weren't carried along by politics, which we were too young to understand, or a rising Malaysian consciousness, which was yet to be defined. What moved us was action, excitement. We were kids, after all. A wildness had suddenly broken out in a city that had always prided itself on social order. Independence from Britain was in the air, and a dozen parties were in collision. The weapons were poster slogans and speeches, accelerating to rock throwing and street fights. We tagged along, calling ourselves the "Raff" gang, a dozen kids, sons of the hotel staff, me, their leader, none older than ten.

We surged through the streets that day, monitored by the constabulary and feeling like real revolutionaries. Then, just after dark, the factions came together until it was a mob—and the noise! Sticks and clubs against the pavement; shouts, arguments; a shaking of fists, macho spitting, changing sides with each forcible speech. Looking for a leader, someone to step across the line from protest to action.

We congregated right here with people pouring in from High Street, jumping the fences of the Cricket Club—to hell with the lawn! Filling up the square, jammed together and looking for an outlet for all that fervor—and there you were, sir, superior, calm, standing above us, looking over our heads to where? Your city? No. *Ours!*

It began slowly with a rythmic chant, picked up by the mob, a channel for inaction—shouting it out.

Off with Raffles' head! Off with Raffles' head!

We were all caught up in the hysteria, bodies giving off terrific heat, faces animated—in thrall to nationalism. At that moment we were comrades bound in common hate of the rich, the white, exploiters, imperialists, anything we weren't. And there I was with this flag of a white face, a rich man's son, shouting with them, for the truth was, growing up with the Chinese and Malay, being imprinted by them, I'd always considered myself one of *them*.

Behind locked doors citizens who *really* owned the city—the ex-colonial Europeans and Chinese majority—heard our shouts and a collective shiver went down their spines. For the fear is always there—will the millions of Malays who surround you, whose place you have taken in their own country, turn and destroy you? Will you be swallowed up in Conrad's Heart of Darkness? As the French, those other colonial entrepreneurs, say: *Après nous le déluge.* The jungle will close in.

But what closed in was the constabulary. That tramping on the cricket grass had done it. Clubs swinging, they cleared the grass and streets in short order. The paper revolutionists ran for their lives, diving in the alleys, the clatter of their feet the only sound. Shoes were left behind by those who literally ran out of them.

I was crushed, near tears. Cowards! I had just witnessed a spiritual bonding as men came together in common cause. Then in the next second they were running like dogs. I was ashamed of them all; shouting that we had to go back and cut Raffles' head off! Show the dogs that we kids could do it!

But my gang went home, back to the hotel, unmoved by a ten-year-old agitator who didn't know what he was agitating about. Furious, I returned alone, taking a hacksaw and rope filched from Raffles' maintenance shop. It had begun to rain and the downpour was enormous, the streets running with freshets, but also empty—the constabulary had gone to cover.

. . .

Raffles stands alone, obscured by sheets of rain. Around him on the pavement are dozens of odd, empty shoes filled with water, poster paper beaten flat by the deluge. A small boy fashions a loop on the rope and after several attempts secures it over Raffles' shoulders. Then, climbing up, he ties himself in a kind of sling. Taking the hacksaw, he places it at the man's neck and finds himself looking directly into his face. Rain swirls down the noble brow, runs to the end of his bronze nose to continue on in a stream. The firm mouth sheds what it can and the eyes . . . the boy has the illusion that they stare straight through him.

He saws. The bronze is not thick and at first it goes easy. Then he hits one of several iron braces bolted on the inside. These take hours to cut through and his arms shake, go numb with the effort. He continues, shuddering with fatigue, and finally, near dawn, cuts through the last brace and the head falls suddenly away. It narrowly misses him, striking the pavement with a hollow thud, then, rolling a few feet, comes to rest, the eyes looking up.

Yes, Slinng says, sighing, I had succeeded, cut your head off. I was instantly uneasy, already sorry. Bawling like . . . a kid. But I'll say this, sir, I picked your head up with great care. You weren't dented and I brushed the gravel out of your hair, putting you carefully in my bag. I had, after all, done what I set out to do—and surely, you're a man who can understand that.

And—oh, yes—they caught me a block from here.

Across town another confrontation was taking place.

Although they came in at different times and entrances, Mr. Kee knew immediately what they were up to. The one who had reserved the room, Mr. Dickey, was tall and thin with a narrow face and blond mustache. An aesthetic young man with a chic Borsalino hat, double-breasted linen suit and just the right tie.

That one went up in the lift alone and here came the other: a dumpy woman in a frilly silk frock, permed hair and bright red lips—nervous and obviously guilty about the assignation. What that elegant young gentleman saw in her he couldn't imagine. But then, he had seen everything in this business. The hotel small, discreet, was tucked into a side street off Moulmein Road. Only Buddha knew what went on in the rooms.

. . .

"I love your hat, Mr. Dickey." Kissing.

"I can't say as much for your wig, Miss Muffy." Laughing. "I had a Sealyham once that didn't have that much curl."

"What? Oh, dear. And I spent such a lot of time over it. Poo!"

"And that dress is awful. It doesn't show your figure."

"That's because I haven't got one, dear." Walking toward an end table set up as a bar.

"Anyone can have tits today."

"Yes, but have you seen them? If you lie down they point to the ceiling like snow cones." Holding up a gin bottle. "Do you want a martini?"

"I used to be mad for them but now they've gone and got popular and been ruined."

"I'll put an onion in and then it will be a Gibson."

"Whatever."

Drinks were mixed and they sat on a low couch made up in a red batik print. A toast was offered. "A week from now and we'll be under way on our great adventure, Mr. Dickey."

"I don't want to talk about it." Tugging the hat down and pouting.

"You're not afraid . . ."

"Oh, no, it's just . . . you know who." Looking around the room, walls a neutral beige with splashy flower prints. "Could he . . ." Gesturing.

"Bug us? It seems unlikely, but let's keep it *arrière-pensée.*"

"A slip of the lip can sink a ship." Giggling.

"Wherever did you hear that?"

"My uncle Ian was a sailor in World War Two. They said it all the time then."

"That reminds me, our intrepid captain is back from Sarawak . . ."

"That horrid person."

"Well, he's a first-rate seaman."

"Being around water all the time, you'd think he'd wash."

"Don't pout, Mr. Dickey—give us a kiss." Offering the red lips. "We'll soon be together in London and stay at the Ritz if you like."

"I hate that lipstick." Wiping it off with tissue.

"The party's tomorrow night, so this had better be the last time we do this."

"Then Miss Muffy's going to have to put out." Lifting up the dress.

"Wait now, don't ruin my panty hose . . ." But slim fingers had tugged them down, releasing an old friend.

"Ho ho! Miss Muffy's dickey is ready for Mr. Dickey's muffy." Ducking her head down to take it.

"Come on," he said, "at least take the hat off." Jerking it up and sailing it across the room. As it did the bundle of blond curls sprang up. Loosing her tie, Mr. Dickey continued.

At eight o'clock, Slinng arrived at Hawker's Center for a last confrontation. Located on a side street where old buildings leaned toward each other as if for support, it was packed with traveling stallholders who peddled food from minikitchens set up curbside. A block long, scrambled buffet; piles of seafood; "moi" porridge, live crayfish, ancient eggs and chili crab coated with thick tomato-chili sauce. The smoke from charcoal fires rose to halo Chinese lanterns and the mingled smells were aggressive. The choked street, an alley really, was too narrow for motor cars and only the ubiquitous motorbikes snaked through with excessive revs and valve pinging. Tonight, as usual, it poured tourists; a flood of permanent press, printed T-shirts and Banana Republic rip-offs.

When his contact failed to arrive, Slinng stepped up to a stall where a grill was kept sizzling by a glowing charcoal pan beneath it. An old Chinese in traditional dress with a belly shaped like Buddha's was cooking "satay," meat that was skewered and dipped in peanut gravy.

"Help you please?" he said in English.

"Thank you," Slinng answered in Chinese. "Your important stomach advertises you."

He was pleased, continuing in Chinese, "From your accent I can guess you come from our city."

"No—from the sea. Like the crab, I crawl ashore from time to time to sample the local menu."

They talked as he ate, watching the crowd. His contact was nearly an hour late now and he was annoyed. Then at the end of the alley there was a rumble of exhaust and a large motorcycle appeared, causing pedestrians to jump aside, cutting a wake up the center of the crowd. It was not your ordinary office-boy transportation. A serious machine with clip-on bars and an uplift of a tailpipe the size of a bazooka. A thing that cost an arm and a leg in Singapore dollars. It skipped to a showy stop and when the rider swung a leg over its stepped tank the name NINJA could be read on the faring. One thousand cc's of big-bike thunder.

The rider was a young Chinese, large, square, with the deliberate movements of the self-assured. Even in the evening heat he was dressed in leathers, black with a design of studs worked in like riveting and a complicated painting of Tripitaka, the handsome monkey king, on the back. He flipped a helmet off to reveal a pancake face blank of expression, a match in one corner of his mouth substituting for character. The small boys were impressed and stood admiring the motorcycle and rider. The leathers fit his tube of a body in sweaty connection and zipping his jacket down for air, he gave it a bit of a fan. The glint of a small automatic could be seen tucked in the belt.

Slinng was disgusted. A cowboy. What were the triads coming to?

What they were coming to was the modern age. The Singapore gangs, the Young Turks and the Ah Kong, were an extension of the old Chinese secret societies that practiced benevolent extortion and the realities of revenge. New attitudes had evolved from movie gangster role modeling and easy access to automatic weapons. Old-fashioned acid throwing and dicing up victims to be sewn back together with green thread had gone out of style. Firepower was in. In the recent "shotgun wars" young warriors stood on opposite sides of the street blazing away at each other. The *Straits Times* called it a "heavy-metal concert" (one killed, four wounded).

Triads had begun out of revolt against the Manchus on the mainland of China in the seventeenth century. From patriotic purpose they shifted to protection and retribution, and became the arbiters of feuds and disputes that the police refused to deal with. A proverb said: "Armies protect rulers, triads protect people." By the twentieth century they had spread out to encompass all areas of Asia and embrace every known crime. They attracted young men who found upward mobility blocked by lack of education or family connection. It was the perfect outlet for the alienated, frustrated and vicious. Billy Hon, the cowboy, qualified. It was not that the older generation were any less ruthless or cold-blooded, but in kidnapping and extortion they still at least endorsed courteous exchange of bargaining as opposed to the current wretched excess of violence. They were vicious, but polite.

Satisfied he'd made a proper entrance, Billy searched the street and identified Slinng by his Panama and silk suit. Tugging an envelope out of his jacket, he pushed through the crowd to the satay stand and rapped him on the shoulder with it. "You Blondie?"

The man looked at him. "You asshole?" He took the envelope.

Billy wasn't sure he had heard right. "What? What did you say?"

Slinng put the envelope away and went back to eating, saying to the chef in Chinese, "Forgive the interruption, sir, some sand inevitably gets in the clam."

"What?" Billy said. "Talk English!"

Slinng turned. "You don't speak Chinese? No, of course not." It was true that most of the young Singaporeans didn't speak Chinese—refused to. The Chinese university had been closed down and a Speak Mandarin campaign launched by the PM, Lee Kuan, in 1979 had had little success.

The chef leaned in. "You must forgive . . ."

But Billy shoved him back. "Keep your mouth out of this!"

Slinng smacked Billy's hand sharply with chopsticks. "Don't touch him!" He continued in rapid Chinese, "How dare you lay hands on your betters!" Startled, Billy stepped back and had the chopsticks jabbed in his chest. "You don't speak Chinese and you don't have any manners! Bad boy! Where is your respect for your elders?" The crowd was amused. Role reversal was pure Oriental theater. They were laughing at him. There was a movement of Billy's hand toward his waist and Slinng's hand shot out, grabbed his wrist and jerked him forward, slapping his hand flat on the grill. A second's smoky sizzle and he was released, staggering back with a howl, clutching his wrist with the other hand.

"Oh! Ohhh!"

The crowd drew apart, shocked, silent as Slinng shoved him along toward the motorcycle in short jabs of the chopsticks, talking now in a low, concise English. "You damned dog! Did you really intend to shoot me in front of all these witnesses? Are you so arrogant—stupid to think you could get away with that? What kind of fool are you? You go back to Mr. Wo and tell him if he ever—ever sends me another like you I will fry his turtlehead—being a real Chinese, he will know what I mean!"

They had reached the bike but when Billy turned toward it, Slinng lashed out and kicked it over with the flat of his foot. It crashed to the pavement in a noisy clatter of metal and plastic. "Oh, no! You're not going to ride!" he said, and aimed a kick at his rear as Billy ducked in the crowd, running for his life. "Run, you bastard! You're damned lucky you don't have to crawl!"

Looking around, he saw that everyone's eyes were averted; even the chef had turned his head away. They were embarrassed for the motorcycle driver, understood his shame, loss of face. "Amok" is a Malay word describing a murder mania. In Mindanao it is called "juramentado" but it is the same throughout the Orient. When a man believes an intolerable injury has been done him, an insult or dishonor which he can never hope to live down, a fit of madness seizes him and he grabs the first weapon at hand and begins killing, starting with the person who insulted him.

The Chinese, Malays, accepted this and knew that the man who had just lost face would not rest until he took it back.

When Slinng returned to Raffles he found a note from Colonel Pynge-Gilbert. He had wrangled an invitation for him to attend a party on the *Sulu* the next evening. He would meet the owner and have a chance to informally inspect the yacht.

In his room, Slinng kicked off his shoes and stretched out on the couch. Only then did he open the envelope that had been delivered to him from the Ah Kong triad. In it was a constabulary report on his father's death, obviously taken from their files. Leaking water had been reported on the hotel's third floor and the body discovered. When inspecting officers arrived he was still in the tub. Conclusion: Due to age and infirmity the victim had slipped while drawing the water, fell in and was scalded, then drowned. It was accidental.

There were color photos attached and they were hard to look at. In one, shot from above, his father looked up at him still submerged in the water. Eyes open, mouth agape, he appeared startled, angry, as if asking, *What have you done to me? How dare you take pictures?!* Slinng agreed. Another showed him stretched out on a table and it was evident from the color of skin that he had been scalded, burned—except for a faint white ring on his hairless chest. He looked at it a long time. What was it? He gauged it to be about five inches across and a perfect circle. It was vague but visible—still, it wasn't mentioned in the report. Why? Had they overlooked it? Hardly. Did they assume it was unimportant, nothing to do with his death? Probably.

He thought he knew what it was. The mark from a toilet plunger.

7

FROM A DISTANCE the *Sulu* gave the appearance of elegant military bearing, a decorator's Coast Guard cutter. This was evident in her skyline of electronic domes and masts: a thicket of Dupletron antennas that culminated at the peak of a raked-back stack sending signals to RX radar, Satnav and autopilots. Two hundred and twelve feet of blinding white yacht with no visible deck guns but announcing she had shoulders and could take care of herself.

Tonight she was party-rigged with loops of full dress lights and the sound of a rock band doing last year's pop hits. Dockside was Clifford Pier with valet parking. When Slinng arrived by taxi, threading his way between Rollses and Mercedes-Benzes, he found the vessel awash with noisy celebrants.

Dress was formal and he was in a beautifully cut mess jacket run up for the occasion by Mr. Chong Sen on Sophia Road, who prided himself on being the "Chinese Ralph Lauren." Coming aboard, he was given a glass of champagne. He stood on the afterdeck in the squeeze, listening to conversation straining in competition with the four-piece band on the fantail. It was a polyglot group made up of a majority of Chinese, Indian, some English and near-zero Malays. Just about the social mix of Singapore. The common denominator tonight was money. They had it or looked like they did.

"I don't think we've met." A young man put a hand out, followed by a nice smile, polished complexion and a minimum of hair, artfully arranged. "Blas Coff."

"Lawrence Slinng." They shook, pressed together by others. Coff wore a nautical blazer with anchor buttons and the ship's logo worked in silver thread on his breast pocket.

"You're the owner?"

He laughed, laying a hand on Slinng's arm. "No, no—the decorator. I've done all of Mr. Hartog's houses and now his boats—ah, forgive— ships. I've been instructed that boats go on ships." He pointed up to the

boat deck overhead. "A Wellcraft, two outboards, three Humber inflatables, an all-terrain vehicle and a Hovercraft."

"Very good."

"Actually I have shops in Melbourne and Sydney. Then, too, Tog and
I jointly own a gallery of Aboriginal art."

"Contemporary?"

"Some, but mostly *maraiin:* realistic carving, ceremonial poles from
eastern Arnhem Land—bark painting. Do you know Aboriginal art?"

"Well, I'm fond of the 'X-ray' things . . ."

"Ye gods, that stuff is terrific! Yes! I can't think of another culture that
depicts the internal organs of animals and humans as art. Well, perhaps
Egyptian funerary displays, but I'm not sure I want to elevate necromancy
to art—in that case we would have to rule out some of the great face-lifts
of the nineties," he added, laughing. He was animated, exuding enthusiasm. Small, less than five six but perfectly proportioned and impeccably
turned out. His accent was urbane Australian scoured to contain not one
whit of trendy outback "barbie" dialect. He examined Slinng more
closely. "What is it you do, if I may ask?"

"Tonight I'm here for Lloyd's."

"Of course, the insurance man. Colonel Pynge-Gilbert called. Will you
want a guide? One of the crew?"

"Oh, no. This is an informal look-over. If you don't mind I'll be on
my own."

"When you get back I'd like you to meet Mr. Hartog."

Slinng thanked him and turned away. As he made his way through
the crowd, Blas looked after him, admiring his fit of jacket and wondering
just what in the world bottomry was.

The overflow of partygoers stretched along the port side under the
boat deck and Slinng snaked through. Knowing the general ship's layout,
he stepped into a midship door where, despite air-conditioning, the
interior had the canned, slightly diesel smell of all large ships. He found
a fire directory and following steps that went from carpet to steel, arrived
at the engine space, entering to the hum of generators.

Electrical panels were exposed and faced with Plexiglas, their intricate
colored wiring and breaker panels looking like a wall of modern art.
Beyond were two M.A.N. diesels in creamy beige, immaculate and unat-
tended. There was the feeling of Chaplin's *Modern Times:* vast complicated machinery running on its own; the ticking of tappets, gauges

fluttering and the oily whine of self-sustaining mechanisms. He walked on, checking inspection and fire tags, and met no one. Then, at the end of the machine space, he opened a door and was suddenly confronted by a dozen men hunkered down on the deck playing some kind of game with sticks and beads. They looked up through a haze of thick cigarette smoke with flat, impersonal stares. All were smoking and all small, of nearly the same size, with identical bowl haircuts. Gurkhas. How remarkable, Slinng thought—a people not known for their nautical bent.

"What's this? Lost our dancing partner, have we?"

A large individual appeared out of the haze. Stepping through the door, he pulled it shut, causing Slinng to move back; a rude face was inches away. "Crew's quarters, mate. The party's topside." Pointing up.

The engineer? Australian again, all business with one of those primitive physiognomies where it seemed a ruler had been drawn across the eyebrows to connect a built-in frown. "Lloyd's—with owner's permission." He wasn't moving, holding his position and not friendly.

"Kee-rist, another one. I don't know what you bloody people want."

"An inspection. Is there an objection?"

He slapped his hand against his leg. "Damn! A man can't get through a meal here—c'mon!" And he led off, pounding his foot on the deck. "Double bottom, honeycomb compartments, scantlings—thirty percent over Lloyd's rating." Reaching over, rapping his knuckles against the exposed hull. "You know what this is, mate? R-fourteen steel—the stuff they make bloody offshore drilling platforms out of—it'll stop a seven point six-two shell—write it down—shall we?"

They continued to the next compartment past the watermakers. "These will do fifteen and a half tons per day and there's a four-hundred-thousand-BTU chillwater AC that'll freeze your dingo like a fudgesicle." He stopped by huge fuel tanks with a complicated Westphalia metering system. "We can burn four grades of fuel," he said, banging on the side of the tank. "It passes into holding tanks where a computer regulates the flow to each engine and filters tidy it up. That means if we're in some scrubby little port where they've only got sump sludge from tour buses we can run on it."

Slinng saw that he had been steered to the ladder leading topside. They paused and the engineer leaned in, summing up. "This vessel was built to one hundred A-1 ratings with on-deck firefighting system, three hundred-pound anchors and one hundred fifty meters of chain for each.

We can steam fifteen hundred miles or lay up for five hundred days without outside assistance. This is a survival machine. A thinking man's yacht built to give pause to pirates and pleasure to the owner—there is nothing we can't handle." He smiled, showing teeth spaced like cow catchers.

"Except possibly bad breath," Slinng said. Thanking him, he went topside.

The bridge was dark, banks of control modules, radar screens all blank. Outside light showed in the stretch of bridge windows and silhouetted the circle of windscreen wipers. Slinng flicked on the instruments, blips coming alive. Range markers and on-screen data in color and monochrome, scanners scanning. He faced the awesome control module: RX radar, Loran and Satnav—every navigational device known to man with backups on the backups.

In the chart room, power-vessel routes for the China Sea were laid out with the tracks for southwest monsoons. Neatly lined up above the protractor was a logarithmic speed, time and distance scale. A greasy cap lay next to them. Somewhere on board was human backup.

Returning aft along the top deck, he could hear music continue relentlessly from below. Here it had competition from the harbor: a counter melody of honks and hoots. Starboard were the lights of Sentosa Island, Singapore's answer to Disneyland. Then, as he came past the massive single stack, a champagne glass crashed at his feet. Jumping back, he looked up the forty-plus feet of stack. Near the top was a vertical fin and a curve that continued on to sprout antenna. Forward of this and facing into the wind was a lookout platform. Just visible were tanned legs dangling between its railing. A girl's voice shouted down, "A full glass if you don't mind!"

Going below into the push and shove of party, he plucked a full bottle off a tray, pocketed two glasses and returned to the top deck. Then, holding the bottle in one hand, he climbed stirrups to the lookout platform. As he went the band played "Guitar Boogie."

She sits back against the stack in a strapless gown that has been pulled up to her waist showing marvelous long legs. The great tumble of hair, lit by the furthermost running lights on the tallest antenna, puts her small face into mysterious shadows. As he comes up through the platform they are nearly on a level and he sighs, knowing instantly who it is, and thinks he has probably never seen anyone quite so beautiful in such a different way. There is something else, an odd focus to those pale eyes that is disturbing. She seems to look through him, beyond. Myopic? Mystic? Dreaming distant dreams?

"God, I hate electric guitars," she says.

Slinng climbs up and, withdrawing the glasses from his pocket, pours the champagne.

"I went out with this rock musician once who played the bass guitar—I couldn't stand it. I remember later reading he had been electrocuted—committed suicide by playing the bloody thing in the bath. I thought that odd because I didn't remembering him bathing."

He hands her a glass. "Still, there's Segovia or Burl Ives."

She begins to sing in a high, quavering tremolo, "Froggy's gone a courtin'—he did gooooo, ah ouuuuu . . . ah ouuuuu . . ."

She goes on to sing the entire song and it occurs to him that her mysterious, magical quality might have something to do with drink, even drugs—then, too, she might just be diffident. She has yet to look at him. Hers is a solo performance, a monologue recited, now sung to the stars.

The band hits a particularly bad stretch and she breaks off. "Haven't you got a hand grenade or a canister of nerve gas we could drop on that lot? Or if you were a gentleman, you might climb down and cut their tendons." She has an upper-class accent, rising and falling in throaty exercise.

"Sorry."

They sip the wine in silence as he marvels at her profile: the fringe of beaded eyelash, perfect nose with a single centimeter of lift. Pursed lips above a superior chin. But it is obvious she is not *here, now.* How to get her attention? He decides on a shot to the heart.

"I saw you the other day in front of Raffles—where those two jumped . . ."

He instantly regrets it. Before he can finish, her face crumbles and she sets the glass down, spilling the wine. "Oh, oh . . . God, that woman's face, I've dreamt of it. Those awful eyes . . . do you know what they reminded me of? The eyes on an upside-down 'Have a Good Day' sign. God, that's horrible . . . horrible . . ." He saw there were tears in her eyes. "It was just . . . so terribly pitiful . . . to die like that . . . there was a purse lying in the street—did you see it? One of those fake Vuittons . . . oh . . ." Shivering, she looks at him carefully for the first time. "Have you ever . . ." Stopping and reaching out with a long slender finger, she touches his earlobe. "What is that . . . a star! Why?"

"Why? For sailing around Cape Horn," he says softly, "It's a seaman's tattoo, an ancient thing. Five times round you have a star on your left ear, ten times on the right—more than that, two red dots on your forehead . . ."

Stretching her fingers, she places them where the dots would be. "Here . . . and here."

Clinging to each other they kiss for a long time, rolling with the gentle pitch of the sea. When they break at last he says, "That first moment I saw you in the car I felt like I'd been struck between the eyes by a hammer. I didn't like that—and I was hoping not to meet you again—or at the very least have you open your mouth and sound like Minnie Mouse."

"I'm Minnie Mouse and I'm fucking Goofy," she says, smiling.

Later he would remember the slant of antenna mast above them, a movement timed like a metronome, a silent ticking that matched their beat together. This time when they break away she quickly stands and pulls the dress over her head. Then, smiling in her enigmatic way, she turns and climbs the rail, jumps. At the last second he reaches out for her but it is too late, she's gone.

"We should really get shut of this language," a beautifully dressed Chinese woman was telling Blas Coff. "It doesn't express our thought or identity. What does 'Keep your pecker up' or 'Chew the rag' mean to us? Nothing. English is too vernacular, full of jargon."

A dark Indian shoved in, gesturing with his shrimp roll. "Slinglish is no better. English patois with Malay and Chinese colloquialisms that bend the tongue. Oh"—he rolled his eyes—"I weep when I think that I cannot speak my own mother tongue as well as I do the English language . . ."

Blas saw the engineer give him the high sign and excused himself. As he did the Chinese lady was saying, "I wouldn't worry about it."

"One of your bloody guests was just in my engine space poking about—I'm not going to have that!" His face was inches away.

"That was the man from Lloyd's."

"Bloody hell! I know that! I thought we were through with that lot."

"That's not my problem, is it? Besides, we'll soon be at sea."

"It can't be too soon for me—have you ever had to bunk with a bunch of Gurkhas? The little buggers smell like wet sheep."

At that moment something hit the water on the starboard side with a terrific whack and they both looked in that direction. "What the bloody hell now?"

Slinng had scrambled up in time to see a credible dive, a clean entrance into the filthy water and a long anxious minute until she surfaced among floating trash. He shook his head and watched as she swam to the ship accompanied by applause from the guests.

He climbed down and, going aft through the partygoers, ran into Blas Coff. "There you are—Mr. Hartog's free for the moment."

"The girl—is she all right?"

"Oh, yes, if you consider having a brain the size of a BB all right. Come on." Slinng followed the decorator, stepping into the quiet of the saloon, off-limits to the deck party. Here glass doors led to an atrium, a dazzling open staircase of shimmering stainless steel, curved glass and mirrors that cut straight though several decks.

Blas saw the expression on Slinng's face. "I admit it's Hyatt, but owners like flash these days. Of course, something had to give and we did lose space in the galley—but it's all microwave cooking down there anyway. We call our chef 'Mr. Chips.'" As they passed a parrot in a built-in cage on the second level, it made a grab. "Nasty bird," Blas said, avoiding it.

At the top level they went down a passageway to teak doors inlaid with elm burl. At one angle to the entrance of Hartog's quarters was a modern secretary's desk with a multiple-line telephone and a huge bowl of mums. "My nest." Lighting was indirect and the rug Mondrian patterns. He opened the door. "Go right in, Tog's expecting you."

The room was done as a library with more of the superb joinerwork in teak. Brass-edged bookshelves were supported by fluted columns and a bar at one end showed Baccarat decanters and antique fittings: neoclassic, designer slick.

A man instantly jumped up behind a desk spread with layers of charts and came around to meet him. "Larry!" Slinng was astonished. *Larry?* He had never seen the man before in his life. He was gripped by the arms and given pats, rubs, nearly a hug. "When I saw the name 'Slinng,' I knew you had to be Neville's son. God, that was a rotten shame about your dad, damn! It's hell to get old." There were actually tears in his eyes.

"Ah . . . thank you, sir."

Hartog was in his sixties, Slinng guessed, tall, spare of limb and dressed in a trendy polo shirt, shorts and running shoes. Newspapers once called him the Australian Onassis and it was true he had the mane of white hair lifting off above a three-finger forehead and the wrinkles and pockmarks of an ostrich wallet. It was a face so ugly it knocked you back—and yes, there was the corrupt blossom of a nose he had seen kissed in the back of a Van Den Plas Princess limousine by the girl of his dreams. He had seen the man before, or at least his nose.

But that face also had the shine of intelligence and a force that demanded respect. He was charming; talking of Raffles; finding out what *you* did, what interested you—nailing it down with the right blend of humor and flattery. "God! A bloody sea captain! Marvelous!" Booming out laughter. Drawing you in so you forgot he was ugly. His was a conversation punctuated by winks.

"C'mon, c'mon!" Pulling Slinng toward the desk, he swung the charts around, shoving books and the anchor of a teak hat box aside with hands that had been blunted, shortened. The tips of his fingers were missing down to the first joint on both hands. "You know our projected course— around the tip of Sabah and through the Sibutu Passage to Tawau."

The chart showed Sarawak on the coast of Borneo in pale greens shading down to tans, then ochre as the mountains began. There, in the interior, the headwaters of six rivers converged and a plateau rose up. It was white—blank. A notation read *Relief data incomplete.*

Hartog punched Sarawak with an abbreviated index finger, "We're going to sail this coast, then put into Kuching, the capital. I want to see Istana, the palace of the Brooke rajahs. I want to steam this great whale of a decorator's barge right up to the doorstep, fire off a sixteen-gun salute! Here's to Jimmy Brooke, the bloody first White Raj, a man with two big ones between his legs who won his own personal country. A man you won't match today. I've read everything I could lay my hands on about him—he's my current mania—the reason for this bloody expensive, jumped-up trip."

At thirty-two James Brooke had inherited an English fortune from his father and in 1838 sailed his armed yacht *Royalist* to the East Indies.

"Does that sound familar?" Hartog asks. "Of course he put out some high-minded yak of bringing civilization to the Malay Archipelago, but then, he was your classic entrepreneur, a man with early PR leanings, a colonial swami. When he reached Singapore he found out the Rajah Muda Hassim of Borneo was in deep dudgeon over a rebellion. The Dayak tribes were taking Muslim heads. Well, Brooke volunteered his irregulars and sailed the *Royalist* to Sarawak, attacked straight off and cleared out the wogs in jig time. Now—and here's the part I love—in gratitude the Sultan of Brunei *gave him the whole damned country!* He became the sole ruler of Sarawak! The first White Raj! It's a bloody fairy tale that's true!"

"It is an amazing story." Like every Singapore kid, Slinng had heard it—but not quite the way Hartog told it. The Sultan had to be threatened, indirectly, by Brooke before he made good his promise. And then he gave over only because Sarawak was out of control—a wild country of Iban headhunters and, worse, pirates. The Seribas and Sakarang tribes owned the coast and no vessel was safe up the uncharted rivers. Brooke turned to the British, and Admiral Keppel arrived in Sarawak aboard the warship *Dido* on May 13, 1843.

The *Dido* anchored off the Seribas River and its crew and marines joined a native force of five hundred men led by Brooke. Continuing upriver in small boats, they destroyed forts the pirates had erected, routing them with cannon and nineteenth-century military tactics. James Brooke secured his kingdom, and the two succeeding White Rajahs (his nephew and the nephew's son took the Brooke name) made an effort to bring it into the modern world without bending the culture.

"They held the country back a hundred years," Hartog said. "Even today with the damned logging and offshore wells at Brunei the interior is still on the edge of the jumping-off place—a trip into the Stone Age." As Hartog bore in on his subject he used the startling face as a weapon, shoving it up at you until every pore and bump on the great nose was magnified, distorted by the eye's lens. He was compelled to hold his listener captive while talking. Laying on hands: pokes, pats, adjusting clothes. The winks. It was an intimate thing, a wooing that demanded reciprocity—made his listener anxious to reassure him. Anything to be released from the suffocating squeeze of his intimacy.

"Can you imagine what it was like?" he said, inches away, searching Slinng's face. "This man, this White Raj owned a country, he was the only law. It was his will that decided life or death, it was his place to do with as he damned pleased. Talk about the use of power . . ." He laughed. "So what if it was full of wild men, headhunters, all the better. Test your backbone against theirs, see who will blink first. Play God!"

After the acceleration of this ride, there was a pause, and Slinng was aware that for all of his conversancy, Hartog had about him the thing that sets apart great actors and the psychopath: the threat of violence. Even smiling he looked capable of anything.

Slinng felt it necessary to add, "For all of their autocracy, the Brookes used their power humanely, judiciously. They held back the exploiters."

"Yes, then they lost it to the champion exploiters, the damn Japs." After the war, Sir Charles Vyner Brooke, the last White Raj, ceded Sarawak to Great Britain and terminated Brooke rule in July 1946, after 109 years. He never went back and died in London in May of 1963.

"Colonel Pynge-Gilbert mentioned you were interned by the Japanese during the war."

Hartog looked at him carefully. "Yes, at Changi—that's where I met your father."

"How's that?"

"He was into smuggling." When he saw Slinng's face he smiled. "For the underground. As you know the Japs kept him on as manager of Raffles and he used to get stuff to us on the sly, food and the like. I was in charge of the pipeline on our end . . ."

A door cracked open to their left revealing the master stateroom. A woman stood backlit in a terrycloth robe brushing wet hair.

"Miri! Come in, I want you to meet someone." She took her time walking across the library and stood next to Hartog, still stroking her hair. He immediately had his hands on her. "Larry, this is Miri Brooke— yes, that's right, she's the grand-niece of old Charles, the last of the White Rajahs." She looked at Slinng with the same maddening myopic stare, not a hint of recognition. "That's what makes this trip so bloody exciting. She's never been to Sarawak or the Brooke palace at Kuching. I'm returning the Ranee of Sarawak to her jungle kingdom. Tarzan and Jane go to Borneo." Laughing, he kissed her neck while his mutilated left hand affectionately caressed her breast. She continued to look through Slinng, stroking the hair.

He turned away. "It's been nice meeting you both." When he reached the door he heard them whisper together and laugh.

. . .

By dawn the debris of the party has been cleaned up. The *Sulu*'s decks are hosed down, and the weary crew turns in to quarters that have been passed by the decorator's magic wand. In the master stateroom the owner lies on his back on a bed he calls "The Enterprise" and snores. It is an awesome sound, projected as it is through nose chambers that rival the tuba.

Miri slips out of bed and, naked, pads through the dark library. Opening the teak doors and turning left, she enters an unlocked door halfway down the passageway and closes it silently behind her. From his concealed position one of the Gurkha bodyguards sees her go and feels the hair on his neck rise. She is a spectral figure in the half light; luminous white skin and a cloud of hair follow like fireflies.

She slides into bed and snuggles up to Blas Coff. "Miri . . . come on . . . ," he groans.

"He's snoring," she says. "It sounds like the Hovercraft warming up. If you dropped a walnut in on his exhaust stroke it would penetrate the overhead."

He laughs, coughing, and reaches for a cigarette. "You're all right?"

"Of course."

"You shouldn't drink so much, dear."

"You go to bed with him."

"We're almost set, a week at most, and you'll be under way." He lights the cigarette and they share it. "What did you think of the Lloyd's man—is he going to be difficult?"

"Don't worry, he's my love slave."

"Another one."

She grabs his penis and begins to wag it in time to her singing. "On the good ship *Lollipop*, it's a sweet trip to a candy shop where the bon-bons play on Peppermint Bayyyyy."

8

AT ABOUT THE SAME TIME Miri Brooke was keeping tempo to "The Good Ship *Lollipop*" Lawrence Slinng was returning to Raffles. He had spent the intervening period at a waterfront bar called "Poochies Hi-life" on Telck Blangah Road. Coming into the lobby of the hotel, he had a bitter taste in his mouth from Nanboku "whiskey" and Hartog's jungle princess. The place was nearly deserted, no one but dozing bell-boys and a mop-up man. It was his intention to steer through the Tiffin Room and go upstairs to his quarters, but he was waylaid by a legend.

A man sat alone at a back table in the expanse of the empty room. As always, eating. Head down, bent into his work with the oiled action of a front-end loader. At six four and nearly four hundred pounds, he was an immovable object unless he decided otherwise. On a wager he once ate all the courses on Raffles' menu, then ate them again in reverse order. He had been known to consume ten gins for breakfast and his record for potables was thirty-six quarts of beer at one setting. His niche in hotel folklore was secured when five friends failed to show up for dinner and he ate for six.

Now as the rising sun pierced the skylight of the central airwell it illuminated the eater on his second dozen eggs.

"Professor Groot."

Eyes rotated slightly upward as he forked in a mouthful. "Larry, my boy! Good to see you—I heard you were back."

Slinng smiled. He had last seen Groot in 1959, when he was ten. "How have you been, sir?"

"Very well—have you heard? They've got ikan bawal stuffed with sambal blachan back on the menu." This was fish stuffed with a thick red paste of putrefied shrimps and hot chilis. It had a penetrating odor and was known to cause temporary skin eruptions.

"Exciting."

"Sit! Sit! Order up." Groot was Dutch, a graduate of Leiden University and once director of the Netherlands East Indies archeological department. He was brilliant and between mouthfuls lectured all who passed by his regular table in a stentorian voice that blew aside a nasty beard like the blast from a whale's blowhole. It was said that during his time in Sumatra he had lived with cannibals and eaten human flesh— and he did seem a man who would eat whatever was set before him.

He was colorful, but he was also something else: a walking encyclopedia of Singapore history.

"Do you know a man named Hartog?" Slinng asked.

The look again. "Oh, yes. He was at Changi when I was."

"You must have been very young."

"Twelve. But I was over six feet even then and not considered a boy by the Japanese. I stayed with the men."

"What about your parents?"

"My mother and sister had gotten out on a boat early in 'forty-one but I hung back with my father. He was a rubber planter, you know—he had a plantation on Bukit Timah Road, if you can believe that. It's all buildings now. His trees were from the first Pará plants smuggled in from Brazil in 1881."

"Weren't you concerned about the Japanese?"

"You have to remember the colonial mentality. This was a British outpost. Warships were out there in Keppel Harbor, huge naval gun emplacements pointed toward the sea—they considered this an impregnable fortress. Of course, the Japanese didn't come by sea. They came overland."

To garrison their "impregnable fortress," the British began a frantic last-minute shuttle of troops from other colonies. These and local volunteers swelled the town with the military and more and more uniforms were seen at Raffles dances. Raffles and Singapore's elite were not pleased. Their town was filling up with louts. Never mind that they were here to save the Empire, they must save it while remaining in their place. Colonial snobbery extended beyond mere racial culling to include class and rank. Raffles asked that military police be posted outside its entrance to keep all those not commissioned as officers out. In the case of Australians, whom the locals found particularly loutish, rank had to be lieutenant colonel or higher.

Neville Slinng was on the desk when Raf Groot and his son came in through the crowded lobby. He was appalled to see the elder in a private's uniform. "What—are you doing in *that?*"

"I volunteered—signed up for the army." Raf was a well-liked man who was a Raffles regular. "I don't report till they get things sorted out. So you're going to have to put me and the boy up, Nev."

"I'm sorry but I can't do that."

Raf was dumbfounded. "But . . . I've been staying here for years!"

"Not as a private."

In those days Neville was tall and aloof with permanently lifted eyebrows indicating that nothing could astonish him. His people had been factors with the East India Company at the founding of Singapore, and his father and grandfather associated with Raffles from its beginning. Being born in Malaya made him strive to be all the more British and his accent became so plummy as to be nearly incomprehensible. He was charming to his equals and courteous to his betters. No one understood protocol better than he. He was the ultimate snob. At the moment his concern was not the Japanese, whom he dismissed as inferior, but the lower-class whites who would shove into his hotel and bring its standards down.

In 1941 there were four thousand Japanese civilians in Singapore, many living around Raffles itself in the textile shops on Middle Road, Hylam and Malay Street. They had established themselves as merchants (to the resentment of the local Chinese), traders and fishermen, and were served by massage parlors, a clubhouse featuring geisha girls rotated from home, and along the coast a chain of small Japanese-run hotels. They were also photographers, a monopoly really, so that after their internment as enemy nationals at the end of 1941 there was no one left to take passport photos.

Yuji Okubo had a studio in the Raffles shopping arcade. He was a courteous man of about forty, always available for parties and popular with the staff. In the years before the war he was the official "court" photographer at Raffles and had taken pictures at the many military balls. From this he built up an extensive file identifying senior Allied officers. He and the file disappeared before Japanese internment.

"Your father was a damned snob," Groot said, "but he was also absolutely loyal to old Raffles 'club' members. He solved my father's dilemma by requesting that the colonel, another club member, raise his rank from private to lieutenant, reasoning that if he was going to be doing nothing he could do it as a lieutenant as well as he could as a private. So we stayed on at Raffles until the end."

On December 6 the Japanese 25th Army was attacking down the Malay Peninsula. When the Royal Air Force base at Kota Baharu fell, Japanese navy bombers roared in to hit Singapore. The attack came late at night, but as usual the town was still awake, blazing with light, and the toll was heavy, two hundred killed and a large section burned out. After the bombers left sirens went off but the keys to the master switches could not be located and the lights burned until dawn.

Groot sat back now, smoking Filipino cigarillos and remembering. "We continued to believe in Japanese inferiority and waited for the mighty fleet to save us. The battleships *Repulse* and *Prince of Wales* had been rushed to the Far East to turn the tide. They had been dispatched by Winston Churchill to show the damn cheeky monkeys the lion's claws.

"They put out of Keppel Harbor at sunset on December eighth and there wasn't a dry eye on the quay. They would seek out and sink the Japanese invasion fleet off Kra Isthmus and stop the assault on Malaya in its tracks. Our hero was its commander, Admiral Sir Tom Phillips—five feet four and known as 'Tom Thumb, all brains and no body.'"

Nothing would do but to have a previctory ball at Raffles to reinforce confidence in the fleet. Neville was in charge of the list and carefully pruned it to include only the worthy. The dances had continued through the emergency (tables were booked into January 1942) and management had been obliged to set up a blackout around the huge ballroom. As for air raids, the hotel engineer now sat on the roof and would sound four whistles when the enemy was overhead.

"I was at that last ball," Groot continued, blowing the foul cigarillo smoke toward the skylight. "Allowed to keep out of sight at one side of the bandstand. I remember it very well—although I confess all the film and television costume balls I've seen since have swirled together in my mind to form one grand sweep of romantic dancers. My memory now is short-circuited with *Gone With the Wind, Doctor Zhivago* and *Die Fledermaus.*

"The music was marvelous. Raffles orchestras have always had style, but this night, lord—the sweet, terrible nostalgia of their playing, the moaning of saxophones. And the slide of feet! The syncopated movement of those locked together in perfect harmony. Bodies held close, words whispered, the press of tomorrows that may not come, the urgency of touch—all the clichés that prove true in war.

"Have I said how they were dressed? Formal, of course, the ladies done up in whatever was fashionable, silks, satins—why is it they seemed more desirable then? Such pathetic vulnerability—and the men, ah! Nearly all military and got up in white mess kit. That's the short bolero jacket that was ruined later by waiters. They were gay, ebullient, confident that the great battleships would sweep the Japs away. After all, they were the English and God was on their side—in those days he was white.

"The ball whirled on with everyone jampacked on the floor, and I must have fallen asleep because the next thing I remember was everyone linking arms and singing 'There'll Always Be an England.' It was very late and they suddenly stopped—dead still—that was what woke me. Neville had appeared and walked to the center of the dance floor. The crowd spread out around him and he read a dispatch from the Far East Command. Both the *Repulse* and the *Prince of Wales* had been sunk by Japanese torpedoes. Admiral Phillips and Captain Leach of the *Repulse* had gone down side by side. Eight hundred and eighty seamen were drowned. There was a gasp from the listeners. They finally understood that Singapore was lost. Then, incredibly, the band played a last waltz. Can you believe it? Talk about your sentimental tearjerkers, it was a piece of bravado that only the British could have come up with."

Neville passes out side doors to the Palm Court where servants stand at windows, peeking through blackout curtains watching the dancers. He pushes past them to a woman who waits in the shadows. She comes to him and they dance to the music drifting out from the ballroom, moving on the dark curly lawn past traveler's palms and coy statues of nymphs. It is an extraordinary thing for him to do and she knows terrible events must have occurred. She is his Malaysian mistress, the mother of his three children, and has never been inside the hotel.

"Singapore was now isolated and in a state of siege. Our impregnable naval base lay in ruins beneath a pall of smoke, and that morning the last pitiful remnants of the last British battalion—Argyll and Sutherland Highlanders—crossed the causeway from Malaya. With their pipers skirling 'Highland Laddie' they blew the bridge and the Johore Strait poured through to complete our isolation.

"On February eighth, in the midst of a terrific thunderstorm, the Japanese attacked with their artillery barrage matching the crash of thunder. A ragtag company of Australians—those same 'louts' that had been barred from Raffles—were our last defense and cut to pieces. Japanese engineers repaired the causeway and troops and tanks poured over."

The town was a horror of bloated bodies, burned-out vehicles and miles of downed electrical poles and wires, some still alive. Fires had spread and more than a million people were jammed in an area of three square miles. Water ran out and the looting began. Worse, Japanese troops had run amok at the military hospital at Alexandra, bayoneting wounded and staff—three hundred were killed. In the town panic was epidemic—Lieutenant Tomoyuki Yamashita, the Tiger of Malay, had arrived.

"At Raffles we poured the contents of the wine cellar down the drain. Rare and expensive brandies, old port, liqueurs—God, I could cry when I think of it—but Neville was determined that the Japs would have none of it. We had already buried the silver roast beef cart in the Palm Court . . ." Groot pointed down the room to the object itself. "That very one." Slinng knew it well. As a kid he had hopped on its smooth dome and skated it down the marble floor of the Tiffin Room—out of sight of the waiters, of course.

"That last day we gathered in the lobby and waited for them. Not many of us were left. My father, a few women, men who had thrown their uniforms away. The staff had done a bunk, deserted, and Neville stood at our head, impeccable as always, determined things would be correct. At noon a car appeared, a large Van Den Plas limousine we recognized as belonging to the governor, Sir Shenton Thomas. Several Japanese officers got out and strutted—that is the only word—into the lobby. When they reached us we saw that the major in charge was Yuji Okubo, our 'court' photographer.

"Neville was stunned but, gaining his composure, said, 'Well, Yuji, being a former Raffles employee you will understand what needs to be done. First—'

"Okubo slapped him hard across the face. 'Who are you to give orders? You are no longer in charge here!' Neville staggered back and we were cowed, unable to look at his face. 'From now on when you address your superior you will bow.' "

Neville puts his hand to his stinging cheek. He is filled with outrage, fury. Never, ever has he seen a white man touched by a yellow who didn't immediately suffer because of it. To have these inferior, rotten dogs in his hotel is bad enough but this—he wants to strike back, smash this insolent bastard into the floor. His own eyes blazing, he looks at Okubo and sees that he dares him to do just this, give him the chance to be a man before his friends. He knows that if he raises his hand he will be instantly cut down—but he will have died for honor. Neville is not a coward, but there is something else—*Raffles.* Who will protect his hotel if he is not there? Is Raffles more important than his honor? Can he humble himself, crawl, to save it? If he bows to Okubo will that make him *and* Raffles collaborators? The eyes of the others are cast down. They wait to see what he will do.

Groot picks this time to pause. He gestures to the waiter and asks for a double dessert of gula malacca. Slinng, caught up in the story of Singapore's fall and his father's role in it, finds it hard to pull back. Stretching, he looks toward the entrance and just happens to catch the Van Den Plas Princess go by. *Was she in it?*

Hartog came out on deck at noon sipping his morning Sambucca. Down the quay, harbor cruise boats were already packing them in for Sentosa and the southern islands. Cameras were out and pointing his way. He waved and smiled, shouting, "I hope the fucking thing sinks and you all go to the bottom!" They couldn't hear him and waved cheerily back.

Walking aft, he had a view of the pier parking lot and saw that the Princess wasn't in its place. Blas Coff was having breakfast under the fantail canopy and Hartog joined him. "Did Miri take the Princess?"

"I believe she went shopping, Tog."

"Jes-sus! She has bloody shopped the town out of business—I can't believe there's anything left on the shelves." He sat down and examined

Blas' plate, picking up a piece of toast. "The woman's a born shopper."

"She's pretty good at it." Blas read the *Straits Times* while he ate, dressed in a neat blazer suit and tie. Using the toast, Hartog mopped egg off his plate.

"I worry about her in town. It would be like her to walk in front of a tour bus and put a crimp in our trip," Hartog said, mouth full.

"Come on, Tog . . ."

"Have you seen her? She never looks where she's going. She's in a daze half the time—catching hold of her is like groping air."

"Are you talking about drinking?"

"No, it's not that, or even drugs—it's just the *way* she is."

"Well, nobody had to tell you she was odd, different. You said it, Tog, it's her way—and anyone that beautiful can get away with it. If she were ordinary you wouldn't put up with her for a minute."

"Well, she's not ordinary."

"She's lucky to have you—she needs somebody who can stay ahead of her, a strong hand."

"Yes, but the thing is, you see, I can't be dodging around shopping and that lot . . ."

"No, but . . ."

". . . so I've got her a bodyguard."

Blas kept his voice very even. "One of the Gurkhas?"

"No, they wouldn't do. Wo got me a proper Chinese, one of his bunch. A tough monkey, so he says."

"Do you think Miri will put up with that?"

"Oh, she'll never see him—he'll trail her on a motorbike."

"When does he start?"

"He started last week."

There was just a half beat. "Well, I'm certainly in favor of anything that will protect Miri."

"Of course you are." He smiled. "You're the cupid who introduced us." And reaching over, he picked a piece of bacon off Blas' plate. Blas hated that.

Miri had the car stop in front of the Isetan Department Store on Orchard Road and jumped out. She entered past caparisoned girls selling "P-Shine" kits and plunged into the crowd of shoppers. As she went she tied a scarf around the abundant hair, tucking it in until there wasn't a wisp showing. A fountain centered in the four-story atrium sent up jets of water that rose to a circular dome lit by colored lights. Behind this were four banks of escalators connecting each open balcony floor, the neon tubes on their railings presenting a glowing, serpentine passage.

Escalating to the top floor, she crossed over to a conventional elevator, dropped to the ground floor, and exited on the street level, buzzing with traffic and motorbikes. Halfway down the block was the façade of a small travel agency. Adjusting dark glasses, she went in. "Tickets for Mr. Dickey, please."

The agent, a pretty Singaporean with last year's curly perm, tapped it out on the computer. "Confirmed, please. Straight through to Heathrow." She made up the package. "Leaving on the twenty-fourth, this Friday, eight A.M. departure, please have your passports ready. Two first-class in no-smoking."

"Thank you."

"Have a good trip, Miss Muffy."

9

"**H**E BOWED?"

"Yes. That was the last time I saw your father until after the war," Groot said. He was back to eating again, talking with his mouth full. "We were taken off to Changi prison on the east coast that very day and he stayed behind to manage Raffles. Later he involved us in a situation that got many of us badly beaten and Hartog nearly killed."

Major Okubo was not necessarily vicious or a bully. He had played a game with Neville and won. He needed his help in pulling the staff back together for the smooth running of the hotel. It was commandeered by Imperial Army Headquarters (Transport and Supplies Section) for the use of high-ranking officers, so at least that remained the same. They renamed it the Syonan Ryokan, "Light of the South," changed the entrance and brought in Japanese cooks from Tokyo for miso soup and other delicacies. The staff, accustomed to the overdressed British, were now exposed to Japanese in loincloths practicing sword moves in the Palm Court. In the evening Mr. Applebaumn and his Hungarian orchestra, stolen from the Adelphi Hotel, played Japanese songs while officers knocked back sake and Kirin beer, singing the popular "Aikouka Koshinkyoku": "Behold the dawn in the east . . . fresh spirits above and below the earth—there leaps the hope of Great Japan."

Neville was appalled at the lack of European manners, squatting on chairs, noisy eating and teeth picking. More serious was the erratic Japanese reaction to the slightest provocation. A cook caught stealing a few eggs was dragged into the Palm Court, tied to a tree and for days beaten by any Japanese who casually passed by. An old room boy who caused offense by being an opium addict had his stomach filled with water from a hose by them jumping on it. Erratic punishment.

Through all this Neville managed his guilt by arranging to secretly slip food into Changi prison. It wouldn't have succeeded without Major Okubo's tacit approval. He allowed it perhaps because his own officers dabbled in the black market where a bottle of whiskey went for $12,000 and a tin of butter $950. And too, many of those in the prison had been his friends and clients in the old days. It went on for nearly a year. Then, late in 1943, Neville received a note from Raf Groot that had been smuggled out. In it he said they were all starving. The food coming from Raffles went into the pipeline of a gang of Australians who controlled it, selling it for huge sums and making slaves of the less fortunate prisoners. Raf wasn't concerned for himself, he was almost finished—but his son was six one now and weighed eighty-six pounds.

Neville was outraged, his sense of white man's justice offended. Those damned Australians again! Here he was risking his neck and those louts were using *his* food for *their* own rotten purposes. He went to Major Okubo. They were on a footing now where he felt he would get a fair hearing. This was a mistake. After much bowing and circumlocution he got his story across without naming names. The Japanese were not at fault, he said, far from it. It was selfish prisoners. Okubo could not understand how the British could be so stupid. Now he would have to act on a thing he supposedly knew nothing about! He would like to take his trusty shin-gunto and cut this man's thick skull with the kami-tatewari—top vertical split.

Instead he sent the Kempeitai into the camp and for three days they scourged the prisoners with beatings and torture. On the following Monday Neville was sent for and found Okubo eating lunch in the Elizabethan Grill (which was now called the Japanese Inn). Standing to one side was a tall gangling young fellow with long hair, an odd nose and skin color he could only liken to a kangaroo's. His hands were tied and he appeared to have been beaten. Two bulky soldiers stood behind him.

"This is the man who takes food from others. His name is . . ." He paused to look at a paper with phonetic spelling. "Hartog. Do you know him?"

Neville was instantly apprehensive. "Why . . . no . . ." Looking in the man's small eyes and expecting to see hatred, he saw instead resignation, a lift to the shoulder that said, "Fuck it, mate, what can you expect from this lot?"

"What do you think should be his punishment?"

"That is not my judgment." He began to sweat, finally realizing the enormity of his mistake.

Okubo got up, wiping his mouth. "Come on." And the whole group—Hartog tugged along by the soldiers—walked through the dining room and, turning left, pushed through the kitchen doors. The cooks and helpers instantly backed off bowing, steaming pots left on their own. Okubo picked up a large stirring spoon and walked along the ranges, clanking pans while he examined the kitchen equipment. "Is it British justice or biblical justice that says the punishment should fit the crime?" No one answered. He stopped by an important-looking machine bolted to the counter that chopped up bone and fat when pressed down through a top opening. It was electrical and when he tried the switch it gave off a vigorous whine of blades. "This will do. Bring the thief over here."

The soldiers grabbed Hartog and pulled him up to the machine. "Wait a bloody minute!" he shouted. "What is this?!"

Neville began a protest but Okubo slammed the spoon down on a pot lid, silencing them. "This man has dipped his fingers into food meant for all. What better method than to punish those fingers?" Flipping the switch on the machine, he nodded to the soldiers.

They jammed first one hand then the other into the whirling blades. Neville stepped back with a cry as a spray of blood, fingernails and bone splattered out the top and hit him. Hartog screamed in long shuddering wails that pierced the walls of the kitchen and sounded down the corridors of the hotel, sent shivers along the spines of the staff. Japanese officers looked up from their beer and wondered.

When it was done the ends of Hartog's fingers had been ground off as if in a pencil sharpener. Fainting, he was dragged away to the doctor for bandaging. Neville, ghostly pale, sagged against the range for support, very near fainting himself. "Now," Okubo said, "please do not tell me that the Japanese are not fair in dispensing justice."

There was a long pause when Groot finished and, stunned, Slinng finally asked, "But . . . Hartog must have hated my father, blamed him . . ."

"No, I never heard him make any such statement in the camp."

"But it was because of my father that they did . . . that to him."

"You have to remember we all thought of the Japanese as the enemy—our hatred was turned toward them."

"What became of Okubo?"

"He died peacefully in his sleep in Toyko. His nephew, Akira, now runs the photo shop in the arcade." His fork scrapped the plate, chasing the last of gula malacca. "Do you know who these new Singaporeans, the young Far Eastern yuppies and upwardly mobile, admire the most? Those they wish to emulate? Not the British who died here defending the city, no, not even the Americans whose culture they flirt with—it is the Japanese, of course. The older ones even now speak with a certain nostalgia of the occupation years, saying that there was discipline then—well, we know that was true, don't we? Certainly Hartog does."

Slinng slid his chair back. "Thank you, sir, for the history lesson."

"The next time I'll tell you an entirely different version of the same events—after all, that is what history is about."

As Slinng turned, Groot stopped him. "Oh, I should inform you there was a constable around yesterday asking for you. I heard him talking to Roberto. Apparently you don't stay here."

Inspector Swee found that hard to believe. But when his man reported back from Raffles he didn't push it, not for the moment. Turning Captain Slinng over to Sri Lanka was a serious thing. There was something else, the father's death. He had never been satisfied with the investigation and perhaps the son wasn't either. He himself had seen Neville Slinng lunching at Raffles with an attractive woman only a few days before his death. He appeared vigorous—not someone who would drown in a bathtub. But the case was not in his department and none of his business.

Perhaps what really bothered him was that the elder Slinng's age was not much off his own. He resented it that "old" and "feeble" were interchangeable in the language of the report.

As his man left he dropped another pearl. He had identified Billy Hon's big motorcycle outside of Raffles. It was not difficult; in a city where the limit on motorbikes was 250 cc, he had wangled a permit for a thousand. They both knew how—Mr. Wo of the Ah Kong. Here was a man they appreciated. He soothed their nerves. There was never any question about his intent; he never made a move that wasn't convoluted, complicated and devious. A genuine Chinese villain of the old school.

Slinng went wearily to his room. The sun was full up and his head ached. He was now convinced Hartog had something to do with his father's death. How could it be otherwise? Now *he* had to do something about Hartog.

In the corridor in front of his door he met a maid, one of his old Chinese "aunties" who had been waiting for him. They bowed respectfully together and she formally extended an invitation, asking if he would honor the family with a visit, tomorrow, Sunday. He agreed but was aware of her uneasiness. Something was very wrong.

The next afternoon, Slinng slipped out of the hotel and took a cab across the Elgin Bridge and through Chinatown. Its center contained enough twists, turns and snaky dead-end alleys to qualify as a genuine Chinese puzzle; packed with restaurants and shops where mah-jonng tiles were stacked like Nabisco Wafers. As he turned on Pagoda Street the smell of incense drifted up from the Sri Mariamman Temple. If you ignored the flagpoles of drying clothes hanging from upper-level windows, and radios tuned to Singapore's Top Ten hits, it was yesterday.

Being modern Chinese, the family Sing lived in the People's Park complex off Eu Tong Road. These were middle-class apartment buildings that might have been put down in Long Island or Liverpool. Slinng paid the cab and took an elevator to the third floor, where the hall smelled of ginger. He was met at the door by his host, the elder Sing, and a roomful of relatives, aunts, uncles, kids, all somehow connected with

Raffles: Hainan Chinese who formed the hotel family. Like the room their appearance was eclectic: Oriental gowns and slippers mixed with Western T-shirts and sneakers.

There was a young daughter, twenty, Kim, a pretty, self-effacing girl in a traditional costume that was perfectly connected to a lithe body. As she bowed, the butterflies in her hair comb set up a fluttering and he was charmed. After the trendy Singapore ladies she seemed positively exotic.

"I've seen you at Lloyd's," she said.

"Is that right?" He was surprised.

"Oh, yes, I'm a syndicate clerk working for Colonel Pynge-Gilbert, that most nice man."

Slinng had to smile; so much for his exotic flower. "You're in marine insurance then?"

"That is true. I transcribed your report on the *Sulu.* Informal but cogent."

"Well, it's a great deal of money for one man to insure with Lloyd's."

"You don't insure *with* Lloyd's, Captain, but *at* Lloyd's." Self-effacing? Pedantic. "It's a gentlemen's club really, the underwriters pay out for the syndicate members—all are private individuals."

"Yes, of course . . ."

She rolled over him. "I worry about Colonel Pynge-Gilbert. He has written a line of seven and one-half percent on a ten-million-dollar ship, accepting seven hundred and fifty thousand dollars of the loss personally."

"Is there something you know that he doesn't?"

But there was the clamor for dinner.

Dinner was shark fins with black bean sauce, steamed garoupa, and fish heads in earthen pots. The chopsticks clicked like drum rolls and conversation was voluble: polite inquiries about his mother's health; sad nods over his father's death. The older family members had worked for him and remembered his "upright dignity" (translated, this meant "stiff-necked").

When the last dishes were cleared and the women withdrew, Slinng settled in with the men and heard the problem. The elder Sing led off. He was a handsome man with raked-back white hair and an established serious expression. They all sat smoking, the Oriental curse, on a narrow balcony looking off toward a view of suburban lights, obscured now by the clouds of their exhalation.

"It is my son . . .," he began, with a sigh that vibrated. "He has gone to the dogs. A young fellow of great promise, he has become a musician—not classical, no—a honker in a band!" This was said with great pathos. "His name is Louis Sing but he has changed it to Cool Luke Han." There was head-shaking over this, mumbles of disbelief.

Slinng smiled but it was not funny to the relatives.

There was a pause while cigarettes were lit off cigarettes, a suck of smoke from the toenails. "It's drugs and gambling," the elder intoned. A breeze of sighs went around the room, each member adding his particular lilt. "He owes money to the—Ah Kong," he whispered.

Then Slinng knew exactly why he had been asked.

"They have addressed the family to pay his debts—some sixty-eight thousand in Singapore dollars!" More groans. "We need time to raise this large amount."

There was no question of the family not paying it. That was accepted from the beginning. No matter what the son had done it was the family's honor to make it good.

"They have asked you to settle it all up—now?" Slinng thought this unusual. That kind of debt was dragged out for years with the interest racing ahead of principal until it became an annuity. Something else was at work here—revenge most likely, an insult called in.

"Yes, *now*. We do not understand. Louis will not communicate with the family. It was our thinking that because he is crazy for all things Western, the son of Mr. Neville Slinng, being fresh from the West, might be taken into his confidence."

So there it was; he was to be the intermediary. In the end it had nothing to do with the West, his father or Raffles. They somehow knew he was involved with Mr. Wo of the Ah Kong triad.

Slinng agreed to meet with Louis at the place of horn honking the next night. Kim would accompany him. He wondered about this. Was there something even more sinister afoot here? Was the family pushing them together, finding her a husband?

She lived only a few blocks away and he walked her home. "I like your way of dressing," he said. "You don't see that much anymore."

"I only wear this home to please the family. You like the old ways, I suppose?"

Slinng remembered Mr. Wo saying, "Our robes hamper speed but give dignity. The young wear trousers for vigor and a hasty gait. They have lost patience without gaining zeal, forgotten old morals without adopting new ones." But he said, "Being in the West with its constant style changes makes you long for a culture that remains the same."

"Ha! That's not Singapore. What is our culture anyway? Malay? Straits Chinese speak Malay and eat their egg foo yung with chili—Malay is supposed to be the national language but who else speaks it? Not us; we were taught to speak English. This is Singapore's schizophrenia. Which culture should prevail? Which ethic?"

Slinng saw that although she was dressed in the old way he was in the clutches of the "new Eastern woman." He tried to change the subject. "Tell me about your brother."

"We kids were raised on Western standards, taught to believe in the rights of the individual. If the old people don't understand Louis, that is the problem. Our Chinese is bad; we like discos, fast food and pop music. Our philosophy is pragmatism—we are rational opportunists. Now they tell us to learn Chinese and study Confucian ethics. The PM says, 'No child should leave school without having the software of his culture programmed into his subconscious.' Ha! Too late for us. Ours is plugged into modern media technique."

They reached her small apartment and stopped in front of its canopy. Across the street were lit shops and a noisy pachinko arcade. Time to say, "Well, it was a nice evening, good night." He was anxious to leave the one-way monologue.

She looked closely at him, smiling as a thought struck her. "It is you who are the Confucian! You look Western, but inside you are more Eastern than my brother, who desperately wants to cross over."

After that there was a pause, and nothing left to be said. They bowed good night. "Don't forget tomorrow night," she said. "Ten o'clock."

"Yes, of course."

As she watched him off down the street she was aware of sexual pressure—sublimated, simmering. It was the old way: to dream of love and expectation, to smile at secret thoughts of coming pleasure.

At the pachinko arcade, the games ding and beep at players' progress. Lines of Chinese and Malay young men hunch over glowing consoles, their narrow behinds boxed into jeans. There is an ongoing chorus of grunts and squeals as they try to walk blips down tortuous electronic paths to glory. The space is dark and the lights from the games give all the eerie look of the possessed.

Billy Hon stands at the front of the arcade under revolving pinwheels of neon and watches Slinng whistle down a cab. He is in his tube of leather and the fierce motorcycle is parked out of sight (with a dent in the tank). After the humiliation of his encounter with Captain Slinng he had not gone to Mr. Wo with his troubles. No. Mr. Wo *knows.* The Captain is one of his favorites.

Despite his brutal appearance Billy is not stupid. Education had been beyond his family's pocketbook but he had been born with that marvelous Chinese affinity for convoluted plots and the patience to outwait enemies. Revenge is best executed not on the victim but his family and friends. It had been difficult with the Captain. His family was not at hand. Then he discovered his family was Raffles. From there it was a question of finding which one was vulnerable and putting the screws on.

He looks at his watch. Time to report for his bodyguard job. He's a busy person these days.

10

INSPECTOR SWEE'S MAN found another pearl. "Did you see this?" He laid a printout of the "People's Crime Report" on Swee's desk. This was a calendar of the week's antisocial events put together from citizens who reported to the police. They were encouraged by the government to watch their neighborhoods and buildings for disruptive persons. It was defined by the P.A.P slogan seen painted on walls around Singapore: *Three-S production plan: Social responsibility. Social attitude. Skill.*

"Here it is, page six. Underlined. 'There was a disturbance at Hawker Centre and several triad watchers recognized Billy Hon and his big motor bike . . .'" Swee read on; witnesses reported he was grabbed by a tall white man in a Panama hat who flopped his hand on a grill, then proceeded to punch and kick him. After knocking his motorbike over, he chased him into the crowd. "What do you think of that? There's a man we should recruit."

Swee was depressed. He had hoped Captain Slinng would go about the business of his father quietly and be gone. There was no doubt he was connected to the Ah Kong; now here he was involved in a disturbance with one of them. "I want you to begin a regular watchover on Raffles. I'll prepare the papers for arrest." Swee was encouraged that his man didn't ask, "Whose arrest?"

The Teddy Disco Lounge was on Lavender Street in the old brothel quarter. Singapore, being an ocean crossroads, had been a sailor town from its beginning, a stopping place for the Flying Fish sailors of Indiamen and tea clippers—the Malay and Chinese crews of the East Indian coasters Conrad had written about. It was famous for samshu shops with Japanese girls from the original Tokyo Yoshiwar. They sat on cushions in shops along Malay Street, attending to bodily ablutions while customers rolled by and gawked in through barred windows.

In those days on the corners of Bugis and Malabar streets, Malay girls posed in stationary rickshaws, coolie runners squatting between lowered shafts while "duennas" in black oil-silk and carrying sunshades haggled over prices with buyers. The area was frequented by white planters, riffraff and the sexually depraved. It was a wild time of Malay ronggeng dancing and the ropey side of night life, where at dawn drunken sailors raced each other back to their ships pulling rickshaws while the coolies hung on for dear life, pigtails flying.

But where colonial morality had winked an eye and missionary zeal went soggy from the heat, nationalism accomplished: By the sixties, Lee Kuan Yew's People's Action Party, the P.A.P., had swept away the visible brothel and its public support system. These days prostitutes were still to be found, but they were discreet and you'd better bring your Visa because they didn't take American Express.

When Lawrence Slinng and Kim Sing arrived by cab at Teddy's, the street was occupied by the young: plastic accessories, Crawford shoulders and ubiquitous jeans. Hair was spikey and, like the music, several beats behind the times. From the outside, the warp of neon into Chinese characters shaped the club entrance and was blocked by crowds of kids in the push and shove of overcharged libidos. There was lots of posturing and threatening gestures, confrontation that was disarmed by friends who tugged the rock warriors away before they hurt themselves.

Dodging motorbikes, Slinng and Kim pushed past loungers spitting and striking attitudes and made the door. Inside it was all noise and steam rising from overheated bodies; searchlights whipped across the barn of a room in confusing patterns. The place was packed, small tables shoved together, jammed with kinetic customers, every one of them smoking. Drinks were beer, tea and something made from coconuts and Kool-Aid. Paper twists of dried noodles with salted squid were sold table to table and their fallout crunched underfoot as Slinng and Kim snaked their way through. The prevailing smell was Brut and soy sauce. Music came from a circular platform surrounded by a forest of amps—cables stretching out like tangled roots. At its center an electric band blasted away in a pitch so atonal that the reverberating *waa-waa*'s actually distorted windowpanes in the overhead skylight.

Cool Luke Han was up front on bass sax; white-rimmed sunglasses, Singapore hip, honking the sax like a long pull on a semi's air horn. He was small and, from what Slinng could see, good looking, slick hair and features like Kim's, a click away from feminine. There was a segue, a drop in intensity and then a beginning wail he actually recognized: "Harlem Nocturne." Luke stepped off the low platform circled by tables and began his big solo.

Continuing ringside, he paused to serenade a Malay beauty sitting with a husky escort. Leaning down, he bent the notes in a sinuous melody, ringing it out in a low, sustained sound connected by breathy intonations. An amber spot picked them up and the girl suppressed a giggle behind her hand. When Luke leaned in closer and the chrome bell of sax nearly touched her cheek, the escort poured a full jug of beer into it and the honks fizzled out, blowing foam.

Furious, Luke swung and the escort shoved him back into a pile of crashing glasses and coconut Kool-Aid. The crowd loved this, laughing and hooting while the band played on.

"Excuse me." Slinng sighed, rose and, squeezing between tables, helped Luke up, only to have his hand angrily shaken off. Behind them the escort grabbed his arm and was smacked soundly in the center of the forehead with the palm of Slinng's hand, knocking him backward off the chair. More laughter and applause from the onlookers. This was the floor show. The escort scrambled to his feet and squared off in karate wig-wags. Now there were cheers and shouts for an East-versus-West match.

His opponent's foot shot out, showing a size-twelve Adidas tread, and narrowly missed Slinng's crotch. But the man was off balance and Slinng caught the foot, twisted and spun him back, upsetting the table and the beauty. The crowd was disappointed at the brief exchange, and there were hisses and the breaking of wind. Thinking it was over, Slinng turned back for his table, then hearing a change to cheers, found the escort charging, out of control. This time a beefy arm swung up for a blow to break the collar bone. Slinng had enough. Turning his big ring around, he stepped through the swing and hit the man with terrific force below the cheekbone, snapping his head around. The sound was like the smack of a large fish hitting a teak deck and he went down, senseless. In the melee Louis Sing had disappeared.

There was an intake of breath from the onlookers, the low rattle Malays make in their throats. They frowned, shocked at the force of his blow. Their hero was only being playful. Half a coconut hit Slinng on the back, then a glass, and insults followed in three languages. He swung around and faced them, walking to the table and holding out the chair as Kim got up. The pelting went on as they walked toward the door, but those protesting saw his expression and big, clenched fists. No one got up to stop him.

Slinng was stunned by the hostility, the hatred that came up. As Kim said, he might like to believe he was more Eastern inside than they were but here he was now, white and an outsider, and he had just struck down one of *them*.

In the cab, Slinng sat perfectly still, breathing deep, calming down. "I'm sorry, Kim—I made a mess of that—it was stupid."

"It is not stupid to react to an insult." Kim could barely contain herself. She was horrified and thrilled. If she was the Modern Eastern Woman in public, here was the white man of her secret fantasies who overpowers the yellow one with pure brute strength, the master who takes what he wants by force. Curiously this was a popular theme in current adult comic books and "historic" soaps on Singapore TV. It had its roots in a strange kind of cultural masochism: the commercial romantic fantasy of aristocratic colonial planters having their way with beautiful servant girls, falling in love with them and becoming their protectors.

At her building Kim insisted that Slinng come up to rest and gain composure. Also she had an envelope to be given privately to Colonel

Pynge-Gilbert. Curious, he allowed himself to be drawn along. When they arrived at the tiny flat he asked about the envelope.

"In doing the traces and contract work on Mr. Hartog's policy I came across many small things—signals—from his various companies. It is a very complicated structure. I think the Colonel should be aware of them." She handed him a envelope.

"Why not give it to him yourself?"

"No, no. I'm a clerk. It would be presumptuous—I could lose my job questioning Mr. Hartog. It must come from you, his friend."

"Well, all right." He took the envelope. "I'd better be going. I'm sorry about not making contact with your brother. Perhaps we can set up a private meeting at Raffles."

"We must talk about it. Here, let me get you a drink, stay awhile—no one will be disturbed. My roommate is staying over with her parents."

"Thank you, but . . ."

"Please."

It was worse than he thought. Sitting him down in the only comfortable chair, she produced a small bottle of Johnnie Walker Black and English biscuits obviously bought for this occasion. Then she sat on the floor at his feet and proceeded to talk while they drank. It had nothing to do with her brother.

"The family was very upset that I chose to live on my own. They did not approve of girls having a flat together. But everything has changed. This is not the old days, I told them, women now strive for independence, here as well as the rest of the world. Our government agrees. My parents were most firm but I resisted. I may appear acquiescent but I am very sturdy in opinions and resolve."

Slinng could believe that. The saying was "The butterfly of spring who is light as a feather will be made of iron by winter weather."

"Here," she said, unlacing his shoes, "take these off and let me massage the feet. I am very good at it."

"No, no . . . please . . .," he protested but she went ahead and he had to admit it was heaven. "I met this young man who came around to the office to administer to the computers. He was Indian, but a native of Singapore like myself . . ." Slinng swallowed a yawn and she went on.

". . . we had fine romance but disapproval from my parents and his. That did not detour us, no, what did was his politics. C. V. Devan Nair, his hero, had insulted the PM and this is all he could talk of. Indians are very high strung and their voices can be sharp as paper cuts. We parted but I was grateful, he had divested me of the burden of virginity."

Slinng winced. Here it was, she was telling him not to worry about the family or her virginity. "Kim . . ."

"I am very bold." She finished her glass of Scotch and put it down. "But I wanted you to know how it is with me." She took his foot and placed it against her slim, flat stomach, the heel resting between her legs. "Press hard," she said. "You'll see how strong I am."

"Kim . . ."

"I have this silly fantasy," she giggled, "where I lie naked and a man places his feet on me. Then . . ."

"Kim . . ."

"Try it."

Instead he pushed himself up, put on his shoes, mumbling lame excuses about the lateness of the hour, early rising, God knows what. He left her hurt and insulted.

In the street he feels rotten, telling himself no matter what she says about her independence he will not put the relentless juggernaut of family intentions in gear. Certainly she's attractive, desirable—and yes, there's something very compelling, naïve in her attempt to be a Modern Eastern Woman. But none of this is the point.

Could he tell her he was in the thrall of a woman whose face he could not shake out of his mind? A great luminous bundle of fair hair; features fine-boned and delicate—the ultimate blond Anglo-Saxon: a white princess.

In his haste to break away he has forgotten the envelope for Colonel Pynge-Gilbert.

As Lawrence walks off down the street looking for a cab, two young Chinese in leathers cross over to Kim's apartment building. They enter the tiny vestibule and, examining the tenants' names, one selects a button and pushes it. To his surprise the buzzer instantly sounds and the door opens.

"I knew you'd be back . . .," a breathless voice says over the intercom.

Returning to Raffles via the kitchen, Slinng found Miri playing pool on the famous table the tiger had been shot under. Or so they said.

Actually like many of Raffles legends it had been stretched. In August of 1902 a tiger had escaped from a show on Beach Road and crawled under the old building. Charley Phillips, headmaster of Raffles School and crack shot, was sent for. Shaken awake from a late night of drinking, he was propelled to the spot still in his pajamas and carrying an army Enfield. The building was on stilts then, and peering into the gloom under the pool room he blazed away, first blowing away a brick support and finally the unfortunate tiger. It was dragged out by its tail and Charley went home to nurse his hangover. It was truly the last tiger shot in Singapore and there was no animal rights group to mourn it. In fact, as late as the 1880s tigers had come into the downtown area to snatch away storekeepers. In those days people were the endangered species.

Slinng had been on his way to his rooms by the back stairs when he heard the click of balls and glimpsed a flash of blond. Going in the pool room he saw Miri Brooke bent over the table, stretched out for a corner shot. One of her superior legs was lifted to show a marvelous connection.

"If you've got a hundred dollars I'll give you first break."

He chalked a cue and broke, sinking six balls. That was his last chance. She ran the table twice and picked up his money. "You're amusing," he said, "but you're a hustler." He replaced his cue and turned toward the door.

"Well," she said, "you're amusing and a sore loser." She followed him out the door and along the corridor toward the stairs. "Where are you going?"

"To bed."

"Can I come?"

"No."

"Why not?"

"As I remember, the last time we met you were spoken for."

"What's that got to do with now?"

He didn't answer and when they arrived at his door she was still following him. He said good night. "I know what it is," she said, "you're one of those kind who can't get it up unless he's in a crow's nest." She thought this was funny and laughed.

"Damn!" he shouted, slamming the door open. "What is the matter with you?!" She followed him inside. "Are you crazy? On drugs? Or just plain immoral?" He began jerking his clothes off, throwing them around, stamping his feet in anger as he went into the bedroom. It had been a full evening dealing with two berserk women.

"Does this mean we're going to fuck?" Trailing him, shucking her dress over her head.

"How can you be so damn beautiful, practically ethereal—and behave like a . . . a . . ."

"Oh, shut up!" And kissing him, she grabbed a convenient handle, shoving him back on the bedspread. "Put your pecker where your mouth is."

It was an athletic contest of heavy breathing and machine-gun bursts that satisfied neither. When they finally lay back and the frantic groping subsided she began to talk in a different, small voice. "I learned pool at our place in Shirr, Ireland. It wasn't a slop table like the one downstairs—it was serious billiards, balkline. My uncle Charley taught me. I had been parked there while my mother traveled the tennis circuit—we were all sports then. They took me in because I was a Brooke, a tag end of the family.

"The house was a marvel. A castle really, but right in the middle of town, with shops and such, straight up against the walls. It made for getting to know the locals. I like the Irish but we cultivated being British among them. The place had once had a zillion acres but of course this was all gone now and everyone's concern was with keeping it going, what with taxes and all. They were an arty bunch, into stenciling and astronomy, and I suppose I learned my values from them. They cared desperately for the mania of the moment but couldn't be bothered with the long run. The family name would carry them.

"I went up to London with Mum. Tennis was over and she kept marrying until she got it right, going off to Canberra with a fellow who was going to introduce waterbeds to the outback. I stayed at schools and got on by being pretty. But it wasn't the kind of pretty that worked in modeling or films. And I really had no special talent for a career, so I became the girlfriend of rock musicians and screenwriters. You know the joke about the Hollywood starlet who was so dumb she fucked a writer— that was me."

"Where did you meet Hartog?"

"In Australia visiting Mum. An antiques dealer took me to a party on the *Sulu.* I was impressed, he was my first big rich uncle. He got all excited about me being a Brooke. The White Raj business. He was crazed on the subject so I fed him what I knew."

"Like what?"

"Not much really, I had never paid attention to it. I knew there was a big family split when Uncle Charley turned the country back to the Brits and Mum told me once that it was written into the agreement that if any of us Brookes returned to Sarawak we would have the honorary rights of the White Raj.

"Is that true?"

"I don't know, but Tog liked it. He began planning the trip right then . . ." She stretched out, looking sleepy at last.

Her story was the modern melodrama of the poor little rich girl—or rather, the poor little *wants*-to-be-rich girl. Attractive, bright and bored by nearly everything and everybody. Drifting along the edge of a demi-social world. Now along as a totem for an immensely rich, ugly man. But how could she stand to be touched by . . . no! He wasn't going to do that. Romance had made its miraculous justifications—he would accept her as she was.

When they were locked together this time it was as though the metronome was in sync again.

They slept and hours later he woke to her crying. He gathered her in, alarmed. "What is it?"

"A dream . . . about a head . . ." Her voice was a whisper and he didn't recognize the eyes.

"Whose head?"

"Hartog . . . I . . . oh, God . . ."

"It's all right—it's just a dream, easy."

"No . . . you haven't seen it . . ." She shuddered.

He soothed her, calling up clichés remembered from films and novels, calming her down, kisses, speaking of his desire for her, his willingness to protect her. She could stay with him, here at Raffles, she would never have to go back to Hartog.

After she drifted off again he lay awake and wondered about her dream of Hartog's head. *What did it mean?*

. . .

When he woke again it was near dawn and she was gone. He got up
and checked the bathroom. A note on Raffles stationery had been tucked
in the frame of the mirror.

Loved the game, said the pocket to the ball.

At Clifford Pier streaks of pink-tipped dark clouds, the spread of
morning light silhouetting tall ships' cranes; chains and cables looped.
Beyond is the outline of solemn warehouses—the *entrepôts* of yesterday
squaring the waterfront skyline now. A cab with a noisy bubbling exhaust slaloms around parked cars and stops in front of the *Sulu*. Miri
pays, stretches long legs and goes on board. Coming up the gangway, she
sees no one on watch and this seems odd. Decks are clear, the atrium
lit by night lights. As she climbs the stairs to the third deck there is the
disconcerting experience of her reflection on the dark, mirrored walls.
Her hair appears as a cloudy apparition rising on its own, her body lost
in overlapping shadows.

She pauses at teak doors of the master suite, then enters the library.
It is perfectly quiet. Crossing to the bedroom she listens again. No sound.
The door is pushed open and Hartog is lying on the bed, face turned
away. But where is the sound of chainsaw snoring? *Is the bastard playing
games?*

Still, the shape of a body appears beneath the sheet. She eases around
the bed and leans down . . .

"G'day!" A booming laugh is behind her, and she pivots.

His face is inches away, the pig eyes squinted shut in laughter. His head
is in the bed. "What a rotten . . ."

He has both of her slim wrists caught in a deft move of one hand. In
the other he brings up a syringe and punches it in a vein at the crook
of her arm. He smiles as he does it, allowing the fluid to be carefully
pumped in. "Nightie-o."

"No . . .," she is crying, ". . . oh, please . . ." But it is already working
and she slides down, caught under the arms and dragged into the library.
Here, deposited in an office chair, she is pushed out into the passageway.
Turning left he wheels her to a door halfway down and unlocks it.

Blas Coff lies naked on the bare mattress. His body is very white and
unexpectedly hairy, penis curled and sleeping. The carefully arranged
hair now stands up like a clown's and his eyes are partly open, unfocused.
Hartog positions Miri's chair by the bed, then, reaching over, rolls Blas'

eyelids back, checking. Satisfied, he hefts Miri up next to him, arranges her limbs and strips her clothing off. Finished, he is unable to resist and leaning down shakes the perfect rounds of breasts with his stubs of fingers.

Next, he circles the stateroom to be sure there is not a piece of clothing left, curtains, towels; the bathroom cleaned out. Then going into the passageway, he locks the door. Wheeling the chair back to the library he passes the Ghurka and receives a salute.

On the pier is the sound of a large motorcycle kicking over. An acceleration up through the gears, a shift down and the buffet of exhaust exiting a pipe the size of a bazooka, then trailing off, fading.

11

AFTER MIRI LEFT, Slinng was too agitated to sleep. Standing at the window over the "R" in the Raffles sign, he looked out past the streak of car lights on the East Coast Parkway to the masts of ships anchored in the Strait.

Two women. He sighed.

Kim had been shocked at his ready violence but he was a veteran of bar wars and had the scars to prove it. In his early days at sea he had lived the life of a common seaman with a vengeance, treating hardship as the norm and drinking and fighting as recreation. Then in Valparaiso he was very nearly killed in a brawl; an icepick perforation had just missed his heart. The German master of his ship visited him in the hospital. He was a bookish man, pedantic and exacting, who had befriended him and now railed at him as a fool who would waste himself with hooligans and booze. Slinng agreed. His wounds had made him mortal and he came of age at twenty.

He had done his best to identify with rough seamen, push down his own background. But he had outgrown seamen's limited goals and now studied for a marine license. In the next years he advanced from third officer and by 1985 had his master's ticket.

Still it was there, this darker thing: violence. He had learned long ago to strike first and with the intent to maim. His strength from the years at sea had made him formidable and he could be ferocious when aroused—overreact—as he had tonight. He wondered about this; was it genes? For all their calm façade the British had always been ruthless in battle. Had he inherited that legacy? They called it the "Pimpernel complex": gentlemen adventurers who quoted verse and struck terror in the hearts of their enemies; cavalry officers who lisped and rode into the guns. He didn't recite or lisp but God help the man who got in his way.

And Miri—what to make of her? He had never met anyone like her. No one so beautiful, so impossible. It had been a terrible mistake to let her get a grip on him. He knew there was no way to hold her. She had gone back to Hartog with his Brooke mania, and yes, his millions . . .

There was a rap on the door and just for an instant he thought she had returned. But no, it was one of the ancient bellboys, another "uncle."

"Charles . . ."

"Esscuse, please, Captain Slinng . . ." He jerked his thumb back over his shoulder in a spastic wig-wag. ". . . Gotta man from Swee catch your name."

Slinng recognized the name "Swee"; he had been a constable in his time. "Where is he?"

"Checka each room—on second floor now."

"Thank you, Charles—my best to the family."

"Daughter worka shop makea 'lectric yo-yos. What kind of job for Peranakan girl?" And he went into detail while Slinng dressed. Then the old man walked him down the corridor at a maddeningly slow pace as he talked, Slinng looking over his shoulder. Finally into the freight lift, down and out one of the many exits. Raffles had been added onto and remodeled many times over the years until it was a labyrinth of passageways, but Slinng had the map in his head. At an outside door, he thanked the old man again. "We'll get together for some nonya soon."

Charles agreed and chuckled, watching Slinng cross the street. "God damn bad kid."

Slinng walked crosstown to Lloyd's, eyes on the morning sky. It was vivid: *Red sky at morning, sailors take warning.*

At Lloyd's he checked the weather report, then the shipping list: The

Sulu had put out at 0600. "What?!" He jerked the paper out of the printer. *"What?!"* He pushed past the brokers and underwriters into Colonel Pynge-Gilbert's office. "I thought the *Sulu* was getting under way on the twenty-fourth!"

The Colonel straightened from his morning brandy and coffee, instantly apprehensive. "Is something wrong?!" His jaw dropped and widely spaced teeth appeared from under the hedgerow of mustache.

"Everything!"

"Your report was clearly affirmative."

"But it was supposed to leave on the twenty-fourth—*next* Friday!"

"But I mean, my dear Larry. The fellow has a perfect right to put to sea anytime he pleases. He filed with the harbormaster."

Slinng was furious, like a damn fool. From the brief time he knew Miri he certainly had no illusions about her erratic behavior. She *knew* last night the *Sulu* was leaving and said nothing. Damned irresponsible bitch! He walked over to the Colonel's bank of weather monitors. The barometer had dropped slightly from its normal of thirty inches, which meant increased temperature and expected wind from the southeast. Isobar patterns were showing pressure areas but the fletch (wave height) was still modest. It was too early to predict a monsoon at two to three hundred miles' distance. The tracks for auxiliary-powered vessels sailing the China Sea were in range of a southwest monsoon. The north equatorial current swept past New Guinea, dodged the Celebes to be squeezed against Java and Borneo until it flowed into the China Sea. The *Sulu* would be following the coast of Borneo along the Palawan Passage. It was too early to forecast—but it was an area where turbulence arrived between eye blinks.

The Colonel, skittish, joined him with his coffee and brandy. "Looks blue sky."

"Red sky."

Colonel Pynge-Gilbert was annoyed. "Larry, what is it that bothers you? Damn it, man! You said the *Sulu* could outrun any storm—was bullet-proof. You gave her an A-1 rating!"

"She's overinsured."

There was actual sputtering at this. "That is my end of business! Do you know something I don't?!"

Slinng was thinking of Kim's envelope—the one he had left behind. "I wonder, sir, if I might use your phone?"

"By all means." Taking his brandy and coffee, he exited the door, nose aloft.

Slinng went through Lloyd's switchboard and asked for Kim Sing. She hadn't reported for work, he was informed, had not called in, and there was no answer from her apartment. Suddenly apprehensive, he phoned the family Sing in the People's Park Complex. There was a long wait and when at last the elder Sing came on, his heart sank at the pathos in the old man's voice. Stunning news: Kim was missing. That very hour the family had received a chilling, handwritten letter. Kim and her brother, Louis, were safe for the moment and in "retreat," it read. When the shame of Louis' debts were paid (S$68,000), he and the sister would be returned cleansed.

Possibly.

Slinng found the Colonel. "Sir, I need the use of a car."

The Colonel looked at him, knowing better than to ask why he didn't rent one. "Well, I've got an old thing of a Morris Estate Wagon . . ." It was a small jewel he cared tenderly for in its dotage, like himself a survivor of better days. He sighed. "I'll call down to the garage."

"Thank you, sir."

"Larry—about the *Sulu* . . ."

Without Kim's envelope—or Kim—he had nothing to back up his uneasiness about Hartog. He took pity. "It's just, well, sir, I'd met a lady who was aboard and . . ."

The Colonel snorted with relief. "Har! My God, boy, why didn't you say so? Damn me, here I'm talking ship and you're talking skirt. Forget her, they run as regular as an opium-eater's nose."

"Thank you, sir, that makes me feel much better."

The Colonel's Morris Estate Wagon was a make that had led the British car invasion of the world market in the fifties and had been promptly run over by the German Volkswagen. It was a smart olive-green polished over the years until the works undercoat showed through in shiny spots. In its favor was real wood framing and body panels varnished until they were deep ochre. Slinng pulled out of the garage and continued up the street. As he went the engine strained with the effort of the constipated—in its disfavor was an eight-hundred-cc power plant that wouldn't pull your hat off.

Nevertheless, once in top gear it proceeded along the flat East Coast Parkway at a reasonable clip. Unlike his contemporaries, he had no interest in cars, had never owned one. But that was not unusual, growing up with Singapore's limited roads, going nowhere really, except in a circle. If you lived on an island then the sea was your highway out of town. He had owned and sailed small boats from the time he was six or seven, had known the freedom of plotting his own course, being out of the sight of land and exulting in it.

Driving, he went over the kidnapping and ransom demand. It was an old game in Singapore and the Sing family would give no thought to involving the constabulary. They would dig out their life savings, a hat would be passed among the staff at Raffles and they would make loans, sell the jade. Still it would not be enough by half. The thing to do was negotiate: Will Captain Slinng please take the money and try to strike a deal with the gangsters? No, he will not. First he will seek counsel with his friend Mr. Wo. *Ah*—this is what they want to hear.

The coast along here had been built up like most of the island; resorts and motels crowded the shoreline with their ancillaries. The place he was headed was called Bedok. Once a Malay kampong, then before the war taken over by Japanese fishermen who turned it into the perfect Nippon village. In those days colorful paper fish fluttered in the breeze when a new baby was born and it was picturesque as a postcard. It was still a port where commercial fishing went on but now there were boatyards, builders of catamarans, pleasure craft, the smell of fiberglass resins and whine of power tools.

Slinng pulled into a yard with a huge wooden shed facing the Strait. Tall powered slings capable of moving large craft from the building berth sat on tracks that led to a slipway and into the water. There was the noise of construction and arcs from welders' torches. A sign below a line of roof transom read EAST WIND YARDS. He parked and walked past shipwrights twisting long ropes of oakum, toward the enormous opening leading into the shed. Two men sat here playing mah-jonng and when he bowed, asking for Mr. Wo, he was led inside past a boat under construction, built in the Chinese way of junks. They continued on to the far end of the shed and as they stepped through a door to the greenhouse, the noisy clatter from the prefabrication shop dropped off. It was built of curved aluminum sections and filled with plants: bamboo and ornamental grasses, odd palms and the umbrella of countless leaves. The humidity caused the atmosphere to be steamy and turned the light into a blurry green.

Mr. Wo met him trowel in hand and they bowed together. "You find me merging with soil."

"With your love of growing things I am surprised that you would not plant yourself." They spoke in Hainan.

"If I did I would be sure to come up smelling of garlic—I have ruined my taste eating Korean." It was true he had a fondness for northern cooking and any kind of eating. He was large, with polished skin and sparse gray hair that gave him a jolly, convivial air. Old age added the look of a scholar and philosopher, and he was that, too. But he had once been something else: the most feared man of the triads.

It began in Shanghai, a very young man learning from Big Ear Tu, chief of the Green Gang. Wo was a cousin of Chiang Kai-shek and had been passed on to Curio Chang, the art collector. He had been part of the Palace Museum movers and, like his boss, a few choice pieces stuck to his fingers. But it was in Hong Kong that he made his reputation. Before the war, the British police there had been able to keep limits on the triads and at one point actually had a gang witness who would testify. It was an unheard-of thing and Wo was sent after him, or so the legend went. At any rate the man's arm was whacked off in the street and carried away. Months later when he recovered and was out of the hospital, he was attacked again and beaten to death with his own arm. It had been frozen and used as a club. This time it was left behind and allowed to thaw. It was the kind of thing that made an impression.

That was the boy; the old man had mellowed and now despaired of young thugs and weapons that reached out instead of closing with your enemy eye to eye. In his old age he had gone back to Zen as founded by Bodhidharma, who had sat and stared at a blank wall for nine years. Slinng thought him the perfect Chinese gentleman and found the stories of his early ferocity hard to believe. It was a mistake.

They strolled among the greenery and stopped by his prize mandrakes, ancient plants whose roots sent up stalks with large ovate leaves like umbrellas, displaying whitish and violet flowers. Their mysterious roots covered a great area, tops exposed and looking oddly obscene.

"*Mandragora autumnalis.*"

"The etymological alter of the middle-English '*mandragora*'—man plus drake." Mr. Wo enjoyed word games. For the Chinese and other ancient races the mandrake had magical powers. The forked root which was deadly poison resembled the human form (hence, the "man" in drake), or more closely the male organ. Dried, it was a narcotic and anesthetic, sold to induce love, pregnancy (because of its shape) and soothing sleep.

"Have you heard shrieking yet?"

Superstition said the mandrake shrieked when pulled out of the soil.

"Not if you uproot it by moonlight with the appropriate prayer and a black dog tied to the plant by a cord." He smiled.

" 'And shrieks like mandrakes torn out of the earth. That living mortals hearing them run mad,' " Slinng quoted from *Romeo and Juliet*.

These mandrake plants were serious to Mr. Wo and Slinng had saved them; that was the basis of their relationship.

As first officer of the *Mauna Key* he had been in charge of loading the plants at Fakfak, New Guinea, on the Vogelkop Peninsula. They were ancient roots and, crated with tons of dirt, were brought down from the Arfak Mountains where they had been cultivated by generations of Ekaris tribesmen. The passage home through the Banda Sea and around the Celebes had been a nightmare. A black monsoon struck off Makassar and the ship nearly went down. The captain and crew abandoned her, but Slinng had gauged the force of the storm correctly and volunteering to stay aboard had saved her.

The ship was owned by a consortium of which Mr. Wo was a principal. In appreciation he presented Slinng with several paintings on silk scrolls and, more important, made it possible for him to lease a ship and begin in the coastal service as a voyage charter. He was aware of Mr. Wo's role as chief of the Ah Kong triad but like many of their operations this one was legal—or so he believed. It *was* true he had delivered arms to Sri Lanka rebels and cut other dangerous deals, but these were done on his own, chances a young man starting a business might take.

When he was in Hong Kong, Mr. Wo's main base, he was his guest and they became friends or rather sailor and mentor. He had asked his help in getting the constabulary report on his father's death. Now he asked another favor, telling him about his family at Raffles whose son put them in debt. They needed negotiations, time to pay. He did not mention the kidnapping of the daughter.

Mr. Wo sighed. "How unfortunate for a son to dishonor his family. But you must understand that Billy Hon has the say in this. He decides when debts are called in." Slinng didn't believe that for a minute. "And there is another, more serious thing—he believes he has been insulted, caused to lose face. What do you know of this?"

"It is true that I found him rude and perhaps overreacted. My temper got away."

"Ah, you see—this young man *is* rude with no education or social ways—but he has pride and you have wounded it. It has to be repaired—but this is something I can't do." They arrived at a table that was set for lunch under a gingko tree. A few feet away a cook worked at a portable gas grill ready to fry prawns. Mr. Wo and Slinng sat down. "Would you be willing to apologize?" Slinng looked at him sharply. "Would you have the humility for that?" There was a pause. "Yes, I think you would." He turned and said something to the man at the door and a minute later Billy Hon came in.

He was encased in the leather armor of a motorcyclist and bowed deeply to Mr. Wo. "Billy, I have spoken to Captain Slinng and he agrees he lost his temper. If you will accept his apology then we might begin negotiations with the family of the musician."

Slinng stood and bowed stiffly. "I ask you to forgive my rude behavior and any damage to your person."

Billy waited and when there was nothing more, he said angrily, "No! That is not enough!" He held up his hand to show the remains of blisters. "This man grabbed me unprepared and burned my hand! Look at it! Then in front of many people he knocked my machine over and insulted me! If you want to beg my pardon, then get on your knees and touch your forehead to the ground! Then I will think about it."

There was an uneasy silence after this outburst and Slinng said in a carefully modulated voice, "I ask your pardon, not to abase myself as a servant. You say I injured your machine—send me the bill. As for burning your hand, how long would you say I held it over the fire? One second? Two? More?" He walked to the portable gas grill, red-hot and greased. The cook had vanished. Pulling up his sleeve he slapped his left hand flat on the grill. There was the sizzle of meat frying. He looked at Billy and began to count, "One . . . two . . . three . . ."

"Enough!" Mr. Wo said in a tone Slinng hadn't heard before. "You will negotiate!" Billy bowed and turned on his heel. Mr. Wo hurried over to Slinng. "Oh, my friend, your poor hand, what can we put on it?"

"I was thinking of A-1 Sauce," Slinng answered.

. . .

Aboard the *Sulu,* Miri came around feeling sick to her stomach and with a deadly headache. She had been out for what seemed hours, swimming up through the soup of nightmares, half conscious. Finally able to focus, she saw Blas sitting on the side of the bed holding his head. They were both naked and the motion of the ship, hum of its engines was evident. "Blas . . .?"

He got up and staggered to the bathroom, shut the door. There was the sound of vomiting. He came back mopping his face with toilet paper. "There's no towels, nothing."

"Why?"

"I was sleeping when I felt a sharp pain in my arm . . . Lord!"

"Yes! Tog! That bastard!" Remembering. They looked at each other, suddenly aware of being naked, the bare mattress, the nearly empty room. There was the numbing sense of dislocation, vulnerability.

Blas opened the closet, jerked the drawers out of chests. "All my things are gone—the rooms have been cleaned out—even the curtains." He looked at her. "Miri—what did you do yesterday?"

"Nothing, I . . ."

"You weren't here all day or for dinner. When I went to bed you still hadn't come aboard."

"I got laid."

"Miri . . ."

"I went shopping, then stopped by a friend's . . ."

"Come on!"

"All right! All right! I'd been thinking a lot about it. I decided I didn't want to do it anymore . . ."

"No—don't tell me that."

"I've *been* telling you! He's crazy—not funny crazy, crazy crazy! I was going home! Enough!"

"*What?*"

"I bought a ticket—for both of us. If you didn't want to go, then I was going alone."

He began to stomp around the room, slapping his hands against his thighs. "Bloody fuckin' 'ell!" Reverting back to his Australian accent.

"Your winkle is cute when it's mad."

He grabbed her up off the bed, jerking her in close. "You think this whole business is funny, don't you? A joke. Well, what is happening now is no joke, you damn silly thing! Feel that motion? We're under way. He's found out about those tickets and by now probably knows about us."

She shoved him back. "You weren't sleeping with him, were you? Do you want me to tell you some of the things he got up to?"

They both turned, aware the stateroom door had silently opened. Hartog stood in the opening. "Well, what's this? Bloody show-and-tell?"

12

THE NEXT DAY Lawrence Slinng received instructions through the family Sing. Negotiations would take place at Woodlands off the Bukit Timah Road that led over the causeway to Malaysia. There was a rough map and he was told to bring cash. Currency would be in Singapore dollars. He would wear a short-sleeved shirt and shorts to show he carried no weapons. He complied; Billy Hon was on a hair trigger and would welcome any excuse to kill him and explain later to Mr. Wo.

His burned left hand had been treated and bandaged and he did his best to drive with his right. The road was busy with trucks on the long-distance haul from Kuala Lumpur and the cities of Johore. Although the oil glut had slowed progress and caused recession, building was still going on along the highway with the roar and shove of bulldozers, flattening what was left of the jungle. If there were once three hundred wild tigers in Singapore and now there were none, other, less spectacular species had followed them to extinction. The flying foxes had ceased to fly; the turtle population was reduced to near zero from egg hunting that had begun long ago on riverbanks by the sultans of Perak; and a mysterious "noisy" rat said to be four times the size of ordinary rats and seldom seen was now never seen.

A long row of betel-nut palms announced the turn onto Mandai Road and he was passed by tour buses on the way to the Orchid Garden and Singapore's Zoological Gardens on the edge of the Seletar Reservoir. Here you could sit and have high tea with an orangutan and her baby, an animal that had never lived wild on the island.

Slinng pulled off to the side of the road at a sign announcing that the last rubber plantation on Singapore was to be restored and would be ready for tourist viewing by the following season. There was a chain blocking access and he got out, dropped it, and drove through. It was a dirt road and very rough, straight for perhaps a mile, then beginning to wind through jungle that closed in on both sides. Here the area had been allowed to remain natural and the landscape was a marvel: the twist of wild orchids, hibiscus, poinsettia; durian trees ninety feet tall with spiked fruit as big as a punching bag that, when ripe, smelled like Limburger cheese; the mangosteen, once so rare that in Victorian times rewards were offered for the first one successfully transported to London (none ever was).

Then a grove of rubber trees, long boles with lovely feathery leaves, chevron marks on their trunks cut by tappers for raw latex. Beyond, the plantation buildings were suddenly visible, done in the old Malay way of bamboo and steep roofs thatched with atap. It was on a sharp rise, backdropped by low palms, and looked as if it were a stage set, which in a sense it was. The road ended abruptly below and teak logs placed as steps climbed to the main building with its crooked porch and railings. Slinng was uneasy about parking the Morris straight in, but there was no way to turn around.

He got out slowly and looking to his right saw the shine of motorbikes behind a shed that had been used in the production of crude rubber sheets. Above, a young man came out on the porch in one-piece leathers zipped open in the heat to his belly button. Sullen, with a thin feral face and a starter mustache, he gestured with the ubiquitous Uzi carried by a camera strap and Slinng climbed the steps.

They stepped into the main room, built like the nipa shack of the Philippines with a split bamboo floor and a square opening in the wall. A shutter was tied at the top and propped up to give light and air. There was no furniture, with the exception of a rough plank of teak on cement blocks used as a coffee table. Billy Hon sat behind this cracking nuts with the handle of a large handgun. There were several cases of Kirin beer in bottles stacked against the wall and three sleeping bags. A roll of toilet paper, comic books and a bottle of aspirin sat next to them.

Billy gave him a curt nod and Slinng returned it. At one corner another leather-bound cyclist squatted. His hair was cut in bangs and he was holding what looked like an Ingram machine pistol, the tube of a homemade silencer screwed in. Slinng hunkered down in front of the table and the negotiations began. "You got the Sing in cash?" Billy asked.

So much for the old, drawn-out Chinese labyrinth of subtle give and take. "Yes, I've got it."

"Sixty-eight thousand?"

"No, no, nothing like that. These are poor working people . . ."

"Their son is a gambler and a spender—who pays for that?"

"The fact that they offer to pay at all shows they're honorable. This can be settled to everyone's satisfaction if you're reasonable."

"Then put what he owes on the table."

They were speaking in rapid Singlish, an English patois of Malay and Chinese literally translated as "On the table sit what you pay now."

"They can pay half."

"What!? You talk about honor!" As he spoke, Billy concentrated on smashing the nuts with the gun butt. The table was scattered with heaps of shell and every time he struck, empty beer bottles rattled together.

"Accept thirty thousand now and they will pay off another ten in five years' time."

"You're joking! Never!" There was more nut hammering, then: "Because you have Mr. Wo's favor we will agree to make it an even sixty thousand."

"You might as well make it sixty million—this is all these people have. If you don't accept it then it will be spent on two funerals. You will have nothing and neither will they."

More hammering. "How do I know you even have any cash? Put it on the table where it can be counted."

"Gladly. But first let me see the two young people."

Billy hit one more nut, popped the kernel in his mouth and shouted to Belly Button outside. "Go get the honker and his sister!"

While they waited Slinng examined the two. Arrested adolescence. In their late teens, early twenties maybe. There was no more dangerous age, full of ego and untried courage, still believing themselves invulnerable, ready to take any rash chance. Perfect fodder for the military or the triads.

There was movement at the door and Kim came in, followed by Luke. She was wearing the same dress he remembered, no shoes, hair disheveled and without makeup, very pale. She glanced at him, head ducked, not smiling. Behind her, Luke reinforced his initial impression. He looked very much like his sister, younger, handsome with a petulant mouth and sly eyes. When they hunkered down at one side of the table he wrapped his arms around his legs and could not sit still, writhing, his body wet with sweat. Belly Button sat behind him, mimicking the shakes.

"Look at him," Billy said, laughing, "he's got worms under the skin. I guess we know where all that Sing went." He motioned to Bangs for a beer. "What a miserable mess this guy is. Who would want to pay a nickel for him?" Two open bottles were put on the table, and Billy slid one over to Belly Button. "Have you ever heard him play that horn? It sounds like farts in a barrel."

The three of them laughed and Belly Button stood up, put the Uzi over his shoulder, and reached between Kim and Luke for the beer on the table. As he did, Slinng saw Luke start to move. "Luke! . . ." But he jerked the Uzi off Belly Button's shoulder, thumbed the safety and fired, shredding the bamboo wall behind Billy. The sound was incredible, brass shell cases climbing, sudden acrid smoke. Everyone scrambled, ducking. Bottles rolled and the harvest of nuts went flying. Bangs, beer bottle poised at his mouth, fumbled the Ingram around and fired back. His shots were wild, chewing up the floor first, then walking toward Kim. Slinng reached out for her, and for that split second the line of slugs seemed to move in slow motion, then one caught up and tore through her abdomen, hitting the floor and sending splinters into his good right hand. Now he scooped her up, and with Luke still firing, stood and ran for the door in the open.

She seemed to weigh nothing and he took the teak steps two at a time, horrified to see she was unconscious and pumping blood. Reaching the Morris, he pulled down the rear door and carefully laying her in the back, stripped his shirt off, buttons flying. Binding the wound as tightly as he dared, he covered her with a canvas tarp. There was still firing from the house and as he came around the car to the driver's side Luke came flying down the steps, long hair streaming back, eyes wild. When he reached him, Slinng slapped him hard twice, knocking him down and took the weapon away.

"You damned fool! Idiot!" he yelled, kicking him hard. "Asshole! Moron! Get in the back!" Billy appeared on the porch above him firing the big handgun with the overlapping TV cop grip. "Fucking cowboy!" Slinng was furious, outraged, and returning fire, forced him into the house as the Uzi clicked on empty. Starting the car, he had to back out twisting to look out the rear past Luke's frightened face, veering from side to side, wheels hopping until he found a spot wide enough to turn. Reversing and going forward in a dozen tight moves was a nightmare, expecting every moment to be shot to pieces. He was using both hands now, oblivious to the pain of his burned left one until it began to bleed and smear the steering wheel. Finally, he was able to turn, rolling up a fender on a tree and getting the car straightened out.

As he shifted up to second, Bangs popped out of the jungle to his left and fired point-blank. Slinng heard the shots hit the front end, climb and shatter the windshield, blowing off the wipers, bending the mirror, whanging out the back to tear up the roof and take out the rear window. He ducked, swerved and before Bangs could move, hit him, breaking both his legs below the knee and hurtling his body up over the hood to bounce off the top and flop on the dirt road behind them, limbs flailed out at odd angles.

He negotiated the sharp turns as fast as he dared, and looking back saw the flash of chrome. Billy was on the Ninja and after him. At the moment he was having as much trouble with the bad road as Slinng was. The bike was a street racer and he had to stand to it, posting like a jockey, fighting the grooves. For the moment Slinng stayed in front, but he knew the straight stretch was just ahead. The heat gauge on the no-nonsense Morris dash was climbing in the red and the hood showed a haze of steam. The radiator had obviously been holed and it was only a matter of time until the engine seized.

When they hit the straight the Ninja accelerated and began to come up on him. In the side mirror, he could see Billy, ducked down behind the fairing, hands gripping the handlebars, the gun in his right one. Slinng's foot went to the floor and the speed set up vibrations that hopped old dirt and lost change up out of the seats. But the motorcycle gained, its dart of fairing growing larger in the mirror, pulling up. He was right behind them now, adjusting his speed to the Morris, tucked in. Billy was not foolish enough to come alongside and risk Slinng swerving into him. He lay back intending to fire though the right-hand quarter of glass into the back of his head.

Steadying the motorcycle with one hand, he raised the gun with the other and aimed. At that instant, Slinng stood on the brakes and flung the driver's door open. The Morris slammed to a stop sending up the smoke of burning rubber. Overshooting, the Ninja smashed into the door, ripping it off the hinges in an explosions of nuts, bolts and a body. Bike, rider and door tumbled end over end up the road, shedding parts in a horrendous sound of wrenching metal. At each bounce the wreckage sent up a cloud of dust and it was possible to follow its progress until, giving a last shudder, it twisted sideways and bounced into the jungle with a muffled whomp. When Slinng passed the spot, all had vanished without a sign, leaving a trail of bent parts, colorful plastic junk and a human foot still in a Fry boot.

A half mile from the Mandai Road connection, the Morris seized up and abruptly stopped, heat ticking, finished. He leaped out, shoved aside Luke, and, picking Kim gently up, began to jog down the dirt road, feet kicking up puffs of dust, breath coming hard. As he went he could feel her blood wetting his stomach and running down his legs. At the busy intersection he crossed the chain and ran straight out into the road. There was a scream of brakes from tour buses and cars, and traffic stopped dead with a cacophony of horn honking. Slinng picked a large Mercedes sedan. Jerking open the back door and laying Kim inside, he got in and directed the startled driver to the hospital. Standing at the roadside, Luke watched them pull away.

At Keppel Road Hospital they came around to the emergency entrance and Slinng was out of the car running. He dashed through the swinging doors and grabbed the first intern he saw, towing him along by his tie. There was resistance to this by the staff, loud voices, calls for security, but he shouted them all down, clearly gone amok. They followed with a gurney, finally understood, and Kim was put aboard, reversed, blood and IV plugged in and raced back into the hospital. Slinng stood outside as they disappeared inside, drained. A nurse, seeing the blood on his clothes and the tangle of a dirty bandage on his left hand, approached. "Are you all right, sir?"

"Yes! Yes damn it!" He was furious, barely under control, outraged at the stupidity that had led to Kim's wounding, the violence that followed it. And last, his own failure to protect her.

"Why don't you come inside," she said kindly, "and let us look at you anyway."

"Just let me catch my breath a minute."

She walked toward the door and when she turned back to see if he was following, he was gone.

.   .   .

Swee's man reported the latest events. A young Chinese girl with gunshot wounds had been brought to the Keppel Road Hospital by a madman. A nurse, Alice Changi, identified him as the seaman who had been admitted with a broken leg earlier in the week. He, too, had vanished.

"The madman is of course . . ."

"Captain Slinng."

"It would seem so." He flipped over his notebook. "Now listen to this, sir. Two young men were admitted to this same hospital at 11:20 A.M. One had his right foot severed, the other both legs broken. They claimed to be riding double-up when struck by a skip run. We found the crashed motorbike, and half mile down the road an old Morris Estate Wagon with the driver's door ripped off. It checked out to a Colonel Pynge-Gilbert of Lloyd's. He says the vehicle was stolen sometime during the morning—and he has an office full of witnesses. Do I have to tell you who the bike belonged to?"

"No." Inspector Swee was puzzled. Was this the result of some kind of gang war? A feud? Initially he believed Captain Slinng had come back to Singapore because of his father's death. Did the Ah Kong have something to do with that? "What about Raffles?"

"I've checked the hotel room by room. He's not there. Oh, on the top floor, in the father's old quarters, were two trunks. The management told me they had belonged to him and were to be shipped to the widow in Hong Kong."

"I wonder that they weren't kept in storage?"

"Yes."

"Are you still looking after Raffles?"

"Not on a regular basis."

"I would. He's going to come back."

Swee's man returned to Raffles, and of course the desk knew nothing of Captain Slinng. He had been thinking about those two trunks in the top-floor room. Going up the back stairs, he let himself in.

The trunks were still there.

Aboard the *Sulu*, Hartog leaned against the open stateroom doorway, relaxed, smiling, shaking his head at the nudes. Behind him could be seen the outlines of two Gurkha bodyguards. He was listening to Blas

Coff rant on. He stood covering his genitals with one hand, waving with the other. Miri sat on the bed, back against the headboard, legs up, apparently unperturbed.

"Enough, Tog! It's not funny! I've put up with some of your bum jokes but this . . ."

"You think this is a joke?" One eyebrow was climbing.

"It damn well better be!"

"Look at this cobber, Miri. Here I thought he was a nancy-boy, a poof, and he's boffin' my sweetie."

"Tog . . ."

"But then, seeing as he's married to her I don't suppose that's illegal." There was silence at this. "I mean, he introduced us, right? It would never have occurred to me you two were married. I mean, you didn't mention it, did you?"

"We've . . . been separated."

"Is that right? Well, it doesn't matter. It wouldn't have bothered me—but then, why not tell me? That's the puzzle."

"Tog, just because Miri and I were married hasn't got anything to do with our friendship, we . . ."

"No? Then why were you two doing a bunk?"

Hartog withdrew an envelope from his jacket. "Here are two Pan-Am tickets made out to B. Dickey and M. Muffy. Cute. You were flying out on the twenty-third—next Thursday—the day before the *Sulu* was to leave."

"No, not me, that's not true . . ."

"I bought those tickets," Miri said, speaking for the first time. "They're for London—Blas didn't have anything to do with it. I was going alone if he wouldn't come."

"Why not take along Captain Slinng, too?" He looked at Blas. "Did you know we were sharing out our little girl? She's been shaggin' the Captain on the side. Yes, that's right. Mr. Wo's man followed her to Raffles."

"Tog, come on, you said it, what does it matter really? It's just, well, Miri being Miri. We've made our plans, let's—"

"Yes, that's the bloody problem. Plans." He held up a brown manila envelope. "Slinng's been pokin' about—hence, our early departure. Plans are changed—and you're no longer included."

"Tog, you're being emotional. What needs to be said here is—"

"Will you two give it a rest?!" Miri shouted. "I've had it! All I want to do is get the hell off this fucking boat!"

"Well, you're going to get your wish, sweets," Hartog said. "Follow me." And he turned away out the door.

"God damn it, Tog!" Blas shouted. "Enough! Give us our clothes!"

"Either you come or these lads will drag you." Hartog continued on. The two Gurkhas moved toward them and Blas and Miri hurried to follow him out in the passageway.

"Look, Tog," Blas said in a shaky voice, "I wonder if you've considered—"

"Miri's right, shut the bloody hell up!"

Going down the atrium stairs it was evident that a heavy sea was running. The night sky had closed down and whitecaps ruffled the tips of waves. On deck there was a sharp warm wind and the strong smell of diesel oil blowing from the stack. They walked in a line toward the fantail with the Gurkhas following. Both were dressed paramilitary style with curved kukris on their belts. Blas began to mutter under his breath, repeating a rambling defense, while Miri said nothing, arms clutching her body, suddenly very cold. They stopped by the stern rail. There was no one else in sight and the saloon lights behind them were out.

"I hope you're not thinking of putting us off in a boat with this weather!" Blas said, eyes darting around.

"No," Hartog said, "you're going to jump."

"What?!" Blas couldn't believe his ears. "Are you fucking crazy? Cut it out! This is not funny!"

"Either jump or the lads will throw you in—you're going to disappear at sea, mate, like in the mysteries."

Blas bolted to the port side but the Gurkhas had him, dragging him back to the rail. He struggled fiercely, swearing, the wisps of hair whipping in the wind, kicking, scratching. They got him up and over but he clung with one hand to the rail and they could not dislodge his fingers. He was now screaming in an eerie wail. Hartog said something and there was a flash of kukri, its blade cutting the hand off at the wrist. Blas fell backward and vanished in the churning foam of the *Sulu's* wake.

Miri stared in dumb horror at the severed hand still gripping the rail. Until this moment she could not really believe it. Then, jerking away from Hartog, she began to run.

13

RETURNING TO the family Sing, Lawrence Slinng sadly describes what has happened and returns the money. There is nothing more he can do, and in fact, his position with Mr. Wo has been drastically altered. There are two badly wounded gang members to be considered and no doubt the wheel of revenge is already turning. Would Mr. Wo understand and protect him? A good question. As for the authorities, at this point they are closing in—time has run out.

The hospital is called and the elder Sing tells him in a tremulous voice that Kim has been operated on and is in critical condition in the room of intensive care.

"Sir, I cannot express the anguish that fills me for allowing this to happen . . ."

"No! You risked your life for my children. What was allowed to happen was the family's indulgence with this son. Love is the matter and we cast it out. We wear white for him now."

"Sir . . ." But what can be said?

At dusk, Slinng walks to Raffles in pouring rain. The storm predicted by the morning sky has arrived. Returning to the hotel is not smart, but he has been drawn back by a sudden compulsion to investigate his father's two trunks, a thing he realizes he's avoided.

His old "uncle," Charles, gives him the high sign and he goes up the freight lift, pausing at the door of the corner suite. Will the police be waiting for him? No. The rooms are empty, the lights left off. Going to the tall desk concealing the entertainment center, he opens its small refrigerator, puts ice in a glass, pours Scotch and goes into the bathroom for water. It is a mistake. There is that great boat of a tub. The picture of his father floating is imprinted on it, looking up at him. *"Damn!"* He has come back to Singapore at great risk to put his mother's mind at rest in his father's death. Beginning by financing the trip with smuggled paintings, he has launched himself in a series of unmitigated disasters. "*Damn!*"

Going back, he squats by the trunks, takes a long draught, sighs and unbuckles the first one. The open door of the refrigerator provides the light. There are clothes, English tailoring run up in Hong Kong by Savile Row clones. Chalk stripes and that kind of windowpane plaid only the Duke of Windsor could get away with. At the bottom two cased shotguns, one a Purdy. An oilcloth is unwrapped and produces a Japanese Taisho fourteenth-year Nambu pistol, a World War II eight-millimeter automatic with the large trigger guard to fit a gloved finger. The clip is full, and even more bizarre are clear plastic grips that show the nude photos of Japanese beauties.

He opens the other, smaller trunk and sighs again. It is full of memorabilia: photo books with the endless identical positioning of his father next to Raffles celebrities, books of newspaper clippings, worn snapshots of long-departed relatives—and a large colored photograph of his parents on their wedding day. His mother with her smile that says, "Isn't this a laugh?" His father holding himself aloof and serious.

In a tin box he finds other puzzling photographs: Here is a pretty woman, pure Malay, with a shy, sad smile; a tiny thing with a superb figure. She stands in native costume, against a background he doesn't recognize, hands extended in a graceful pose. A dancer? There are many pictures of babies, three small children growing up. They are dated on the back in his father's handwriting and appeared to have been taken every year at Christmas. Is the dancer the children's mother? There are no pictures of her after 1945.

Slinng knows with a sudden shock that this is his father's *other* family, a thing he had pushed out of his mind all of his life. It is such bitter irony that this stiff-necked man, this colonialist, this ultimate snob would have a native mistress and three kids. There are years of checkbook stubs circled with rubber bands. No doubt a down-to-the-penny accounting of what it cost to maintain a second family. There are other current photos, Christmas again, right up to the year of his father's death.

Looking at these strangers, now adults in their forties or fifties, it is difficult for Slinng to relate to them as kin, half-brothers and -sisters. Had his mother known? Probably. In the last photo, an attractive middle-aged woman sits with her adult children and Chinese husband in the uniform of a constable. They pose in front of Christmas ornaments strung on a palm tree. On the back is written: *Clair—1989*. Below is an address: a health salon in the Shangri-La Singapore.

Clair Wong turned out to be a tall woman with a strong body shown off in tights and leotard; powerful legs and upper arms. She was physical instructor for the hotel's health club. Behind her, Nautilus machines and sleek modern equipment were being wrestled with in an evening session by hotel guests and regulars wearing trendy workout costumes.

"I've been half expecting you—come on, let's go in the office." He followed her to a glassed-in space with chrome furniture and a wall decorated with client photos labeled "Health Successes." "I thought you or your mother might be at the funeral."

"No, I was in Britain and it took some doing to get back. Gladys was in the States—at Johns Hopkins for blood work."

"Why now?"

This was a bit blunt. "She was uneasy about the way he died and asked me to look into it."

"It was very straightforward. He was an old man and slipped and fell in the tub. Just as the police said. He wouldn't let anyone help him after Benny died—I tried but he was stubborn, nasty—well, you know how he could be."

Slinng was put off by her directness and economy of emotion. Looking at her, he saw carefully drawn on eyebrows, bright lipstick. Hair pulled back gave her features a Malay cast, but the height and arrogance surely came from his father.

"What about his other children?"

"Leo's a commercial fisherman in Penang. Nev, the oldest, is—I don't know where. Last I heard he was a rigger on one of the oil platforms off Brunei."

"I'm sorry not to have known you—or him really. I was sent off to school early, then when I was sixteen went to sea—I never saw him again."

She softened a bit. "Yes, well, we all suffered from his neglect—not money, no, he provided that. But after Mama was gone we were raised by relatives. So, it turned out. I have good children and a serious husband."

"I'm glad to hear it."

"You're a ship's captain?"

"Yes."

"That's important."

"He didn't think so."

"No, he wouldn't. All he could talk of was the old days at Raffles before the war. Big people."

"Do you remember any of that?"

"Before the war? I was just a little kid, three or four—then after Mama was killed he—"

"Killed?"

She leaned forward, her voice showing emotion for the first time. "Oh, yes, the Japanese shot her."

"*What?*"

"That's right, for smuggling food out of Raffles, or that's what they said. An officer was in charge, a major called, ah—"

"Okubo."

Aboard the *Sulu,* Hartog fought his way to the bridge. Hanging on to the railing he braced himself against each counter roll of the ship, then proceeded until the next. The sound of the wind through the stainless-steel rigging was a series of untuned whistles and each time the bow crashed down a cascade of foam came up in a spectacular curtain against the night sky. He made it to the bridge door and, jerking it open, plunged inside. "Is this it?"

A Malay helmsman stood up tight to the wheel, bare feet wide and braced, eyes dead ahead. Next to him was a stocky man with a white wiry beard and a ragged cigar. He wore a dirty jumpsuit and fisherman's cap with a long bill that was stained by sour sweat. His face was up against one of the bridge windows looking through the circle of windscreen wiper. "It's a bonzer, mate." He turned away and, steadying himself, gripped a handle next to RX radar. "Lookit here."

Hartog got across the bridge and joined him. "Typhoon?" They had to shout over the noise of wind and sea.

"Believe it. The barometer's off three and a half mb's." He twisted the range scale to change the distance intervals between rings. "See that?" There was a green swirl of thick cloud images centered by their dot of position. "There it is. It's moving at about twelve knots in a northeasterly direction, sixty-four-knot winds. The naval meteorological station at

Brunei is sending out force-five warnings. It's on a track for the whole Borneo coast. Coming up around Cape Datu and traveling west up the Palawan Passage and dodging through to the Sulu Sea. They expect hundred-mile-an-hour wind conditions and fifty-foot-plus seas."

"What's our position?"

"We're running in front of it at eighteen knots about ten nautical miles off Cape Sirik."

"Damn! Perfect!"

"We may not get another chance like this. It's going to blow for two days, then move inland. Just what the doctor ordered."

"Well . . ."

"Come on, mate, have you got hair on your balls or what?"

Hartog looked at the tough face and they grinned together, old friends since his early days as dock boss. He was an Australian like the chief engineer, another pal. "You know you're as wacko as I am."

"To be that I'd have to shove a pogo stick up my ass and join the 'roos."

"All right! Let's go!"

"Now you're talking!" He shoved the helmsman aside and taking the wheel began a slow turn that took them out of a trough to buck waves and wind. Evading a typhoon called for determining bearing from the direction of swells and adding 115 degrees from the direction of true wind. The idea was to bring the wind on the starboard quarter (160 degrees relative) and try to turn out of the dangerous semicircle of the storm. He was turning the ship *straight back into the eye of the storm.* The two of them screamed at the top of their lungs, enjoying every minute.

As they came about against the force of the sea the ship shuddered and everything that wasn't secure moved; rattles and clanks and bangs that traveled the length of the *Sulu.* In the glass atrium the parrot's cage was adrift and slamming back and forth. Terrified and hanging on by bill and claw, he saw his own image multiplied in the mirrors, hundreds of parrots, swinging. Below decks, the Gurkhas, who weren't good sailors under the best of conditions, were all sick. The crew members, seamen, cooks and stewards, looked up wide-eyed. *The ship was turning into the storm!* They couldn't understand this.

In the engine space, the engineer understood but it didn't make him any easier. The M.A.N. diesels were thundering wide open and temperatures were soaring. The deck below him was vibrating with such torque from twin screws that it unscrewed bolts and sent the soles of his topsiders buzzing. It was an itch you couldn't scratch.

Outside the Shangri-La health salon, Lawrence Slinng considered his next move: to get the hell out of Singapore. He had come to investigate his father's death and ended up where he began. Nowhere. Hartog had sailed away and his newly found sister had told him the old man fell in the tub and drowned himself—just as the police reported. So be it.

He realized there were two large Chinese at his sides, conservatively dressed in dark suits and ties with middle-aged, serious faces. "Will you please come with us, sir." They took his arms.

"Wait a minute!" They didn't.

There was a car waiting at the curb and although the street was busy they expertly bent his body into the correct angles and levered him into the back seat. He sat between the two while a driver wearing white cotton gloves pulled carefully away from the curb. The car was a large Toyota, black with starched antimacassars on the back of the seats. It was the kind of vehicle used by republic officials and the constabulary.

As they continued through the city Slinng was puzzled and then alarmed. They had passed Constabulary Main and all the other public buildings that might be an official destination. He began to sweat. *Ah Kong triad?* These two had the appearance of policemen or prosperous wrestlers, but there was no triad type: United Bamboo.

They entered the old section and went down a twist of streets to a remarkable sight: a bizarre confection of plaster, cement and garish polychrome paint: the Tiger Balm Gardens, built in 1935 by two rich Chinese brothers who had been instructed simultaneously in dreams, so that an image jumped full-blown into their minds and was translated into a quasi amusement area—with a message. A pale Buddha squatted atop a mini pink-and-blue pagoda looking down on grottos, tableaux and garish murals. They illustrated an odd medieval morality: a series of brightly painted hells as a reminder to the young and susceptible that punishment awaited transgressors. Each section carried its own lesson: punishment for cruelty to animals, to old parents and to the defenseless in general. It had the unpleasant attraction of freak-show posters and primitive religious icons.

Slinng was extracted from the Toyota by his escort and walked through the entrance and up a ramp that led to bridges crossing plaster streams. Below, painted water raced past with painted foam cresting painted rocks and sculpted painted figures fishing for giant painted crayfish. The place thronged with visitors, a great many children at this still early hour and grouchy tourists expecting Disneyland.

There was an explosion followed by a sharp staccato rattle and Slinng jerked his head to the left, ready to break free and run for his life. But it was a fan of fireworks lighting the sky over a small lake with actual water in it. There was a pavilion facing it and the backs of people were silhouetted as they watched. One back standing apart was familiar. Mr. Wo.

They bowed together. "Please forgive my impoliteness for bringing you here in such a rude manner. But I must tell you my colleagues are very aroused over recent events. I felt that only secrecy and the help of my lodge brothers"—he indicated the two conservative moose—"could assure your safety."

Slinng bowed again. "I am once more sheltered by your consideration. My own anguish at the disaster of negotiations is complete. May I ask about the victims?"

Mr. Wo sighed. "The young men were seriously injured but survived. Both are in the hospital and Billy Hon has lost a foot—ahh! Why anyone would ride a motorbike is beyond me."

"May I report Kim Sing is also in the hospital in guarded condition— shot in the confusion by the young man with the bangs."

"Terrible, terrible. Am I correct in being told this disaster was begun by the musician?"

"Yes."

"Ah . . . what a shame! Who can say if honking loud music in a horn does not disturb the brain's connections? Do branches rattle at the wind and break off? This honker has broken branches—but then, others lose their limbs."

This was rather heavy but Slinng responded, "Perhaps they may be repaired."

"A good point. Those who would retaliate by breaking more bones might be persuaded to wait if that was possible." There was a pause as a particularly loud sky rocket burst and was followed by the *ooh*'s and *aah*'s of the crowd.

Slinng picked up the thread. "Perhaps the young men injured might be paid an indemnity in the way of compensation." Another orchestration of colorful bursts, the trails falling away to be mirrored in the lake.

"Good thinking. What do you suppose the fixing of bones costs these days?"

"Well, without the bandage of medical plans it comes high. Would you say fifty thousand Sing?"

"Low, I think—have you seen a doctor these days who does not look like a banker?"

"No."

"I would have to say twice that. Does that sound high?"

Did he have a choice? It was an interesting figure, S$100,000, as though someone with X-ray eyes had peered into the safe at Raffles. That was just about what was left from the sale of the Chinese paintings. Here was the perfect Oriental circle: Mr. Wo, who had been in his debt for saving the mandrake roots, gives Slinng the Chinese paintings. Slinng sells the paintings. Mr. Wo takes the money to halt the circle before it stops on revenge (he says). They are now even: where they started.

Not quite.

In due time an educated buyer from the triad will call on Mr. A. L. Ting and buy the paintings back for a price he can't refuse—the S$100,000. Now Mr. Wo will have paid his debt to Slinng and ended up with what he started with.

Beaten, Slinng bows to his better. "I am honored at your careful negotiations on my part. I, of course, accept."

They stay on for a few minutes exclaiming over the fireworks and smiling at the enthusiasm of the Chinese for blowing things up. When they part Slinng inquires about one piece of unfinished business. "May I ask what will become of the musician?"

"No."

He found a telephone booth in the Gardens and dialed Colonel Pynge-Gilbert's home number. No answer. If he was going to get out of Singapore he would need his help—also, he owed him an explanation for the ruining of his Morris. He tried Raffles and had him paged. He was not there. Then the Army and Navy Club; not there. Although it was long after business hours he called his office at Lloyd's. The rain had begun again, blowing in a sharp angle against the booth, rattling against the glass panes. While he listened he watched visitors running for cover. The monsoon season had arrived.

He was ready to hang up when the Colonel answered, his voice flat and curiously stilted. "Pynge-Gilbert here . . ."

"It's Slinng, sir—I'd like to come round to see you if I may."

"You've heard then?"

"Heard?"

"The *Sulu*'s gone down."

"*What?*" Trying to hear over the rain.

"Sunk, old son, bottoms up."

14

THE STORM lashed the sea to a frenzy, then moved inland in blinding sheets of rain to cause destruction and the interruption of tourist business. It was called a black monsoon and although the city dwellers on Borneo's coast, like civilized people everywhere, blamed the weatherman, the Iban and primitive Sakai tribes in the interior knew better. It was the gods pissing down wind on them, and for those caught out it seemed like it.

The Republic of Singapore Navy (RSN) had its hands full. A great many craft had been tossed about. Several fishing boats floundered and at least a dozen pleasure yachts were lost. Three times that many were wrecked while in poor anchorage close to shore. And of course there was the *Sulu*.

They had tracked her with patrol aircraft, a Fokker-50 and a DeHavilland DASH-8, but they were unable to get down on the deck and it was too dangerous to fly the helicopters. Still, floating wreckage was sighted and it was clear the *Sulu* had sunk. The crew was picked up by a Lürssen missile corvette pressed into rescue service. The survivors had weathered the storm in a twenty-five-foot Wellcraft put off the yacht. This was a powered boat, cabined especially for lifesaving. With the exception of a sprain and bruises the crew was in excellent shape. Others were not that fortunate. The second launch was found, swamped. The owner, guests, captain and engineer were all missing and presumed drowned.

When Slinng arrived at Lloyd's he didn't know this. It was after midnight and he was let in by security. Crossing the shadowy outer rooms to the Colonel's private office, he followed the sound of a television voice and found him sitting in the dark in front of the set. The glow of tube lit him in pale hues, shifting with flickering images. Glass in hand, he drank, watching Singapore's round-the-clock news. Slinng slipped in a chair next to him, and neither man said a word.

The survivors were being interviewed at the RSN station on Sentosa. The Malay boatswain spoke first, dark hair slicked down, smooth face belying his age. Awakened by the motion of the ship turning, he said, feeling the battering of the sea, he thought the rudder broken or jammed. He called the bridge and was told that the RX navigation systems guided by storm tracking had indicated a course change to outrun the eye.

The second engineer, a young Chinese, agreed. Steering and rudder were correct. It was the diesel engines. About an hour into the storm the port engine broke down. They had trouble in the past with water and sediment in the fuel and the chief engineer put him to clearing filters. But it was no good, they couldn't restart the engine. Then the second quit.

When that happened they were dead in the water. The bottom was too deep for their 150 meters of chain and attempts by seamen to set a sea anchor were unsuccessful.

The cook said he and the messboys were told to put on their life preservers and report to the boat deck (no one had to tell them twice). Everyone's eyes were as big as moonstones and there was praying in six languages.

Where were Mr. Hartog and his guests during all this?

No one knew.

Slinng straightened in the chair. "What?

Then no one had seen the guests, Miss Brooke or Mr. Coff?

No.

"What?"

Distress signals were sent as the twenty-five-foot Wellcraft pulled away and the crew had a last view of the ship wallowing and taking on water.

No one had seen the other boat launched, but then it was difficult to see even five feet away.

"Miri?"

"And Hartog," the Colonel said, "and the bloody captain and bloody engineer."

The commentator summed up: The *Sulu* had gone down near the fix of her last distress call six miles off Cape Sirik, Sarawak, where the offshore trench was several miles deep.

Slinng was up and pacing. "Something is very wrong!"

"You can say that again, old son. Yours truly also just went down with the ship. This is the one that will take that last button. Seven hundred and fifty thousand dollars of loss on my account and God knows how many millions from the other syndicate members. Old Tan Lark, the CEO, will have me diced like octopi, he'll bloody eat me for breakfast. I'm done in."

"Two diesels do not fail in tandem. And M.A.N. are especially reliable."

"I read your report."

"And that business of the navcom and radar giving a wrong heading—that means they *both* failed, too."

"Spare me the autopsy."

"Was anything said about the Gurkhas?"

"The what?"

"When I was below inspecting the *Sulu*'s engines, there were a dozen or so in one of the compartments."

"Like fairies at the bottom of the garden." Although the Colonel was very drunk his speech hadn't been affected and he seemed to find the whole thing slightly amusing.

"Damn it! Who's to say Hartog wasn't up to something rum here? Kim suggested there were irregularities . . ."

"Kim?"

"Kim Sing, one of your clerks."

"My dear fellow, Hartog is the original irregular. That's how he made his pile. He has half the money ever minted."

"As I remember, most cases of maritime insurance fraud are fire or sinking by owners."

"Hartog didn't own the *Sulu*—it was leased."

"What?" He was knocked back by this.

"That's right. The payout will go to the leasing company, not Hartog." He poured his glass full.

Slinng sat down, slumping back. The Colonel passed the bottle. "You're going to have to take it about the little girl. She's gone."

There was a long silence while the television rambled on in the dark room, sending its flashes of changing light; kids screaming out a Japanese sausage commercial, *"Veenieees!"*

Finally Slinng gave one of his sighs and said, "Sir, I came here to ask you one more favor. I'm going to need help clearing Singapore."

"Yes, well, you've come at the right time, haven't you." He got up, crossed the room and unlocked a steel cabinet. "I mean yesterday I might have had scruples, but by God there's nothing like going doggo t'unscruple you." He shuffled several envelopes. "We have special couriers travelin' back and forth to Hong Kong and keep permanent identification on hand. Ah, here's a Dutch chap in liability that might fit your description." He handed it over. "You can mail it back."

"Thank you, I—"

"Look here, if you can hang on till business hours tomorrow I can get you an airline ticket through Lloyd's."

"Sir, really . . ."

"No damn it, let me do it! Meet me in the coffee shop downstairs tomorrow, say ten o'clock."

"How can I . . ."

"Larry . . .," he said, putting his hand on Slinng's shoulder, "there's one thing you can do for me. Don't be too hard on the old man's memory. We were all like that back then, thought the world made for the white man. Young people don't understand that today. Everything's cut an' dried to 'em. But the best of us thought we were meant to lead 'em out of the jungle—what did we know?" They embraced and Slinng thought he saw tears in the rheumy eyes. He wondered: If he'd been able to embrace his father like this, might things have been different?

Still, there was a hurdle. Slinng had to return to Raffles to retrieve his funds from the smuggled Chinese paintings. Mr. Wo must be paid the annuity for the wounded warriors—then, too, he had decided he wanted to take away the albums of personal family pictures. So he crossed town again, this time in a taxi while the rain hammered on its metal roof.

At Raffles, his "uncle" Charles was not on duty but he took the back way to the top floor, corner suite, and once again paused in front of the door. *Was somebody waiting inside? No? Yes.*

Opening the door, he was promptly kicked in the head.

The blow skidded past his cheekbone, tearing his ear and sending him flat on his back in a thud that sent up carpet nap. Instantly jerked up, he was dragged across the room toward the corner window over the "R" in the Raffles sign. It had already been opened, drapes raked back, gassy effluvium from Beach Road reaching up. Slinng was not unconscious, but numbed, dislocated from the blow. He was hauled up, hoisted in a fireman's carry. His assailant shifted his weight at the window edge, prepared to toss him out. It was a full three stories to the concrete drive.

His head at the man's shoulder, Slinng opened his mouth and bit him, clamping his teeth on the trapezius muscle, twisting to tear. There was an agonizing scream and the man stumbled back, loosing his grip. Slinng instantly kicked him, slamming home with big feet, terrible blows that ripped his pants and took the skin off shins. He groped at his belt for a weapon but it was too late. Slinng was now slamming into him with thick fists, forgetting the burn, forgetting everything, furious, amok, releasing all the pent-up anger and frustration of the last days.

He beat the man insensible, drawing back only when he was unconscious on the floor, finally stepping aside, breathing hard, still outraged. *To be attacked by a perfect stranger!* But . . .

Was he? Despite the mess of blood there was something about him . . .

Opening his jacket he found a small automatic holstered at the waist. Why had he tried to throw him out the window rather than shoot him? Then a wallet. The man *was* police. Identification showed him to be a sergeant working out of Inspector Swee's office: Edward Wong. *Wong?* Suddenly Slinng had it, knew who he was, why he was vaguely familiar. He was the uniformed constable in Clair's Christmas picture—*he was her husband.*

Going through the wallet he found dozens of business cards, police contacts, he guessed, some notated. One stood out from the others, embossed and expensive:

H. Hartog Ltd.

On the back was a scribbled number. Slinng recognized the marine prefix; it was the satellite telephone connection for the *Sulu*. So there it was. Hartog *had* been involved in his father's death. Were the Wongs blackmailing him? Or vice versa? He would probably never know. Hartog was gone for good and there was no way he could present himself to the police and demand an answer.

He went in the bathroom, avoiding the tub, and washed the blood off his hands and face. His knuckles were raw and there was a vicious bruise on his left cheekbone from the initial kick. The earlobe had been ripped up a few centimeters and he stuck it together as best he could with a plaster from the medicine chest.

Gathering up the few clothes he had bought, he stuffed them in a hotel laundry bag along with the photographs selected from his father's trunks. Then, hesitating, he added the Nambu pistol. Ready? Slinng corrected his tie, smoothed down the rumpled silk suit and slanted the superior Panama over one eye to distract from the bruise. It was just dawning when he stepped out the door, and the rays of light slatted by blinds fell over the battered policeman, eyes fluttering, nose snuffling.

Going down the freight lift, he discovered his ancient "uncle" just coming on shift. "Charles, a policeman has fallen down in my room and injured himself. I wonder if you'd mind calling an ambulance?"

For some reason Charles found this funny. "Damn dumb feet."

The manager, Roberto Triestino, was in his office, still in a bathrobe, having coffee. "Larry! Glad to see you. I'm sorry we haven't been able to get together."

"Consider yourself lucky, Robert." Slinng smiled. "I'm leaving now and want to thank you for all you've done."

"Nothing! Nothing! I'm sorry it's been such a difficult trip for you— next time we'll have that dinner."

"Next time."

"Let me get your property." He opened the hotel safe and handed over a sealed envelope. Slinng quickly withdrew several bands of hundreds and, leaving the bulk, resealed the envelope and wrote Mr. Wo's address on the front. "I wonder if you'd mind seeing this was delivered?"

"Of course."

"Well, thanks again . . ."

The phone rang and Roberto waved, picking it up. "Hello, yes . . ." Holding his hand over the speaker, he said, "Larry, wait a minute, it's for you. The desk man says they've called several times during the night but won't leave a name."

Slinng was going to refuse, then thought it might be the elder Sing with news of Kim. "I'll take it."

"Is this Slinng?"

"Who is this?"

"This is somebody he should know, yes."

"I'm going to hang up—"

"Oh, no, man! Please not to do that!" Then he lowered his voice. "Luke—Louis Sing."

Slinng realized he didn't recognize the voice because he had never really heard it. Not at the club or in the frantic escape from Billy Hon. "How is Kim?"

"That is just it—the big problem—I was over there at the hospital to see her and these guys from the triad came after me!"

"I'm going to tell you something, and I want you to listen very carefully—I don't care. Good-bye."

"Oh, man! No! These people are going to do bad things to me! Think of my family, man! Yes, my sister!"

"Why should I? You didn't."

"You were the negotiator! You put me in a bad place with these people! Oh, yes! Kim said you would help me! You must do it now! I've got to get out of Singapore to Hong Kong!"

Slinng tried to control his temper. "Where are you?"

"At McDonald's . . . ?"

"Oh? Are they having a jazz festival there?"

"What are you talking about?" Among his other character flaws, Slinng thought, Luke did not have a sense of humor—well, not a Western one. "I am in the kitchen at the back—I've got a friend in the way of a salad chef here—but those guys are waiting outside in a car!"

Slinng gritted his teeth. "All right! All right! I'll come by in a cab in about an hour. Be waiting by the kitchen door, ready to jump in the minute we stop—got that? What kind of car is it?"

"A green Proton Saga."

"A what?"

"One of the kind they make up at Kuala Lumpur."

"Be ready."

"You wouldn't have any of the pharmaceuticals they call Eastern Sun or Blue Doves, would you?"

"Be at that door."

. . .

As promised, Slinng arrived with the cab at McDonald's on time. "Pull around back to the kitchen door, driver, I'm picking someone up." The driver, a Malaysian in an L.A. Dodgers cap, stopped talking long enough to comply. He was a small shriveled man who looked like he could be a hundred.

"Sure thing, tuan, you got a date with a fry cook? Heh, heh, heh."

They passed broad trademark windows jammed now with all races digging into early-morning Egg McMuffins; Malay kids whose grandparents once ate raw fish, skinned crocodiles and took heads. The parking spaces were filled with cars, bikes and even trishaws. At the back, they dodged around plastic garbage cans and found the double doors to the kitchen. Beyond, where the drive circled the building, a small green car was parked in position to view those coming and going. The Proton Saga. Two young Chinese men were visible through the windshield sucking on malteds.

The cab stopped directly by the kitchen entrance and the driver opened the left rear door by engaging a lever mechanism from the front. This was a feature of Singapore cabs along with a sign in the back that requested in four languages not to spit on the floor. From appearances, passengers were not multilingual. They waited for several minutes with the engine idling but no Cool Luke Han. The two Chinese in the car watched them, mouths poised over straws. Then one opened the passenger door and got out wearing a yellow jumpsuit.

"Sound the horn," Slinng asked. It sounded, the kitchen door opened tentatively and Luke's head appeared. His long straight hair was parted in the middle and fell to both sides, cupping a delicate face. He was wearing mirrored sunglasses, jeans and a T-shirt that advertised Great Wall Canned Chicken Claws. "Come on! Come on!" Slinng shouted. The Chinese in the jumpsuit was walking faster toward them with his hand held down by his side.

Luke darted out the door and climbed across Slinng, dragging a beat-up black case. "What in hell is that?"

"My horn, man, I go nowhere without it. Oh, no!"

"Get in! Hurry up!" He slammed the door.

Then like magic a sawed-off shotgun appeared through the open window. Another man stationed on the opposite side of the drive had come up on the cab's blind side. Slinng's hand shot out and grabbed the abbreviated barrel just as the man fired. The noise in the back seat was terrific, pellets rattling off the opposite window frame, acrid smoke burning the nose. He had a glimpse of pock marks and bad teeth as he jerked the weapon out of the gunman's hands. Slamming back with the stub of stock into his breastbone, he knocked him down. "Drive! Drive!"

The cabby stomped his foot down, burned rubber and very nearly ran down the one in the yellow jumpsuit coming toward them. He leaped for his life as the cab screeched around the corner of the building and whipped past the Proton Saga. Slinng leaned out the window with the shotgun and fired off the other barrel, blowing out the front tire. The man at the wheel chewed through his malted straw.

At the sound of gunfire, customers in McDonald's went on eating their Big Macs and fries. Once out of the jungle and kampong and into modern urban life they had developed a new survival skill: indifference. As the cab tore past the big window with a white man hanging out the rear window holding a shotgun, few looked up. It was a thing seen on television every day.

Turning up the main road the cab driver was near hysterics. *"I'll find the police! I'll find the police!"* he cried, his Adam's apple working, heart pumping.

Slinng leaned over the front seat and, speaking with calm assurance, flashed a wallet with his Maritime Union ID and picture. "I *am* the police—Triad Squad."

"What? Who?"

"Shhh, easy—this man"—indicating Luke—"is a protected witness. Please take us to Lloyd's on High Street."

The cabby's eyes were very large and his knuckles gripping the steering wheel went white. He had nearly swallowed his cigarette. In the back seat Luke kept repeating, "Man, you almost got me killed, oh, yes, yes!"

When they stopped in front of Lloyd's, Slinng put the shotgun in his laundry bag and got out. Leaning in the driver's window he talked very confidentially to the driver. "I don't have to tell you to say nothing about what's happened—this man's life depends on it." He peeled off two hundred-Sing notes. "This is for any damage." The driver took the money and floored the accelerator. The question was, would he keep quiet or go straight to the police?

"You're on your own," Slinng said, but Luke followed him into the coffee shop.

"Oh, no, man, this is not good enough, I must, yes, get to Hong Kong!"

"Not with me you won't." Slinng found a booth and Luke slid in opposite him with the awkward sax case. He was shaking and sweating badly. Drugs? Slinng looked around. Colonel Pynge-Gilbert hadn't arrived yet so he ordered coffee.

"Listen, man . . ."

Slinng showed his teeth. "Call me 'Sir' or 'Captain Slinng.' But if you call me 'man' one more time I will smash your face." It was quiet after that and a half hour later the Colonel came in looking terrible. He sat next to Slinng, raising his eyebrows at Luke. "Your man?"

Slinng had to smile at that. "It is his favorite word. What's happened?"

"Just what you might expect. Been retired. Didn't get the watch though, or set of clubs, no, got the wing tip of a Chinaman's boot up m' bum."

"Terribly sorry, sir."

"Ah, well, it's the game." He smiled. "Lloyd's travel agency is just down the block. If you'd like I'll walk you down and fix up a ticket."

"Thank you."

"Where's it going to be?"

"Hong Kong. I can make connections from there."

The Colonel started to slide out and stopped. "Oh, got an odd cable at the office just before decamping. Can't make it out. He handed it over and Slinng read:

> One of the Iban up near Rumah Bujana had
> a dream. He saw a prav big as a longhouse
> on the Rajang heading south. The thing to
> remember about these fellows is they tend to
> mix waking and sleeping. Be advised.
>   R. Arrowjoy, Dis. Officer.
>   Kapit, Sarawak, N. Borneo

Slinng was electrified. It was a fantastic notion, out of the question, impossible! But there it was! "You don't understand what this means?! Hartog has taken that yacht up the Rajang River into Borneo! Sarawak! He's doing what he told me he would do—following the tracks of James Brooke, the first White Raj! The *Sulu* did not sink!"

"Why the devil would he do that?" the Colonel asked, too weary to be galvanized.

"Who knows, it's insane! But it means he's alive and by God, I'm going after him! For my father, for Miri—and if you'll permit me, sir, for you and the insurance money."

"Fine," the Colonel said, "but you've got your priorities reversed."

15

CHANGI AIRPORT is on the east coast of Singapore, in the same district as the infamous Changi prison. Here in the 1940s, Lawrence Slinng's father, Neville, had smuggled food from Raffles and Hartog had ruled the camp with tough Australians. Today a part of it has been restored and painted a cheerful green. Tour buses stop on their way to visit the popular Crocodile Farm, so passengers might visit its crude chapel (except Sundays and public holidays; proper attire necessary). As they climb back aboard the buses, the sonic boom of jets can be heard climbing out over the Strait toward the South China Sea.

Lawrence Slinng pushed through the crush at the airport terminal doors and into a jammed interior. Luke Sing was right behind him. "Man, ah, Captain Slinng, I must get to Hong Kong."

"Fine. You do that. The ticket counter is right over there." Slinng kept moving through the crowd. As in all Asian airports the prevailing smell was cigarette smoke and the accumulated clouds that rose to the ceiling were a visible gray. Malaysia Airlines, the feeder line that serviced Sarawak, was at the far end of the field and reached by connecting corridors. He plunged into a boxed labyrinth that seemed to go on forever at odd, oblique angles.

Luke still followed. "I have no Sing, man—how am I going to get there?"

"That's your problem, isn't it?"

"Come on! Damn! You can't just desert me here! I have to go to Hong Kong!"

Slinng stopped and did a remarkable job of keeping his temper. "Do you have any brains at all? Don't you understand that there are twice as many of the Ah Kong triad in Hong Kong as there are here? It's their home office. Their rook! You wouldn't last five minutes." And he turned and continued on.

They walked in silence, passing few people, baggage handlers, befuddled passengers. Luke shook his head. "You're really going to Sarawak?"

"Correct."

"That's terrible."

They arrived at a small plain counter with a friendly clerk, a young Malaysian girl with a button that said, "We Put the Born Again in Borneo." She bowed. "Greetings, sirs, from the careful sky fliers of Malaysia Airlines."

"Thank you. I have a reservation for Kuching." He showed his Lloyd's courier pass. Kuching was the capital of Sarawak, an hour-and-thirty-minute flight across the Strait of Singapore to the coast of Borneo. "This is not right!" Luke whined. "I cannot stay here—you promised my family—"

"*All right! All right!*" he exploded, frightening the girl. Then he soothed her, smiling. "Sorry . . . forgive me—I don't suppose I could ship him in baggage?"

"Oh, no, sir! Only for dogs!"

"No? Too bad. But we wouldn't want to offend them." Luke had hit a nerve talking of the family Sing. Still feeling guilty about Kim's wounding, he reluctantly bought the brother an extra ticket and they hurried out on the field. "When we arrive you are on your own!"

"I must protest, sir, I do not want to go to Sarawak—I know nobody who does."

"Yes, you do—*me.* I want to go!"

"Very odd." The aircraft, an Aero Commander, stood warming up. Its low tube of cabin required only a few steps up and they climbed aboard with six other passengers.

The plane took off with a roar of piston engines and, turning south, cleared the island in a blur of skyscrapers, heading out over the Strait of Singapore. It was an area (connecting with the Strait of Malacca, sweeping between Sumatra, then on toward East Malaysia) that had attracted vigorous sea action in past history. Here the Confederate raider *Alabama* had captured and burned Union trading ships during the

American Civil War. In World War I the German cruiser *Emden* had sunk a dozen British craft before the Australians ran her on the Cocos reef. And most recently, the Imperial Japanese Navy had destroyed the Allied Far East Fleet in early victories in 1941—then three years later met their own final defeat when Admiral Toyoda steamed up from Brunei Bay to attack the American Third and Seventh Fleets off the Philippines. It was a sea once bloodied and crossed in many days, now in hours by passengers looking down and seeing a blued surface, swept clean of blood and battles.

Lawrence Slinng, worn out from his own battles, laid his head back against the seat and closed his eyes. *Good-bye.*

Next to him Cool Luke Han clutched the sax case between his knees like a totem. Still shaking as the rush of Eastern Sun pharmaceuticals wore off, he asked the steward for a martini cocktail and six aspirin.

For Slinng, the island sliding away below was his second troubled farewell from Singapore. The first, begun long ago as an exile, had changed his life forever.

Good-bye.

It is dawn at Raffles and a constabulary car idles at the new entrance, exhaust bated, parking lights shimmering on water-slicked streets. There are drips from traveler's palms plunking the car roof and the driver dozes. Inside, the hotel lobby is dimly lit, shops dark, but—most unusual, lights show in the manager's office.

Ten-year-old Lawrence Slinng waits with his mother outside his father's office. They sit on opposite benches, he dried off from the wet night, tugging a blanket around his shoulders, head ducked, she wearing an elegant peignoir complicated by bows and ribbons, hair tied in a voile scarf. She does not move to comfort him or speak, but when he looks up she smiles with that odd cant of head that says, Well, what did you expect?

Slinng's view of his mother has always been from a distance. Her role as manager's wife is as hostess to the great hotel and it is constant; every minor celebrity or political figure has to be entertained. As a boy, his memory of her is rushing out beautifully dressed to some sort of an event. As a result he is left very much in the care of nannies or amahs—his hotel family.

They can hear muted conversation rising and falling from the inner office. The arresting sergeant tells the hotel manager that at this moment Sir Thomas Stamford Raffles' bronze head is being temporarily rewired to his body. Until it can be permanently affixed, mum's the word, it will not do for the local disturbers to know it was removed.

Neville is nearly apoplectic, his handsome face distorted by anger. He holds it in, a pull of mouth, puff of cheek, eyelids ticking. Whatever the damages he will pay, the boy will be punished. The sergeant has no doubt of it, any sentence a judge could propose will not be as harsh as the father's.

Later Slinng waits outside his parents' bedroom hearing the mutter of their voices: the trial. Then the door opens, the jury is in, the sentence read. First a long speech by the judge, laying out the proper conduct of an English gentleman, taking into account that unfortunately he *is* half-American (a slur as revenge on his mother's plea of leniency). Nevertheless he will be sent away to an English school. A thing that should have been done long ago to cut off unhealthy mixing with locals and a flouting of discipline that flirts with anarchy. The school is Gordonstoun in Scotland.

Where?

To be jerked away from friends, family and transferred from Singapore's mild latitude to the frigid clime of Gordonstoun is a giant slap. Shoved up into the North Sea on the Moray Firth, the school stands in 150 acres of woods; stiff stone buildings, one built in a hollow circle and called the Round Square. All is manicured, managed and, to young Slinng, totally foreign. Neville had been impressed by the royals who had gone there but ignored one of the school's principal aims: independence of judgment. It is a thing that will undo both father and son.

If Gordonstoun is a spin of the globe to Slinng with its rigorous academic life that forces high performance, codes written and unwritten, one thing is the same: the sea. It stretches out beyond sandstone cliffs, crisp and windblown, the curl of sharp waves traveling, outward bound. The fishing fleet of Lossiemouth ranges the horizon; giant oil rigs are towed by to new anchorages in the North Sea. And there is a school sailing yacht, the sixty-six-foot *Sea Sprit,* cutters and Devon yawls.

For all of his early homesickness, the bitterness of exile, he perseveres and receives an education. The tone is moral, Christian with a layer of Greek and Roman virtues, citing public service, honor and self-sacrifice, and a code that states a gentleman is one who, understanding what is good in himself and what is bad, subordinates the bad.

His family arrives in London once a year from Singapore, staying at Claridge's. He comes up for Christmas but nothing has changed. They are on the social run, dining at Mirabelles and a round of society parties that leave him on his own at the hotel. It is at this time he has his first real sexual experience with a black student from Lake Rudolf, Kenya. She wins him by saying *her* first time had been *inside* the skin of a twelve-foot crocodile. He is impressed.

At sixteen Slinng has taken four A-levels with decent honors and is ready to pass on. He writes his parents of his ambition to go into the Royal Navy. Neville is horrified. Great God! Not the navy! It might as well be the tuna fleet. He arrives in London, alone this time, and takes Lawrence round to the East India Club to set him straight.

The club is at No. 16 St. James's Square and has seen great days. The Prince Regent had heard the first news of Waterloo from its balcony; later it formed up to become the home for the East India Company and the military serving in India. Then when the empire fell away it had to merge with other failing clubs until now it is sadly called The East India, Devonshire, Sports and Public Schools Club. Never mind, the view is still of St. James's Square from the dining room, and when Neville settles in with his gawky son the waiters act like they remember him.

"This is it, isn't it?" Neville asks. "Didja see that great whacking portrait of the Bombay Raj in the hall? God, can you believe the power we once had? Well, it will come back. History travels in a circle."

"We'd have to lose a war first, wouldn't we, sir, like the Japanese or the Germans?" He is smiling.

Neville looks at his son, sees no malice and laughs. "With this mob running the government that shouldn't be too difficult." And he launches into the old days, working it around to the long line of Slinngs in Singapore's history, their years at Raffles. "Here's the good news. I've talked to M. Blachard, the head at École d'Hôtel in Bern. It is absolutely top drawer—totally current in managerial accounting and hospitality service, and he sees no problem in registering you for the—"

"Father, I don't want to go into the hotel business."

Neville leans in, massaging his glass of sherry and holding his temper. Around them club members chat in low-keyed conversation. "Do you know what a great opportunity it would be to follow me into Raffles?"

"Raffles was my home—it no longer is. I would like to be allowed to stay here and go into the Royal Navy."

"What have you been watching on telly? *Dames at Sea?* The navy is no longer a fit place for a gentleman. It's full of wogs and sons of plastics salesmen."

Slinng was furious at this; for him it squeezed his father's prejudice to a head. "Do you think being behind the desk of a hotel makes you a gentleman? Do you know what they called me at Gordonstoun?" Slinng can see his father's face tighten and knows if he goes ahead they will both regret it. "Bellboy. Gentlemen don't go into trade and they don't turn down bedcovers." Once started it all came out; speeches rehearsed in private should not be spoken aloud in public. "Raffles is not a national monument, sir, it's a place to sleep over—and it's not always been full of gentlemen—it even surrendered to the Japanese, remember?"

There, he had said it. But young Slinng wasn't prepared for the look on his father's face, the awful contortion, and realized with a start just how old he was. He was instantly sorry. "Father, I . . ."

Neville spoke in a modulated voice, his eyes cutting to other diners to make sure they weren't listening. "By marrying your mother I made two mistakes. One, she was American and two, she had you." Lips were pulled back from his teeth; his diction for once was as sharp as a band-saw. "I want you to get up and walk out of here. I never want to see your damn silly face again."

Slinng paused, then under the terrible scowl, got swiftly to his feet and walked out of the dining room, face flushed. When he had left, Neville called the waiter over. "Clear the other place, please."

Many times since, Slinng thought about that last conversation with his father and winced. They had both said things they couldn't take back, blows that struck to the heart. He hadn't meant it to be that way but father and son never saw each other again.

He spent his seventeenth summer at Lossiemouth chopping whitefish at the cannery. Then in the fall he signed on as a "decky learner" aboard a North Sea trawler and began his professional career as a seaman. There was no more arduous task than to be aboard a trawler in frigid seas where the weather was so cold men put their hands in the icy water to warm them. When he moved on to container ships and tankers it seemed like a holiday—or almost.

Now as he dreams, flying high over the South China Sea, the names of the ships he's crewed blend with the sound of aircraft engines and sing like a litany: *Fallow Champion, Golden Phoenix, Hunter Armistead, Lyness, Tarbatness, Sirius, Stomness, Caribe Enterprise, Austral Eatente, Mauna Key anddd* . . . A rumbling bump and he wakes with the whispered name of his own ship on his lips: *Singapore Exile* . . .

In the next seat Luke is watching him. "What are *you* on, man?"

There is another rumbled bump and the squeal of passengers as lap trays rattle. Still blurred with sleep, Slinng asks, "What's happening?"

Luke points down, smiling for the first time. "Good news, sir, Borneo's disappeared."

Kim was still in intensive care and the family Sing trooped up the hall of Keppel Road Hospital to her room. They brought gifts, pomegranates and the elusive mangosteen. She was unconscious and they silently stood and watched her. All the aunts and uncles, nephews, kids, quiet for once, marveling at the snake of tubes and ping of life-support systems. She had the look of a phantom diver plugged in to descend to some terrible depth. Her skin was white as the sheets and her long eyelashes lay on her cheeks as though they had been tattooed there—to remain forever.

They all wondered if she would be whole again but no one had the courage to say it out loud.

Ironically, down that same hall lay the young man with the bangs who had shot her in the confused flurry of response to Luke's erratic burst of gunfire. Both legs and a shoulder had been broken, but those could be fixed. Unfortunately, after being tossed by the Morris he had landed on his neck in the road. He would now be a quadriplegic. He had a trachea tube inserted and was strapped to a Stryker frame that could flip him every few hours like a flapjack to prevent bed sores. No more bike rides, but with luck he might graduate to a wheelchair.

Next to him was Billy Hon, recovering from his loss of a foot but still feeling it was there, reaching down to itch empty space. He was bright and spent his time reading romantic comic books and going over the same nano-second of time. *How had it happened?* How had a person, the musician, he considered unworthy of serious attention begun the thing that ruined them all? Then he thought of Blondie—hitting the brakes of the car, seeing that door open, from there the blurred jumble of noise and flying parts, sharp pain and the numbness that ended in the destruction of his motorbike—and his foot. Curiously he didn't bear him any grudge—no, it's just what he would have done.

But he did wonder where he was, at exactly this hour, this moment.

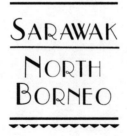

SARAWAK
NORTH
BORNEO

16

THE TWO MOVED ALONG the razorback ridges and deep ravines, slipping between fallen trees with roots entangled and connected into a thicket of underbrush, all under the roof of giant rain-forest trees. Boles rose like columns to a hundred feet overhead, supporting a leafy canopy that blocked out the sun. Only feeble vertical shafts of it streamed through to illuminate the upper branches, creating a yellowish haze, an eerie mist in the deep gloom. The smell was of damp earth and rotting vegetation—but it was familiar and they never missed a footing.

Then, as tributary streams filled and raced toward the river, the two slowed. They were not river people and mistrusted deep unclear water; did not like to venture out of the shade of their forest where the sun might strike them directly. As if to heighten their discomfort there was the scream of a female gibbon, an animal that was cautious at this time of day. Then came a sound that raised the nap of hair, stiffened movement, brought them to a halt. Blowguns were raised. Their ends, worked into spears, were held out to reveal the honed blades. *There it went again*—talk at the treetops that sent the birds up in a flurry, mysterious voices that sang *"Surfin' U.S.A.!"*

Cool Luke Han seemed to be right. Borneo did appear to be missing. The Aero Commander rode all the way in on a dense monsoon cloud, letting down over the coast. Wet jungle and rivers rose to meet the falling rain in a lift of moisture that put them nearly underwater. Below, the rivers were huge and muddy, branching off and looping through the jungle, arteries pumping. It was still a country of few major roads and the rivers were the main highways, towns built as junctions. As they banked for the slice of runway there was a wet shine of corrugated-iron roofs and at a distance, in jungle clearings, Chinese farms and longhouses of the Land Dyak. Buildings began to multiply and cultivation showed its face: big trees logged out and hillsides stripped and planted with rice.

Kuching was an ancient river city of the East, a place Joseph Conrad had written darkly about and where Somerset Maugham placed the archetypical white planter. Although it was lurching into the twentieth century like a runaway water buffalo it still had the look of the nineteenth century stamped on its character. As in Singapore its population was a split of Chinese and Malay with a drift of tame tribesmen, and now the new entrepreneurs who came to sell them what they didn't need. The plane landed and splashed along the runway to a small airport shed with a tin roof painted with a greeting: *Welcome to All Sorts.* This was the connection for Djakarta and Pontianak in West Borneo, or Kalimantan, as they were calling it these days. A Land-Rover from the hotel bumped out to meet them with noisy honks, and passengers and luggage were piled on.

"Chop-chop! All aboard!" The driver was the hotel publicist and greeter, Alstair Eames, a Peking-born British subject, one of those thin young Englishwomen with an awkwardly large bosom that's allowed to shift for itself unencumbered. She was bright and cheery with a glib tourist spiel and the wit of those inured to dealing with tourists and the simpleminded. Not quite pretty but with round metal-rimmed glasses for myopia that gave her eyes a look that conveyed a steamy compliance.

She had spied Lawrence Slinng's raffish looks and contrived to get him seated next to her. "What do we have here?" she asked, shifting up the Rover and moving off. "Selling tape machines or birth-control devices?"

He smiled. "Is that what's needed?"

"We have quite enough of one, thank you, and not enough of the other."

"Can I guess which is which?"

"You will hear which is which."

"Oh, I hope not."

"What happened to your face?" She noted the bruise and torn ear.

"Ran into a door."

"Boor?"

"Door."

"Well, welcome to Borneo—here for the monsoon?"

"Actually I'm interested in the Brookes—the White Raj."

"Oh, dear, all gone. What the folks hereabouts are interested in these days is the future, not the past. The Brookes are looked at as benevolent foot-draggers. In their anxiety to protect the indigenous of Sarawak—the Iban and other tribes—they held back progress, even to the extent of limiting education."

"A barefoot-and-pregnant program."

"Are you a writer?"

"Oh, no, a looker—the visual is my game."

"I could take you on a tour of Istana—the palace of the Brooke Rajahs—later if you'd like."

"Thank you, I would."

"My name's Alstair—but just call me Al."

"All right, Al." He smiled back, thinking it had been a long time since he'd met anyone with such an open, sensual nature. In the seat behind them, Luke was shivering from withdrawal, feeling miserable. The minute Sarawak and Kuching had appeared in the cloud opening he'd hated it. This most rural backwater represented all he was trying to get away from. If even Singapore had not had the urban swank he lusted after, what in God's name could he hope to find here? Certainly not pharmaceuticals. And he hated the English girl with those glasses, with her cheerio, thumbs-up attitude. He was going to have a rotten time.

Warm tropical rain slanted in, dimpling the Kuching River as they passed on the road along its bank. The color was a reddish-brown, Slinng noted, and filled with flotsam, or was it jetsam—entire nipa palms and the battered sections of bamboo buildings being swept from downstream while tambangs, river taxis, expertly dodged around them in the roiling water, boatmen standing to oars crossed over the bow. Shops and markets were stilted on the bank and their garbage and open pipes went conveniently into the swift sewer of the river.

The old town had been built in a pleasant style of colonial architecture, plastered buildings connected by the arches of an arcade. The new was squeezing in while Iban from the interior, showing blue-black floral tattoos and distended earlobes, stood in front of video-shop windows watching "Lifestyles of the Rich and Famous" on color TV sets. Here, plastic shoes sold better than leather ones and everyone wore a T-shirt with a logo on it. Still, merchandise was displayed along the arcade in the old way, in baskets holding staples: rice, dried *bêches-de-mer*, and prawns. On the street, hucksters cooked in the open, sending up the smoky smell of frying fish and palm oil. People stood and ate while small birds snatched at crumbs on the wing, flitting in and out of the arches.

Proceeding up the main block, the Rover maneuvered among blue-and-white buses, motorbikes and darting pedestrians. The rain began to clear and the last rays of sun struck the golden dome of the Great

Mosque. Once it rose above the town as its tallest landmark; now it was surmounted by the new tourist hotels on the surrounding hills, buildings reflecting international architecture that blended East and West together to produce unsuccessful elements of both. Below, the raw public housing being built would supplant native kampongs as it had in Singapore. The interaction of tribal longhouses would be replaced by the anonymity of apartment cubes.

They were delivered to a hotel done in a kind of Malay Holiday Inn style with four-inch hissing cockroaches. In the lobby a manager and desk clerk bowed as if joined at the hip and asked for Captain Slinng's choice of accommodations.

"I would like the best room in the house. As for him," he said, indicating Luke, "put him in a closet over the kitchen."

Luke was hurt. "Wait a minute, sir! That is not most congenial! Hey, no!"

"Then you pay or go bed down in the trees."

"Is he your servant?" Alstair asked.

"No, he is an anvil around my neck."

"Hey! Like . . ."

Slinng turned on him. "Like? Like? Do you think people actually talk that way in the West? Next you'll be saying 'hip' or 'dig' or, God forbid, 'cool.' I'll give you an anachronism. 'Get lost!' "

He stomped off. "Shit!"

"And they don't say that anymore either!" The officious manager and desk clerk were uneasy at this exchange, eyes cutting back and forth. They were not used to Occidentals who abused Orientals these days.

"You were a bit hard on him," Alstair said.

"What would be hard on him would be my using a hammer on his skull."

"You're not a couple then?" She was smiling.

"Are you going to take me to see the palace of the White Raj?"

"Be outside at dusk."

He was, and they drove off in the Land-Rover. Light was fading and streaks of rain clouds blended into the lowering night sky. Catching the last hints of sunset, the river appeared as polished jacinth.

She had changed her dress and her short brown hair was nicely brushed. "You look fresh," he said.

"If you want to make your fortune in Borneo, bring us a deodorant that will stand against the smell of fermented prawns, dirty feet, crotch rot and sump oil hair slickem."

"As we used to say at school, 'Clean mind? Or clean body? Take your choice.' "

"What school?"

"Why, Gordonstoun."

"Yes, come to think of it you look like a Brit. You've got Leslie Howard hair."

"Leslie Howard was Hungarian."

"What a shame, he always seemed so 'us.' " They continued and she asked, "Why the interest in the Brooke Rajahs?"

"Oh, lately I've run into people who talked about them—my interest was piqued." There was a distant, solid boom. "What's that?"

"Perfect timing. That's why I asked you out at dusk. Each night a cannon goes off at eight—it's a tradition going back to the White Rajahs—listen." There was the note of a martial bugle call and the lights began to flicker on in the town and kampongs. "See that building up there at the bend of the river?" Whitewashed battlements were blocked in against the green of jungle at what once was a strategic point in the river. "When the Sultanate of Brunei gave Sarawak to old James Brooke, it included creative headhunters in the interior and out there—off shore—pirates who would dice your eyes for the salad. So Brooke and his gentlemen adventurers had their hands full. Putting the fort there to block river access they fought off pirate raids, bad breath and athlete's foot. Then there were expeditions to the interior to discourage the tribes from taking heads—starting with their own. It was no fun, but you have to remember at that point in history the entrepreneur carried weapons other than a big mouth. By eighteen forty-seven the British government had made him consul general for Borneo and he had won his country."

"That's very good, Al. You know your history."

"Actually, it's my tourist rote. That will be three-fifty Sing, please, with one in the box to buy condoms for the poor."

Then ahead appeared the irregular shape of rambling buildings, whitewashed plaster again, the brace of timber in the British way but translated to a Malay shape. A blending of cultures, a time warp of centuries. The jungle held at bay: cultivated, clipped; trees throwing mysterious shadows, beyond, the shimmer of the river. Istana, the palace of the

White Rajahs. Here it sat as it had for a century and a half, rolled English lawn, window mullions shaped as diamonds, Malay good-luck symbols carved into lintels. There was a silence about it now, the quiet of a missing family. It had been deserted by its last generations with the Japanese invasion of Kuching in 1941.

They enter the house, going up grassy steps to a proper English porch, stepping past a dozing watchman. It is a national treasure now—well, at least to the English-speaking. Through a broad door sagging teak floors slope away to wide windows. It's their faint light that illuminates original furniture. There have not been government funds to restore the interior into what it might have been, instead of what it was: fussy provincial taste. There are English pieces but most are nineteenth-century Malay reproductions. Certainly an original Wornum piano with a badly warped lid, odd sideboards and later Victorian additions, scruffy rugs. But what impresses Slinng is *that it's still here at all!* Outside this very window a furious river roars to the China Sea. Once it teemed with pirates and headhunters and there were those who dared to live among savages and murderers and prevail: *Alone and afraid in a land I never made.* Who will stand bold among armed, hostile strangers four thousand miles from home and make demands? Outnumbered a thousand to one, who will behave as though they had superior strength? The Brooke Rajahs.

It is exactly where Slinng stands that Charles Brooke stood. Roused from his sleep at midnight by chilling yells, he had looked through the venetian blinds (at this very window), then run for his life. It wasn't pirates or headhunters that put the fear of God into him but Chinese with big swords.

Chinese colonists had been a mainstay in Sarawak and the Chinese Gold Working Company in the interior at Bau was particularly successful. Forming a "second capital," they had resisted the Rajah's authority. The Kungsi, as they were called, also formed a branch of the Tien-Ti-Hué (Heaven and Earth triad), a secret society outlawed in Sarawak. There had been a scandal in 1856 involving opium smuggling, and traffic had been suppressed by fines and the cracking of Chinese heads. This and the news that the British had been forced to retire from Canton in humiliation encouraged the Kungsi to insurrection. In February of 1857 five hundred armed Chinese came downriver to attack Kuching with the intention of killing Brooke and taking over the country.

The whites in town were slaughtered: an officer, the constable, several civilians and their children. It was nasty. A Mrs. Middleton had hidden in a large water jar while the Chinese cut the head off one young son and threw a second son into the fire as the house burned down. Victorious, the insurgents paraded through the streets with a pike showing a head identified as the Rajah's. Actually it was that of the young officer, Mr. Nicolett, who had rushed to his chief's house and was killed in his stead.

Brooke had got out and, dashing across the lawn, slipped into the river and swam to the other side. There, he was able to rally support among the loyal Malays and in several weeks of vicious fighting drove the Chinese out of the country. When chided later about his ignominious swim, he said testily, "I had quite enough common sense, and lack of heroism, to make my escape when opportunity offered."

In one room that must have been the family office are pictures of the generations. There's a reproduction of the painting by F. Grant in the National Gallery, London, of Sir James Brooke. There are pictures of his successors, the nephew Johnson who changed his name to Brooke, and finally the last White Raj, Charles Vyner Brooke, who ceded the country to the British after the Second World War and raised a furor in the family.

Slinng looks at the snapshots of anniversaries and reunions, searching the faces for a clue to Miri's background, but finds no such beautiful predecessor.

There is a large map of Sarawak showing the twist of its lifeline of rivers—marvelous-sounding names: *Rajang and Balui and Baram and Tinjar.* They converge at the rise of mountains, turning to rapids, fed by waterfalls from the highlands. Here the mountain interior shows no town or village. A blank. Slinng bends in and sees that like Hartog's map aboard the *Sulu,* the muted green of jungle is marked *Relief data incomplete.*

"Is that still true?" he asks Alstair. "That this section is unexplored?"

"Oh, yes. The teak harvesters haven't got there yet. But no doubt they will and before the decade's over, supermarkets will sprout where the rain forest was and sell artificial Christmas trees."

"Is it inhabited?"

"Supposedly by the Tantu, a people so remote and shy they avoid contact with all other tribes. They've been described as looking African or Papuan and living in the trees. They are known to still take the occasional head and are possibly cannibals."

"You're serious?"

"Well, it's a story the tourists enjoy. Actually they're the last of the hippies—it's like the elephants' graveyard—old hippies go there to die."

Slinng kissed her.

"What was that for?"

"You've never heard the expression 'Kiss a fool for luck'?"

"No, let me try it."

Returning to the hotel, they had dinner on a terrace that had a long overview of the town. The sky had cleared and a sliver of a moon sent enough light to trace the river's flow. The meal was fishy and they finished with kopi susu, a Malay version of café au lait. "You were born in Peking?"

"Yes, my father had worked for the Rockefeller Foundation there after the war. He went there to write about Sir Edmund Backhouse—do you know about him?"

"An Orientalist?"

"Yes, and also an outrageous forger and con man—they called him 'the hermit of Peking.' Fascinating fellow. My dad worked for years on the book, it was to be his scholarly masterpiece, but before he finished it, Hugh Trevor-Roper came out with the definitive volume, soo . . ."

"What about you—are you in hotel management?"

"Good God, no. I was to be an ornithologist but I never finished my master's and without at least a doctorate in that game you don't count. I came down here to work for a fellow preparing specimens and drifted into this job—but come on, talk about you—you're not really just a tourist?"

"Well—it is a business trip. I'm doing a job for Lloyd's, following up a claim."

"I'm crushed—an insurance man! I thought you'd at least be an international jewel thief or a spy on the run from Interpol."

"Not quite—how about a seaman and smuggler who's just one step ahead of Tong hatchetmen and the Singapore constabulary?"

"I know you're not a writer or you'd be able to make up something better than that lot."

.   .   .

They returned to his room and went to bed as if it had been decided on the ride from the airport. It was natural and easy and they both enjoyed it. No points had to be made and love did not get in the way. When she ponied up for a second ride she accidentally smacked his head with one of her large breasts. "Sorry about that."

"My pleasure."

"They're such a bother, always in the way. They were an inheritance from a long line of Eames women with large frontage. They are terrible to deal with in clothes, and I've thought many times how pleasant life would be without so much of them." She sighed. "But they are popular these days and people seem to enjoy them, so I guess I'll persevere."

"Good thinking."

The bedside phone rang. "Don't answer it."

"I better—I gave the desk this number." Still astride him, she picked up the receiver. "Al here. What? Oh, blart! All right—yes, right now." She swung off him.

"What's blart?"

"Oh, just another way of saying 'fuck' or 'shit'—those two become so tiresome." She began to dress. "That Chinese anvil of yours is causing a disturbance in the bar. We better get down there before they call the police."

"Double blart!"

"You've got it."

The hotel lounge had been decorated with carved Malay screens and seats tricked out with bongons, tree-bark baskets, in an effort to warm up slick modern fittings. The action was up at the bar but blocked off by patrons crowding in to watch. They were a split of tourists, Far Eastern salesmen and roughneck construction workers hired on from New Guinea for a public housing project going up. There was a loud voice and laughter; apparently humor was involved.

Slinng shoved through the crush with Alstair, already angry that Luke was involved. He saw now that a tough-looking worker in an orange hard hat had a hold of Luke by his face. His arm was stretched out, fingers and thumb of a large hand clamped around Luke's mouth, squeezing it open in a figure-eight shape. He made a gurgling sound, twisting the man's wrist with his own small hands, but made no impression.

"There you are, you rascal," Slinng said to Luke, smiling, then to the hard hat, "I hope he hasn't been causing any trouble—he loves a joke."

"The booger owes me fifty Sing." Two leather dice cups and scattered dice on the bar told the story.

Slinng shook his head sadly. "You didn't gamble with him, did you? He's a bit . . ." He tapped his head. ". . . Hasn't got it up here—or in his pocket." He smiled again.

"By God, he's got a gold tooth and I'll have that in payment." This is where the humor came in and the crowd laughed. But Slinng also saw a Swiss Army knife in his other hand with the plier configuration out. He raised it as Luke squirmed. "I can see it glinting in the back there." Whether he would have gone ahead was hard to tell. He was easy to dislike on sight with skin the texture of a geode, and the arrogance of cultivated ignorance. Slinng laid a hand lightly on his arm.

"No, no—you don't want to do that—you wouldn't want to hurt the handicapped."

"The fuck I wouldn't."

"All right—look—he's my charge, let me take care of the punishment."

"Are you going to take care of the payment, too, mate?"

"Look at him. You should know better than to gamble with the simple. Why don't I buy you a drink and we'll forget it?"

"Why in the hell should I do that?"

"Well, it would just make it so much easier."

"What makes you think I want to make it easier?—and get your fuckin' hand off my arm, Blondie, or you'll get a big kiss." More laughter. The patrons liked this.

Well, there was nothing for it and he swung. But the man was quick, ducking, and Slinng's hand smashed into the hard hat, his big ring denting it. It was a terrific blow and broke the grip on Luke, but he thought it might have also broken his hand. He fanned it, holding it out. Damn! It hurt.

The hard hat was swinging now and Slinng raised his shoulder and took two paralyzing blows in the upper arm. His opponent was fast and strong, a boxer. That called for feet and he shot one out, kicking his heel into the man's shin. He responded with a kick of his own and the heavy bridgeman's shoes knocked him down, sending out a wave of spectators who jumped for their lives, spilling drinks and laughing at the good-natured mayhem.

Before Slinng could scramble up, another kick was aimed at his head but wasn't delivered. Alstair had picked up a stainless-steel tray off the bar and struck the man over his hard hat with all she had. It made a resounding gong, then was repeated in a series of blows like a drum tattoo, ramming the hat down over his eyes. Standing behind him and battering away, she moved deftly in a circle as he tried to get hold of her.

Slinng was up, and holding one wrist with the other, smashed an elbow in the man's chest that knocked him through a carved screen and along the floor toward the barroom door. Jumping on him with both knees to the ribs and getting a grip on his ear, he bit down. There was a howl, and they broke free tumbling into the lobby, skidding luggage along the tile floor and sending late tour-bus arrivals scampering for the elevators.

Furious, the Chinese manager and desk clerk chased after them screaming as they pummeled each other across the lobby. Both Chinese now began shoving until the two combatants went out the front door and flopped onto the drive. At the bottom, racing up, was a police car. Its lights uplit the frantic tableau and the participants paused. As they did, their eyes picking up the light took on a feral gleam.

The manager was apoplectic. "Now you see come big justice! Police shoot dead with pissholes!"

"That's pistols," Alstair said wearily.

17

ALSTAIR JERKED SLINNG to his feet, swaying with his weight. "Come on, Tarzan! Up!" But as she turned toward the hotel entrance the officious Chinese manager and clerk blocked the way. The police car approaching from the drive below had turned on its red light. "No, no! He out! No more guest! Bad! Bad!"

"Mr. Hai . . ."

"You out, too—you bring 'em! Out! Out! Bad! Bad!"

"Oh . . . up your blart!" and she towed Slinng around the corner of the building to the parking lot.

"Al—I'm sorry, I . . ."

"Who cares, the little prig! You know what I really hated about Mr. Hai? He kept using the word 'global.' " They stopped by the Land-Rover.

"Doesn't this belong to the hotel?"

"I've got the keys, haven't I? Get in." She started the car and they swung around heading down the opposite drive—away from the entrance. Suddenly Luke came up in the lights waving his sax case.

"Run the bastard down!" Slinng shouted.

But Alstair stopped, hopping the wheels. "You don't mean that."

"Oh, yes I do!"

Luke climbed in the back. "Sir, that was most terrible! He was a dishonest person! That game was badly unhip! Oh yes, let me say . . ."

Slinng reached over the back and began shaking him by his collar. "If you say one more word I'm going to disconnect your head from your chicken neck!" His teeth were rattling now.

"Larry," Alstair said, "that's no way to treat the handicapped."

Slinng shook him loose and, turning around, settled down, taking out his handkerchief and dabbing at wounds. She looked at him out of the corner of her eye as the Rover continued down the drive. The police car had stopped at the hotel entrance as the Rover went up Kuching's main street. "That was a bit rough back there—is that the way Lloyd's insurance people behave these days?"

"Oh, yes, it's a very competitive field. If the bastard had been from Metropolitan Life you'd have really seen something."

"You said earlier you were a seaman—was that true?"

"What makes you think so now?"

"Well—at one point I noticed you were trying to bite the fellow's ear off—did they teach you that at Gordonstoun?"

"Quite. Plato said if you can't catch a man's ear—bite it."

Alstair had, at that moment, a revelation. A gulp, a spine shiver that many people feel when they suddenly discover their companions are not only not what they say they are, but may be downright dangerous.

They came by the lights of storefronts, noisy pachinko parlors, and turned toward the river, passing out of town. The lights of the Rover were filtered by brush that reached out from the road side and the crushed-stone road turned to dirt. "Where are we going, Al?"

"I've got a friend we can stay with tonight. In the morning I'll return the Rover and pick up our things. All right?"

"Fine. I'm headed for Kapit tomorrow. Do you know where that is?"

"A couple hundred miles up the Rajang—is this insurance business?"

"Right. I'm to meet the district officer there."

"Really."

They were on the riverfront with lopped-off palms carrying utility wires and shadowy enclosures of bamboo. Alstair stopped in front of a house built in the Malay way, shoved in between native warehouses: godowns. Slinng was reminded of the nipa shack in Woodlands and the shoot-out with Billy Hon. This place did have glazed windows and showed dim light. A three-speed racing bike was chained to the porch railing. "Who lives here?"

"A friend, Beata Po Ba."

"Sounds exotic."

"She's an Italian from New York, Bernice Rizzo, who came out here in the seventies and married a Burmese. He's done a bunk but she has a grant from UNESCO to do research in herbal medicine—it was her brother Kevin I was collecting bird specimens for."

"She's a scientist then?"

"Without the degree. One of those naturals with the brights and push to pull it off. I've got to warn you—she's also a bit stiff, very involved with the supernatural, local superstitions, that sort of tripe." They got out of the Rover, but Luke stayed in the back pouting. "Aren't you coming in?" Alstair asked, "We're going to have a nice time," but he wouldn't answer, hands shoved down in his pockets to still the shaking.

"Leave the sorehead."

They went up on the porch, and after rapping, Alstair opened the door. "Beata?"

The room was hung with baskets containing dried plants, and the commingling of odors was a powerful, pungent assault of dozens of different species. There was a workbench to one side stacked with plant presses and in the center of the room a low table with a portable Hermes half buried in reference books and loose paper. The room was nearly dark and a light wavered from a back room, showing its progress through cracks in the paneling. A woman appeared in the doorway holding a pressure lantern. Its light illuminated narrow, small features and an astounding head of dense black hair. A single braid as thick as a man's wrist reached below her waist. Although in her late thirties the initial impression was of a child's body with an adult's face.

"Alstair, baby! I knew you were coming—I've had the wim-wams all day." Her expression was serious yet with a hint of sly wit and shared secrets. As she spoke she kept her eyes on Slinng. They were large and liquid and showed wariness, suspicion. She turned a switch for a single electric bulb hanging on a cord from a beam.

"This is my friend, Larry—we had a bit of a fracas up at the hotel and that old blart of a manager threw us out. I was wondering if you could put us up overnight, until we can get straightened out?"

"Of course." Her eyes were still on Slinng. "Sweet Jesus, you look like you got the worst of it. Want to wash up? I've actually got an inside john—right through that door."

He found a small room with a slatted floor stilted out over the river. There was a single iron pipe with a faucet and basin that drained into the river, and in the corner, a toilet that did the same. A candle provided the light. He ran the cold water over his right hand. It wasn't broken but very tender, the knuckles bruised. The big ring on his third finger was tight with the swelling and, using a sliver of soap and the water, he worked it off. Fine. A burned left hand, now the right one bent. Looking at his battered face in the wavy metal mirror he could understand the suspicions he saw in his hostess's eyes and couldn't blame her.

"Who is that?"

"He works for Lloyd's. Down here on some kind of claim investigation."

"What? Come on! Don't believe it for a minute. Look at that face! Can't you feel the vibrations coming off him?"

"Yes, they're marvelous."

"I'm not talking about sex—he's brought some kind of heavy spirits with him—wherever he's headed there's going to be bad news."

"You know what you sound like, Beata? One of those storefront fortune-tellers."

"I'll accept that, baby. They're connected to a special wavelength—and I'd like to think I can tune in on it, too. Hell, there's nothing wrong with that—and in fact, if your karma is right you can do some good."

"My idea of good karma is fourteen stone of dirty blond with an alert winkle."

"Still the sex-crazed bird woman. Kevin always asks about you."

"Kevin has his head up a drongo's cloaca."

Slinng came back in looking a bit more tidy. "Thanks for the use of your facilities."

"Yes, well, nothing like a straight chute. Never have to worry about clogged pipes." She plugged a hotplate into the one overhead light cord, immediately dimming the single bulb. "Let's have some tea." She filled the tea kettle and put it on.

Slinng was examining the herbarium. Besides the baskets full, there were clouds of dried plants hanging from rafters that brushed his hair. "Quite a collection."

"Forty species for healing, a hundred and fifty for food—on and on."

"All of them with impossible Latin classification," Alstair said.

"True. The local names are right on the money—chicken soup tree, cigarette tree, and I love this one, crotch-hair vine."

"My favorite is bachelor's wild banana . . ."

"A primitive erect fruit, of course."

"Then you're not looking for new species."

"No, just rediscovering old ones the people here have known about since the Stone Age."

"And they have modern application?"

"That depends. Some also require belief."

"You mean if you didn't believe aspirin would work, it wouldn't?" He smiled.

"Something like that. Autosuggestion."

"Metaphysics?"

"In the original sense, as concerned with first principles and ultimate grounds—time, substance, equals thought, medicine. The people here understand the connection between the two instinctively."

"Do they still? From what I see of their T-shirts and Sony Walkmans I would gather the new metaphysics is pop culture."

"Don't you believe it." As she talked she broke tea leaves and herbs in the pot. Three chipped enamel cups were set out. "Do you know that no new construction project is started here without calling in a dayung, a shaman, to make a blood offering?"

"What?"

"It used to be a Kenyah tradition before starting a longhouse—blood would be poured on the ground to bless the building and placate bali tanah, the spirit of the earth. In the beginning, of course, before the Brookes interfered there was human sacrifice. Nowadays this ritual has been carried over to modern bridge building and hydroelectric plants. Each has its own spirit: bali jambatan is the spirit of a vehicle bridge; bali rummah jambatan, the spirit of a high-rise and so on. And believe me, the local workers won't go on the job until blood has been spilt."

"You're not talking about human blood?"

"Not officially, but yes, it's considered essential for a real fix. The belief was that a longhouse needed the blood of one person as an offering. Now, well you might ask: How many people are needed to supply the blood for a high-rise, or a dam? What about one-hundred-person office buildings? Five-hundred-person dams? Pertamina, Indonesia's national oil company, has a permanent dayung on retainer, that's how serious they take it."

"But where does all this blood come from?"

"Ahh, that's the rub. The quoted price for, say, ten pints is two million rupiahs—about three thousand U.S. dollars. But the forest people believe a *bali saleng* does the collecting."

"I don't think I want to know what that is," Alstair said.

"Just what you'd guess—half-man, half-spirit. A black ghost who wears spring-powered shoes for jumping over the trees. He can be anyone, look like anyone. That's why you want to be careful in the rain forest . . ." She looked at Slinng. "The people in there are very superstitious about the matter and more afraid of the *bali saleng* than they are of the authorities. They kill strangers if encountered at the wrong time or place."

"What makes you think I'm going into the rain forest?"

"Aren't you?"

There was a pause as she poured the tea, a thick brew with a dense, mysterious smell. At that moment the door popped open and Luke came in unannounced, hands in his pockets, sax case carried over his shoulders by a strap.

"It was most unpolite to leave me out there."

"Come sit next to me," Alstair said, smiling.

He settled in and Beata examined him. "Now here's a real jazz musician."

"How do you know that?" he asked, brightening.

"Our hostess is a practicing psychic and a licensed tea-leaf reader."

"No, I read the name plate on his instrument case: Dixie Melody Master."

He tried his charm on her. "What most terrific hair. That braid is as thick as a rope."

"Thank you, it's my annuity." She gave it a toss. "Every six months I cut it off and sell it—it grows right back."

"Marvelous. You would not happen to have any pharmaceuticals— Eastern Sun or Blue Doves?"

"No. Try the tea, it will help." Then she turned back to Slinng. "If you *do* go into the rain forest, see a dayung first and he'll give you a charm or a dream stone. It can't hurt and it may help."

"What's a dream stone?" Alstair asked.

"A special smooth brown stone that is held in the hand when you dream. Then you take it to a dayung and he holds it and interprets your dream."

"Thanks for the advice," Slinng said, with no intention of taking it. As a seaman he had been exposed to his share of superstitions and managed to resist them all.

"Larry already has a charm," Alstair said, as if reading his mind. "That star tattooed on his ear."

"That is not a charm," he answered, annoyed. "It's a memento for a particular number of voyages."

"It won't work on your next one," Beata said, enjoying herself.

They slept in hammocks slung in the main room, each alone, twisted up in sisal and looking like cocoons. With the light out, a sliver of moon was reflected from the river and sent a pattern to dance on the ceiling like the mirrored globes of ballrooms. Slinng was dead-tired and fell immediately into a troubled sleep, and then disturbing dreams.

A shimmer. A slide of light that uncurls, stretching out, snapping as a whip might. A flog of turbulence that roils and rushes before the wake of a sleek white shape. A ship? There are masts and staffs and forestays. Trucks connected by spider-web lines, a scurry of arachnid legs up rat-lines. Then, the breakout of cobweb sails, the bloom of puffballs; a cloud of gassy effluvium that propels the ship forward on a river's silent surface.

He recognizes James Brooke's armed yacht, *Royalist:* caparisoned gentlemen adventurers with the faces of cannibals daubed with white dots and the jagged flashes of lightning bolts. At their head, a lofty bird with a black countenance and headlight shine of monocle. The White Raj? He talks in bombastic gibberish and becomes Hartog: banana nose, porcine eyes. His head turns and the spotlight of monocle beams a canoe on the river's mirrored surface. Behind it the jungle bank rushes by at a blur and the canoe stands still. In the stern a bend of back, blued tattooed arms digging a paddle in, head tucked; cockscomb ruff, a sawtooth circle against the light. At the bow a bright flag streams back, feathered and golden in the light, a great luxurious swirl twisting in the air.

The tattooed arms are his arms, the view his view. At the bow the show of flag is Miri's great bundle of hair, flooding out from a head propped up in the bow: bloodied neck, blanched face, looking at him. Staring.

In the water, a plunge into calmness. Below, a blue black that ends as night. Above, a light that dapples a swimming figure, graceful, shining with a green phosphorescence moving toward him from a great distance. He increases his effort and swims toward it. *Miri!*

Only at the last instant he sees it as a huge crocodile, jaws open; then it is too late and he is swallowed.

Slinng woke up in a cold sweat. Jesus! His eyes popped open and took a second to register the room and hammocks. His hands were squeezed tightly shut and when he opened the right one he was holding a smooth brown stone. Witch! She had placed it there, but it still gave him a start. When he looked toward her hammock, she appeared to be asleep, the sag of small frame showing a backbone's curve against the swag of sisal. What a ghastly dream! The tea had helped, along with a pinch of bella donna no doubt, or the local equivalent. Witch!

Early that morning Alstair took the Rover back to the hotel and returned on the bus with their luggage. At the shack there were good-bye tears, hugs and gifts of herbs. "You're going with him, aren't you?" Beata asked under her breath. "You're going into the rain forest."

Alstair was surprised. "Why, I hadn't really thought of it."

"Oh, yes, you have."

While she and Luke waited in the road, Slinng said his own private good-bye to Beata. "Thank you for letting us stay over—and working your magic—I got your stone."

She smiled at him. "Here, magic is called life."

"I'm sure." He reached in his pocket. "Oh, I'd like to give you something in return." And he handed over his large ring.

She was taken aback. "What . . . ," she began, looking at the odd symbols engraved on the face.

"It was my father's Masonic ring. I was never a Mason but I wore it for luck. Mine has been rotten lately so I'm passing it on to someone with a talent for superstition—maybe it'll work for you."

Her eyes got big. "Wait a minute—I can't accept this—I'm a Catholic!"

"Is that right?" And laughing he went down the steps to join the others.

"Bastard! You're trying to put a curse on me!" She was shouting after him and shaking her fist, but holding on to the ring as if it were impossible to let go.

"What was that all about?" Alstair asked, waving as they walked on.

"A parting jest as they say."

"You certainly got her all steamed up."

"She needs the exercise."

The road was still muddy from the rains but the air was fresh and they decided to walk rather than take the smelly bus. Luke didn't agree. "Hey, tuan"—this was his new word to replace "man"—"what are we doing?"

"We're walking, Cool Han, that's when you put one leg in front of the other and move forward like scissors."

"I don't like it. I'm a person who needs to sit when he moves."

"Then sit on that stump and wait for a bus."

"But I don't have any Sing."

"Come on, Luke," Alstair said, swinging her bag up and adjusting the straps to make a backpack. "Let's have a jolly hike."

"That's the first time you've sounded too English."

"Sorry."

"Is that all you've got? That backpack and the duffle?"

"The rest is in storage. I travel light."

"You're traveling?"

"Larry . . ."

"Yes, I'd be glad to have you accompany me. My pleasure."

"I can be of help, I know some Malay and I'm good at wash-up, you know, camp routine."

"There is one thing—maybe two. I've told you I'm here for Lloyd's. Actually I'm here for a friend who was fired by Lloyd's, Singapore."

"Well, that's close."

"I owe it to him to try and chase down this claim. But I have to tell you I have no idea what we're in for. The district officer up at Kapit wrote that one of the Iban had seen my claim on the Rajang in a dream."

"What is the claim?"

"A two-hundred-foot motor yacht painted a blinding white."

"Oh."

He said nothing of his father or the hunt for Hartog and certainly not the ache of Miri's disappearance. He was a man who found great difficulty including others into his confidence.

As they continued, there was a honk behind Slinng like a bus horn and he jumped. "Jesus!" But it was Luke playing the bass sax. He had the case strapped over his shoulder, the instrument held out, its bright chrome bell catching the morning light. As he fingered the complicated keys, his feet kept time slapping the mud. His mouth pulled at the reed and the sounds issuing might have been water buffalo bellowing at mating time but actually were an old Vito Musso killer, "Come Back to Sorrento." "Oh, my God!" Slinng said.

"Actually, he's not bad."

"Oh, my God!"

Four days up the Rajang, two days beyond the trading port of Kapit was Rumah Bujana, an Iban kampong isolated in the deep space of the rain forest. It was literally the jumping-off place; and for the river Iban, the world ended at the edge of their kampong. Unlike the tame Land Dyaks or Sea Dyaks on the coast they made few compromises and lived much as they always had. This was rare nowadays and the district officer, R. Arrowjoy, was proud of them. He did his best to protect their independence, holding off recruiting parties from the lumber harvesters and tourist groups.

Now they were threatened by something more ominous, a spirit that invaded the kampong and got inside them. He could see it in their eyes, in the way they moved. It had begun with the dream of a white prav big as a longhouse moving on the river. A ghost in the rain; a thing that couldn't be where it was. Arrowjoy called them together and explained that he would go down to the trading town and bring back a man who would explain the dream—exorcise it. They said nothing and he knew there was more. Something had occurred deep in the rain forest to change the way of the old spirits. He knew it was bad because they refused to put a name to it.

18

TICKETS BOUGHT, Slinng and company settled in with the pigs. They (the pigs) were put aboard the *Ovaltine Super Express* in baskets, four-foot-long cylinders of rattan that were swung aboard the ship by a crane. Their squealing was pitiable, a chorus to rend the heart. Lowered into a shallow hold, shoulder to shoulder they would make the trip facing aft.

The human passengers faced each other, but accommodations on the river trader were not deluxe. There was a dirty day trippers' cabin filled with rurals who sat on long hardwood benches piled with woven packs and twisted bundles of goods. Some were Iban returning up river with nose plugs and jungle knives, wearing jeans and T-shirts, "gold" watches and fountain pens clipped to ear loops. They ate homemade sandwiches of squid and garoupa on sago bread and stared at the odd newcomers. The place reeked of cigarette smoke and the deck was slippery with spent chewing tobacco.

"Why is it primitive people instantly pick up on the worst of our habits?" Slinng asked.

"Why? Because they're the ones that offer forbidden pleasure, of course. I'm sure before the missionaries taught them it was bad, making love and raising hell weren't nearly as much fun. See that fellow staring at my topside? Now if I went around bare-breasted as their wives do, he wouldn't look twice."

"I most sincerely doubt that, lady," Luke said, giggling. He had finally recovered from his shakes—perhaps it had been Beata's tea—but he was modestly alert without acting wired and seemed actually pleasant.

"Well," Slinng said, "don't tell me he's got a sense of humor after all."

"What I have is an artist's sense of beauty."

"What he is, is a tit man."

Slinng bought sandwiches from a vendor and left Alstair and Luke puzzling over contents that contained a glazed meat that might have been used as tire plugs. Going topside, he stepped over rolls of lashed-down linoleum and white vinyl furniture, chrome legs reflecting the late-morning sun. There was a bridge that was little more than an abbreviated enclosure open to the sky and piled with cases of Coke and Medicated Brylcreem. He was welcomed and found the captain, another Australian, congenial, bored stiff with a turn-around run and anxious to talk about soccer. They reminisced about the three-game series between El Salvador and Honduras in 1969 that had started a war and Slinng eventually worked it around to the recent black monsoon.

"Oh, that one was something, a real bowser. We were tied up at that floating fuel dock at Sibu and it rolled near to a gallop. I mean it jerked out hoses and broke loose a two-thousand-gallon tank. I thought I was aboard a derby winner and that is fair dinkum." He was a large man with cultivated mustaches and dressed in a billed cap advertising Eveready, flower shirt, white shorts and sandals. Like the helmsman and nearly everyone on board he also wore mirrored sunglasses. At some point a company must have dumped its entire output in Sarawak.

"Let me ask you—and this is hypothetical—would it have been possible for a large vessel, say fifteen hundred tons, to navigate the river that night? Would it have been visible?" Slinng tried to imagine it.

A blur, bow down, diving into the trough of raging water, ripped by rains, a howl of wind that would bend metal and pull tears out of your eyes. All the radar, range-finders would be full on—pings and blips sounding the danger. And there would have to be a master helmsman, a seaman who was guided as if by the wire—on instinct and electronic marvels.

"What in God's name would it want to do that for?"

"Just supposing it had?"

"I'll tell you, mate, when typhoons sweep inland and lash up these rivers the change in temperature sets up a fog like downtown London. You couldn't see the bloody *Queen Mary* in front of your knob."

What would you hear? Runaway props lifted out of the water by the roll of river. A clatter that shakes the vessel, a thrust of torque as they reenter the water: all invisible in the fog.

As the river trader proceeded, the brown river grew wider and the jungle came down to the shoreline. Barges drifted past stacked with great piles of hardwood logs and shoved by greasy tugs. Freighters and fast passenger launches appeared, their aluminum hulls powered by twin 500-horsepower Detroit diesel engines. These boiled up the water, sending out a furious wake and, going by, the bass blast salute of air horns, a *honnnkkk!* that vibrated the teeth. The river here was a superhighway: long-haul freighters, chugging buses—longboats and dugouts, kumpits and pangkangs squeezed in between. All were overloaded with families and produce on the way to market, hunting dogs standing in the bow.

Kapit appeared at a turn in the river, first as a smudge of stack smoke hanging over the jungle, then as noise. Jammed with shipping, there were the steamy toots of dockside cranes and whine of cables taken up, dogs on drums clacking as they set. The *Ovaltine Super Express* backed down, screws churning the water, and began to maneuver around tugboats pushing log rafts downriver. There was a docking problem with a line of rusty coastal steamers and small trading craft shoved up to the loading wharfs. But they nosed their way in with bullhorn honks and the passengers were discharged. These went up a ramp that led to a raised walkway around the main square of town. The smell was creosote and rotting fish, and the air full of clouds of white choking dust as stevedores manhandled wooden pallets of cement swinging up from the hold of a freighter. There were shouts and whistles, and from somewhere Radio SING blasting out *"Breaking up is hard to dooo."*

As Slinng came up the ramp with Alstair and Luke following, he stopped dead, backing up the others.

A huge crocodile lay on the splintery walkway above him. Nearly at eye level, the mouth wide open, the ragged sawteeth marking out a throat as big and dark as a drain pile. It was the monster of his dream. The one that had swallowed him.

"What's the matter?" Alstair asked behind him.

"Ah—that crocodile . . ."

"Oh, poor thing."

He saw now that its jaws were propped open with a wet stick and there was a large-caliber bullet hole between its eyes. Still, the malevolent, vertical slits of eyes were on him. He could not shake off the horror of his dream.

"This may be the place to have a bag run up," Alstair said.

He stepped gingerly around it onto the level of walkway where several

Iban were unloading other fresh game from a longboat: a deer, delicate hooves crossed as if in the ballet position *croisé*; wild pig carcasses with tangled, coarse hair and tusks that circled back to snouts; skinned monkeys, their pink flesh looking distressingly human.

Although the men were dressed in tank tops and ragged shorts they had a different, wilder look than other Iban seen so far. Amazing tattoos of serpentine floral patterns were surmounted by a half moon and stars; tortoise-shell tracings on the backs of hands, and the stalks of plants that rose from the collarbone up the throat to blossom and support the chin. Hair was tousled, a mushroom cap, shaved up the sides.

As they worked, their eyes avoided contact with him—except for one, a young man with smooth, hairless skin that included no eyebrows. Instead, they had been tattooed in, and curiously, frown lines added. He looked straight into Slinng's eyes, held them for a split second. The eyes were a dense black, liquid, and, Slinng thought, seductive. His was the look of a lover. When he raised his own eyebrows the contact was instantly broken off and the Iban continued their unloading.

Then he become aware of another watching him. This man, white, leaned against a rude railing, sinewy arms crossed, short and wiry with a crooked nose and a face as square and fixed in expression as the Iban. When he spoke, lifting the curtain of a chewed-off mustache, gold caps showed in front.

"Slinng?"

"Yes, that's right." He stepped over and shook hands.

"R. Arrowjoy. The boy here recognized you right off."

"How could he do that?"

"Why—he's the Dreamer."

He was dressed in the military style, a green jungle hat and shirt missing its insignia. "This is Miss Eames and Louis Sing."

Arrowjoy was obviously taken aback and not polite. "I hope you don't think this is some kind of a damn tour?"

Slinng was not in the mood for temperament. "Here's what I think it is: An insurance investigator, me, has flown all the way from Singapore to the Borneo jungle in answer to a cable sent by you about a dream. What it probably also is, is stupid." There was a pause. As aboard his ship, Slinng liked to get matters of command and purpose straight at the beginning.

Arrowjoy understood the tone of voice and saw a look that demanded respect or else. He had served under many officers with that look, those who would tear a stripe off you or save your life with equal aplomb. "All right, I've got it. But don't expect the bloody Ritz."

"I was thinking more of Claridge's," Alstair said, smiling sweetly. "I've brought my Vuitton."

Arrowjoy wouldn't look at her. "Let's give the boys time to trade. I'll shout you a drink." And he turned abruptly toward the square.

"You know what he looks like with that broken nose and awful mustache? A dyspeptic porcupine."

"Well, you're just going to have to put up with him—in case you haven't heard, Errol Flynn is dead."

"Not in my mind."

Arrowjoy led them off the dock and across the street to a café facing the river. The shops here were stuccoed brick, arcades crowded with shoppers. Signs on canvas awnings advertised chainsaws and male potency pills. They sat down at a table with a pink Formica top and Arrowjoy ordered beer all around from a Malay boy. The Chinese owner lay flat out on a counter in the back sleeping with a cloth over his face to fend off the flies. As they drank their beer in silence the ceiling fan above them rotated in an unoiled squeak and swatted bugs with its wooden blades. It was necessary to cover the glasses as their body parts descended.

"Just how much farther are we going?" Slinng asked.

"Couple of hundred kilometers—past Long Murum—the last of the big longhouses before the mountains."

"The river is navigable?"

"From there maybe another sixty kilometers until the Ambun Rapids, then it's the end of the line. Beyond, the mountain ridges get up to thirteen thousand feet and that's the border between Sarawak and Kalimantan—West Borneo."

"You're the district officer for the Iban there?"

"That's right, from the Hose Mountains up to the Tamabo Range."

"What does that mean?"

"Mean?"

"Your job."

"It means I try to keep the poor buggers off the oil platforms at Brunei or sawing their dinks off at the lumber mills."

"Then the government is protecting them?"

"Did you ever see a government that gave a toss for anybody that didn't pay taxes? My job, among other things, is to keep them from being exploited."

That seemed to be the end of that.

"Maybe they're bored living in the Stone Age," Alstair said, flicking the buzzing thorax of a giant cicada off the table. "I'd guess gathering berries or whatever and not being able to flush might get to be hard cheese after a while."

He looked at her as one might a child. "You don't understand."

"Really? Why is it we're always trying to save other people from themselves? They have as much right to pig out on bad taste as we do. Do you suppose Romans who invaded Britain gave a whatever for those primitive tribes who painted themselves blue? And that was us, wasn't it?"

"As far as I can see of this rotten world we'd be better off still blue. These people have been ruined by our ideas. There was a fanatical Christian revival here in the seventies that had them throw away their heritage—priceless icons, charms and dream beads—the old head-hunting swords were dumped in the river because they didn't go along with Christian beliefs. Singing and dancing were forbidden and the heads that had hung in the longhouses for centuries were broken up and buried."

"Yes, well, it's hard to work up a nostalgia for the good old head-hunting days."

Slinng saw the look on Arrowjoy's face and tried to turn the subject in a different direction. "Certainly there was more to the change than missionaries."

"Greed. In 'seventy-nine the hardwood prices doubled on the world market and there was a logging boom here and the need for cheap local labor. They left the kampongs for jobs. Now timber operations are about fifty percent of exports."

"That's good for the economy, isn't it?" Alstair asked, refusing to be shut out of the conversation.

"Have you got any idea what they do to the rain forest? It looks lush in there but the ground is infertile because of the heat and the leaching of the soil by the constant rain. After they tear it up with their logging trails and cuts, nothing will grow but mud. Then what are the tribes going to eat?"

"Well, they can always go back to eating each other."

There was a dead silence and Luke took this moment to ask, "Say, tuan, do you know if there's a pharmacy where I might get drugs without a prescription?"

Arrowjoy looked at him. "Who is this individual?"

"He plays the sax," Alstair answered. "He's really very good."

"Of course," Arrowjoy said, getting up, angry, "that's just what we need in the jungle! I hope somebody else thought to bring a bloody piano!"

"No, but I'm a strong whistler."

As they followed Arrowjoy back across the street, she kept in step whistling the "Colonel Bogey March."

"Why are you doing this?" Slinng asked.

"Because he's such a misanthrope. Talking about missionary zeal and loggers ruining *his* country. He wants to keep the Indians down on the reservation and everyone in place. For him any change is automatically bad. He's the kind who would welcome the end of the world so he could say 'I told you so'—even if there wasn't anyone left to tell."

"I thought you were coming along to help me? Is fighting with the man who's going to be our guide and sole contact with wild men helping me?"

"He's also sexist, treating me like a helpless woman."

"That was a mistake all right."

The longboat was forty feet long and carved out of a single tree trunk, meranti merah, the very best timber for boat building. Each side was built up with overlapping planks toenailed in, ribs as stiffeners, then the whole thing caulked with fibrous bark and tree resin mixed with sump oil. Not many were built like this anymore and Arrowjoy was proud of it, fitting for a man who liked to embrace the old ways. However, his enthusiasm didn't extend to paddling and the boat was fitted with a fifty-horsepower Mercury outboard.

The Iban had gathered together their trade goods and piled them in the boat. There were no seats and they went into the bottom on duck boards: moks of rice, mats, axes, pots, sugee: Lombok-brand chewing tobacco, bars of Sunlight laundry soap, bamboo sections containing pig fat for cooking and five cartons of Skyscraper Filter Cigarettes. There were also two cases of arak in old brown beer bottles that Arrowjoy personally loaded on board. His face was still stiff with disapproval at bringing Alstair and Luke.

As they worked, Slinng began to sort them out. There was an old man, a bit gray and stringier of muscle to whom the others deferred, Ubang Deng, whom Arrowjoy called "Salt," and three younger men. The one with the eyebrow tattoos was Salt's son, Bit Ubang—the Dreamer. The other two who seemed interchangeable were called Gong and Den.

"Why does that cute one keep giving you the eye?" Alstair wanted to know as they stood on the walkway and watched the loading.

"I don't know but it's a bit eerie."

"Looks to me like you've got a sweetie," she said, as the Dreamer smiled. Slinng had had his share of schoolboy admirers at Gordonstoun and later as a young man aboard ship fought off seamen looking for "wives." However, none had their eyebrows and frown lines tattooed in, and none carried a wicked twenty-four-inch knife called a parang. "Just my luck to lose my hunk to a jungle bunny," she added.

"I suppose you think that's funny?"

"I'm crying on the inside but laughing on the outside."

They roared away from the wharf, dodging river traffic, bow cutting through oil slicks thrown by the rusted-out coastal freighters, riding over cola cans, the drift of rattan and spent Family Friend condoms imported by the thousand gross by the World Health Organization. As dusk fell other shipping had been left behind and the river flow stretched out ahead, closed in by the trackless jungle that pushed down to the edge of the water. The sound of the outboard became a monotonous drone and made conversation impossible.

Arrowjoy sat at its tiller smoking and staring straight ahead. Alstair was partly right in her instant character analysis, Slinng thought: He did behave like a misanthrope, ready to put the blame on mankind in general and whoever was closest in particular. But Slinng was more sympathetic; he had known men like this before. The sea was a great refuge for those who wished to distance themselves from civilization. It was possible on a long solitary cruise to believe only you and the world of the ship existed. Arrowjoy had chosen this jungle to be his sea. Like a captain who controls his crew with life-and-death decisions, he had the power to keep others away from those primitive people he held sway over. And this is what bothered Slinng. He knew why *he* was there—but what did Arrowjoy have to gain?

It was quickly dark now and ahead, beyond another of the graceful curves of the river, a hint of red tinted the sky. It was not a place for the sun to set and seemed beyond explanation. When he looked at Arrowjoy he got no acknowledgment. "What is that?!" Alstair shouted over the outboard.

"I don't know!" Then as they came closer there was a waver to it and they saw it was fire, the smoke hidden in the night skies.

"Can the rain forest burn?" she wanted to know.

He had no idea. It didn't seem possible, but what else could it be? The flames grew brighter and now there was the sound of crackling wood. Coming around the long sweep of river the bank straightened and the view was of hell. It was a panorama that might have been an end-of-the-world scenario for the large screen.

It stretches nearly a mile deep along the river, barren raw ground, denuded, treeless, a colossal scoop taken out of the rain forest. The flattened red earth has been soaked with thousands of gallons of sump oil to keep the sawdust down and has taken on the color of rotten salmon. At the center of this desolation a fire burns fiercely, fed by tons of branches and brush not worth marketing. Around it bulldozers grind and push and giant machines with wheels taller than men grasp huge logs in mechanical teeth and deposit them in piles. In their enclosed cabs the faces of the drivers, Malay and Iban, are uplit by the flames. They work the levers and gears as effortlessly as they once did the snare or blowgun, and they are thrilled by the power they control.

Behind them a dozen logging roads fan out into the slaughtered hillsides, paths into the heart of the rain forest. The bulldozers push ahead sending up the wild birds and shaking the gibbons out of their trees—opening it up for the logging trucks and men with chainsaws. When they are done, what was once mysterious shelter cooled by the fan of interlocking trees and offering a hundred varieties of edible plants is now sterile eroded ground fit only for parking lots.

As the longboat passes, the workers are visible, Iban again in bright orange hard hats and company overalls. They carry their chainsaws like weapons and swing off the big logging trucks, coming back from the wood lots. Squaring one side of the compound are prefab barracks and a pair of eighty-kilowatt diesel generators to supply electricity. Overhead lights on tall poles throw everything in flat relief and long shadows stretch out behind the men as they walk to the mess hall. The Iban in the longboat wave, but there is no response. Can the Iban on shore see beyond the glare of lights? Or, locked in as they are into their new world, do they want to see? Farther on, tugboats and log barges are tied up to a crude wharf along the bank and show Singapore registry and the company logo, MALTEC.

Then, as the longboat passes the noise of the log station and the night goes to black, they hear a strange, haunting sound rising even above the sound of their outboard. Luke sits in the bow with the sax, legs propped as a brace against the motion of the river, and plays his heart out. The song is "Harlem Nocturne," and he travels its swoops and lifts honking and hooting, dropping to sweet toots, twisting them off, then returning to the line and ending in a long, sustained, fading note that might be the epitaph of the rain forest. The Iban are enchanted, stunned. Slinng looks at Arrowjoy and even he smiles.

After another mile downriver they nosed into a brief grassy bank and the Iban leaped ashore to set up camp. There was a hustle of action, parang whacks, and shelter was cut from the jungle: sapling shelters, pondoks, with raised platforms to provide ventilation and space above the snakes, leeches and fire ants. Mats were laid down and a fire begun. Cubed pork, left over from a wild pig, was shoved on skewers and put over the fire along with its liver.

Slinng and Alstair stood watching. "You'll have to admit, Al, he was right about the logging."

"That was horrible, wasn't it? Now if the world will just end, it will make his day . . ." They turned at the sound of a bubbling exhaust and a twenty-foot power boat suddenly appeared out of the dark, its white sides nearly luminous against the night. A spotlight was turned on and the bow beached against the bank behind their longboat. A heavy man in a hard hat jumped ashore followed by two Malay carrying shotguns. They wore overalls with the MALTEC logo.

"What in hell are you people doing here?"

Arrowjoy straightened up from the fire. "Who are you to ask?"

The man pushed in closer. He had a sunburned face and very pale blue eyes. A plastic tag on his shirt pocket read Brenner—Security Chief. "You can't camp here, this is company property."

"These people have been camping along this river for as long as any can remember." The Iban had stopped what they were doing and all looked at the intruders.

"I don't give a good God damn what they used to do—this property is leased by Maltec now for five miles up this side of the river." He swung out his arm. "Now I want you people to get off it." He had an American accent and the demeanor of a tough cop.

"Oh, no," Arrowjoy said. "I'm the MFS District Officer for Long Murum and—"

"Well, now, why don't you get the fuck up there then? You have no jurisdiction here, mister." He had moved very close to Arrowjoy, his bulk overshadowing him. Behind him the two Malay watched the Iban, shotguns held toward the ground. "We've had a lot of trouble with these people, we've lost a couple of chainsaws and canned goods. I am not going to allow them—or you—to come within five miles of our camp."

"Just a minute! These—"

"You're not listening!" And he began to thump Arrowjoy on the chest with his index finger. "I want you to—" On the third thump Arrowjoy's hand shot up like a snake and, grabbing the finger, broke it with a deft backward snap. "Ohhh! Jesus!" The man staggered back holding his hand. "Christ!"

There was a double clack as the two Malay jacked shells into their shotguns and raised them. Behind him, Slinng saw the young Iban swing up their jungle knives while the old man reached for an ax. He also noticed that the Dreamer was smiling at him.

19

"BELAY THAT!" Leveling his shipboard voice, Lawrence Slinng stepped out of the shadows and placed himself between the Malays' raised shotguns and the Iban jungle knives. "These people are under my command!" There was a second's hesitation as the Malay guards looked toward their security chief. Guns remained pointed but it was obvious no one wanted to shoot. The Iban, by contrast, were only held back by Arrowjoy's presence. They would have been delighted to start chopping.

"Who in hell are you?" the security chief asked through gritted teeth. His finger was still bent back and he was in pain.

"Captain W. Lawrence Slinng." He withdrew an envelope, shaking out a bogus letter. It was on Lloyd's stationery and had been written at the last minute by Colonel Pynge-Gilbert to speed him on his way. In it, the undersigned was authorized to pursue Lloyd's matters in Sarawak and Borneo. He held it up. "Are you aware that all indemnity and liability policies for Maltec Mills are handled by Lloyd's underwriters?"

"What's that got to do with—"

"Just listen! There is a rider that those policies may be withdrawn at any time because of increased accident rate or faulty security enforcement."

"Wait a minute . . ."

"It is my job to monitor these properties—that is why we are here. A bad report can mean your company will be *without insurance*—do you understand what I'm saying?"

"Nobody told me about any—"

"Did you intend shooting down these unarmed people?" He gestured at the Iban, who stood holding their twenty-four-inch jungle knives and an axe.

"This bastard broke my finger!" He stabbed it at Arrowjoy.

To Slinng's consternation, Alstair pushed past him. "Let me look at that, please!" Stepping up to the security chief she gently took his hand. "I'm Sister Goodnight, medical person aboard—I'll have a bang at it."

"No, don't—" She suddenly snapped the finger back. "Ohhhh! Jesus God!"

"That's got it." Whipping out a soiled handkerchief, she bent down to pick up a stick as splint, and bound up his finger and hand in a complicated bandage.

He jerked away and hurried back toward the launch with the two Malay following. "You can be damn sure I'll check with the office!" In the next minute they were aboard the launch and backing off shore.

"Sister Goodnight?" Slinng asked.

"I thought I was very good in my part."

Arrowjoy looked at them both. "Was any of that true?"

"Absolutely none," Slinng answered.

They then heard an odd sound: Arrowjoy laughing.

The next days were spent in river travel. Long hours under way listening to the roar of the powerful outboard—nights camped on the bank with the ominous noises of the jungle to fall asleep to. Slinng had begun to sound the river as they traveled upstream, using a line with knots tied on it and a heavy bolt at the end for a sinker. Tossing it in at the bow he walked the length of the longboat to gauge river depth. Pigfat smeared on the bottom picked up mud or sand and indicated conditions. He was discouraged.

"It's sand and there's barely enough water here to float a vessel with any kind of a draft," he said to Arrowjoy when they broke for an afternoon meal.

"River conditions constantly change. During a monsoon it can be twice this deep, but full of floating logs and snags. Now it's average. With too little rain it will expose long stretches of rapids. One thing is certain: It's always dangerous."

"The vessel I'm thinking of has a double bottom and heavy scantlings. It could survive a rough passage."

"Yes, but why would it want to? Why would it be here? There's the question."

"What about your Dreamer? Didn't he see that in his vision?"

"No, that's your job to interpret."

"Me?"

"For these people that dream had a profound and disturbing effect. A thing has come into the rain forest they can't understand. It is a feeling, a spirit that consumes them these days. I can't deal with it—but I'm hoping you can convince them this ship is real."

"The way we can do that is find it."

"Yes."

"When will I hear this dream in detail?"

"We'll be at the longhouse by tomorrow—then we'll have a gathering of the men. Understand that these matters must be treated as seriously as a Vatican Council."

"Let me ask you something." Slinng was uncomfortable with this but went on. "Why is it the Dreamer keeps looking at me, smiling . . . ?"

"This is an important thing to him—a spiritual matter. He has been told you will explain his dream. If you can do that, then he will be released from its spirit. He looks to you as a dayung from the West, a spiritman. He smiles because he wants your favor, he is in your debt."

"But that's wrong! I can't promise anything! What if he's not satisfied with my explanation of the ship?"

"Well, in the old days he would have taken your head. Now, I'm not sure; an arm or a leg maybe." Arrowjoy chuckled; this was his idea of a joke.

While Arrowjoy and the Iban loaded the boat again, Alstair asked, "What were you and the porcupine going on about?"

"It turns out I don't have a sweetie after all. The Dreamer is looking for someone to explain life's deepest meanings."

"Is that all?"

"That's all."

"You could start with the reason bread always falls jam side down, and why the one you love always loves another."

"Thank you."

By noon they had reached the fork where the Rajang turned from its main course toward the mountains. They raced past the few river towns, heading on the final leg of a journey that would take them to the last of the big kampongs at Rumah Bujana. As they got closer the distant ridges of mountains were visible rising thirteen thousand feet to merge with the clouds. The river was deserted here with no commercial vessels and only the occasional native craft. It narrowed, but judging from Slinng's sounding was deeper—fifteen feet in some spots.

Then suddenly the power of the outboard was cut back and Arrowjoy nosed into the bank. It seemed to Slinng they would hit and he braced himself and Alstair, but the old man, Salt, parted the overhanging branches and they ducked through on a tributary. Here the trees were interwoven and travel continued through a tunnel of green leaves reaching out to brush the longboat. Another mile and the motor was shut off and the Iban leaped to the bank and pulled them ashore.

For Slinng it was indistinguishable from any of the other places they had passed: a tangle of vines and trees that rose up to block out the sky. There was no sign of habitation. "This is Rumah Bujana?"

"Another kilometer. We have to walk in. Give us a hand with this gear."

When everybody was loaded down, the Iban carrying huge packs, they set off. There was no trail that Slinng could see, but they moved over the vines and around the boles of trees in the rhythm of those who know where they are going. It was very difficult to keep up with their pace, and they obviously weren't waiting for anyone.

"I say, are these people going for some kind of cross-country record?" Alstair was breathing heavily, picking herself up after falling down.

Slinng helped her up. "Shall I yell at Arrowjoy to slow down?"

"Heavens, no. That's just what he wants."

Luke was a good twenty-five yards behind. Just then a flash of T-shirt showed. "Come on!" Slinng shouted. "The crocs always pick off the last man!"

"Is that supposed to be Western humor?"

Straggling along they were aware of an increase of light, then patches of sky through the canopy of trees and finally, breaking out of the dense vegetation—there it was, the longhouse of Rumah Bujana, a great land-hugging structure blending into the environment, a structure modernists struggled for and failed—the perfect people place. Centered in a broad clearing and raised up on ten-foot hardwood posts, it stretched out two hundred feet long, softened and made human by irregular lines out of square sections and indigenous materials. The roof was thatched with atap and raised in several sections to let air in and smoke out. In the old days longhouses had been elevated for defense, the only access up a greasy notched pole. Although the time of tribal war and headhunter raids was over they were still built off the ground as protection against snakes, and worse, a vicious bacterial fungus that eventually swallowed up anything laid on the jungle floor. Garbage and sewage were dumped through trap doors and animals ranging underneath picked it clean.

As they broke out of the jungle into the clearing there were shouts, blood-curdling screams at their appearance. Slinng and Alstair drew back, uneasy at the violence of welcome. There looked to be a hundred people whooping it up at fires below the longhouse and they all started forward to meet them at once. Small children rushed ahead holding up babies while dogs raced along, snapping at their heels. The sun was just setting and its color added drama to the wild medley. As they awaited the onslaught, several runners fell down, legs tangled, rolled a dozen yards, recovered and happily got up. Then they were engulfed, carried along by the exuberant mob.

"What's happening?" Alstair asked, clinging to Slinng. "Human sacrifice?"

"It's a party," Arrowjoy answered, "to celebrate our safe arrival."

"It looks like they started without us," Alstair said, accepting kisses, pats and head rubs.

"This day also happens to fall at the end of mourning for those whose relatives died within the last six months—they do tend to cut loose."

Arriving at the fire, Salt as headman did the honors, introducing his wife, a tough-looking lady covered with sweat and grease from a cooking fire that crackled with entire pigs. She gave Slinng a penetrating stare, a look that said, "What are you doing here, and what can we expect?" It was not friendly. Like the other Iban women she was bare-breasted, and the sweat and pig fat gave her torso a greasy shine in the firelight.

There were pau, blankets spread on the ground and heaped with food: charred hunks of wild pig, varieties of eggs; mounds of gummy, glutenous rice and slick fried bananas. They were given an honored position. "Oh, dear, if there's one thing I can't abide it's a fried banana," said Alstair, pronouncing it "bahnahnah."

"It may not be the worst thing you eat tonight."

"Is that a sexual or culinary observation?"

Luke sat to one side, engulfed by young girls and giggling children. "Hey, tuan! Is this one of those places where they have hallucinogenic plants?"

The tribe was arranged squatting around the fires and already drunk on tuak, rice wine. The cases of arak were brought out and the brown bottles passed around. This was a wicked distilled spirit put up by the Chinese merchants and locally called "Brain Dart" after the blowgun poison that would stun a crocodile.

"Before the main course, there's a blessing," Arrowjoy said. Salt walked among the seated drinkers and tapped bowed heads with a live rooster, holding it by its neck while it squawked in protest. "In the old days they would have its throat cut first."

"It would have been better off." In the beginning the taps bestowed were light, but encouraged by taunts, became harder, slamming down and whacking heads to the screaming delight of the crowd. Then, after a particularly solid blow, the recipient leaped up and, grabbing one half of the rooster, tried to jerk Salt off his feet. The bird tore apart and they fell back on the drinkers, each with a bloody half of feathers. The crowd thought this was hilarious.

"What a clever way to liven up a cocktail party," Alstair said.

"Is this what usually happens?" Slinng asked Arrowjoy.

"No, sometimes it can get rough. They're being polite because you're here. But it's all in fun."

Now came pig passing. A heavy haunch of meat was volleyed around the group as each receiver cut off a piece and threw it along, with whatever speed he could muster. On the last pass it went through a drunk's arms and hit an old lady in the back, knocking her flat. More hearty laughter.

Alstair tried the arak and it was minutes before she could catch her breath. "My goodness!" she finally said, but drank it, doing her best to keep up. As she did, he noticed her left eye drifted toward the center as the muscles relaxed.

Impromptu dancing, ngajat, began. Men suddenly leaped up with chilling battle cries, swinging parangs at invisible enemies. Accompanied by three-stringed sapehs, nose flutes, and a bamboo version of a Jew's harp, the music was wild, dancing intense and the knife swipes hazardous.

Old men danced into the firelight, pantomiming life's tragedies: a failed erection, a scratch you can't itch, the last drop in the bottle—and as a finale, death creeping up as a crocodile. To illustrate this, the performer backed into the shadows as if consumed, cleverly folding in his arms until he realistically vanished.

The young women danced with their backs to the men, decorous, showing only the shimmer of hair and subdued movement. All, that is, but a bold unmarried girl who pushed through, planting herself in front of Slinng. Rolling her breasts and using her hands in original ways, she had his attention. He was close enough to count the petals on the hibiscus pattern of her sarong.

Alstair was drunk and not amused. "If she gets any closer you're going to have that thing in your face!"

"She's just being friendly."

"Is that supposed to be dancing?"

"Alstair . . ."

"Does she call those legs?!"

"Alstair . . ."

"Does she call those tits?! I'll show you tits!" she shouted.

Slinng tried to calm her. "Al—easy, we're guests."

But she wouldn't have it, lurching up and shouting at Luke, who sat smoking a huge cheroot with the young girls. "Luke! Get that bloody horn out!"

"Al, come on—fun's fun, but . . ."

Alstair pulled her T-shirt over her head now, flinging it away. Shoving the girl aside, she moved onto the mats slippery with food.

"God," Slinng said, rubbing his forehead

At the first honk of sax the Iban were riveted. Wherever the instrument had been heard, it was yet to premier at an Iban longhouse in the vastness of a rain forest. Its basso tones honked out the traditional sliding line of burlesque strippers, an invitation to seduction. Alstair, throwing her arms up, twirled (a bit unsteadily) into the center of the group and began a combination of disco moves and early ballet training. As she went, the globes of breasts crossed in figure-eight patterns. The viewers were stunned. Bare breasts were nothing new. However, as in all sexual connections, the difference was the difference. Mouths gaping, they watched transfixed.

The sax rose and dipped in concert with the principal dancer. It was not great dancing, but never mind, the message got across and when she finally became dizzy and fell back into Slinng's arms there was the rush of young bucks. He and Arrowjoy fought them off with feet and elbows smiling all the time: thuds and slaps, bumps and grunts. Arrowjoy shouted that this was the white dayung's spirit wife—a virgin! They backed off and Slinng threw a blanket over her.

"That was a bloody stupid thing to do!" Arrowjoy snarled.

"Yes, I suppose it was," Slinng answered, "but then, it fits right in with hitting people over the head with chickens and knocking old ladies down with pigs, doesn't it!"

Alstair slept and Slinng sat next to her as the party roared on. A fat woman, the tribe's singer of legends, stood in the middle of the firelight and began a long song of the forest spirits. As her voice moved up and down in dramatic tones the tribe quieted down. It seemed a solemn moment. Then, nearing the end of the song, one of the Iban sneaked up behind her and, reaching around, smeared her face with handfuls of black muck. There were screams of laughter.

"Why would he do that?" Slinng asked, puzzled.

"For fun! This is a time to puncture pomposity, to bring everyone down to an equal level. If they're a bit rougher than usual it's because of the spirit of gloom that's been hanging over the place since the dream."

"What is that stuff he smeared on her?"

"Oh, pot black mixed with motor oil, or sometimes for a real joke they use pig shit."

"Cute."

Now they all were doing it, running back and forth chasing each other with black soot rubbed from the pots, flinging it, grinding it in hair and clothes. Three young men struggled and fell in the fire. A sarong caught, and while the one on fire frantically beat it out, the other two happily urinated on it. This was considered the high point of humor for the evening.

Slinng dozed off, then started awake at a man howling like a dog and dogs answering. When this continued his friends stuffed a rag in his mouth and tied him down. Toward dawn he thought he saw Luke, wearing a loincloth, disappear into the jungle with one girl—then later, another. There was gunfire through the night, war whoops and the sound of crazed laughter. At the last, snoring—a concert of snorts and wheezes, coughs and prolonged bursts of flatulence whose velocity rivaled chainsaw decibels. The party was over.

He woke to Arrowjoy shaking him. "Come on!"

"Wha . . . ?" It was still dark with just a hint of pink in the east. "Where are we going?"

"It's time for the dream."

"Now?!"

"Now. Don't worry about your girlfriend, she'll be all right."

Slinng got up and felt a weight shift from his toes to his head. "God . . ." He smacked his lips at the bad taste in his mouth.

"Here." Arrowjoy handed him a beer. They walked back across the compound below the longhouse. Bodies lay where they had fallen, arrested in midflight, passed out and asleep. Pots were overturned, bottles broken, and there was the sickly smell of sour rice wine in the air. Surviving chickens pecked at spilled grain while dogs slunk off with bones. The fires were dead and ashes caught a slight breeze off the river, blowing up in a fine sift of dust that settled on the sleepers. From inside the longhouse there was the cry of babies and soothing tones of children, their little brothers and sisters taking care of them.

Slinng entered the jungle behind Arrowjoy and a curtain dropped. Coming from the feeble morning light of the clearing, they were suddenly plunged into a dark, verdant green. He followed at arm's length, knowing that if Arrowjoy chose to dodge away he would be totally lost. Although only a hundred yards from the longhouse he would never find it again.

They went perhaps half a kilometer, and came to a small circular clearing. There was just enough of a break in the overhead canopy to allow thin shafts of light to penetrate, beamed down like the keylights of a theatrical production. At dawn when the upper, cooler air merged with warm ground currents, a fog occurred. It rose in wispy curls at the forest floor, weaving around a dozen seated figures. Partly obscured by its mist, blankets were pulled up against the morning chill and they sat waiting, expressions unreadable.

Yes, Slinng thought, this is stage-managed. Coming after the drunken party when everyone's head was altered, it was a deliberate move. He was entering the realm of metaphysics again. Seated opposite the Dreamer, he recognized Salt, the headman, Iban from the trip and other young men not yet identified. Next to him, Arrowjoy said, "I'll translate for the Dreamer." Slinng looked across at him, seeing a face that seemed not quite in the whole, blurred at the edges as if the fog had eaten away at it. His eyes were glazed, whether in drunkenness or spiritual euphoria, it was hard to tell. He stared not at Slinng but through him, eyes red-rimmed and not tracking. His voice was a murmur overlaid by Arrowjoy's whisper—even the audio was contrived to heighten the effect.

"I went to where the two rivers meet," the Dreamer said, "to trade. While I was there the black storm came. It was worse than any I ever saw, winds that swept in full of themselves, taking the tops from houses, rolling up tin roofs and blowing the people off their feet. Waters rose and made that place a lake.

"It went on one, then two days. The things that make electric light failed and the air was so filled with water that fires would not start. I wanted to get away because I could not stand that place. But it was impossible and they told me not to go. Then on the third day I went anyway. But it was a mistake. The water moved on the river as if shot from a hose and my prav made the speed of one with motors. I could not control it and was rammed into the bank. I lost all my trade goods but I got the boat up on the land and, turning it over, crawled underneath. Now the winds increased and the sound blew through the jungle with the rush of waterfalls, exploding the trees and sending them crashing down. Even where I was, ten arms above the river, it began to rise and swirl around me. I was very afraid and shivered a long time, then at last when the night came I fell asleep. That is how I had my dream."

Slinng looked at the others, heads down, lips moving in unison, reciting along with the Dreamer. They had all memorized it. Telling dreams, bringing back the subconscious, was probably man's oldest entertainment. But few dreams were as meaningful to listener as teller. He thought of the vividness of his own dream of the crocodile and Miri's head—it was still with him.

"First I heard another voice, not one the storm would cause: a humming roar, the sound machinery makes when angry. In my dream I raised the side of the boat and peered out. It was very dark and the wind whipped a froth from the top of the water, sending it whistling along as a cloud might go above the earth. Then the thing appeared, looming out of the night as a spirit on the river—riding the water on that lift of froth. It was a huge size—as big as our longhouse and white—the white of a cloud, and that is how it went—its shape shifting, stretching out. As it passed in front of my eyes I saw holes punched in the sides and lights shining out. Above was a building with more squares of light and the heads of men. Over them sat a big round ball, and behind them a tower slanted back, the half moon of a giant's bite out of its top. Then in the next moment it was gone, swallowed up in the black night, with the wink of a firefly high above it that flew along."

When the Dreamer finished there was mumbled accord among the Iban that this was truly a singular thing to appear in a place where nothing like it had ever been seen before. It had brought with it a bad wind that was still blowing,

"What do you think?" Arrowjoy asked.

"He's got it right. That ball is the sat-com dome, and the bite, the curve of mast above the stack. He's seen it."

"Tell them that."

"All right, let's go."

With Arrowjoy translating, he began. "I know this white boat, I have met it," he said. "I have entered it and walked among the things that make it go. I know the man who drives it. It is a boat made by men like yourselves. It is not magic or a spirit."

There were head shakes and eyes cast down. "They want to know why it was here—that is the puzzling thing. If no one else saw such a big thing on the river, how can it be real?"

"Tell them this."

"This boat is running away," he continued. "The man who drives it has done wrong things among his own people and is escaping—he had a part in my own father's death. He thinks if he comes here no one will find him. He doesn't know the Iban are great trackers and hunters. That is why I ask *you* to lead *me*. This boat *has* to be hidden up the river, it is too big to turn around and back out like an animal in a burrow. We must find it and show the spirit as bad."

There was a pause and more mumbling. The Dreamer looked into his eyes now, but did not smile. Salt as headman got up and made a speech. He had an offhand way, evident by his tone, of making Slinng feel insignificant, at his sufferance. He went on to dismiss his appearance, reasoning and philosophy. It took a long time.

"What did he say?" Slinng wanted to know.

"They don't believe you," Arrowjoy answered.

"Why?! My God! My explanation was absolutely rational!"

"That's just it—they are talking magic and you're talking reality. They believe the Dreamer because he says it *was* a dream. You are saying it wasn't, but this is inexplicable to them. You have to understand that the Iban believe in the omniscience of thought. Anything that can't be explained to their satisfaction has to be supernatural."

"Will they help us look for the ship?"

"Yes, if I ask them. But are you sure you want to find it?"

"Of course! Damn it, man, this is fantastic! The Dreamer has seen the *Sulu* on this river! That's incredible! That crazy bastard Hartog has sailed a two-hundred-foot yacht right into the middle of the rain forest! We've got to find it!"

"If we do, I can't predict their response one way or another. It may be dangerous."

"Nothing could be more dangerous than that party."

When they got back to the longhouse, Slinng found Alstair gone. He stood for a moment expecting an explanation or a clue. But no, the fallen slept on and shouts brought only dogs barking. She had disappeared.

20

"SHE'S GONE!" Slinng shouted at Arrowjoy. "Alstair!"

In turn, he yelled at an old woman who was moving around at the edge of the compound. She shook her head, flapping her hand behind her in a casual gesture and giggling. *"Muee-loto!"*

"What's she saying?"

"Well, roughly translated, 'Wiping her rear end.' She hasn't seen her but guesses she's gone into the jungle to relieve herself. Come on!" And Arrowjoy was off and running.

"Wait a minute!" Slinng shouted, running after him. "Maybe we should give her some privacy!"

"You still don't understand, do you? If she walks ten yards into that jungle she may not come back!"

He whistled up the dogs, several of the savage breed the Iban used to hunt with. They were not pets and were kept half starved to sharpen their noses. They raced ahead as Arrowjoy and Slinng trailed after them, breaking through the bush. Arrowjoy was right. Once again when they entered the jungle he was lost. The overall vista was in terms of yards and everything looked exactly the same. There were no landmarks and with the sky closed in by the canopy of trees their sense of direction became hopeless.

Ahead, the dogs were baying and there was Alstair, back up against a tree as they harried her, snarling and snapping. Arrowjoy beat them off with a stick. *"Blart!"* she said, angry and frightened by their ferocity. "A person can't have a moment alone without other people siccing the dogs on them!"

"I'm sorry, Al, but we were worried about your getting back."

"You think I can't find my way a few yards back?! I've been camping before, you know!"

"All right," Arrowjoy said, annoyed. "Lead us back."

"Of course!"

And they set off. Ten minutes later they were still walking. "It must be just ahead, I remember that frumpy plant."

"No," Arrowjoy said, "you're going the opposite direction." And he turned around. "I haven't got any more time to waste."

"You're the one going wrong, it's that way!" She pointed. But they followed him and minutes later broke into the clearing. "Well, I would have gotten here. Mine was the scenic route."

Arrowjoy stopped for a lecture. "Look. In 1975, a friend of mine, Bruce Sandilands, got lost near here. His guides were disoriented and they panicked—when he couldn't keep up with them, they abandoned him. He died eighteen days later and was eaten by animals. He had been going in circles. Bruce was a government surveyor for twenty-three years out here. Now if a man like that couldn't find his way back, what do you think your chances are?" And he walked off.

"I was just testing you!" Alstair called after him.

They left this time in two longboats. Salt, the Dreamer and the same Iban made up the crew of Arrowjoy's boat. The other was commanded by the young man who had fallen in the fire and burned his sarong. He was now called Hot Tail. The six other warriors had been chosen by their current status. Everyone wanted to go. Moks of rice were loaded aboard, the bamboo tubes of pig fat, and seven packages of the favorite Sky-scraper Filter Cigarettes. As the boats pulled out the women who had walked down from the longhouse waved good-bye. They were uneasy. Salt's wife (whom Slinng had christened "Pepper") led the opposition. It had been her experience that white men's dreams were wrong. Now here was this stranger with ugly hair the color of bananas and a beard like a fox's rear end, putting his dream ahead of theirs.

Slinng settled into Arrowjoy's boat with Alstair, while Luke went along with the other younger men. He had made a big hit with his horn playing and they treated him with respect, sharing sugee. Like the coca leaves of South America, a pinchful was shoved under the upper lip. It made work easier and the day go faster, they said. Luke, who was always anxious to shove any foreign substance in any opening, thought he'd try it.

Two dogs were taken, one to a boat, and each stood on a pile of goods and sniffed the air for wild game. They were not friendly and to touch them meant being bitten. Invaluable to the Iban for hunting, they were carried as a knife or a spear—a weapon.

With the sun up it became hot midstream and the boats were guided along under the shade of huge branches that hung over the river from shore. Birds flew ahead of the noisy motors and their brilliant colors could be seen interwoven with trees, a thread of reds and yellows stitching the green. There were no other boats or commerce here, and ahead the mountains continued their climb, a series of green ridges overlapping and blending into sky.

"We're beyond the area for profitable exploitation," Arrowjoy said. "Ahead, upriver, it has always been treacherous in dry spells and then there are the rapids and the mountains. Above are the Apo Kayan and central highlands. Even the most aggressive traders and loggers gave up because they couldn't get past these obstacles, so it's remained isolated."

"I've seen that area on Hartog's charts and a map at Istana. There was a blank spot and both said 'relief data incomplete.' "

"Oh, yes, that would be an ONC—Operational Navigation Chart. It was put out by the British Ministry of Defence during the war. It's forty years old but still the standard work. Those areas have never been properly surveyed. Rivers are misnamed and there are question marks next to trails and villages that have long since vanished."

"What about the people in there? The tribes?"

"The Kenyah farm the highland plateau on the edge of the jungle and there may be other scattered tribes of nomads in the deep rain forest."

"The Tantu?"

Arrowjoy looked up sharply. "Where did you hear that name?"

"*National Geographic?*"

He was not amused. "Keep your mouth shut about them around the Iban. They frighten their children with Tantu—it's their version of the bogeyman. They believe the Tantu are the embodiment of *bali salengs*."

There was a frantic, ripping howl from the dog in the bow and he launched himself off the boat, hit the water and scrambled up the bank. The other dog was after him in a nearly perfect double volley, both howling their heads off.

"*Pig!*" Salt shouted. Arrowjoy put the tiller over, touched the bank and the Iban were out of the boat after the dogs. Arrowjoy was next with Slinng behind him.

Alstair stood up in the boat calling after them. "If you don't mind I'll

pass—I'm not that fond of pork! If you should happen to be attacked
by a lamb, though, count me in!" She looked over at the other boat. Luke
sat in the stern alone, puffing up one of the ghastly stogies. "Not joining
the pig stick?"

"No thank you, lady, that stuff makes me sick." The increased barking
of the dogs could be heard now as they closed. "Listen—do you happen
to know what we're doing out here?"

"Why, looking for a ship—the *Sulu*. Didn't Larry tell you that?"

"No. I thought he was selling insurance to these guys." He considered
it for a minute. "What kind of ship?"

"Well, from what I understand, a big white yacht."

He looked worried. "I knew he was on something."

"You're wrong."

"Then we're in big trouble, lady."

An hour later the hunting party returned carrying a large pig. It had
been speared to death and its head hung down showing tiny eyes and
an unpleasant complexion of bumps and wiry bristles. The snout was wet
and the mouth gaped, exposing bloody teeth and wicked curved tusks.

"Ooh," Alstair said, "what a shame. It's got little ears like Porky Pig."

"Look at those tusks!" Arrowjoy said. "They're sharp enough to cut
your toenails."

"I use clippers."

The pig was flopped on palm leaves and the Iban went to work
butchering it with the smaller parangs they called nak, "knife children."
"We'll camp here," Arrowjoy said. "What we can't eat or smoke tonight
will be rotten by tomorrow." A smoky fire was built and helped to keep
down the hordes of sand fleas. These, plus fire ants, leeches, mosquitoes,
tiger wasps and a thousand-and-one unidentified species, were constantly
on the move. It was not possible to sit for one second without having
a bug crawling on you somewhere. At times it was impossible to eat
without swallowing dozens at a gulp.

"One of the reasons Borneo has never been explored in depth is not
because of wild animals—the crocs and snakes and boar or even headhunters. Do you know the single most dangerous animal in the jungle?
A fuzzy red caterpillar. If you step on it it enters the foot and drills a hole.
Its nearly invisible fine hairs enter and create a crippling septic wound
that can kill you months later. It was insects that defeated expeditions.
Millions of the bastards swarming over you, pushing into every crevice,

worms that got into the food and then intestines, bringing sickness and sapping strength. I would rather hunt boar with a switch than deal with a horde of damn bugs. And it's no different today. Commercial applications don't work for long. Urinating on your hands and rubbing it in the hair can help if you're up to it."

"I'll bet that's where the word 'pisshead' comes from," Alstair said.

The boar's hide had been skinned off and its delicacies laid out: a tongue that resembled a razor strop, liver and the heavy-duty muscles in the rib cage. They were jointed, boned and threaded on skewers to be smoked over the fire.

"I'll do salad," Alstair said. Taking a basket, she walked along the shoreline with Slinng following her. Bending down to test plants, she plucked one here, one there.

"You do know what you're doing?"

"Oh, yes, this is wild ginger. I told you I'm a camping person."

"You're sure that's not something that will mummify the winkle."

"Would I pick that?"

Ribs had been propped over the fire and while they crackled she whipped up the salad, using a coconut shell and stone as a pestle to mix the dressing. Salt was pinched in, plus chili, and it emerged as sambol, a peppery ginger toss. "This works wonders with those who have lost their sense of taste," Alstair said.

"I can believe that," Arrowjoy agreed, fanning his tongue.

They sat eating the ribs, bent over, grease running down their arms. The dogs had been tossed the bones and guts and everybody was content. Iban, in the lee of the smoky fire, made their own jokes while the round eyes parleyed. "Are you married, Mr. Arrowjoy?" Alstair asked.

Uncorking one of the brown arak bottles, he took his time answering. "Yes, of course. My wife's the district sister—nurse—in Penang."

"That far?"

"The opportunities are there."

"English?"

"Malay—she hates the jungle. We take our holiday in Brisbane. They have a Fairy World that beats Disneyland all hollow—or so I'm told." There was a pause. "What about you, miss . . ."

"Al."

"Al—married?"

"Twice." She looked at Slinng. "Once to a Peking businessman who imported IUDs shaped like question marks and the next time to the wagonmaster of an Airstream trailer caravan. He was a nephew of Wally Byam."

"Interesting."

Later when they were under the mosquito netting together she said, "He's an alcoholic, you know."

"What? Come on."

"Oh, yes. If you watch him you'll see he's constantly taking a pull off something. It's so quick it seems a reflex. I know that sign—I've seen it before."

"Was that true—about your being married?"

"No, I've never been married. I've lived with a few fellows—the drunk and another one who couldn't make up his mind about being gay. I was always a fool for flawed men, but I wasn't dumb enough to marry one."

"Good for you."

"I didn't hear you volunteering marital statistics or mention a main squeeze."

There was hesitation. Slinng could not bear to say Miri's name. To him she was nearly an illusion—someone who had appeared out of his subconscious to vanish again when reality shoved its cold nose in. He held her in close to his heart and would not show her to anyone. "No, I've never been married. I'm a sailor after all, and it's your duty to have a girl in every port."

"All right, then, you be my Popeye and I'll be your Olive Oyl." They kissed quietly, without moving to alert the sleepers, and used their hands inventively.

They continued on the river for two days, and those days became the same, with the passing landscape mirrored in the approaching one. As they moved under the overhanging branches of flowering aran trees, their pink petals drifted into the boat and lifted by the wind spread out on the river to tint it their color. Their passage was pleasant but uneventful and showed no evidence of the *Sulu*.

They camped each evening when the black cicadas tuned up, signaling an hour of light. On the third night Slinng was ready to give up. "Certainly if that enormous white whale of a yacht came up this river we would find it."

"Not necessarily." Arrowjoy was drinking in the open now and it was ongoing. However, Slinng could discover no changes in his behavior. He remained rock steady and showed the effects only in his eyes, which had moved an increment from misanthropy to the merely pessimistic. He was anxious to encourage Slinng to go on. In that way it might be proven whether the dream was real. He had said it might be dangerous if they found the ship, and it would be. The Dreamer would be reduced in stature from a mystic to merely an eyewitness. Worse, the magic would go out of it. It would be like telling armed, dangerous children there was no Santa Claus. Still, he was gambling that it would defuse the undercurrent of bad spirits that had moved in with the dream of the ship in the first place. Now he set about the unfamiliar task of being optimistic.

"Let me tell you something about hide-and-seek. This happened in New Guinea but the conditions there are very much the same—endless jungle rising up in a series of razor ridges. In 1938 the Third Archbold Expedition discovered the Grand Valley of the Balim River and fifty thousand people. This in a place thought to be uninhabited. These were Papuans still living in the Stone Age who had no idea there was anyone else in the world but them. What's all the more remarkable is they were only 115 miles from the coast. And here's the heartbreaker. Earlier, in 1922, another bunch, the Kremer Expedition, using eight hundred porters and two hundred tons of food, had taken six months to get four of their people to within a few miles of the Grand Valley. But they passed to the west and because of the intervening ridges and jungle never saw them.

"Now, if you can miss fifty thousand people by a mile, what is a two-hundred-foot yacht? If it's there we may find it. Tomorrow will tell the tale. We're going to be running out of river and the rapids will begin. Also, the river will split off into dozens of tributaries and that would be the place to hide it, up one of those twisty turns."

The next morning they had only gone a few miles when disaster struck.

Sweeping around a long curve in the river they were struck by an enormous hardwood log. It was partly submerged and suddenly lifted the front of the longboat at nearly a forty-five-degree angle, spilling everyone out. They were followed by all those items not tied down: a rain of arak bottles and pots, bamboo sections of pig fat and the dog. It gave Slinng a nasty whack as it went by. There was not even time to shout. He was aware of the runaway frenzy of the outboard blade as it went under, then the rush of the river pounding in his ears as he struggled up through clouds of bubbles. The river was swift here, rushing down from rainstorms in the mountains. When he surfaced several hundred yards downstream, he was tumbled along fighting and gasping for breath. Rocks banged at his legs as he reached out for the shore whipping by. When he finally caught hold of a twist of branches and pulled himself up into the tangled roots that clutched the bank, he was alone.

The river was empty. The boat, Alstair, Arrowjoy, the Iban—all had vanished. The other boat had been ahead of them and, masked by the curve of the river, was probably unaware of the capsizing. He felt sure the others had made it. Like him, they had been swept away and would be strung out along the bank. Gnats were already crawling over his face and, wiping them away, he saw a flash of tan fifty feet down the riverbank. *The dog!* It scrabbled up from the river, legs going, long ears and tail slicked down, soaking wet. Front feet clawing, it got traction and crawled up on the firmer ground.

Slinng whistled and shouted, wishing for Iban words. But the dog ignored him and, shaking itself, headed upriver at a trot, never once looking back. He set off after it, thinking it would lead him to the others, and immediately fell down. Trying to make his way along the edge of the riverbank over the slippery tree roots and mossy rocks was treacherous. A misplaced step and his foot would skid off, plunge through the tangle and trip him up. In the next hour he fell heavily a dozen times, battering his knees and elbows, and eventually wore himself out. The dog had disappeared, and in an effort to make better time he moved inland where he could still follow the river and have secure footing. But he couldn't catch up with it.

Alarmed that he had been gradually moving away from the river until it was barely a shimmer, he backtracked and came again to its bank. But something was wrong. It was narrow here and the sun at another angle. *It was a different river.* Stumbling after the damned dog he must have curved around and followed one of the tributaries flowing into the mainstream by mistake. If that was true, he would either have to cross it—swim to the other side and try to pick up the trail—or backtrack and find his original position. He had made a bad mistake ever leaving it.

He wasn't up to the swim and, after resting, set off again to try following his own spoor. He very quickly lost all sense of direction. He had thought by following the flow of the water downstream it would eventually lead to the main river. But now there was a confusion of other tributary streams running to all points of the compass. They rushed along in torrents, spilling over mossy ridges in dozens of waterfalls. These sent their cold mountain spray against the warm forest floor, rising in a mist to the interlocking trees high overhead. Slinng was shocked at the effort it took just to walk. On this maddeningly irregular terrain you needed another kind of coordination—a sense of ground levels—to know where to put your foot. A misstep could break your leg. He also knew that to go on was foolish. What had Arrowjoy said about his friend the surveyor? He had lasted eighteen days walking in circles.

Exhausted, he slumped down, and the smell of rotting vegetation and damp earth came up. He was enclosed in heat and mist; the humidity hovered around 99 percent. It was the ultimate greenhouse, the perfect hothouse to grow orchids and tropical disease. He also saw that his legs were covered with leeches. *God!* Shuddering, he found two small flat stones and did his best to grind them off. The thing to do was stay in place, wait for the others to find him. Using his seaman's knife (that and a belt full of Sing were his only resources), he cut saplings as he'd seen the Iban do and built a crude platform, a pondik, lashing it together with rattan vines.

Slinng climbs on his pallet and, pulling broad palm leaves up as you might covers, tries to rest. The black cicadas sing out the hour before dark, and lying as he is, with a view through the saplings to the forest floor only two feet below, he sees a large snake. Highly colored (usually meaning venomous), it slithers past his field of vision. Will it climb his feeble platform? He doesn't care. There are sounds: a chorus of female gibbons, the snap of a barking deer and birds—a last glimpse of Brahminy kites against the sky. He sleeps, or does he? Eyes flutter and at one point he thinks he hears the distant snarl of the outboard on the river. He raises his head but it is the wing beat of an ornate bug that has entered his palm leaf enclave.

Near dawn there are other sinister sounds. Drums. He comes around slowly, listening, unsure if it is in his head or some trick of nature. No, it has a regular, man-made rhythm. Do the natives here signal with drums as in jungle movies?

Then he recognizes the beat. *Reggae.*

21

I T WASN'T THE FIRST TIME Arrowjoy had been capsized and he kept his head. Stay with the boat was the rule. Exploding to the surface, he swam after the overturned hull and managed to get a grip on the propeller shaft housing. Hanging on and kicking with his legs, he gradually directed the longboat toward the bank. The river's pull was swift but after another kilometer he nudged the hull into the overhang of low branches and touched bottom. Using a rocking motion, he wedged it ashore.

Alstair popped up, arms and legs going. She was a strong swimmer and struck out after the Iban who had surfaced in front of her. They helped her up the bank and watched as the boat whipped around the turn of the river tugging along Arrowjoy. Breaking their way through the jungle, the group arrived at his position in under an hour. Salt was there and even the dog. Now all were accounted for but Lawrence Slinng.

The other longboat looped back and began a search. Following the rapid course of the river miles downstream, they covered the bank on both sides whistling and shouting, the dog adding his bark. It was nearly dark when they finally returned. A camp had been set up and Arrowjoy was working on the waterlogged outboard when the search party returned. Their faces told the story.

"I can't believe anything happened to him!" Alstair wailed. "He was a sailor!"

"There are sailors who don't swim," Arrowjoy answered, not looking up. He had the carburetor parts laid out on a palm frond and meticulously wiped down each spring and gasket.

"No! He could swim! He had swimmer's hair!" If this was strange, her behavior gradually became even stranger, more erratic. Pacing back and forth, arms clutching her bosom, she kept stumbling and falling down on the uneven ground. The Iban reacted as they alway did when death blew its breath—they ignored it. Luke sat on a mossy stump and his only concern was how this would affect him.

"You're not going to stop looking?!"

"Even a good swimmer can get caught underwater on a snag—old roots or submerged trees. He might not come up for days—weeks."

"Don't say that!" Her vehemence caused the Iban to jump, then look away. Any outward display of temperament was considered bad manners. Salt turned his mouth down.

"Maybe he made it to shore—maybe you just can't find him because of all these . . . these blarty bushes!" She flailed about with her arm.

"Well, if he made it to shore and had the good sense to stay in one place, we'll find him."

At the sound of reggae, Slinng slides off his platform and goes toward it—a distant mumble rising and falling among the treetops. Voices? A *wa-wa* of distortion that might be beamed from outer space. High above, the rhinoceros hornbill cocks its head uneasily at the competition and a chorus of monkeys protests. The jungle here is awesome, two-hundred-foot hardwood trees, palm fans, ferns, and climbing every supporting vine are orchids as common as weeds. Underfoot, the fungus shows vivid colors: orange and luminous fuchsia. Slinng makes his way, more careful now, each step calculated, marching with the caution of a minesweeper. Then a sudden surge of butterflies, hundreds in bright yellow that rise up in a fluttering wall, whipped by acrobatic precision to shift in sudden graceful patterns, swooping one way, then another.

Going upstream, he stays close to the curve of tributary that ambushed him away from the main river. Occasionally there is a break in the density of trees and it is possible to see sheer rock walls climbing toward the mountain—they begin here. Using the seaman's knife to hack through the most difficult places, he continues on all day, and by late afternoon has come only one mile. His only guide is the music and he moves to its beat. The rhythms change and occasionally he hears a voice, a mumble that ends once in a laugh. An eerie sound to come echoing down from the trees in the middle of trackless rain forest. Then it stops.

Slinng stops with it, listening, hearing the beat of his own heart, breath coming hard. Jungle sounds cut in: a waterfall and the tattoo of a woodpecker. He can actually hear the drops of sweat from his forehead hit the broad leaves of a plant. He remains motionless for minutes, then sags back and flops onto the damp earth. A lizard crawls over his boot and, using the edge of the knife, he scrapes off the day's accumulation of leeches. What now? Not for the first time he wonders if he has *really* heard music. The heat? Delirium? Maybe it's an animal—a strange bird; the jungle carries its own odd distortions and magic, too. Mysterious, dangerous—civilized man has always been afraid of it. One of the first acts of the settler is to cut down the woods surrounding him. There were probably less than a dozen stands of original, first-growth trees left in the world. This was one of them. Magic reminds him of Beata and her warning about meeting the *bali salengs* in the rain forest. Well, that hadn't happened—*or had it?* Was that evil spirit traveling with him?

Then suddenly the voice cuts in again, singing. This time he can make out the words. "Down in the ghettooo . . ." He stands and shoves his way through the brush using his body as a break. The river is close on his right and the sound is channeled down its open trough, wavering, clear sounds; ridiculous words in a booming baritone—ye gods! *Elvis!* Laughing out loud, he shouts to the trees, "He's alive and well in Borneo!"

Slinng falls, gets up, takes a dozen steps and falls again, panting, wearing himself out. He waits, rests, then continues at a measured pace, listening now to a commercial for Dinty Moore Beef Stew in family-sized tins. "It tastes soooo good!" Next a hint of white, a shock in the green hue of jungle—more, the dot of a porthole, a complication of slack cables, the tatters of a flag and as his vista opens up—there it is:

The *Sulu.*

He stops and stares. As he parts the palm fronds at the edge of the river, his view is stern on. The vessel has been rammed into the bank and sunk to the upper deck. It lists fifteen degrees and the overhang of trees and vines is so complete that even from a dozen yards away the vessel's shape is nearly invisible. Midship, the rake of stack and electronic mast reach up through the roof of green to the sun. It is from there the music continues, playing disco favorites now. Slinng wades out and breast-strokes the few yards to the ship, climbing over the submerged fantail to the boat deck. The boats are away and the heavy crane is angled over the starboard side, its hook twisted back on itself. The deck is strewn with ragged line, greasy rags and heavy tools: a sledgehammer and spanners, a bent pry-bar. The remaining small boats—two twenty-foot outboards, an all-terrain vehicle and a twenty-five-foot Hovercraft—are all missing.

He pauses and goes forward on the incline of deck toward the stack.

There is the crescent bite out of the mast that the Dreamer described, the antenna with its firefly tip of light. Slinng takes his time, breathing evenly, eyes straight ahead, afraid to look up, then, stopping at the bottom of the stack, he does. A pair of tanned legs are visible forty feet up the stack on the crow's nest.

He climbs up and finds Miri.

She stretches out sunbathing: white visor, bikini bottom and grease. There are Perrier bottles and empty cans of cocktail tidbits surrounding her. A large portable keeps the beat. "It's about time," she says, turning the music down as his head pops up though the ladder opening. "You look terrible—did you walk from Singapore?"

"Something like that." He drags himself up and flops against the mast, exhausted. They are above the insect line and it is pleasant, if hot. Opening one of the bottles, he takes a long drink.

"I hope you brought something decent to eat. I'm sick to death of tinned kippers and Cadbury Tea Biscuits."

"Miri—weren't you worried, afraid?"

There's a pause. "I was terrified—but I knew someone would come. I mean, you don't lose a whole yacht and not come looking for it, do you? It's been, what?"

"I've lost count—five days?"

"God! You know what's been the worst? Worrying that the batteries would run out in the portable. I hate the sound of the jungle, don't you? What *are* all those things in there? It gives me the shivers."

"Did you listen to the news? The storm and the sinking were on all the media."

"No, I never listen to the news. It depresses me."

What a maddening, impossible girl he thought. Is this an act? Is she behaving in this offhand, casual way because she is brave? Or just can't be bothered to get excited? He had visualized their meeting as an explosion of passion, flying into each other's arms, a smother of kisses, instant lovemaking. Instead, they sit, backs against the mast, talking as calmly as if on a resort liner. One thing he realizes: He never believed her drowned.

"What happened?"

A pause, a slathering on of sun block. "He went crazy."

"Hartog?"

"He killed Blas, had him thrown overboard."

"*What?*"

"That's right. God, it was awful. He clung to the rail and one of those bodyguards chopped off his hand.

"But . . . why? What caused it?"

"Nothing! I told you—Tog just went crazy. Remember me talking about the head? He was crazy."

"What about you? How did you get away?"

"I don't think I want to go into it now."

"Oh, yes," he said, very firm, "you've got to."

"Well . . ."

The minute Blas disappears into the roil of wake, severed hand still gripping the rail, she breaks violently away from Hartog. Dodging past the Gurkhas (who are reluctant to touch her), she bolts into the saloon and up the atrium stairs. She hears Tog behind her—actually laughing, shouting, "Come on, Miri! Everyone in the pool!" At the top she dashes out the door onto the boat deck. It is dark and difficult to keep her feet as the ship rolls in high seas. The view from the top deck is to the horizon and the sea spreads out to meet black sky. As each wave presents a white cap the effect is of a vast, endless pattern of furious scallops. Forward, the bow dips and takes on a crash of water that sends spray to the second deck. The sound is terrific: wind singing in stainless rigging, whistles and howls. Beyond the stack is a lighted porthole in the bridge door. It seems a welcome beacon.

"But I didn't trust that dirty old man of a captain with his greasy cap. I never understood why he was allowed on such a beautiful boat. Tog did have a good sense of swank and the man was impossible." She was doing her nails now, pulling a brush tipped with vermilion across a surface that had already been buffed and filed. "Thank mother, I found this P-Shine kit above the water line."

"What was his name?"

"The captain? Wittenoon. He and Tog were chums from way back, so that was the answer. Still . . ."

"You went up the mast."

"Uh-huh."

.   .   .

She crosses over to the stack on a rigged safety line and even then very narrowly misses the first stirrup as the ship rolls. Hanging on with both hands, her feet are carried out from under her, then swinging up, she begins to climb hand over hand. At night, in bad weather, the perspective is daunting, forty feet straight up and angled back. It moves now with the motion of the sea as the vessel plows a trough. Clinging onto wet rungs as the wind tears at her, Miri keeps an eye on the running light atop a slender aerial at the very top of the mast. Its red glow travels the distance between each swoop and dip with perfect grace. It is as though some maniacal conductor waves a baton in concert with the furious sea. Few pieces, including the cannon thunder of Beethoven's "Wellington's Victory," have the impact and sheer terror of this performance.

Miri gets halfway up, fingers locked, desperate, when Hartog comes on deck below her. He has fallen, banging his knee, and the fun has gone out of the chase. When he gets to the boat deck and she is nowhere in sight, he gives up. Where is she going to hide in any event? Grasping the rail, he carefully makes his way past the stack toward the bridge. He stops every few feet to try to gauge the pitch of ship as the deck falls away beneath him. Finally catching hold of the bridge door, he jerks it open, falling inside with the next dip of the ship.

"I watched him come by below, practically hanging by the cheeks of my arse, sure that he would see me—but he never looked up. I've read where people tend not to, and it's true. By now I was nearly frozen; tropics or not, that rain was bloody cold. Once on the platform I went on hands and knees and got this little door open in the mast." She rapped a three-foot square behind her.

"The inspection panel for the radar connectors."

"Yes, there's all sorts of cables and switches and things in there, but just enough space to squat down. There's even a light. I had stashed towels in there before for sunning and was able to rub down, and wrapping them around me, warm up a bit. I was starkers, you know."

"What?"

"That damned dog had taken my clothes."

Slinng didn't want to know about that. "What next?"

"I got sick."

. . .

Miri is a good sailor, has never been seasick. But enclosed in the tight space of the mast housing with its canned air and long loops of motion she is soon violently ill. Cracking open the inspection door, head hanging out, gasping and choking, she rides with the wind in her face until at last, empty, dehydrated, she collapses back inside, exhausted.

The motion of the ship increases, a battering now that indicates they are turning into the storm; a violent pounding that shakes everything and causes the light in her space to flicker.

"At some point I woke up and realized the engines had stopped. My light went off. I opened the door. It was lighter now, morning, but the storm hadn't let up, visibility was at arm's length. Still, I could hear activity on the boat deck—the whine of that big crane. They were lowering boats. Do you know what I thought? Bloody hell! We're sinking!

"But we didn't. Later I heard one engine kick in, then another. And we started swinging around, changing direction once again. I couldn't care less at that point—I slept through it."

"Actually slept?"

"Oh, yes. Wrung out. It didn't matter what happened. When I woke up it was night again and the feel of the ship was, well, different. The storm was still howling around us but the terrific rolling was gone. When I opened my door, fog had closed down to the water level. It was as though we were suspended in space with no up or down. And the sounds were terrifying, a kind of thunder that was ongoing—the wind rushing through trees . . ."

"You were on the river."

"I knew that because there was no taste of salt in the air. I stayed in my hole and drifted off again—the thing was, I felt like being awake was the dream—or nightmare—and I might find some peace asleep. I desperately wanted to lose myself, but I was awakened several times during the next day by a horrible wrenching that sounded as though the bottom of the boat was being torn off. It stood my hair up. When I looked, the storm was still ranting about and I couldn't see a thing. We were stopped dead with the engines winding up, peaking. Finally we moved ahead with awful scraping sounds. Afterwards there was a lot of vibration."

"You were hung up on rocks and probably bent the props."

"Whatever. Then on the third day . . ."

"Weren't you hungry?"

"God, no! I never wanted to see food again. Just the thought of it made me ill. Anyway, the last time I was awakened by a jolt it very nearly brained me. I shot out the door and was ready to jump for it when I saw a remarkable thing. The sun. The sky was clear and I could reach out from here and touch the trees. They had rammed the boat ashore."

She hears voices on deck and pulls back in the cable space to hide, listens while they load and lower the remaining small craft. It takes nearly all day and finally, with the sound of engines, she knows they are moving away from the ship and up the river. Creeping out and lying flat on the platform, she sees them as they pass by. It is a terrible moment: abandoned, left behind, alone in the middle of millions of acres of rain forest. If she stands up now, shouts now, they will hear her. Stop. But if she does, she knows for certain that Hartog will kill her.

"Could you see who left?"

"Oh, yes, Tog and the captain and some of the Gurkhas in one of the twenty-foot outboards. That all-terrain thing had been loaded in the other one and they towed it. The engineer was behind them in the Hovercraft with the rest of the Gurkhas."

"A convoy. How many Gurkhas?"

"Oh, ten or twelve."

"What then?"

"I rushed down the mast and ate anything I could find. I was famished." She held out her painted fingernails fanning them. "Well . . . they're dry . . ." And suddenly she burst into uncontrollable sobs. Slinng held her and did his best to soothe but it took a long time before it was all out. At last she said in a small voice, "God, you smell vile."

He had to agree. They went down the mast, Slinng throwing off his foul clothes and shoes, diving over the side. The water felt marvelous, and here in the inlet where the captain had chosen to ram the *Sulu,* they were out of the river's swift pull. For the first time the jungle seemed friendly, a travel poster: sparkling blue water, the swag of orchids from overhanging trees, happy monkeys chattering in their tops. True, there were huge deer flies to be batted off and a nagging reminder in the back of the mind of snakes and crocodiles. But never mind, after what they'd both been through it wasn't worth worrying over. They splashed and shouted, embracing underwater, legs intertwined until they couldn't stand it. Climbing back aboard and racing the bugs, they ducked into the upper saloon, diving on one of the luxurious couches.

It was the ultimate romantic experience, the classic coming together of two lovers after days of terrible trial when they never know if they will see each other again. A time before the intrusion of bad habits and differences of opinion, when each believes the other flawless—or at least not capable of deceit or betrayal. The thrill of electricity passing between bodies that surpasses ordinary bedding down, transforming pure pleasure into love—before love becomes duty.

They were silent a long time after this. Then, holding Miri close, Slinng said, "I've told you I'm a seaman. I ship out of Port Moresby and sail a coastal charter that takes my ship, the *Singapore Exile,* around New Guinea and the Solomons up to Hong Kong. My base is a small place at Manu Manu. It's on the Gulf of Papua and backed up to Mount Victoria and the Owen Stanley Range—the view is quite spectacular."

"Sounds lovely."

"Or, I suppose I could work at marine insurance for Lloyd's—we could live in London." A month ago he could not have imagined making this statement.

"Whatever." She sighed.

He sighed with her and got up. "I'd better see what I can do about getting us off the *Sulu* while it's still light."

"I'll be Mum and do dinner." Kissing, they parted.

He went forward to the bridge and entered, facing its array of electronic marvels. There was every current navigational aid: a radio that would probably reach the moon, satellite connections that allowed you to phone any place in the world. He picked up the mauve receiver and looked at its buttons. A call to Kapit and they would have a boat here in days, a helocopter in hours. He hung up the phone. All this elaborate, sensitive equipment ran on power from the generators and they were sunk underwater, three decks below. It was useless junk. All yachts this size carried H.D. batteries on the bridge for the radios—but they were missing. Had Hartog carried them off?

The bridge deck was strewn with charts, coffee cups, the detritus of a fast getaway. He searched the charts until he found what he wanted. A very detailed hand-drawn map of Sarawak's inland rivers. Beginning with Cape Sirik on the coast, a course was charted up the Rajang onto the secondary rivers and unnamed tributaries. It was marked for depth, channels and currents. There were handwritten notations on the width of the river at crucial points, landmarks indicated, and the position of river towns or remote kampongs. At each twenty-four-hour segment, time estimations were inked in.

So it had not been a daring dash up uncharted rivers by a madman. Every kilometer had been carefully laid out in advance by a pilot who knew what he was doing. Captain Wittenoon, no doubt. Then with all the radar and depth finders to aid him he had taken his chance. It would only be possible to travel that distance undetected at the height of a storm, and that's what they had done. It *had* been one long chance but he had made it—almost. Slinng looked for a map that might indicate Hartog's direction from the *Sulu*, but there was none.

He opened the bridge lockers, searching for the battery radio and emergency sender, and found them missing. Even the Aldis lamp was gone from its cubbyhole. There was a flare gun but only two magnesium flares. They were in a canvas bag and he took it along. The best time to try it would be after dark.

In the captain's sea cabin, aft of the bridge, he discovered clothing left behind in an airline bag. A pair of clean shorts, too big, that could be cinched up with his wide belt. A white short-sleeved shirt still in its Darwin laundry bag showed four stripes on epaulets. And at the bottom, in its pristine plastic cover, a captain's cap with an Australian navy device. Wittenoon was navy, not maritime.

On the boat deck the three Humber inflatables were still in place but there were no outboards. If he and Miri launched one, they might be able to navigate that rush of a river downstream with the aluminum paddles. The cicadas announced one hour to dark and he went into the saloon wearing his captain's getup, cap cocked at just the right angle.

"Marvelous! That's the way you should always look! Never take it off! Captain Crotch of the Sea Horse Marines!"

"Who are you?"

Miri had wrapped a flowered tablecloth around her waist as a sarong, and breasts bare, put an orchid behind each ear. She pushed up against him. "I am Tondelayo, white man, jungle princess." They kissed. "Is Captain Crotch glad to see Tondelayo or is that a parang in his pocket?" They laughed and she broke away. "Let me put some music on and we'll dance."

The upper saloon was a long cabin intended for informal entertainment. There were loose-pillowed couches, cocktail tables and a huge television set at one end. At the other was a wet bar and small galley. With the power off none of the appliances worked and the frozen food had gone bad the second day. Still, there were tins of caviar, pâté de foie gras and cocktail delicacies. Cases of Perrier supplied the water and the bar carried all varieties of liquor.

Miri set a table with silverware and plates bearing the ship's name and arranged the cans and biscuit boxes artistically. Candles had been found and lit, and the room took on a nice glow. She tuned the big portable until she found just the right music and they danced. There were wide square windows on both sides of the cabin and beyond them the last fading light before evening settled on the border of jungle. For Slinng, whirling around the candlelit room with a glorious, half-naked woman in his arms, the incongruity of the moment was not lost. It was something Noel Coward might have appreciated, or Maugham—two very civilized people a wink away from God knows what dangers, dancing on a ruined yacht a million miles from nowhere in the depth of the Borneo rain forest.

He was suddenly reminded of Groot's description of that last dance at Raffles. Enchanted women, beautifully gowned, officers in white mess jackets, dancing their hearts out as the Empire's battleship saviors were turned into scrap by Japanese dive bombers and their world changed. At the last, did his father really embrace his Malay mistress like this and dance in the shadows of Raffles' Palm Court? Had Groot embroidered that, sweetening history?

Mouth close to his ear she whispered, "Can I say that I love you? Is that too easy?"

He was stunned. "I didn't think people said things like that anymore—I was afraid I'd sound silly."

"Sound silly." He did.

As they whipped around in a showy turn, skimming by couches and tables, Slinng caught the blur of faces at one of the windows. When his head snapped around again, they were gone. But he knew in that instant exactly who they were.

The Tantu.

22

ALSTAIR KEPT AFTER ARROWJOY. He had sent half the Iban, Hot Tail and those of the other boat crew off early that next morning when Lawrence Slinng still hadn't been found. Alstair sensed something in their manner, averted eyes that wasn't right. "Look! Maybe you don't see it, but I do. These people are acting funny." Arrowjoy wouldn't answer, fitting the cleaned outboard to the righted longboat. "Something's going on. I don't think they want him to come back!"

Arrowjoy had to give her credit. She was right. They considered the capsizing and Slinng's disappearance as bad signs. It was time to go home. He agreed.

Working on the outboard, thinking it over, it hit him like a hammer. He suddenly knew how the Dreamer could have given an accurate description of the white prav and not see it. It was simple: He hadn't returned from trading at the fork until several days *after* the storm. By that time pictures of the *Sulu* were in the papers and on television. He had probably seen them in town, and impressed, made up the dream. Arrowjoy felt guilty and uneasy having put the whole thing in motion. They were on a wild goose chase.

When he didn't answer her, Alstair got mad. "If you're not going to do anything about it, we will! Luke!" She startled Luke, who sat on a stump cuddling the sax. "Come on! We're going to look for Larry!"

Arrowjoy sighed. "Please, don't be silly . . ."

"It's your responsibility as district officer to get off your blart and—"

"*All right! Enough!*" The others looked up at his shout, and gathering his gear he called out in a weary voice, "*Hati, hati—tidak apa.*" Picking their own gear, Salt, his son the Dreamer and two other Iban followed him into the jungle whistling up the dog, who eagerly ran after them.

"What did you say?!" she yelled after him.

" 'Hati, hati' means take courage, have a good liver," Luke answered. He began polishing the sax, mirror chrome reflecting back his distored image.

"Have a good *liver?*"

"That's right, lady, the Malay think the liver, not the heart, is the core of the body. If you're bad you've got a sakit bati, a bad liver."

She was impressed. "How do you know that?"

"It's basic Malay, bahasa pasar. If you're from Singapore you know it, like slang."

"What was the rest of it?"

"Oh, something about your mouth being as big as your—"

"It is not!" Frightened birds rose up from the trees in a rattle of wings.

In the late afternoon they found the crude sleeping platform Slinng had fashioned. Squatted around it, the Iban tapped the ground with their parangs, eyes on the jungle, uneasy. The dog circled, nose to the ground. This was not his country. And if the territorial imperative was strong among animals, marking trees and leaving feces, the Iban had their noses in the wind, too, like the dog, sniffing enemies. They were here. Arrowjoy knew this. Of course, as district officer *he* also had the authority to be here—but what did that count for with a blowpipe dart in your throat?

They moved on, following a clumsy trail. "He went on the wrong river," Salt said, discovering the tributary that had lured Slinng away.

"Maybe not." The Dreamer was still Slinng's champion despite his disappointing dream explanation. If they lost him, his own importance would vaporize. "A man follows his own trail."

The Iban rolled their eyes at this. The Dreamer, impressed with his recent celebrity, was beginning to toot off like an oracle. Anyone under sixty who spoke in proverbs was a fool.

They came to a message stick and were riveted. It was freshly whittled, about four feet long and stuck in the center of the trail. There were notches cut along its sides and fitted with feathered rattan and designs of leaves and twigs. The Iban sucked their breath in. It signed "Bata'oro. Strangers in the forest." Arrowjoy wondered if they meant *them* or Slinng? Had he come this way? It didn't look like he would find out. The Iban would go no further.

"Just a minute, Miri . . ."

Miri was startled out of her mood. "What?"

The door opened at the end of the cabin and two angular figures stood

in the half dark looking at them. Unlike the Iban, they were black with
a flare of nostril and a heavy boned ridge over the eyes. Both were naked
except for a few beads, feathers and—most startling—a prop that held
the penis erect and was tied around the waist with twine.

Miri laughed. "What are those things on their things?"

"A cure for the old ennui, no doubt." He went forward cautiously,
smiling. They smiled back, but their teeth were filed and this was terrifying. Slinng tried his Malay. *"Ma-hat ku koo-ee.* Let us know who you are."
They continued smiling but there was no answer. He tried again. "My
ke medai—jee-an ako ee-tto. Don't be afraid—I am a good person." Their
eyes were curiously flat and close together, made sinister by red paint
ringing them. Now those eyes suddenly opened wide and mouths gaped.
They had just seen Miri's hair.

Moving into the candlelight, the great halo of hair was illuminated,
backlit in a sudden flare that seemed to have an inner light of its own,
a mysterious glow that stunned the Tantu. They had never seen a head
like it.

"It's your hair . . . you've got their attention," Slinng said, uneasy.

"Can't say it's mutual. I hate the teeth."

The Tantu were smiling again and making the familiar come-with-me
gesture. "They seem to want us to go with them."

"Do we have a choice?"

A good question. Were they friendly? Both men carried jungle knives,
but more serious, tall blowpipes tipped with spears. His only weapon was
his seaman's knife . . . and yes, the flare gun lay on the couch in the
canvas bag. If he could load that . . . "Miri"—he was still smiling—"stay
just where you are. I'm going to—"

"Ahh—there's one inside, behind us."

"Right." He had come in the door leading to the bridge, carrying a
blowpipe and dragging a large plastic bag. The two at the door continued
their sign for "follow me," growing restive. "Miri, have you got something else you can wear?"

"Yes."

"Put it on quickly and cover your hair, will you?" His eyes on the
Tantu, he was smiling.

Miri had found one of the crew's bright blue jumpsuits with *Sulu*
stitched on the back. Shedding the tablecloth sarong, she quickly put it
on, zipping up. The Tantu watched every move. A large damask dinner

napkin was tied over her hair for a scarf and sneakers a size too big pulled on. When she finished, the one with the sack moved forward and she backed off with a wave of the hand. "Larry . . ."

Slinng stiffened, but the Tantu went around the bar and began to throw cans of soft drinks in the plastic bag.

"I don't like this," Miri said.

"It's possible they want to help us."

"Do you believe that?" He didn't answer.

Outside, the full moon was up and its light sailed ripples across the water. There was a romantic unreality about it, Slinng thought, another clichéd travel poster, hardly apt. They followed the Tantu off the ship on a log thrown across to the bank and entered the rain forest. Back into the dark primeval world. Only this time it was lit by shafts of moonlight that pierced the treetops in erratic blue-green shadings; a path that found its own way. They moved fast and Slinng and Miri struggled to keep up with them. If it was difficult walking in the daytime it was impossible at night. When they fell or faltered the Tantu urged them on, aggressive and urgent, still smiling, dipping their heads in jerky bows when Slinng complained, but not slackening the pace. The long blowguns were carried as batons and the first man towed the sack of Yoo-Hoo. "What's the bloody hurry?" Miri wanted to know, panting.

"I don't think they like to travel at night any more than we do."

Miri looked at him in a way that he never forgot. "They're going to kill us."

"No! Of course not!" But this was said with too much emphasis.

After an hour of walking they had fallen in line with one Tantu leading, Miri, another behind her, then Slinng and the third man straggling several yards back. Once again he felt totally lost and at others' mercy: a man who navigated the high seas, who found his way in any fog or storm and now, by God, was turned around in ten feet of jungle. But the jungle was another kind of ocean that showed no steady wind direction, no landmark, and rarely a glimpse of sky or stars. You navigated on instinct and genes. He stumbled, fell behind and when he got up, Miri and the Tantu ahead were gone. The man behind him had vanished. *"Miri!"* he shouted, and with no answer, plunged into the green mass, caught immediately up in a tangle of vines. *"Miri!"*

· · ·

The blade of a parang slices past his ear, detoured by bouncing off a tough limb. Slinng throws his right arm up against the downward stroke, striking the man's wrist and slamming his other fist in the crook of his elbow. The arm bends, he grabs the wrist and they go down in a tumble. The Tantu is on top, his face inches away, and Slinng is stunned by the ferocious mask, eyes squeezed to slits, lips pulled back exposing black gums and sharpened teeth. Neck muscles are stretched in cords, muscles knotted; unyielding, indurate. The smell hits him, smoky, unwashed, the scent of an animal.

He wavers, caught up in the grip of a numbing psychological force: a game that gives way at attack by predators—overwhelmed and at a disadvantage on another's territory. *No, by Jesus!* He's rolled on barroom floors in all kinds of hostile territory, fought it out with rotten bastards in the world's worst sailor towns! Been stabbed with an icepick, knives, had his eyes thumbed, teeth sunk in his ass. Is this animal of a Tantu any worse? He is sprung steel with the breath of a jackal, but Slinng is twice his size. Damn! He lunges, letting go the parang arm, and rolls free. The Tantu is up instantly and chops down. Slinng is on his back and in the classic knife-fighter's defense kicks out with his feet (better toes than nose). The parang slashes through his left foot, cutting away leather, sole and a slice of foot. But he has his seaman's knife out now. Eight-inch blade, honed to a feather edge. Holding it in the fencing grip, he is up and attacks.

Body in the crouch he strikes out and slashes the Tantu across the wrist. He retreats, again, another quick bloody cut across the forehead. Moving forward without hesitation, crowding in relentlessly with the intent to kill. The Tantu chops down with the parang but each time he does, Slinng slashes him in a rapid stroke, drawing blood. He closes, grabbing the parang arm and driving the knife up under, going for the kidneys. Because his opponent is small he misjudges and the big knife goes between his two bottom ribs. He jerks away, and the blade, up to the hilt and caught on its notched back band, is jerked out of Slinng's hand. The Tantu staggers back, breath blowing, turns, walks into a tree, falls, struggles up to his knees and crawls off into the jungle. Slinng reaches out for him, but he is gone, disappeared with his knife.

Silence. He takes up the bloody parang and leans against a tree. Are there more? Will there be another attack? When it doesn't come he shouts Miri's name again and again. Silence. *My God, they've taken her for that hair!* He knows he must move, follow them . . . but which way? What can he do? Then he remembers.

By sheer force of personality, threats, sweet-talking, Arrowjoy flogged the Iban along the trail until after dark. He could not bear to go back to camp and face that damn pushy woman without some clue to Slinng's fate. But once night had fallen there was no holding the Iban and they turned back toward camp. All were subdued, frightened to be in enemy territory. Even the dog sensed this, going with his tail down.

Then a thing occurred that stopped them cold. A bright red burst in the night sky. Shooting up first in a single red line that blossomed with a hollow pop, sending out plumes of burning magnesium; dropping back to earth in pink, smoky tendrils. Even with the canopy of trees overhead its fiery ascent couldn't be missed. Its position was less than a mile away to the east.

"Come on!" Arrowjoy shouted, turning in that direction. When they hesitated he shamed them. "There is the sign you've waited for! That's the white dayung telling you where to find him! *Come on!*" Reluctantly they followed, the dog bringing up the rear.

When the Tantu saw the flare they increased their pace, half dragging Miri along. Finally she rebelled and began to flail out with her arms and legs, kicking. "Stop! Stop! Stop! No more! Damn you! That's my man! He's coming! He'll punish you!" They knocked her down and tied her wrists with rattan, looped more around her ankles in a hobble like those used on pigs. Then jerking her up, with one pulling, the other pushing, they set off again. She screamed at them, furious, tears streaming down her face. "Bastards! Pygmies! Cocksuckers!"

They found Slinng still against the tree, covered with blood, holding the parang. The Iban were impressed. "What in God's name happened?" Arrowjoy asked.

Slinng knew he had to be rational, calm if they were to help him. "I found the *Sulu* . . ." He saw their faces change at the sound of its name. "There was a woman still on board—"

"What?"

"Yes, a young woman, Miri, I knew from Singapore—then just as it

got dark those people"—knowing better than to use the name Tantu—
"came . . . I thought they were going to help us . . . but they attacked
me and took her." He held Arrowjoy's eyes. "We've got to go after
them . . . they're going to take her head—I know it . . . she is very
beautiful . . . Arrowjoy . . ." His voice broke, giving way at the last.

"All right, yes. First let me bind that foot or you'll slow us down."
There was a large chunk of flesh missing from the side of Slinng's foot.
Looked like a slice off a pig's haunch, Arrowjoy thought. Working with
a pocket flash, he packed the wound with folded leaves, then bound the
whole thing, shoe and all, with tough strips of palm fronds. "If this isn't
properly treated in a day or so it's going to be septic and you'll lose the
foot or even your leg—but it will last the night."

"Good enough! Let's go, for God's sake!"

Before they started off Salt laid his hand on Arrowjoy's arm. "This is
not right for us. This is not our place to be."

"Listen to me," Arrowjoy said, speaking slowly so they would be sure
to understand. "Other people have come and taken his woman away.
Would you let others come and take *your* women? *Is that what you would
do?* Now. We will go alone without you and try to find her if you wish.
But I have to say that when we come back I will tell the story." Grumbling
they went along. "Pure blackmail," Arrowjoy said. "I hate that." But
Slinng was already pushing ahead.

They were moving upland now, climbing the ridges as the mountain
began. Then an hour later they came to a well-defined trail. A path had
been cut about six feet wide. The marks of axes and chainsaws were
visible on small trees and bush. It detoured on around the major obstruc-
tions and up the mountain. "Look here," Arrowjoy said, kneeling with
Salt and beaming the pocket torch on the ground. "Tire marks."

"Hartog," Slinng answered, looking to the west where the trail cut in.
"We must be miles upstream from the *Sulu.* He had an all-terrain vehicle
with him. The Gurkhas probably cut the trail for it."

"Gurkhas?" Arrowjoy frowned.

"He had ten or twelve as bodyguards."

They continued, moving quicker now on the cut trail. A mile or so
later, the Iban stopped, pulling back. Something dark was hunkered
down ahead, its shape picked out in the shafts of moonlight streaming
through the trees. "Looks like a hippo to me," Arrowjoy said, joshing
the Iban.

They went ahead cautiously, Slinng on point. "It's the ATV." An axle had broken and the machine bogged down. The Iban kicked at the six doughnut tires while Slinng and Arrowjoy examined it. It was stripped clean but had *Sulu* stenciled on the back. There at last was hard proof of the yacht's existence. Arrowjoy had to admit that the Dreamer was right, he *had* seen it.

"These things are not much good out here," Arrowjoy said. "They get tangled up. The poor boogers had to cut a path all that way for it, and look where it got them."

"They must have gone ahead on foot—what? Five or six days ago? Where were they going?"

Arrowjoy wasn't interested, they were all exhausted, burnt out. "Listen," he finally said, "those people are moving a lot faster than we are. We're not going to catch them."

"Oh, yes! If you think . . . !"

"Wait a minute! Have you got any more of those flares?"

"One."

"All right. Now maybe if you fire it off you can scare them into leaving the woman behind."

"It also might spook them into killing her."

"True. Are you willing to take the chance?"

Slinng thought about this moment many times in the weeks that followed. Lying in his hammock staring at the rafters of the longhouse, he went over and over it. Had he made the right decision in firing off that last flare?

Loading the gun with an eight-inch cartridge, he hears its clack, remembers even the maker's name circling the brass end with its copper firing pin: ACME PRO. EQUPT. CO. PITTSBURGH PA. He cocks it, aiming up at an angle over the trail, sighting in on the moon. For just a second he hesitates, then fires.

There's a muffled shotgun sound and the brass tube is projected in a steep arc. Reaching proper height, it bursts in an impressive pomegranate color, showering down burning pieces of magnesium. The Iban stand and watch its progress through the tops of trees, and what sticks in his mind is the refraction of light that tints their upturned eyes blood red.

23

LATE THE NEXT AFTERNOON they straggled into the river camp. Hobbling on one leg, Slinng was supported by the Dreamer and another Iban. Alstair was horrified and even Luke reacted.

"Oh! Oh!" she kept saying.

"Was it a snake?" Luke wanted to know.

"No, no. Just a bad cut." Arrowjoy went for his medical kit and they laid Slinng on one of the sleeping platforms. Alstair saw that his eyes were glazed and he was in great pain. They cut the lace boot away and cleaned the wound. By now it was a nasty purple color. Arrowjoy sprinkled on sulfa power and carefully bandaged it, then gave Slinng a shot of morphine. She watched as his eyes closed and he passed into sleep without speaking.

Alstair stayed with him while he slept, then near dark went to sit with Arrowjoy, watching the river. He drank and she kept quiet, not asking questions. He admired that. Finally, he said, "He found the *Sulu.*" Seeing her look, he continued. "Yes, that's right. We saw it, too, came back that way. It's just as the Dreamer described it—although it's half sunk now." Another long swig from the brown bottle. "There was a survivor on board—a young woman . . . apparently she was very beautiful."

Of course.

"She'd been with the owner—Hartog."

"Where is she?"

"That's the thing. The Tantu came and took them away. Slinng was wounded and they killed the girl, we found where they had done it."

"But—that's . . . astounding!"

"Yes. He's taken it very hard—wanted to go after her body. He knew her before in Singapore."

He had never said a word.

Later she walked back and, standing, looked down at him while he mumbled in his sleep. Well, she thought, I've done it again. Found myself a flawed lover. This one has Leslie Howard's hair, Tarzan's muscles and is in love with a dead woman. How long will it take him to get over her? Never? She was gorgeous, of course, with a head of hair like an explosion in a Dynel factory. It should look marvelous on some Tantu's mantelpiece. Hard cheese? Yes, blart it! Alstair was a bad loser and knew she had lost. This poor sap would go around mooning over the beauty the rest of his life. The worst kind of love was the kind that ended before it was over. That kind lingered in the memory and grew more perfect with time. No woman could fight that.

They were back at the longhouse in Rumah Bujana by the end of the week. Alstair stayed with Slinng, being Sister Goodnight until the wound healed properly. She was cheery and irreverent as ever and he finally began to laugh with her, but they didn't sleep together and he had changed. The romance was over. "They're going down to Kapit on Monday to trade," she said. "I think I'll go along and make connections for Kuching."

"Really? Well, I don't blame you, it's been rough—I'm afraid we've put you through a lot."

"Oh, no, shipwrecks and headhunters and heat and a zillion bugs? It's been grand. If we could get it up as a tour we'd make our fortune. They'd especially like the part where Iban rub pot black and pig shit in your hair."

"What will you do?"

"Oh, I don't know. I started out to be an ornithologist. I suppose I should get back to that."

"Good idea."

"Why don't you come along? Your footsie is nearly well but you could have it looked at by a real doctor."

"I'm fine now."

"You're going to stay then?"

"Yes, for a while."

She took a deep breath. "She's dead, Larry." She deliberately did not use a euphemism. "Let go of her." They had not talked about it. All her carefully rehearsed speeches had fallen away with the expression on his face. He was somewhere else, not with her.

"Maybe she is . . . but until I really know, have proof . . . I'd like to wait."

She very nearly said, "What do you want? Her head?" But she restrained herself.

On Monday Alstair was ready when the Iban had the longboat loaded. Slinng and Luke walked her down from the kampong to the river carrying her things. "Well, I'm off." She shook Luke's hand. "Good luck with the sax and all."

"Thank you, lady." Luke had decided to stay. He was having a romance with a beautiful fifteen-year-old. Each night they sat out in the jungle smoking the huge cheroots and making love. The tribe was delighted. They were hoping she'd get pregnant and produce another horn honker.

"Larry." They kissed. "I'll be staying with Beata. If you want to write, I'd get it there."

"Yes, of course."

She got in the boat and turned back to them smiling, eyes glistening. "Well, I guess it proves one thing."

"What's that?" Slinng asked, hoping she wouldn't say something sentimental.

"Tits aren't all." And, waving, she sat down as the outboard kicked over and the boat pulled away.

Arrowjoy also had hoped Slinng would go. He said as much but didn't press it. Instead they played Chinese checkers with the help of the longhouse kids. A baby swallowed one of the marbles but it was passed, buffed off and cheerfully returned to the game. As they played they talked about what their actions should be concerning the discovery of the *Sulu*. Arrowjoy was in favor of forgetting it.

"*What?* How could you get away with that?"

"I will tell you that the people I report to are not going to want to hear about head-hunting and cannibalism. Can you imagine the effect on Sarawak's modern, progressive image? The tourist business? Nobody thinks these subjects are of folk or cultural interest. No, they wouldn't like it one bit. Now, I don't give a damn for them, but my concern is for these people here, and it's not in their interest either—in the public view they're all suspect savages anyway, and they don't need any more bad press. Of course I know you have different motives."

There was a pause and Slinng said, "I came out here because I believed Hartog was alive—that he was involved in the death of my father. Then, too, to find that yacht and prove he had deliberately scuttled it. Well, I did, and he did. But where's the proof? Where is he or any of the others involved in the fraud?"

"They're all up on that mountain, Slinng. Bones. That helicopter was going to take them off. Instead they were ambushed by the Tantu—they chopped them."

"No, there's more to it than that, much more. Hartog's scheme was complex. The timing of the typhoon, navigating these rivers. No, I can't believe he let himself be slaughtered by wild men, headhunters and cannibals in that primitive place. No."

"Believe it."

"Miri was the only eyewitness and she's—"

"Dead."

"We don't know that."

"Let's accept it. Because there's no way I know you're going to prove it otherwise."

"Well, then, you don't know me, do you, mister?" and he jumped up, stalking off.

If Arrowjoy saw in this the refusal to let go of the dead woman, grief or obstinacy, he couldn't say. But he knew it was bound to cause trouble. In that he was right.

Luke passed Slinng and came to squat next to Arrowjoy. "Tuan's got problems."

"Haven't we all."

Luke sighed and leaned back against the railing. "That's true, I'm worn out with love. Who would think two people could keep up the pace." He was wearing a smile that went along with his recent vigorous sexual activity with the fifteen-year-old. He was pleased with himself.

"Lovely girl." Isteri Jalong, Salt's granddaughter. "Has she asked you when you're getting your palang?

Luke looked blank. "My what?"

"A penis pin. They drive a hole through the distal end of the pecker, then insert a piece of bone or bamboo in to keep it open . . ."

"But . . . why?"

"When it heals you can insert pig's bristles, or a string of beads— whatever pleases the ladies. The friction you build up really gets them."

Luke was horrified. "You are serious, sir?"

"Take a peek under some of these loincloths. The real lovers have two pins like four-bladed props."

"Is this a manhood ritual?"

"No, no—the women insist on it. You can't get married without one."

"How . . . could that be done?" He shivered.

"You stand in cold river water until your dobber shrinks, they slip on a katipution, a bamboo compressor—with two guide holes—then, when you're ready, a sharp rod is shoved through."

"Ohhhh . . ."

"There are other ways. Up on the Bahau River they cut the head with a knife and rub in ash to raise scars. Or leech oil . . ."

"Please . . ."

"Buffalo leeches are marinated in coconut oil. Your shaft is scored lengthwise until it bleeds, the leech oil applied and a bamboo section shoved over it. The idea is the pecker swells to fill the bamboo and the leech oil doubles its size."

"Ohhhh . . ."

"For the weak sisters there's mata kambling, the eye of a goat. The eyelash ring is cut from a freshly killed goat so that the stiff eyelashes face out in a circle. It's soaked in warm water, then shoved over the head of the pecker—nature's tickler . . ."

Luke was up and gone with a weak wave.

"I'd talk to Salt!" Arrowjoy shouted. "He's the local palang puncher." He smiled, thinking what these sexual customs said for the Malay character. In other primitive cultures—in Africa and the Middle East—women had once been deprived of sexual feeling by clitoridectomy and infibulation. Here, men underwent pain and mutilation to give them pleasure.

Slinng was determined to learn the jungle and each day went with the Dreamer and Hot Tail to hunt. They carried a homemade twelve-gauge shotgun made of pipe, a rough carved stock, pieces of inner tube, clock springs and a Bic pen firing pin. It was a weapon as dangerous to hunter as hunted and gave game a fifty-fifty chance as to who would be shot.

Slinng presented them with the sawed-off shotgun taken from the triad gangster at McDonald's Singapore. They were impressed but rarely fired it because of the noise. Even talking was discouraged while on the trail. They communicated in gentle calls and whistles. Loud sound was like a stone dropped in a pond, sending out ripples and warnings. Birds flew up in sudden shuddering flight and the gibbons hooted indignantly.

How to navigate the rain forest? When Slinng showed them a map they laughed. Paths were not made in straight lines; no, course was directed by contours. The Dreamer pointed out landmarks—enormous epiphytes, mossy plants that embraced host trees and created green crossroads; a glimpse of sun against a rock to indicate shadow, read like a sundial; the flow of streams. He came to believe it an art, inherited, like their powerful legs and feet as broad and thick as floats, prehensile toes. He was learning where to put his own clumsy feet, planning each footfall.

They heard the odd cry of the mouse deer, plandok, a shrill "E" sound, and killed it. It looked to Slinng like a large rat provided with slender legs, cloven hooves and a tiny delicate face. A fire was built and the animal put on. After boiling rice the deer was chopped up and the delicacies shared: the lips, tongue and eyes. Slinng passed. The Iban finished up by splitting the skull, and while they sat talking, scooped the brains out with fingers, trailing them into mouths.

They were fascinated by Hartog, the man who steered the white prav, and wanted to hear again why he had sailed into the rain forest. Slinng repeated the story: He was a scheming person who came into the jungle to hide the prav. That way he would be paid insurance for it by other people who traded in those goods. They understood treachery but could not grasp what insurance was.

"You buy it to protect your goods. Take your longhouse: If you bought insurance on it and it burned down, then they would have to pay you to build it up again." But what if it didn't burn, they wanted to know. Would you still pay? "Yes, you go on paying as long as you want protection. If you stop, it ends." They shook their heads over this. What was to prevent people from burning down their own houses and getting new ones? "The law." Then the law was on the side of the insurance people? That couldn't be argued. Then they understood.

"It is like gambling without the fun," the Dreamer said. A person would have to be crazy to pay for something all of his life without getting anything in return. If the man in the white prav had been in insurance trading in the first place he would have stayed rich off other people's worries and not have to wreck such a fine boat. They all nodded.

Slinng encouraged these sessions to improve his Malay. Bahasa pasa was the basic trade language in Sarawak. With three hundred words and a concept of sentence construction you could converse. He realized if he was to find out what had happened to Miri, he would have to be able to ask questions and listen to answers without the distortion of translation.

They came back from a hunting trip of several days and found the kampong changed. Not visibly but indirectly. The people were nervous and excited. A storyteller had arrived from the connecting inland Penan tribes with an electrifying story. Arrowjoy was apprehensive and annoyed. "This kind of thing happens periodically. The last time it was the 'Holy Spirit' movement. The people believed that through trance they would have direct access to God. They prayed night and day and were taken with fits, passing out and screaming. They thought they were talking in tongues and even tried their luck at faith healing. It got so popular there were Holy Spirit cassettes coming in from Indonesia and Brunei. Recordings of people ranting and carrying on."

"Religious fanaticism?"

"Adapting it to the old ways. In those days they used to say, 'The longhouse is getting cold.' What they meant was they needed fresh heads. And warriors would go out and get them. Let off steam and experience the emotional excitement of a barbaric act. Now when the longhouse gets cold they take up the latest religious fad."

"Is that what this storyteller has brought?"

"Yes, only this is more dangerous. It has nothing to do with missionaries or Christian faith."

"What then?"

"Wait" was all he would say.

They began with drinking. Arak passed around in the brown beer bottles and a local brew called "sweat of armpits." It was late and only men had gathered around the fire. This was a solemn drinking occasion and the women had been excluded. The storyteller sat in the place of honor. He was a Penan from the highland plateau and had a different look than the Iban—smaller, with distended earlobes and hair cut in bangs and falling to his waist. His eyes were bright and darting, his face as smooth and hairless as a girl's.

He had come here, he said, to bring word of great elmu bitam—magic—at work in the mountains. There a thing had happened to revive faith in the old ways. He and a few others of his kind had gone to a neutral place to trade with those who live in trees. There was an uneasy shift from the Iban, but the storyteller politely did not mention the Tantu by name. "We are the only ones to see these people who are half wild and take apes as wives. They also wear springs on their feet and can jump over trees." This was a direct lift from the *bali saleng* bogeyman tales, crossed with the Malay's belief that the orangutan was the old man of the woods and everyone's ancestor.

Why wasn't he afraid? they wanted to know. These people still took heads and ate long pig. "Because I have my jeemat." He fingered a bag tied around his neck. "It has very strong obat, medicine. And I am a brave person with happy ways. I am liked."

Who brings this new spirit? they asked, getting him back on the track. "A man whose spirit is more potent than Jesus. He preaches that the tribes should be as they once were—follow the path of those original people who owed nothing to strangers and took heads to cleanse their livers. His head tells them this from under his arm."

There was an audible intake of breath at this and Slinng felt his scalp tighten. "They have seen it and say he walks with it under his arm as you and I carry coconuts."

"What does this man look like?" Slinng asked, barely contained.

"Where his head would be it is black and on top, ghost hair. He is as tall as two men and the rest of him is many colors, red and blue and—"

"*Hartog!*" Slinng shouted, standing up and startling the others. "He's in there! By God, I should have known! This is his hocus-pocus! He's alive and you can bet she's in there with him! Yes! He sent those Tantu back to the yacht to get her! They didn't kill her!" All this was said in rapid English to Arrowjoy. The Iban and the storyteller looked from one man to the other as they continued.

"Slinng . . . listen, this business about carrying a head is an old folktale. I've heard it many times."

"Right! And so had Hartog. Listen to this: Miri talked about Hartog's 'head,' had nightmares about it. He's had a replica made of his head and is using it to get control of the tribes."

"Come on! You're not thinking straight. I . . . ."

But Slinng was pacing around the fire now, carrying his bottle of arak. The Iban loved drama and they sensed that something unusual was about to happen. They sat as expectant as a first-night audience. He began speaking in Malay, taking his time to keep the words straight, face animated in the firelight, eyes wild. "You know that I have come here following the man who rode the white prav into the rain forest." He shook the bottle. "This is a bad person dishonored by his own people who now wishes to dishonor *you*. We thought he was dead and found his bones. *But we were wrong!*" There was complete silence at this. The Iban drew up as though instantly sober. The storyteller frowned at this man who would steal his story.

Slinng continued pacing, then stopped and took a mouthful of the arak, filling his cheeks. Turning, he suddenly spit a stream on the beaten ground, marking the outline of Borneo. "This is your country!" There was a thump of feet at this artistry. Heads nodded. Taking another mouthful, he punctuated it with a single accurate daub near the upper middle. "And this is where my enemy is! *He is the same man who carries his own head!*" There was a shocked reaction from the Iban, who hadn't seen this coming. "This man sent your enemies, those in the trees, to take my woman! He sits there now laughing at us as cowards who turned back and were afraid to follow! Do you remember the old ways?! Do you have the backbones of your fathers—or your mothers? Would *they* allow this to happen?"

A moan went up and the Iban rocked together, seeing death clearly. He had challenged them, and as human beings against those in the trees—they would have to go, lead him to his enemy.

"You damned fool!" Arrowjoy shouted, furious. "I hope to God you realize you're very likely to get us all chopped and eaten! Look at these people! Look at their faces—they've already crossed over to the dead."

"I don't give a good God damn!" Slinng shouted back, I'm going to find Miri whatever it takes! She's alive!"

In the longhouse, the women had listened to the shouting and understood something terrible had happened. Pepper, Salt's wife, saw Slinng standing in the light of the fire, face contorted, and blamed him. The minute he had arrived so had the bad news. She began to think about how to do something about it.

24

WHEN LAWRENCE SLINNG came out of his sleeping space in
the longhouse the next morning he found a small, bleached skull at its
entrance. It sat looking up at him. He staggered back horrified. *It was
Miri!* Her thick blond hair had been plaited and was woven through the
eye and nose openings, ending in a knotted handhold on the top. *Monsters!* He went closer, bending down to it, then suddenly straightened,
furious, and jerking his leg back, kicked it. The skull sailed off the porch
and hit below, where last night's fire had been. It sent up a puff of ash
and rolled to a stop. "You bastards!" Slinng climbed down the ladder
and stormed over to where Arrowjoy lay by the dead fire. He had passed
out after the evening's dramatics and slept where he dropped.

"Is this your idea!" Slinng pointed at the skull. In the light it could
be seen that the "hair" was woven corn silk.

Arrowjoy pushed himself to a sitting position, rubbing his head. It was
gray from the ash and his face stippled with a three-day beard. Reaching
for a beer left open since last night, he took a long drag, and spit out
a mouthful of slugs. "Damn! That will wake you up." He wiped his
tongue.

Slinng would not be put off, bending in, face contorted in anger. "Of
all the rotten, damn—"

"No, I didn't have anything to do with it. My guess is, it was the
women. They're trying to tell you something."

"If you think this is going to stop me . . ."

"No, I don't think that! You've got a hold of this thing now and won't
let go of it. But look at it from their point of view. What they see is their
men have been shamed into going against a mythical enemy. Facing what
they fear the most—the *bali saleng.* They expect to be widowed by forest
ghosts and here that means your spirit will be sewed up in a pigskin for
eternity."

"That is a lot of cock! The Tantu are men, small ones at that. I know;
I killed one! They're human, they bleed. They don't have springs on their

feet or magic powers. They're totally primitive and not very bright. They're the monkey's uncles, remember? Isn't it time the Iban faced up to them and shook off this *bali saleng* crap?"

"That's not why you want them to go in there."

"Right! You know the reason."

"And you're willing to risk all our asses to do it?"

There was a pause. "I will do anything I have to."

"Yes, I guess you would." Arrowjoy got up and dusted himself off. "One thing is accurate. That man with his talking head is disruptive. It will only be a matter of time before his word spreads like the Holy Spirit frenzy."

"Does that mean you'll help me?"

Arrowjoy looked at him evenly. "You're a hard case, Slinng, a tough bastard, tricky. And that's a fooler, because you look the gentleman. You know, you remind me of that fellow who played the perfect Englishman in films, ah, what's his name . . .?"

But Slinng had turned away.

In the end twelve of the Iban agreed to go. These were young men led by the Dreamer and Hot Tail who accepted the challenge. They now boasted about it around the fire, each outdoing the other in bravado, farting and joking so the women and girls would know they weren't afraid. Salt would have nothing to do with them. He did not speak out against them because that would mean the bad spirits might hear him. This was true of all of them. Instead of talking about going on the trip, the young men would say they were going *"tie neet-neet,"* which meant they were going into the jungle to pull their foreskins back and urinate. It was not wise to talk aloud of real intentions because bad spirits might be listening. They never mentioned their destination, weapons or, God forbid, the Tantu.

The women knew better and walked around with long faces. Gloom settled over the kampong and the men worked hard to leave as soon as possible. By the end of the week the two forty-foot longboats were loaded and ready to go. It seemed a lot to Slinng. "Where we're going, we can't be sure of the hunting," Arrowjoy said, "so we have to carry everything in. Figure it out—eight ounces is one mok and a man eats three moks of rice a day. Multiply this by a month on the trail for fifteen men, then add in all the other equipment."

"How much can one man comfortably carry? Fifty pounds?"

"Just about. And remember we're going over unknown ground straight up that mountain. In 1983 I escorted a team of scientists into the Hose Mountains. It took us two weeks to penetrate seven miles." He saw Slinng's eyebrows go up. "Yes." They were also taking Arrowjoy's portable sixty-cycle AC transmitter. "If, or I should say, when, we get into serious trouble I can raise the MFS Air Base at Bakenu and they just might come in for a medical emergency or if we bring this man Hartog out."

"Or Miri."

Luke wanted to go. Arrowjoy was amused by his reason. "Well, it is this lady, sir, Isteri Jalong. She is a fine person, but now talks of our life here together. Of sons playing saxophone in the kampong. Can you see that? Out here in the jungle? Blowing jazz to pythons and birds? I am a city person bound for greatness in London or New York. How could I live in the woods and have a group with little kids? But the trouble is, she is crazy for me and I don't want to break her heart."

"She'll get over it."

"I doubt that. She's never met anyone like me."

"When you get back you can send her a cassette of you honking—or name a song after her. How about 'So Long, Jalong'?"

He wrinkled his nose at this. "Yes, but in the meantime, I had better go on this trip with you."

"It's going to be dangerous."

"Not as dangerous as here."

True, Arrowjoy thought. Anything was better than having your penis drilled for palang pins.

The women and the older men would not come down to say good-bye. The dogs were to be left behind and only they stood on the shore barking a farewell. The longboats left at dawn as the mist cleared, returning on the same rivers. The water level had dropped and the river grew rocks where rapids thrashed. They got past these with the Iban still in good spirits, shouting insults at boulders and testing each other's nerve, leaning out as far as possible to push rocks aside; taking chances; jumping in when necessary to shove the boats past difficult passages. The roar of the water was terrific and it poured in while everyone bailed with plastic dinner plates.

When the mountains showed themselves as a green wall rising up to be blurred by clouds, they quieted, became sober. These were lowland people, river people, and the highlands were ominous and forbidding in their folklore. As in most cultures they mistrusted strangers and the distant places they came from. Camping at night, Slinng became their cheerleader, entertaining them around the campfire with rope tricks and seaman's knots—talking up their courage while Luke played the saxophone. But the bass instrument was not meant to sound gay and when its mournful sounds drifted up with the smoke to the treetops, eyes cut toward the depth of rain forest. *Were they in there watching?*

By the end of the week they had arrived at the conjunction of tributaries where Slinng followed reggae and Elvis to the *Sulu.* The longboats were pulled ashore and unloaded. The trip inland began on Hartog's trail to the lava bed. This took nearly two days, made easier by the path the Gurkhas cut for the useless vehicles. Everyone went silently, heavily loaded. As they pressed upward and the incline increased, the fifty-pound packs doubled their weight, straps pulled taut. Slinng was toughened now, surefooted, memorizing landmarks, learning to navigate the rain forest. Behind him, Luke hauled his sax case and a pack that included cheroots and Baby Ruth bars tucked in by his fifteen-year-old lady love.

When they approached the lava bed near dusk the mood altered. Although neither Arrowjoy nor Slinng had described what they would encounter, those of the Iban who hadn't been there instantly sensed the menace of the place.

"Like it or not," Arrowjoy told them, "it's the best location to camp. It's the only one where the helicopter could land if we need it." Their eyes went to where the burned-out carcass of the last helicopter sat. They were not encouraged. The goods were unloaded and stacked up at a distance from the ashes of old fires and piles of bones. They worked quickly to build a fresh fire before night fell and settled in with weapons close at hand. There was no loud talk and no sax playing. Although they were still many days from the highland plateau and the vast wildness of Apo Kayan, spirits might be listening. Now, as the sun set, the group sat around a cooking fire and looked across the lava bed to where it sloped to meet the wall of jungle. From here the climb was straight up the mountain to a place with no name.

.   .   .

Far ahead in that place with no name, in the dense wet of mountain rain forests, the mist lies about, tufts tugged aside by a breeze to drift into the high valleys. Smoke from cooking fires rises and merges with it in a gray smear that hides the setting sun. Here is a kampong of an ancient kind not seen on the slopes or flatlands. The jungle pushes in with only the briefest clearing and is circled by a fence of stakes. From a distance these appear to have odd, ornamental tops. Then, closer, it can be seen they are heads, an even dozen, each turned to face the longhouse. They wear the berets of Gurkhas and the ribbons at the back flutter in the light breeze.

Inside, at the center of a long room, at a place of honor, a hammock is strung. In it lies a straw figure dressed in a Lacoste shirt and shorts. Nike running shoes are placed carefully at one end, and at the other is a realistic head done in plastic, correct in every detail down to the gross nose, pig eyes and flag of white hair.

Around it women squat, chattering as they do their chores. They are smaller than the lowland tribes people, with dark skin, filed teeth and the fierce built-in scowl. All are naked, and as babies nurse, they spit and smoke Davidoff cigars. There are no men here. They have gone off to meet the enemy.

Before they left the next morning, Slinng and Arrowjoy examined the helicopter again. "Even though there was a helmet with the Aussie air force insignia, the chopper is civilian," Arrowjoy said.

"The pilot was ex-military, then."

"Maybe. The poor bastard had a large set of balls to fly in here—this would be an easy place to miss."

"Probably beamed in by radio location."

"Probably. Hartog had it all figured out, didn't he? Charting the rivers, the vehicles, the bodyguards . . ."

"Yes, but what went wrong?"

"My guess is the helicopter. The Tantu saw it come in and were waiting. They are not a people you negotiate with. There is no passing around of trade goods or white man's magic. They kill you silently on sight."

"They didn't kill Hartog."

"That is your opinion."

They walked past the piles of bones to where the Iban stood at the edge of the jungle. "When we come back—if we come back—you should select some of the most recent bones and take them with us," Arrowjoy continued. "You may be able to get some kind of scientific proof as to who was who."

They were all impatient to leave the lava bed and its unpleasant aura. Half of the food would be left here for the trip back. It, along with the radio, had been carefully covered and they started up the mountain without a backward look. As the angle increased to thirty degrees, the plaited straps of backpacks began to cut in and everyone streamed sweat. Trees were a tangle of exposed roots and progress difficult. From above a patter of drops rained down, hitting the broad leaves of plants, and the humidity soared as the greenhouse effect closed in. From around them came the sounds of insect hum and birdcalls: the Beethoven bird who sang the four opening notes of the Fifth Symphony, the chatter of twenty kinds of cicada. Even the ground was alive with movement and noise—termites, two thousand per square yard, gnawing away at the eight hundred species of tree.

But they heard none of it, were blocking it out. Concentration was on getting up the mountain. To help they chewed sugee, shoving it up under lips, chewing, spitting out old pieces, jamming in new ones like replacing spark plugs. It was a drug that numbed the pain of exertion. Level of difficulty was rated by how many pieces of sugee were needed to overcome it. This was a fifty-sugee climb. By evening they had reached the beginning of the highland plateau at two thousand meters. Its enormous area stretched out ahead into central Borneo and from there six major rivers flowed downward to the Celebes, Java and the South China Sea.

"The border between Sarawak and Kalimantan is somewhere along here," Arrowjoy said, "but we aren't going to meet any border guards asking for passports." Arrowjoy and Slinng lay exhausted. The whole troop had collapsed after they made camp. "During the unpleasantness in 'sixty-two when Indonesia tried to keep Brunei out of the Federation of Malaysia there were intrusions over the border, but it was just too difficult for both sides and they gave up. Oddly, this area up here has become more remote in recent years because traders and missionaries now fly over it rather than walk through it."

"If they're so dangerous, why aren't the Tantu and other hostile tribes policed by the government?"

"We are probably talking no more that fifty or one hundred individuals and up to this point they have only preyed on each other. The kind of effort it would take to hunt them down in a million acres of rain forest just hasn't been worth it. Besides," he said, smiling, "they're considered an endangered species. I mean, how many genuine headhunters and cannibals are left? Like the crocodile they should be protected—they're just lucky their skins make rotten handbags or they'd have been extinct long ago."

As they entered this part of the highlands there was a dramatic drop in sound level. Here was a moss forest with enormous hardwood trees, bosky greens in every shade, complicated, interwoven vines—and silence. "This area was hunted out generations ago as the tribes moved on. That's another reason the Tantu have it to themselves."

This lack of comforting animal noise and bird sounds bothered the Iban. If they were uneasy before, now they were stony and sullen. Lips pulled down, they began to reconsider the whole adventure. Slinng caught hard looks. Only the Dreamer remained resolute and it was he who held the rest together.

Luke noticed none of this. He was delighted with the quiet. Birds annoyed him with their off-key attempts at song. In fact he was enjoying himself. After the early days of his arrival in the rain forest, when he thought each step would be his last, he had hardened until he could keep up with the others. It was a new feeling to be competent among men. He began to whistle and the Iban froze; for them this was the worst kind of bad luck.

"*Listen!*" Arrowjoy said, twisting his head around. Slinng thought he meant the whistling and looked toward Luke. Then they heard it, the sound of wind. Next to the red caterpillar, the most dangerous thing in the jungle was wind: a sudden blast coming out of nowhere, rushing through the thousands of trees. First it sent down a torrent of huge dead branches from overhead to hit the ground like bombs, a crackling explosion of heavy timber. Then the trees themselves would begin to go, enormous top-heavy monsters, roots jerked out of the feeble topsoil with horrendous creaking sounds. When they went, they slammed into others in chain reaction, taking them down, too. As the toppling of trees built to a crescendo, the giants fell like dominoes until acres of rain forest were flattened. The sound was incredible—a thundering as deafening as an artillery barrage.

While the trees crashed around them, the men clung to ground that shook under the assault like the violent vibration of trains roaring past. Then it was over: one minute of pure undistilled terror. The survivors pushed up from the damp ground and counted heads. There were casualties among the Iban: a broken arm, a man knocked senseless with his right ear torn off—and one dead. After the worry about the Tantu, this unforeseen violent death seemed wrong. Fate was awry. They held council and it was decided that two of them would carry the body down the mountain to where it could be buried with dignity. The wounded would accompany them.

The survivors continued, glum now with reduced company, cautious, listening for the sound of wind—and when the rare birdcall was heard, wondering if it really was a bird.

Approaching from the other direction, they infiltrate the jungle nearly silent, imperceptible, emerging from the trees as though part of them, an extension of greens and browns in startling body paint and feathers. Jagged patterns of lightning shooting up arms, faces quartered in black and white, eyes red-lined—in full war regalia. Each man carries a seven-foot-long blowpipe with a spear tip and a bamboo quiver for poison darts. Parangs and lesser knives are at the waist. There are only twenty-five, representing all the young warriors and able-bodied men of the tribe—the last of what was once hundreds. Moving forward in a straight line toward their enemies, they are the ultimate savages, a blend of animal instinct and human cunning without the complications of conscience or the burden of mercy.

At dark the Iban huddle together and eat their rice cold. Having a fire is now too dangerous and sentries have been posted. Slinng and Arrowjoy lean against the same tree, legs stretched out. A bottle is passed.

"Damn me," Arrowjoy said, letting out a sigh, "I'm getting too old for campaigning. I thought that was behind me when I left the army."

"Were you born out here?"

"Yes, Brunei. My dad was an oil rigger. He came in with the boom in north Sarawak—that was the first strike. It's petered out now but the refinery still processes oil pumped down from Brunei. It's the world's richest welfare state—oil income generates something like a hundred million Malay dollars a month for eighty-five thousand people. They've all got pensions and free medical care."

"You didn't gravitate to the oil business?" Slinng was squinting up at a narrow gap in the treetops, a hint of sky. There was actually sun up there, blue sky.

"No, I wanted the army. I'd missed the war and went off adventuring, hunting pirates on the coast. They were a real problem in the sixties— still are for that matter. Hijacking and murder is a trade handed down from father to son. The Celebes and Sulu seas were full of them. We once pulled over a fishing boat off Tawau—they were chumming for shark— and we wanted to ask about a missing coastal steamer. They claimed to know nothing about it and we were ready to shove off when we discovered the chum was human body parts. They'd chopped the crew and passengers up and this was their way of getting rid of them and turning a profit. They had a nice catch."

There was a pause after this. Then Slinng asked, "When do you think we'll meet the Tantu?"

"It's hard to tell. They're nomad-hunters and who knows where their current camp might be? I hope we'll start finding message sticks and we can gradually make contact without frightening them into doing something rash."

"You've never made contact with them before?"

"No, and I don't know anyone else who has either—alive, that is."

The next morning they started out in a fog that clung to the ground and created the eerie effect of torsos moving through the jungle without benefit of legs. The going became increasingly difficult with a dense tangle of tough springy vines that parangs bounced off. These vines had caught up dead trees and branches and held them captive, interweaving them in a mass of foliage that bristled with thorns and barbs like sawteeth. The only thing to do was cut a tunnel though this patch, and going single file they whacked away, ducking down and finally crawling through the impossible parts. Enclosed on all sides in a cocoon of lush vegetation, they all began to feel the edge of claustrophobia. It was possible to imagine yourself a fly caught in a spider's web.

Behind him, Luke labored along on his hands and knees dragging the sax case behind him. "This is not good, tuan. I could be meeting a snake eye to eye."

"Hang on, we should clear this piece in a minute . . ." But they didn't. Slinng crawled over a rotten log that came apart in his hands, and thousands of winged termites swarmed out and up his arms and body. He brushed them off frantically and tried to stand but the heavy limbs of fallen trees crossed above him forced him to his knees again.

Then came the clear whooping sound of the gibbon, followed a minute later by a more distant answer. He was riveted; it was the first animal sound they had heard in a place where there were no animals. Ahead, he heard Arrowjoy shout, *"Tek-kenay?* Who are you?" There was no answer, then *"Ma-hat ku koo-ee!* Let us know where you are!" Nothing. All chopping of parangs had stopped and those swallowed up in the tube of jungle seemed to hold their breath. Slinng thought of Major Okubo's old Nambu pistol in his pack. Could anything be less useful? The last thing he heard Arrowjoy say was a rather plaintive *"My ke put koo* . . . Don't shoot us with your blowpipe . . ."

Behind him, Slinng hears a small gasp and turns to see Luke staring at the jewel of a bright bug held in his fingers. Its wings are feathered and carefully tied. There is a drop of blood on its tip and another on his neck. Opening his mouth as though to speak, he looks at Slinng and his head drops softly into the wet grasses. In the next instant Slinng slaps at the back of his own neck. Then, nausea and blackout.

The darts come in on feathered wings with unerring accuracy. Penetrating the dense enclosure, they fly to their mark, silent, and in their graceful arc are beautiful: a tiny burst of bright color streaking through the muted shades of nature; a flight of man-made insects; wasps with the venom of snakes, tipped with a poison that will paralyze or kill.

Behind the swarm come the Tantu. Blowpipes are put aside, and taking up the twenty-four-inch parangs, they begin to chop away to get at their victims.

25

VERY SLOWLY it comes to Slinng that he's staring at the moon: flat on his back, mouth open, a catch-all for bugs, eyes fixed on the pale disk. It is directly overhead, peering down at him through a narrow opening of jungle, an eye blinked by shifting tree branches. He tries to get to a sitting position but can't find his arms. When he does, pushing up in an awkward sideways motion, he sees a figure lying next to him. Luke, curled up, hand locked to his sax case. Slinng tries to get hold of this but can't quite grasp it. What is he doing here?

Gradually his view plane expands to take in posts supporting a long-house. They seem to curve in a convex sweep but he knows that can't be. A man sits back against the far post and appears as distant as if viewed though the wrong end of a telescope. He is looking at something straight ahead. Slinng wants to turn his head in that direction but it takes nearly a full minute. In the center of a small clearing are silhouettes of women against the burn of fire. This is where the sear comes from. They rake out a long bed of coals, bodies shimmering with the waves of heat—outlines diminished as if the fierce glow had begun to melt their edges. Beyond is a half circle of stake fence mounted with heads, the hollows of eye sockets directed toward him, mouths agape.

When he looks back at the seated figure, the perspective has straightened and he recognizes Arrowjoy. His head is at an angle lolling against his shoulder, eyes fixed, staring past him. Slinng turns. At the far, dark edge of jungle fireflies dance in a long, vertical line: a curious action; a bobble that moves forward and now elongates. As they come on, increase in size, he sees they are the beams of flashlights, held upright, pointing toward the sky, and that each beam illuminates a single head. These heads move in concert toward him. Now he can make out the bodies, naked and painted in grotesque patterns, whites and blues and reds and greens—a palette of shocking combinations, lightning bolts and the twist of serpents on arms and legs, heads topped with a fan of yellow and orange feathers. The effect of the light uplit on white-painted faces, eyes outlined in red and filed teeth, is terrifying.

At the head of the procession is a tall figure. Aloof, regal, naked as the others and illustrated with startling designs. The face is painted out in black and above it a mane of white hair flaps in the breeze as of a bird in flight. In the crook of his left arm is his head, and a flashlight held in that hand illuminates it. The other hand holds a bullhorn. As the retinue reaches the longhouse they split off and take positions around the fire, hunkering down and watching the women.

Hartog squatted next to Slinng. Setting the bullhorn and plastic head on the packed ground, he snapped off the flashlight. If Slinng thought he would be addressed by a madman he was disabused. "Did you people bring up any D batteries? This bunch are crazy about the flashlights but I'm just about out of batteries."

Furious, Slinng tried to get his mouth working. "Uhhh . . ."

"Easy . . . easy. That's the darting. It will take a bit to get over. All that film crap about poison arrows and instant death by curare is just that. The idea is to stun prey, keep it breathing in a kind of suspended animation until ready to cook. It's their answer to freezers. The poison comes from frog sweat." He laughed. "That's right, there's a certain kind of tiny tree frog that produces a toxin that'll stun a moose. They torment the little buggers until they sweat—work up a white froth—then scrape it off on dart points. It remains deadly for five or six months and one frog will supply about fifty darts. Interesting, huh?"

Slinng's mind had cleared but connecting words was laborious—it was as though he'd had a stroke. "Hartog . . . you . . .!"

"I hope you don't think I had anything to do with what's happened? I'm not in control here. I couldn't have stopped it if I wanted to. I survive because of my head." He patted it. "And let me tell you, these are wild men, erratic and dangerous. By God, they took out those Gurkhas right off. Can you believe it? Combat veterans with automatic weapons!"

After the ATV had broken down they got out and walked. This was rough. Hartog was in his late sixties and in good shape. But Wittenoon, the captain, had atrial fibrillation and hypertension so that Hartog and the engineer, Dirkes, had to carry him most of the way up the mountain.

They arrived at the lava bed exhausted but still on schedule. The Gurkhas set up a defensive perimeter and called in the helicopter. It was a big old Sikorsky S-61L commercial job that Qantas leased out. With twin turbine engines and a useful load of 7,700 pounds it was capable of flying from Darwin across the Celebes to Borneo and lifting out the twelve Gurkhas and three Australians. While they waited they rested, and Wittenoon got his wind back. Near dusk (as planned), they heard the vibration of blades and the chopper appeared over the clearing and let down, blowing up ashes of the dead fires and exposing more bones. The pilot, an ex-military, was another Australian, an old friend of Hartog's, famous as one of the mercenary pilots that Swedish Count Carl Gustav von Rosen led against the Nigerian air force during the war in Biafra.

He was a big man, tanned and broad-featured, wearing his battered "lucky" flight helmet. Hopping out of the pilot's canopy, he and Hartog met in a contest of dusty back slaps and knuckle-bruising hand shakes. The four confederates, captain, engineer, pilot and Hartog, joined arms and did a little victory dance, sending the ashes up in sooty puffs and laughing their heads off.

The Gurkhas watched the ebullient greeting, laughing with them, excited at what they thought was the conclusion of an arduous passage. Then the first went down unnoticed, stumbling and falling, and for a moment there was a suspension of belief. A comrade bent to help him and he collapsed, behind him another and another. What was shocking was the lack of noise. These were hardened veterans used to incoming fire, heavy weapons, rockets, grenades. This death came on the air as silent as a fatal inoculation. There were shouts now and the automatic weapons opened up, spraying the edge of jungle. *But where were they?* It was nearly dark and in the half-light no enemy was revealed. The action happened in seconds and those slow to react fell in the first flight of darts.

Hartog dived for the lava bed, scrabbling among the packs, pulling them close for protection. Around him the Australians and their Gurkha protectors were decimated. Burrowing into his pack, he found his head and tentatively raised it up. The pale plastic skin, gross nose and flutter of real hair were gradually elevated with his outstretched arms. As the darts ceased he straightened, holding it as high as his arms would reach, one head mirroring the other.

. . .

"It was like Custer's last stand," Hartog said. "There I was surrounded by dead, or actually the paralyzed. They didn't dart me, but they wouldn't show themselves either. My arms were getting tired, and remembering the bullhorn, I reached down and got it with one hand, clicking it on while I held the head with the other. Then I called out to them, 'Me Hartog! Me friendly!' You know, Tarzan talk. I had it on extra loud, and by God, they took off! I could hear the little bastards running away! I had scared them to death. All that noise from the guns hadn't bothered them; they knew what those were. But my bloody big voice coming out of the horn really spooked them."

Hartog sits at the center of his fallen troop all night. Bodies surround him, arms thrown out, faces pressed to the ground, arrested in the position they dropped. Automatic weapons are strewn about and when a breeze comes up the rotor blades of the helicopter whisper around. Occasionally there is an eerie groan, a gurgle or escape of wind from one of the fallen. He still grips the bullhorn and plastic head, but his own head nods and he dozes off and on through the night.

At dawn he jerks awake and sees the Tantu warily approach, moving toward him very slowly, blowguns held out. He smiles and tries to remember his trade Malay. *"My ke medial . . . jee-an ako ee-too!* Don't be afraid—I am a good person!" Several of the elders relax their weapons and sit at a distance observing him, while others build a fire and drag the bodies toward it. Later he hears the thud of parangs and realizes they're taking heads.

"At first I thought, Hartog, they think you're a god! You've done it! You're going be king of the jungle like in the films! But no, they're not dumb. For a few days they examined my feces carefully and sent their women to sleep with me. When they were sure I was a man like them, I was accepted. The head saved me, of course. They were curious about that—their sense of drama is keen. What I've done is got up a bloody act. Look at me! I'm on stage. I talk, trying not to move my lips so the buggers will think the head's doing the talking. Damn silly! They know this head is not really mine, not talking, but they like the idea of it— they want to believe in it. It's the old business of religion-magic. They've self-hypnotized themselves into believing. They'll keep it up as long as it suits them, then—zip!" He drew his finger across his throat.

There was activity at the edge of the fire, and two of the women tugged something out from under layers of palm leaves at one side. Behind them heat waves rising from the bed of coals gave the scene a distortion and Slinng tried to push himself up to see what was happening. His limbs wouldn't respond. "Wha . . .?"

"Easy . . ."

Slinng saw now that they were dragging a body toward the fire. One of the Iban. *"Hartog!"*

Hartog shoved him down. "Shut up, you bloody fool! What is it you think you can do? Take his place? Look at their hungry faces with those filed teeth and smacking lips—would you like to enter a vegetarian's plea? You've been invited to dinner—don't offend your hosts."

After the men had ceremonially taken the head, the women did the butchering, chopping off limbs and cracking ribs with a minimum of lost motion. Their victim had been kept drugged and there was no struggle or outcry at death—only the clutch of muscle against the knife's pull. The body was quartered, bones chopped with a heavy parang and the entrails and delicacies laid aside. The women worked naked and were covered with blood and visceral slime. In the firelight their bodies took on a dark cherry color as though they had been dipped in some exotic sauce. Once more the coals were raked out and choice parts put directly on the fire. There was an instant sound of sizzling and the smell of burning flesh.

"The thing is," Hartog said, "the meat has to be cooked over an open fire. If you try to boil it or stew it the poison will rise to the surface, affect the taste, and in turn poison the eater. So that old joke about cannibals putting missionaries in a pot is just that—what they like is a barbie."

Slinng was aware of the severed head lying to one side of the fire. He saw its expression very clearly. *It was the Dreamer.*

That night the three of them were carried into the longhouse and dumped on the floor. Arrowjoy and Luke were still incoherent and lay where they fell. After the horror of watching the Tantu glut themselves, Slinng collapsed, and doing his best to block it out of his mind, fell into a troubled sleep. The Tantu came and went, shadowy figures stepping over them in the wide communal room to go into narrow sleeping cubicles. These were curtained off for families, with the young men rolled up in sleeping mats outside on the rough floor boards. The place was spare and in the dark showed the shapes of cardboard boxes and baskets, pots lined up in odd irregular sizes, cans of soft drinks.

The only decorations were skulls. They hung from the beams around the big room in a line that stretched to its end. Hundreds, interwoven with rattan to hold them in place and arranged in such a way that the black eye holes looked down at the living. Even in the dark there was a shine to them that circled the room, a ghostly blur. When Slinng awoke this was what he saw. Light was just breaking and they grinned down, picking up a pink hue from the dawn. His own head had finally cleared and, shaking off the effects of the darting, the first thing he thought of was Miri.

At the far end of the room a single hammock could be seen, hung in a central position. Around it were a toss of canvas packs, the twist of web belts, uniforms and piles of clothes—last effects of victims. Even from this distance he could see Hartog's large frame asleep in the hammock. Luke and Arrowjoy were still out and Slinng checked their vital signs; pulse slow but regular, skin clammy. He rolled Luke's eyes back and from what he could tell, he seemed normal. Arrowjoy was another thing; there was something seriously wrong with him.

Stepping over the two, he went straight up the middle of the room, past the early risers, old ladies and little kids. They looked up as he passed but raised no alarm. The warriors slept on after the night of feasting and even the dogs were listless. Reaching Hartog's hammock, he gave it a violent shake. "Hartog! God damn it! Where's Miri?!"

Hartog groaned and unwrapped himself from a young girl. "What in hell . . .?"

"You bastard! What have you done with Miri?"

Hartog eased his feet over the edge of the hammock to the floor. He was still in the ludicrous body paint, his face as black as a minstrel's. "Christ! Stop that bloody yelling. I've told you—these people don't like noise." He was right, there was mumbling, and the warriors began to unroll from their mats. *"Tidak apa,"* Hartog said, smiling at them. "It doesn't matter." And stooping down, he picked up a can of Yoo-Hoo from a sack. "C'mon, mate, let's go out on the porch." They crossed the room and went through a narrow door to a long verandah that stretched the length of building. "Thank God I had some trade Malay before I got involved in this mess."

"What about Miri? What happened to her?" Hartog leaned against the log of a railing, relaxed easy, while Slinng, agitated and frantic, could barely contain himself. His instinct was to instantly throttle the man. The view was across last night's smoldering fire to the stake fence topped with Gurkha heads.

Hartog rubbed his face and took a swig from the can. "Christ—I've got to stop drinking after dinner."

"*Hartog . . .!*"

"Easy . . . easy. I have no idea what happened to Miri—well, not true, we had a row on the ship and the silly bitch ran out on deck in the middle of the typhoon. I assume she went overboard. We searched the ship later but couldn't find her."

"She survived, you bastard! When I found the wreck of the *Sulu* she was still aboard . . ."

"What?" Hartog's head snapped around, smiling. "That's bloody marvelous! What a girl! But . . . what happened to her?"

"I'm asking you! You sent those Tantu down to the *Sulu* to get her!"

"Oh, use your bloody head! I had no idea she was there. I sent them after sodas"—he held up the can—"and some decent canned grub—and D batteries. Do you think I would have had her killed? Why? My God! With her here it might have been a holiday—me and my baby, king and queen of the cannibals." He laughed and took another swig.

"Three of them took us off the ship. On the trail they got away with Miri and tried to kill me. I killed one but I couldn't catch up to the others."

He shook his head sadly. "Only two came back with the stuff—telling me the other was still hunting—and as God is my witness they said nothing about any woman." There was a pause and a sigh. "None of this has turned out as I planned, cobber."

Slinng was half listening, staring off at the edge of jungle, eyes unfocused, trying to grasp the reality that Miri was gone. *Was this it then? Had Miri been killed? Had she paid the price for a head of hair like Rapunzel's?*

"I met her through Blas Coff, you know," Hartog was saying. "He introduced her as one of the famous Brooke family and that's how I got caught up in the whole bloody business—the White Raj, Sarawak, all that rot. It evolved into a plan, his plan—we would use her and the Brooke name as a cover for our insurance scheme. If we were discovered on the rivers in Sarawak—and there was a good chance we would be—

that would be our reason for being there—following old Brooke's route."

"So it *was* insurance fraud."

"Oh, yes, I can see now that the whole thing was badly flawed, but mate, I was desperate and stony broke."

"How could that be?"

"How? The oil glut. The tankers went first. Then the corporations, gutted to float what was left. Each investment, stock and bonds, rolling the next one, collapsing in turn like dominoes."

"But how could you get away with it?"

"Playing one creditor off against the other. When you owe such tremendous amounts nobody wants to pull the last brick out and tumble the structure. And by God, I did a near-miraculous job of concealing it. Let me tell you a secret: It's easier to be in debt for a billion than run a bill of a thousand on your credit card."

"And no one caught on?"

"Oh, they were snapping at my ass. That was the rush to get out. That little girl in Lloyd's office . . ."

"Kim Sing?"

". . . she picked up on it. My guess is, right about now it's hit 'em. They've been flogging the computers, galloping through a badland of holding companies and bad debts trying to put it together . . ." He chuckled. ". . . And some cobber of an accountant is slapping his forehead at this moment and saying, 'Holyyy shit!' " He laughed out loud.

"Colonel Pynge-Gilbert told me you leased the *Sulu.*"

"True enough, the leasing company was a blind for Blas—my trusted business partner. They never would have found it. There were more twists and turns in that trail than a barrel of snakes. The yacht was just about all we had left. Although it was worth a bundle on paper we couldn't get ten cents on dollar for her in the depressed market. But old Pynge-Gilbert was greedy to get the commission from those huge premiums and overinsured her."

"As simple as that."

"We couldn't sink her at sea and show up with our hands out. No, *we* had to disappear, too—our lives insured, of course. I still had a big piece of land—a hundred-thousand-acre station in the outback—in Miri's name. After we hid the yacht upriver the chopper would lift us all out to Aussieland. There, me and my jungle princess would lay low and when Lloyd's paid off, Blas would skin down to the Caymans where the knicker was to be funneled into our joint, secret account."

"Miri said you killed Blas—threw him overboard."

"What? C'mon! The little bastard is hiding out someplace right now—first class you can bet—waiting for the payoff. He was out to skin us all—including Miri."

"She said the Gurkha chopped off his hand when he clung to the rail."

"And you believed her? Did she also tell you they were married—a bloody man-and-wife team of con artists?"

"*What?*"

"That's right, cobber. They were a couple of beauties, they set out to screw me from the beginning. Can you imagine! The chickens eating the fox? And it would have worked, too, but she got crazy that first night at sea and blew the whole thing—she was into drugs, y'know? Oh, yes, I had a helluva time with her. I was holding back the stuff, trying to get her straight, and all this came out. That's when I found out about it. Now here's the crusher—she's not even one of the Brookes."

"Wait a minute . . ."

"There *is* no 'Miri' Brooke. Her real name is Jan Smight and her dad's a jockey in Queensland."

Slinng was stunned. "But . . ."

"No buts about it. When you get back you can look it up."

"*When* I get back?"

Hartog had another hearty laugh at that.

Luke recovered fully by the next day but Arrowjoy never did. The left side of his face was paralyzed and he lost the use of his left arm and leg. There was confusion, loss of speech, and severe vomiting. Slinng and Luke did what they could to nurse him but he drifted into a comatose state. Hartog shook his head. "I've seen this happen once before. The dart must have pierced his spine at the base of his neck—it's like a stroke—what do they call it? Cerebral hemorrhage."

"We've got to get him medical help."

"Just how are you going to do that, jocko?"

"Go down that mountain to the lava bed—there's a transmitter there—we can call in an airvac from Bakenu."

There was a pause and Hartog looked at him. The whites of his eyes were startling against the black face paint. "Do you think these people are going to allow that?"

"They don't pay any attention to us. We can slip away at night. There are no guards."

"Why should there be? They would track you down in hours. They'd love it, real sport, pig sticking. And even if they didn't do you think you could find your way through that bloody rain forest?"

"I'd give it a try. Anything is better than this—and with your plastic head and that bullhorn maybe they wouldn't bother us."

"I wouldn't be too sure."

"Are you telling me you would rather stay here than go back?"

"What would I be going back to? I don't fancy spending my old age in the lockup."

"For what? Insurance fraud? If Lloyd's doesn't have to settle the claim and you pay out what you can with your hidden assets . . ." He saw the look on Hartog's face. "Unless, of course, you really *did* kill Blas Coff. But then if you didn't, and as you say, he's lying low, surely he can be found to give testimony . . ."

But Hartog had gotten up and left.

Four nights later as the ritual of feast began again outside, Slinng sat with Luke inside the longhouse feeding Arrowjoy. The food was cakes of wild sago flour moistened with blood, then flopped into an iron pot of sizzling fat. This was their main staple and barely possible to choke down with cans of Yoo-Hoo.

Hartog came by on his way outside. The sounds of cracking bones could be heard. "Not going to join the fry tonight?" He squatted down. "Sorry—bad taste—but my dad was a butcher in Melbourne and I grew up watching him chop meat. Did some of it myself when I was a kid. So maybe that's the reason I'm not so squeamish."

"It's just a little more than being squeamish, isn't it?"

"Oh, I don't know. If you sat down to dinner with cows and pigs would you speak out against eating beef or pork? Of course you would. I'll tell you there's not a whole lot of difference in chopping up and eating one kind of meat or another—human or animal."

"It's the difference between being savage or civilized," Slinng said, barely under control

"Is that right? I read somewhere that the Aztecs were cannibals. Would you call them civilized? It said all that hooey about sun gods and human sacrifice was a cover-up to put meat on the table."

"You don't know what you're talking about."

"Why do you think these people are cannibals? Ferocity? Meanness? That nonsense about taking on a dead man's spirit? No. Hunger. They don't get enough meat to eat. Protein deficiency. Game was hunted out on this mountain generations ago. The tribe's been dying off, hunted down by enemies. It's why they're secretive and ferocious—it's also why they're small, undernourished. There's only forty or so left—once there were hundreds but they've been forced into isolation. They're not farmers and what they can gather is not enough to sustain them."

"The government would support them as it has other tribes."

"Do you think so? Look at them, their color and features are different. They don't look like the Malays and are much more primitive. The Iban hate and fear them—you've heard the talk of *bali salengs*. If they give up their weapons, go down the mountain and accept government hand-outs—become beggars—then they will lose their manhood and their culture. And how long do you think they would survive among their enemies?"

"Nothing you've said can justify murdering other human beings and eating them. If this is what their culture is, then by God, it *should* be destroyed."

Hartog bent in closer and Slinng saw that dangerous countenance he remembered from their first meeting. His voice had lowered to a hoarse whisper. "There were eight Iban darted but one died right off and the meat was spoiled. After tonight two will have been eaten. That leaves five. At one a week you should be able to figure out when your turn will come. Then you'll have a chance to be part of that culture—you'll be swallowed up by it." Laughing, he straightened. "Bon appetit."

As he went out the door Slinng saw Arrowjoy's eyes follow him. He leaned in, looking closely at his face. It was the first sign they had that he was responding to stimuli around him. "Arrowjoy! Can you understand me? It's Slinng!" There was a slight nod. He felt tears sting his eyes and gripped Arrowjoy by the shoulders, his face inches away. *"Listen! You've got to hang on! We're getting out of here! I promise! We're going to make it, and we're going to take that son of a bitch with us!"*

26

THE WOMEN SIT GOSSIPING, chattering together with the remaining Iban between their legs. They smoke Hartog's Davidoff cigars, finishing up by chewing and swallowing the ends. Backs braced against trees, Iban heads rest on their shoulders, mouths open. While one hand manipulates the throat, they shove sago "noodles" down their gullet with the other. These are long slippery strings of wild sago flour soaked in blood and water. This is an art practiced long before anyone could remember to keep game alive and fattened in the same way as turkeys and geese. It is a laborious process but they enjoy the social occasion. When they finish each day, the Iban are sloshed down, cleaned, and placed between palm leaves to keep them cool until needed. Fresh meat.

Slinng began by retrieving their packs. A tricky maneuver of timing: slipping through the longhouse when the Tantu and Hartog were elsewhere, then working the packs out of the pile near Hartog's hammock. They were hidden in the narrow corner he and Luke occupied. That night, Slinng opened his pack and took out Major Okubo's Nambu pistol. There were seven eight-millimeter shells in the eight-round clip. Had Okubo fired the missing bullet? If so, at whom and how long ago? Would the weapon still fire? Unlikely. Looking at it he realized what a clumsy piece of work it was. How inelegant compared to the long, slender blowpipes and their ammunition of delicate, brightly feathered darts. What possible good would it be against them? None.

However, this blunt gun with its yellowed Lucite grips showing naked Japanese beauties was a focus, a straight line into the past. Slinng had begun his Singapore quest to discover the truth in the death of his father. In the end, Miri, Hartog and the voyage of the *Sulu*, Borneo—all were detours on the emotional trail of a man he really never knew. A father who exiled his son and then totally rejected him. Here was a self-confessed snob, colonialist, manager of a great hotel and, curiously, in the eyes of some a hero. He had collaborated with the Japanese for the sake of that hotel—and defied them—smuggling food to prisoners of war.

Hartog had been one of those prisoners and because of his father, brutally handled by Major Okubo. Certainly he had every right to hate Neville Slinng—but had he killed him? Slinng put the Nambu in the pocket of his ragged shorts and went looking for the king of the cannibals.

He sits soaking, knee-deep in a hollow rock basin sprayed by an erratic slipstream of water tumbling down the mountain. A waterfall blown off its course on the descent, a frizz curling out like Farrah Fawcett's late-seventies flip. It was not a waterfall or pool to inspire tropical dreams. Dottie Lamour would not appear in a sarong. Still it was a blessed relief from nattering Tantu. There were times when he thought he might go starkers with the sounds and smells of the little buggers.

They knew where he was but let him alone. They were not water babies, would not bathe and mistrusted the glassy surface of pool that showed them who they were. Now, as Lawrence Slinng comes up and stands silently behind him, his wavering image appears on the water. "Come for a scrub?" Hartog says without getting up or turning around.

Slinng hunkers down by the side of the pool and draws the Nambu pistol out of his pocket. Its barrel lengthens in the reflections. "Actually, I wanted you to have a look at this." He pointed it.

There was a long pause. Then: "Okubo's?"

"You recognize it?"

"Oh, yes, the grips."

"It was in my father's things."

"I didn't know that—but I suppose it made some kind of sad sense to him—after what happened."

"What *did* happen?"

"You know, of course, that your dad was smuggling food into Changi prison camp . . ."

"Yes, and because of him, Okubo had you beaten and your finger tips ground off."

"True enough. Neville was one of those bloody officious nits that go by the book. Everything has to be just so. Me and my mates were running that prison, seeing to the food distribution and taking our bit for managing it."

"And he turned you in to Okubo."

"He didn't understand how it worked. With our lot parceling out the smuggled goods we may have taken a skim off the top but at least the others were getting some, we controlled it. After they did me, nobody got anything. The end of the war was on the way and the Japs squeezed our rations down to a trickle. We were desperate. If it hadn't been for Sivi most wouldn't have survived."

"*Who?*"

"Why—Sivi Guan—your dad's squeeze. A beautiful little thing, a dancer."

Slinng realized he had never heard her name. "What did she have to do with it?"

"She was the one who got the food rolling again. We considered her nothing less than the bloody food fairy."

Neville Slinng took the weight on his shoulders. It had been his bungled attempt to bring justice to the food distribution that had caused the break. His influence with Major Okubo had vanished. No more card games or mah-jongg. He had withdrawn his limited friendship. It was tough on both of them. As commander of the Transport and Supplies Section he was aloof and rigid with the officers under him and did not encourage intimacy. Curiously, his social life had evolved over the occupation years into the day-to-day contact with Neville. Now he was lonesome.

Neville knew this and considered how to regain his patronage and get the food moving again. A thought occurred and he dismissed it first as caddish, reprehensible. Then going over it, he gradually reduced its status to possible, necessary and finally a noble sacrifice. Major Okubo was fastidious and correct and Neville doubted if he even visited the nearby House of Nippon Joy as did the other troops. Women were not allowed in officers' rooms at Raffles and houseboys cleaned their quarters. Still, Okubo had an eye for the erotic. He had shown Neville the clear Lucite grips for his Nambu pistol that revealed photos of naked Japanese beauties. They had been run up by a wag in the machine shop and he thought them amusing.

Neville waited until a particularly good meal of ikan merah—red snapper done with white wine—was eaten and, standing by to supervise the serving, asked, "Tell me, sir, are you interested in the classical Malay dance?"

Okubo frowned, picking his teeth behind a napkin. "What do you mean by classical?"

"I mean in the same sense as the Ballet Russe. Serious art."

"Why do you ask?"

"There is in Singapore a very great dancer. A young woman who was an artist before the war. I thought you might be interested in seeing her perform."

He thought for a moment. "You're not suggesting anything lewd or improper?"

"No, no. The dancing is done in full costume—it is very reserved. Artistic"

It was arranged for the end of the week and the major was enchanted. The dancing itself was accompanied by the rattle of gongs at a very slow beat, stylized movements appreciated only by the aficionado or tone-deaf. But Sivi's beauty transcended the dance. Moving to the sedate rhythm in the Palm Court with the pale shadows filtered across a mysterious face, eyes suggesting heavenly treats, she captivated. The major was enthralled and Neville moved his plans ahead.

Her performance became a weekly thing and she was allowed to join him afterward for tea and cakes. They sat in full view in the Palm Court while he told her about his homeland and Neville discreetly watched from the arcade. After a month of this the major wanted to show his appreciation and suggested a gift. She shyly demurred but sadly mentioned her two young brothers, foolish boys now in Changi prison. They were very thin . . .

"That's how we got back in the smuggling business," Hartog said. "And just in time. It was the summer of 'forty-five, and we knew the end of the war was near one way or another. Sivi was allowed the use of a beat-up Ford truck from Motor Transport and once a week would drive down the east coast to Changi with the scrapings of Raffles' kitchen, stale bread and cans of grease. It saved us."

"Were you still in control of who got it?"

"No, Okubo had nearly done me in. It was a long time before I could use these." He lifted his mutilated fingers clear of the water.

"You must have been very bitter against my father."

"No, I understood what he had done and why—the rule was to look out for number one. Your dad didn't put my fingers in the grinder. No, it was that bastard Okubo I was after.

"We had been getting air raids and a dud fell in the fields beyond the prison. I got it smuggled into the compound and we turned it into a bloody antipersonnel bomb. There was no shortage of demo lads in camp and they rigged it with a detonator that worked off a plunger connected to a brass hinge in the lid of a box. We turned a whiskey case into a proper chest. One of the Malay boys, a carver, did the cover and sides in rising suns and chrysanthemum mons—all that Jap cock. It was bloody marvelous, stained and hand-rubbed with wax. Inside it was fitted with lift-out trays and lined with felt. The TNT and shrapnel were concealed in the false bottom."

When Sivi came out the next time she was secretly shown the box and allowed to open and examine it. It was a present, Hartog said, for Major Okubo from the prisoners for his humane treatment and gift of food. Would she deliver it? It must be done without the knowledge of any others because it would not do for them to know the major permitted the prisoners to receive unofficial food. She agreed and when she left took the box. In the meantime the mechanism had been cocked and a wooden dowel placed in the hasp to close the lid.

At Raffles, Sivi carried the gift upstairs and, avoiding the servants, went into Major Okubo's empty quarters. She could hear the officers and men at dinner below in the Tiffin Room. She placed the box on the major's desk, carefully aligning it for the best view. A note had been pinned to the top saying that it should be opened *only* by him. She left unnoticed but at the end of the hall looked back to see his room boy enter. She turned to continue and in the next instant there was a muffled explosion and the door blew off, sending out a sheet of flame and smoke.

The hall was filled with running men, shouts and confusion. Major Okubo had hold of her wrist demanding to know what part she had played in the explosion. Badly frightened, she did her best to explain about the prisoners' gift but he only shook his head and ordered her taken to the courtyard. Neville followed and when they reached the grassy space and Okubo drew his sword, he began a desperate plea.

"Major Okubo, please! This woman knew nothing about any explosives! She did as she was told, thinking it was a favor for you—she's being used! She's too simple to be involved in any plots . . ."

"Don't you think I know that? Do you think me stupid?"

"But—"

"All attention is focused on her role and myself as commander. I must act to reinforce discipline and security right now! This minute! If I do not it will be said she made a fool of me and the army."

"But surely not to kill her!"

"Oh, yes. That is the penalty for a civilian attacking a Japanese soldier. She must be summarily executed here in front of my troops and hotel witnesses." He shifted the sword and nervously licked his lips. It was obvious he had no wish to whack the head off this beauty. The sword was not a family jewel, just a common gunto, but it was heavy and sharp. He took a step forward. Sivi knelt in the grass, head bowed, crying. The soldiers stood in a half circle in various stages of uniform, rifles lowered, all watching their commander. The air was electric with awful expectation. Around the arcade and in the windows that faced the courtyard could be seen the faces of the hotel staff, expressions held in suspension. All were lit by the flickering fire on the second floor and the shouts of those putting it out.

Neville pushed in front of Okubo and their eyes locked. "I am the one who brought her here to dance—it is my fault then—take my life."

"Oh, no. That would not do. These witnesses know better. They know who is accused here. Stand aside!"

"Not the sword then—don't take her head!"

"That is the way it is done!"

"Please! Understand! For the Malay this means he may never have peace, that his spirit will remain with his severed head. That is why headhunters take heads—to destroy an enemy's spiritual life. It is a deeply religious belief."

Okubo thought about this, then had the solution, one that would take the pressure off him and be fitting. "All right, I can understand this. She will be shot—but under one condition. You shoot her." And he undid the flap of his holster.

"*What?*" Neville had gone very pale.

He cocked the weapon and took off the safety. "That way you may atone for your role in introducing her. It is a sad but ideal solution." He handed over the gun.

Neville felt its weight in his hand and could offer no further pleas. He quickly took his place behind Sivi and carefully placed the barrel of the gun on the last knob of her spine. He did not want to ruin her face. Then he fired.

It hit him hard. A thing completely unexpected, unacceptable. *His father had shot and killed his mistress, mother of his three children.* My God. It was so out of character . . . so pitifully tragic. All those years he had dismissed him as rigid, dispassionate—then this. When they addressed each other that last time across the table at the East India Club, the son had despised him, insulting him *and* Raffles, concerned only with his own limited aims. *Would he have had the courage to shoot a woman he loved under the same circumstances?*

It occurred to him that Hartog might not be telling the truth. No, he believed him—it explained a great deal. Now he must settle the final doubts about Hartog's role in his father's death. "Before I left for Borneo I was attacked and nearly killed by a constable at Raffles. The bastard tried to throw me out the window. It was Edward Wong—Clair Wong's husband—Neville's daughter by—"

"Yes, I know."

"When I searched him I found your card with the *Sulu's* number on it."

Hartog sighed. "Yes, he came to see me about your father's death. He was concerned I might get talky—I was the only one who knew the whole story. Even that bloody blimp of a Groot didn't have it right."

"Had *what* right?"

"Clair was in the courtyard at Raffles that night."

"*Clair?*"

"Sivi had left her and the other kids there while she delivered the chest to Okubo's room. She was only—what? three or four—but she saw Neville shoot her mother."

"God."

"Yes. She never recovered. As time went on she got a fix on me. She knew my part and thought I might help work a revenge. Instead, I tried to talk her out of it. What she couldn't grasp was that in the end only you and the enemy really understand what *your* war was about and you come to cherish each other." There was another pause as he raked the white hair back with wet hands, then went on. "She had this picture imprinted on her mind and used to run it off like a bloody film—Jap soldiers with rifles, Okubo strutting about with a sword, their father pleading and their mother crouching in fear below. God! Then just when things seemed calmed down, the gun is passed to Neville and he shoots her. She could still describe the spurt of flame from the barrel, the impact, and how her head jerked when she pitched forward in the grass . . ."

Hartog picked up a bar of soap he had placed on a leaf and began to lather up. As he did the runoff spread around him in the shallow basin. Slinng, staring absently at his own reflection in the water, was startled to find it suddenly clouded.

"So when her policeman husband came out to the *Sulu* after you had arrived in Singapore—and began to question me about my contact with you—I knew right then Clair had killed him. He was protecting her. Neville didn't accidentally drown in that tub—she held him under."

There was nothing more to be said. Slinng felt a terrific letdown. The moment called for drama. Should he rear back, wind up and let fly—give it all he had and throw the fatal gun as far as he could, wing it off into the jungle? It was the sort of thing they did in films. Or should he place the barrel at the back of Hartog's head and blow his brains out? After all, he was the cause of his troubles, why he was here. And in spite of his humanity in his father's case, it was clear he was prepared to let the rest of them be eaten by the Tantu.

In the end he put the weapon in his pocket and walked away. Behind him he could hear Hartog splashing in his bath.

27

IN THE NEXT DAYS they collect food, sago cakes and cans of sardines, Beluga caviar stolen away from Hartog's hoard. These are hidden in the packs with water gourds and cans of soda. But the problem is Arrowjoy. He has improved to the point of awareness but his left arm and leg are still useless. They get him up and try short walks in the longhouse but it is impossible. His leg drags and both Slinng and Luke have to support him.

"It's not going to work, tuan. We'll have to carry him down that mountain."

"No, no, he's going to make it on his own—come on, Arrowjoy, think that leg! Imagine it walking!" But it is no good and the three of them collapse, pouring sweat. The Tantu enjoy the walking sessions. Their idea of fun is watching Arrowjoy staggering along, kids running after him, dogs barking.

Slinng thought about it and remembered that stroke victims often had a brace, a splint. He set about making one, splitting bamboo and binding it up with rattan to Arrowjoy's leg. It helped, and with a stick for a cane, he began to make progress. Each day he would set out down the room swinging the leg like a dead weight, one half of his face contorted with the effort, the other half slack. Hartog came in and was amused. "Well, by God, here's a man determined to walk to the barbie. Good for you."

"We're walking out of here, Hartog," Slinng said. "Count on it."

"If you do, mate, it'll be in someone's belly."

By the end of the week they were ready. Slinng would not wait until one more Iban was killed and eaten. "We're going tonight," he said to Luke.

"Oh, Jesus boy, I do not think I'm ready for this."

"Yes, you are! There's a full moon and if the sky is clear, I'll be able to find my bearings and navigate the jungle." He leaned in to Arrowjoy. "Do you understand what I'm saying?"

"Go!" The word exploded.

"All right. Damn straight!" Laughing for the first time since they arrived.

Hartog lies in his hammock drinking and entertaining the Tantu. They are gathered around him. Warriors laugh and stamp their feet as he does his act, mothers nurse babies, the old people rock on haunches smoking, and kids scamper about: the headhunter as a family. Hartog has the plastic head cradled in his arm and in a high tenor voice asks it questions in his limited trade Malay. Then, answering in baritone English, he shakes the head to add motion. They don't understand a word but are exhilarated by the sounds and acting. It is a new dimension in storytelling for them and they insist on a performance each night. This hammock is as close as they come to the concept of a chief's throne. While Hartog goes on, a thin young girl lies alongside him playing with his penis. She stretches out his testicles and holds up the flaccid shaft for the admiration of other young girls. They are awed at its great size.

This last night, Slinng watched the performance from a distance, leaning against one of the center posts that supported the roof. From here the profiles of the Tantu were sharply defined. They looked up toward Hartog with complete attention, their expressions expectant—the look seen on the faces of children watching television.

Sadly their only skills were hunting and body painting. Unlike the Iban they were not wood carvers or builders; their women did not weave, sew, make pottery—and beyond the use of wild sago flour, cooking consisted of scorching meat. The loghouse they occupied had been built by another tribe long since vanished. Slinng remembered the storyteller saying they lived in trees as apes. He thought that once might have been possible. They were still in the Stone Age and here came Hartog with his talking head to bring them the TV age.

Slinng gestured to Luke and they entered the group, squatting down, Luke sitting on his sax case. "Sorry you missed the act," Hartog said from his hammock. "All those years of watching rotten ventriloquists on the telly have paid off. The secret of keeping an audience is to keep giving them the same thing. People hate to be surprised in life or entertainment."

"What's this? Show-biz philosophy among the cannibals? I'm beginning to believe you're actually enjoying yourself!"

Hartog frowned. Slinng's tone was . . . different; something was up. "Why wouldn't I? It's the ultimate experience! I've been everywhere—done everything—shoved whatever they had up my nose and kazoo, spent a fortune trying to amuse myself. And nothing even remotely compares to this! Bloody hell, I couldn't even get it up without doing some pretty weird things—here weird is a way of life. If you want sex as it was originally intended, try one of these wild beauties, they will lead you back to Eve's bed." However, he removed the girl's hand from his penis. "Easy, dear. You're going to wear the bloody thing out."

"So you've turned the clock back to the Stone Age and discovered the heart of darkness is man's primitive soul—if you'll forgive the hyperbole—that his beastly nature is the secret that he hides from himself; that anything is permissible if you are to survive."

"I didn't know that was a secret."

"I'll tell you what I think," Slinng said, and looking at him, Hartog grew increasingly uneasy, realizing that he was being challenged, that whatever happened would end in violence. "I believe you *deliberately* came here, Hartog, to this place. That whole elaborate scheme about the *Sulu* and the insurance was just the excuse. You had no intention of going back to your zillion acres of outback. You were going to be the White Raj, the jungle king, the god. When we first met you were caught up with the idea, on fire with it. Remember? You made it happen."

"No," Hartog said evenly. "There is no way I could have planned this . . ."

"I agree . . . but somewhere along the line a few nuts and bolts came loose and the idea took hold. You've climbed the tree and joined the savages . . . up here." He tapped his head. They looked at each other for a long moment, Slinng squatting on the floor, Hartog in the hammock. "But the problem is, what happens when you run out of Yoo-Hoo and the batteries go dead? When your act dries up? How are you going to entertain them then?"

Another pause. Their eyes were on each other as though no one else was in the room. "Well . . . how about this?" Hartog asked. "When the last Iban is eaten and stomachs begin to rumble I've thought of a diversion for you three. Instead of a crude cookout I'll suggest that we might take a tongue out here, an ear there—work our way up from your fingers and toes to small parts, then the limbs. That way I might be able to keep you alive as long as possible, and if you like, you might dine on yourselves—so to speak." He laughed. "I think the Tantu might find that entertaining."

Slinng laughed with him, then suddenly jumped up, startling Hartog and causing the Tantu to shift in expectation. Although understanding nothing, they followed each man's facial expression carefully. "I agree. If it's entertainment these folks want let's provide some." He very slowly reached down and picked up a parang, smiling at the warriors and winking as Hartog might. Straightening, he suddenly tossed the blade in the air, catching it by its sharp edge when it came down. There was a gasp of appreciation. Next he flipped it behind his back and caught it between his legs. More squeals.

"Cute," Hartog said tightly.

"It's the kind of thing every kid in Singapore practiced in the school yard. I did. It helps if you hide a piece of bamboo in your hand. I used to trot it out aboard ship or in bars to win bets. Now—you talked about cutting us up in small parts. I like the idea of intimate hors d'oeuvres. But I think to spice it up we should have a little knife action like those chefs at Benihana." He reached down and picked up another parang. "Here is what I propose. That you and I give them a preview. Each of us takes a turn and whack something off the other. A finger say, or a nose to put on the barbie—surely you brought cocktail toothpicks from the *Sulu?* No?" He pressed the parang on Hartog. "Who'll go first?"

"Why in hell would I do that?"

"Because I'm challenging you in front of the tribe. Isn't that what they do in jungle films?"

"Get the hell away from me! The joke's off!"

"Not quite." Slinng swung one blade in a showy arc, making it sing and missing Hartog by inches. He bailed out of the hammock with the girl, flopping on the floor and sending the dust up. The Tantu laughed, enjoying this. In the next swipe Slinng brought the parang around and cut the rope on the hammock. One end dipped and the bullhorn bounced onto the floor.

It was very quiet now. He had their attention. "That will conclude our main show, I think, but we should have some music for the finale."

"Slinng!" Hartog said in a low growl. Getting up and shaking the girl off, he straightened to his full height. But he had lost the stage to Slinng, who now turned toward Luke, squatting on his sax case.

"Cool Han, these people haven't heard you blow. Why don't you get your sax out and lay a number on them?"

Hartog took a step forward. "I'm warning you . . ."

"With *what?* When a person is slated to be chopped up and eaten by cannibals, what do you threaten them with?" Hartog took another step. "But if you move one more foot I'm going to chop your toes off." This was said smiling. "What do you bet they'd enjoy that?" Hartog stopped.

Luke unsnapped the case and got the sax out. There was an intake of breath at the brightly chromed instrument with its complication of disks, valves and the elegant sweep of bell. They had no idea what it was, and when Luke wet the reed down with his lips, thought it might be a marvelous pipe for smoking.

"Tell you what, Cool Han, why don't we have a little amplification? A sound system." And he picked up the bullhorn. Turning the switch to high, he laid its mouthpiece in front of the sax's big bell. "Go get 'em! Blow!"

Luke drew his breath in, expanded his cheeks and blew. At the first sustained honk the floor actually vibrated. It was a sound louder than the blast of an airhorn, segueing into the trumpeted shrill of a bull elephant. Coming as it did, totally unexpected and (for them) out of nowhere, it literally blew the Tantu back. Panic followed terror and in minutes they had leaped out of the open sides of the longhouse: the ferocious warriors, women, children, hobbling old, all cleared out.

Slinng found it amusing and while he laughed and Luke blew, Hartog shouted at the Tantu that it was a trick! To come back! But he couldn't be heard and by now they had disappeared into the jungle. When Luke was out of breath and sat panting, Slinng and Hartog still faced each other. "Now," Slinng said, "we're going."

"Oh, no! Not me. I stay here. They'll catch up to you in an hour."

"Not if your head goes along."

"You'll have to kill me first and carry my body down that mountain. Are you prepared to do that?"

"No. What I have in mind is this." He spoke very softly, holding Hartog's eyes. "I'm going to cut your head off and take *it* down the mountain—that's the head I meant. It will serve just as well as a plastic one, I think—I'll tell the authorities that the Tantu did it, of course." Hartog understood then that he absolutely meant what he said.

They pulled their packs on and got Arrowjoy up and moving. Standing in the clearing, Slinng looked up at the stars. It was a familiar seaman's world. He had no sextant now to shoot it, but he had his compass and a dead-reckoning position could be determined by checking the leading star of Orion's Belt which rose east to west. It did this at essentially the same angular distance, and true south was midway between. Compass error would be the average rising and setting azimuths compared with 180. From this he would establish a rough position line—checking it as they went—if he could find a break in the jungle.

They came past the fire, dying out now, walking at Arrowjoy's pace, Hartog leading, Slinng behind him, Luke bringing up the rear. He'd left the sax case behind and the instrument was carried over his shoulder like a rifle. To their right were the blankets of palm leaves the Iban lay under. They slept on, paralyzed—silent. Slinng could not bear to look in that direction. If any were to be saved it depended on *his* navigation, their speed down the mountain. Then, single file, they plunged into the jungle and were enveloped.

The Tantu waited until they were gone before emerging from the jungle on the opposite side of the clearing. They stood for a long while looking after the spot where the man with the head had disappeared. They were puzzled. Finally, the warriors broke off to follow, their long blowpipes bobbing.

It was impossible to tell how long it would take to get down the mountain. If it were measured in pain, exhaustion or sheer determination, then it might be forever. Or it might be never. They traveled day and night, dropping when they could no longer go on, eating the God-awful sago cakes washed down by tepid Yoo-Hoo. Only one thing made it possible to continue—going downhill. Still this was dangerous: slides and falls, faces and legs whipped by sharp grasses, knees scarred on sharp rocks, wrenching sprains. The smells and temperature changed with the altitude and the air became warm, sending off the sharp stench of rot. Orchids curled up dead trees and the wind brought flowers down from the treetops, petals spinning like tiny autogiros.

Slinng did his navigation, taking sightings at night and by day using his watch: pointing the hour hand toward the sun and drawing a line between it and the twelve-o'clock position to indicate north. But now more and more he followed signs he'd been taught on hunting trips with the Iban, looking for footprints or a chopped vee where a parang had whacked a tree on the way up. When they got lost he would patiently retrace their steps to a spot he had marked and try again. By now he had confidence in his instincts and had begun to read the jungle as he had the sea.

The Tantu did not show themselves but no one doubted they were there. One early evening as they lay sprawled on the ground trying to recover their wind there were odd sounds and Slinng clicked on the bullhorn while Luke blew a long blast. Then, hideous squeals and the air above them exploded with the bodies of flying foxes, bats. They had been hanging, head down, from the trees all day and now filled the patch of sky like black rags, gliding from tree to tree, complaining, snarling, showering those beneath them with guano. If there were Tantu out there, they now knew where the prey was.

Slinng carried Arrowjoy the last three days. He simply gave out, could not go on. It had been amazing that he lasted as long as he had. They lashed his wrists together, and arms around Slinng's neck he was half carried, half dragged on his back. Their pace had slowed to a crawl with frequent rests, collapsing, until the time became a blur. They sat numb with fatigue and only when Slinng got up would they reluctantly follow. No one wanted to be left behind. Then on the last day Slinng didn't get up.

It's over, he thinks. Food has run out and from that Slinng calculates they have passed the lava bed. Missed it. Well, what were the chances of finding one particular acre in the middle of several million? Not good. They sit propped against trees, Arrowjoy flat out on the ground. He has failed, he tells himself. There isn't the strength in them to go another mile. He puts his head back against the tree and is too tired to brush the flies off his face. A breeze comes up growing to gusts and he remembers the blow that toppled giant trees and killed a man. *Who cares?*

He begins to squirm as insects discover him. Ants now crawl up his legs investigating a food source, detouring around leeches. How long will it take them, and a zillion other kinds, to reduce his body to bones? One day? Two? Suddenly the thought of being consumed alive by insects fills him with dread: beetles, maggots; the delicate touch of a butterfly, powered wings fluttering, tongue exploring his eyeball: all unacceptable, more horrible than being snapped up and swallowed by the croc. *God!* He pinches his nose as a fly tickles. When you can no longer defend yourself they will crawl in every body opening . . . swarm over you . . . the pistol is still in the pack. The Nambu . . . *What was that?* He opens his eyes, then shuts them. He thinks about the gun for a minute but is too tired to find it, go through the bother of killing himself . . . the bugs can have him . . . *there it goes again.* What . . .? And then he has it. *Damn!* Shoving himself up, smacking off the bugs, staggering, bracing against the tree. "Listen!" His voice is hoarse; none of them have had the energy to really speak for days. "Don't you know what that is?!" He lurches around, kicking Hartog, then Luke. "Come on, God damn it! Get your asses up! *What is that? Tell me!*"

28

"GET UP, DAMN IT!" Slinng laid about him, kicking Hartog and Luke until he finally worried them up on their feet. "Come on, hurry up! Help me with Arrowjoy!" Stumbling like drunks they hoisted him up on Slinng's back and staggered after him as he broke the way downhill. Using his body as a ram, he kept moving. On his back, Arrowjoy's feet dragged behind like a travois, cutting a groove in the damp soil. "Don't you hear that? Are you deaf?" Neither answered, too worn out to talk. Nothing mattered but putting one foot in front of the other. The sound was a high-pitched squeak that varied with the force of the breeze. It was mechanical.

Slinng navigated by its sound, stopping every few yards to get his bearings, praying the wind wouldn't drop off. It was early morning and when the density of light began to increase, sending shafts slanting through the trees ahead, he knew he was going in the right direction. Then suddenly they broke out onto the lava field and stopped, unable to believe they had made it. Ragged figures squinted against the sun as it cut across the bare clearing. The wind lifted a fine sifting of ashes from dead fires, sending it scooting across the bones to greet them. The packs of supplies were still at the far end of the bed—and dead ahead was the burned-out helicopter. Its rotor blades were into the wind and as they went around, free-wheeled, the unoiled gears made the squeaking sound.

They crossed over to the supplies, ruined boots slapping on the hard flat surface, knees buckling, awkward after the days of navigating the soft, uneven jungle terrain. Ripping the tarp off the food left for the trip back, they sank down and ate. Shoveling in rice and pig fat, boxes of biscuits, washing it down with tepid water. Then they flopped back against the packs, panting, eyes squeezed shut against the glare of sun after the deep shade of the rain forest. Finally, Slinng roused himself and pushing up, uncased the transmitter and got it working. Watching the output meter he began a low-power tune-up, nursing the batteries. Twisting the dial on the antenna, loading from coarse to fine, he went on full gain, sending from the frequencies Arrowjoy had taped on the front of the set. He repeated the call letters, adjusting the gain, but got no answer. It was a powerful transmitter, one hundred watts with bands from 160 through ten meters, and he should be getting out. At last there was an answer, garbled, then in the clear from the MFS Base at Bakenu. The voice was maddeningly casual, and speaking in a Malaysian accent asked for coordinates. Slinng repeated these. Then: "This is Arrow-One, we have an emergency! Repeat! Emergency! We have wounded men and need immediate medical evacuation! Do you read me?!"

"Are you sure?!"

"Am I sure? God damn it, man! We have been under attack by headhunters! We have three dead and nine more including us who will be if you don't get here right now!"

There was a long frustrating pause and Bakenu came back on. "Sorry, Arrow-One, but the only helicopter we have of a size to make that run up the mountain is at Victoria Island on typhoon patrol. It will take time to recall. Over."

"Well, do it! Get going! The bastards are out there! They're going to attack at any moment!"

"We'll do our best, Arrow-One. Keep your transmitter set at the following band and continue on-hour signals at this frequency." He gave Slinng homing coordinates for the helicopter. When they were finished he said, "Bakenu signing off—have a good day."

Slinng stared at the receiver. *"Have a good day?"*

He heard Luke laughing. "It is funny what is funny, tuan. I can't remember when I last had a good day."

"That makes two of us." He got up, taking a parang. "Come on, we've got to make some shade." They went to the edge of the jungle and cut poles. As they did they kept an eye out, expecting any minute to feel the sting of a dart.

"Are those people there now?" Luke asked.

"I don't know," Slinng said honestly. "We probably won't know until it's too late."

They carried the poles back and tying the tarp to them arranged a sun screen. Slinng took some of the water and cleaned Arrowjoy up, washing his face gently. He was beginning to put together words but it was painful. "S-sorry . . . uh . . . I can't do . . . for myself . . ."

"No, no. I'm the one who's sorry, desperately sorry. You were right, of course, about coming up here—the Tantu. I've caused us all a lot of grief. It was, well, my obsession with . . . Miri." He spoke her name softly. "Refusing to believe she was dead . . . I still find that hard to accept. I hope you can understand."

"No . . ." Slinng looked at him, but he went on. "Nobody . . . put a gun to . . . my head." He closed his eyes, tired out with the effort of speaking.

Slinng looked at Hartog, wondering if he was all right. He hadn't said a word in days, dragging his tall frame along like a zombie. He was so gaunt you could see his ribs. It was amazing he had come through at all—the man was up in his sixties but still fit, tough. With the sweat and rain his body paint had run together in a blurry smear that looked like camouflage. He wore a pair of filthy ragged shorts and heavy jungle boots. Like the rest of them his body was covered with scratches, cuts and insect bites, calves stippled with bloody marks from leeches. His head was back against the packs, eyes closed.

"Hartog—are you all right?"

He laughed, a deep rumbling sound. "Oh, hell, yes, bloody perfect. Whizzo."

"There's some water here and disinfectant if you want to wash up."

Hartog opened his eyes and looked at him. "What for? What possible difference would it make? We'll all be toes-up by sundown." And he sagged back, closing his eyes. Slinng was ready to turn away when he said, "You know, in the end they got him, too. Nothing turned out as he had imagined. Nobody really understood the great thing he'd done. All they went on about was bloody scratch. They thought that was what he was after, too. Nothing like it. He spent his fortune here and never got it back. We're alike in that, you know. Back home the bozo looking after his affairs was screwing him—another Blas—and then the government started in on him like they did on me."

"Who . . .?"

"They charged him with cruel and illegal conduct. Got that? Because he went after the bloody pirates, the Iban, sent them running . . ."

"Are you talking about the Brooke Rajah?"

"Can you imagine it? He risks his life going against a bunch of murdering dogs and gets slapped on the wrist, called cruel, for God's sake. What in hell did they know? Sitting safe at home in powdered wigs, fingers up their arses. He was cleared—but never forgave the bastards—never trusted the bloody government again. He had wanted to turn over Sarawak, have it included in the British Empire, but they refused—there wasn't enough knicker in it for them. After all that he had done they cut him off. I know exactly how he felt, the whole rotten bunch ganged up on me, too."

Slinng wasn't sure what response was expected. In his recital of the Brooke Rajah's career, Hartog was evidently drawing parallels with his own. "Is that right," he finally said.

"He finally went back to England worn out by the bastards. The family was in a snit as usual and he was looked after for a while by a lady who had helped him with his cash flow. Then when another old girl showed up to visit, the two of them got in a fight over him. Can you imagine it? These two biddies fighting over the old boy? Anyway it must have been too much for him because he stroked out and gave up the ghost. There was a squabble in the family, of course, over who was to inherit what, and in the end, the nephew who had changed his name to Brooke got Sarawak. When his heir, Vyner, finally turned the country over to the Brits after the war, the bloody British lion was a pussy and they couldn't hang on to it. It was too late.

"And what about the people? The Malays he rescued from piracy and headhunters, the ones he protected from the exploiters? Did they even remember his name six months later? Not bloody likely." He laughed softly. "After all I did for my little buggers—introducing them to Yoo-Hoo and flashlights, giving them a music hall turn with my talking head—are they going to remember me? Who the hell cares! So what! I was a White Raj, too, for a while, King of the Cannibals, the Big Wazoo . . . in the land of the blind the one-eyed man is king . . . that was me, by God . . ."

"Hartog, what you are is an opportunist, a crook and a murderer. Worse, you encouraged your poor little buggers to take heads and eat other humans, so you could play king." But Hartog wasn't listening. His head had flopped back and his eyes were closed.

. . .

By late afternoon Slinng had begun calling the MFS air base in Bakenu on the half hour—forget the batteries, soon it wouldn't matter. But this time he got a different operator, and the whole procedure had to be repeated, sorted out, his request passed down the line once again. The helicopter, a big Sikorsky S-65 heavy transport, had been finally redirected from Victoria Island, but first it had to refuel for the long trip. ETA was not yet calculated.

Slinng tried to keep the frustration and anger out of his voice. "Listen! It's got to arrive here before dark! Repeat—*before dark!* It will be difficult enough to find this location even with a homing signal in the daylight! It would be impossible at night—*and we cannot hold out another day!*"

"Confirm. I will pass your message up. Have a good day. Over."

"How would you like to take your . . .!"

"Maybe the Tantu aren't out there," Luke said, fingering the sax silently. "We haven't seen any sign of them."

"I told you, we won't until sundown," Hartog answered, eyes still shut. "The little buggers hate the sun. They've lived their whole lives in the shade of the forest. They attacked my bunch at sundown."

Luke looked toward the angle of the sun as it dropped to the top of the tree line.

"About an hour," Slinng said, answering the unspoken question.

"There they are, mates." Hartog was alert now, sitting with arms resting on his upturned knees. "Dinner may be a little early tonight." He laughed.

Slinng jerked his head up. From their position at the bottom of the slope, they looked to where the lava bed rose to meet the edge of the jungle, then connect with the mountain. As they watched, the Tantu emerged from the curtain of green. The sun was behind the tree line now, filtered through the top branches, light dancing, then fading. They were visible in the twilight, twenty-five of them moving slowly ahead, painted bodies, the long blowpipes held out, the bob of feathered head crests. They were still too far to send a dart on the wind—about a football field's length away—but a dozen more yards would make the difference.

"Luke! Get on that horn!" And he scrambled up, already fingering the keys. Slinng clicked on the bullhorn, positioning its mouthpiece in front of the sax bell. Luke drew his breath in, puckered up and blew—but the sound in the open was not nearly as effective. It wavered off-key, hesitant.

He's sounding his fear, Slinng thought. Still, at its shrill notes the Tantu retreated back to the edge of jungle where they stood and waited.

Hartog jumped up and waving his arms began shouting, *"Come on, you ninnies! Come and get them! Here! Now! We'll have them on the barbie tonight!"* He was laughing. *"Come on! My kee medai! Don't be afraid!"*

Slinng got him by the arm and jerked him down. "You damn fool! Shut up or I swear I'll break your . . ." Furious, fist cocked back, it occurred to him Hartog was an old man nearly his father's age. Looking at him, just then, at that instant, it *was* his father. He drew back.

The Tantu understood little of what Hartog shouted but his sounds and gestures were enough. Encouraged, they came forward again, faster this time.

For all the delay the rescue team had come well-prepared. There were two Chinese medics and a half squad from the First Infantry Battalion, PDF (People's Defense Force). They were in full battle gear, berets, camouflage jumpsuits, and armed with automatic weapons. The pilot was British, on detached training service, and the copilot Malaysian, one of his students. Both were uneasy because a sudden twenty-four-hour weather alert had put a monsoon in their area. It was moving with the Indian monsoon current, coming down across Sumatra toward the southern end of Borneo. Following the homing signals from the Arrow-One transmitter they had let down to one thousand meters for a visual sighting of the clearing. If they were caught out by the expected torrential rain and the rotors filled and stalled, they would be unable to restart them at this altitude and 33,484 pounds of S-65 helicopter would drop in the jungle like an anvil.

Worse, they had been unable to raise Arrow-One on their transmitter. Either they had gone off the air or the poor bastards had been done in. The pilot, Gillies, tried again, his mustache working like a rabbit's whiskers. "Arrow-One, Arrow-One! Do you read me? This is Air-Vac Six, come in." No answer. He tried again on another band with the same results. "Looks like the evac is off the blower. Damn. Even with the homing signal we're not going to find that bald patch in all this bloody flora until we're right pork, on top of it. Our daylight's going too. B-a-d, bad!"

The weather came on from Bakenu and the two pilots raised their eyebrows. It was serious. "Bloody hell." If they turned back now they would still only have an hour to clear the front. "I'll tell them we're going to abort." They could not risk the helicopter and the lives of the crew. And who knew what they would find? That is, if they could find it. "This is Air-Vac Six, Bakenu. No contact. Repeat, no contact. We are return-ing to base, over."

The Tantu were nearly in striking distance, strung out in a vee. The bravest warrior was on point and when he raised his blowpipe the others came up, tubes presented like lances, spear points gleaming. Now they began to chant, a low hooting sound like the gibbon. *"Houu! Houu! Houu! Houu! Houu!"*

Slinng fumbled Hartog's plastic head out of his pack and holding it by the hair doused it with kerosene from the can they carried for a single Coleman lantern. Jumping up, he jerked one of the poles out from under the shade tarp. Luke was still playing the sax in sputtering, short bursts. The Tantu were halfway down the slope now, blowpipes raised. "They're going to dart you!" Hartog said, laughing again, beating the lava with the flat of his hand in a loud smacking sound, keeping time with their hoots. "You're going to be on the barbie tonight, mates—how would you like yourself done? Medium, rare or well?"

"Oh, boy, tuan, oh, boy . . ." Luke stopped playing and crouched down behind the packs, gripping his sax.

Slinng jammed the head on the end of the pole and lit it off. The resins exploded in flames and sent up a dense greasy smoke. He then held it up and began to wave it slowly back and forth. As the fire grew hotter the plastic melted down, eye sockets elongating, sagging, until the glass eyeballs bubbled to the surface in a stare. Finally, the white hair caught, and fanned by the waving motion, blazed up, flapping like a bird in flames. Imitating Hartog's voice, Slinng shouted, *"Obat! Obat! Magic! Magic! My ke put koo!* Don't shoot me!" The sight of Hartog's talking head burning stopped the Tantu in their tracks. A sound went up from them like the rush of wind.

"Look at that! Six o'clock!" the pilot shouted, turning the helicopter on its own axis in a shuddering buffet of wind. The last streak of sunset was reflected on the Plexiglas bubble of canopy, traveling in a complete circle. Below, a thin line of smoke rose barely a quarter of a mile away.

There was no movement of air and its path upward was straight as a string. In the next minute the big machine came over the crown of hill filling the sky and began to let down in a furious whacking of blades. As it did, the Tantu turned, and ran for the edge of the jungle. Getting into the clearing was a tight fit and the pilot had to descend at an angle on the slope, blades tilted, fanning the ground and sending the ashes of old fires up in furious plumes.

The instant the S-65 landed, the starboard door flopped down and the squad of PDF were out and formed a perimeter, automatic weapons pointed toward the jungle where the Tantu had disappeared. The sergeant used hand signals and they stayed in place holding their fire. The two medics were out next and met the survivors as they hobbled toward the helicopter. Arrowjoy was helped up through the door and Luke next. Slinng had turned toward Hartog, behind him, when Hartog suddenly broke away.

Later it seemed to Slinng it had been run off in slow motion, a silent horror film or perhaps one of his bad dreams. Hartog is away and running, long body stretching out, the white hair stringing back, dodging past the startled soldiers, running downhill to where the Tantu have vanished. His mouth is open, shouting after them, exhorting them to come back! Kill the thing! Wipe out the bastards! Slinng looks toward the pilot in his Plexiglas bubble and sees he is shouting, too. A warning. The terrific noise creates the illusion of a silent film, erases human sound. As Hartog continues, Slinng realizes what the pilot is shouting about.

In the next instant it happens.

Because of the downhill angle, the blades are about five feet off the ground on one side, rotating, slicing the air, and Hartog runs straight into them. The first whacks his head off and the second punts it in a long loop into the jungle where it drops behind the green curtain. There's a second's horrified disbelief, then Slinng and the sergeant dash after his body, and ducking down, drag it back, neck pumping blood. They hoist it into the helicopter with difficulty, trailing a red smear, and before the door is up the pilot lifts off.

Below them in the deep shade, the Tantu creep forward and look down at the head. It has landed nearly at their feet, face-up in the grass, and they see a last flickering expression, a movement in one of the dead eyes that seems to be a wink. Reaching down, a warrior gently picks the head up, then, stretching his arms, holds it aloft so that Hartog might watch his spirit depart.

Slinng squeezes himself between the pilots, urgently explaining about the Iban left behind. He has the position coordinates in his head, he says, to navigate to the Tantu longhouse. "Look," the British pilot answers in his command voice. "You people are bloody lucky we got *you* out. Leave it at that! We've got a monsoon chasing our tail. I'm going to clear this area, now! Do you understand?!"

"No," Slinng continues in a tone which gives the pilot pause. "I'm sorry, but I don't think *you* understand. *We* are going to get those Iban out of there—one way or another."

The pilot looks at him quickly. The man *does* have a pistol in his belt, but makes no move toward it, hands on the back of the seats. No, it's his appearance: filthy, bearded, face scratched, scabs—and the smell coming off him—but really it is all in the eyes. Red-rimmed, unpredictable. Probably off his head at this point, willing to do anything. He remembers his terrorist scenario: Don't fight it. "All bloody right! Jesus! We might as well find a flea on a bloody elephant!"

But Slinng knows what he is doing, and following the stars still visible in the skies ahead, they navigate up the mountain. Behind them the broad, black front of the monsoon moves in, rolling the stars up. An hour later they approach his fix on the Tantu kampong. Incredible, he thinks. It had taken them how many mean days to travel these few miles? Days that seemed endless. Vicious days, wringing them out, and nearly doing them in. Now, here they are in a nearly effortless flight

"I'd put down," he instructs the pilot. "The longhouse should be coming up."

The pilot does as he is told but with raised eyebrows that say, "Not bloody likely." But amazingly, there it is! A brief clearing and the stretch of building surrounded by a sea of black jungle. Powerful landing lights are switched on and they come in over the longhouse in one pass, wheels nearly touching, blowing the atap off the roof in a flurry of dried grasses that fills the air. In the beam of lights, Slinng sees the Tantu, women, kids and the old, pour out of the building, mice flushed by a cat, streaking for the jungle, terrorized.

They land and the door is snapped down. "Go! Go! Go!" the pilot shouts and with Slinng leading, Luke and the medics following, they jump down and run past the staked Gurkha heads to where the Iban lie darted under palm leaf covers. They are hoisted up, limbs flopping, put over shoulders in a fireman's carry, others on stretchers. Carrying them back, Slinng is surprised to see the troops torching the longhouse. Tins of gasoline are poured and they race back and forth lighting it off. Last, the Gurkha skulls are tossed in and they climb back aboard, hands shielding faces against the fierce heat.

As the helicopter takes off, creating an updraft of air, the blades fan the flames and the interior becomes a roaring inferno. Ancient wood and mats explode in a combustion that will level the building in an hour. Inside, the blaze consumes the main room and reaching up, incinerates the rattan tying together the long lines of skulls on the beams, burning along like a fuse. As this happens they begin to drop into the flames one by one, then in dozens and finally in concert until the beam, too, comes down in a shower of sparks, and the fire turns white-hot, reducing everything to ash.

As the big machine climbs into the night skies, navigation lights blink and the thumping whack of its blades beats like thunder against the air. Twisting around, Slinng looks down and is startled to see animals silhouetted in the tree tops, lit by the vivid flames. Then he realizes they are the Tantu.

29

COMING INTO CHANGI AIRPORT, city towers drenched in sunlight, one would think the dark of the rain forest was eons away, but it's only a wink away. All Lawrence Slinng had to do was close his eyes. He was left with nightmares, daytime hallucinations—a fever came and went, making him wonder if he had contracted some obscure tropical disease. But he knew better, knew he had contracted the disease of fear, primitive fear. If Conrad had melodramatically written about fear of the

unknown in *Heart of Darkness*—the horror that lurked in the depth of
man's soul—then Slinng had come face-to-face with it. It was *not* unknown to him. What had begun as adventure, romance, had ended in
horror, violence and guilt. Men had been killed and injured because he
had to untangle the cloud surrounding his father's death; *had* refused to
believe a girl was dead.

The helicopter evacuated survivors to Kuching, where an ambulance
van took them to the Sarawak General Hospital. There they were
treated for exhaustion, malnutrition and, in the case of Arrowjoy and
the Iban, severe toxic poisoning. Slinng and Luke were released four
days later and said good-bye to Arrowjoy. He was improving and his
wife would join him to continue therapy. He felt he had to make a
speech. "I deplore . . . what happened . . ." He picked among the
words in a halting voice. ". . . I blame you . . . and I blame
myself . . . I wanted to find that damn boat . . . but . . ." He clasped
Slinng's hand, tears filled his eyes. ". . . You brought . . . us out . . .
me on your back . . . not many men could . . . have done that . . ."

The Iban had come around from their loss of time as though it had
not occurred, and, as the doctor said, smiling, seemed well rested. They
appeared recovered but it remained to be seen if there was brain damage
or other ill effects. They would be kept for tests. Slinng passed among
them to thank each man and give him a hundred-dollar bill. These they
rolled up tightly and stuck in the loop of earlobes. It was impossible for
Slinng to hide his emotion at the parting but they were distant, wary.
A shadow had fallen between cultures.

Hartog's body had been removed to Arrowjoy's District Office and
placed in the frozen meat locker. He, Arrowjoy, would personally supervise identification and final dispersal of the remains. As they left the
rambling one-story structure Slinng looked at his hospital bill. Four days
came to twenty-five dollars.

While they waited for their flights, a hard rain hammered down on the
corrugated tin roof of the airport Quonset hut, sounding like a machine
gun. Slinng and Luke sat at a table with a fly-specked top drinking Peking
Four Star Beer. Plans had been made. Luke was flying to Tokyo. Slinng
had advanced him money and a letter to a friend, Masaki Iizuka, a
producer with links to the popular music world. Slinng would go back
to Singapore to report to Colonel Pynge-Gilbert before returning to his

ship in Hong Kong. Word of the *Sulu*'s fate and Hartog's death had not been leaked yet and it was his intention to be clear of the country when it was.

Luke's connecting flight left first and they said good-bye in the rain. Slinng would visit Kim in the hospital and relay to the family Sing what had happened and where he was. Waving, Luke jogged toward the small plane, carrying the sax wrapped in a plastic garbage bag. At the door under the wing he looked back, and seeing Slinng's expression, shouted, "Hey, man! Lighten up! Things could be worse!" How, Slinng wondered? Soon he would find out. And then Luke was gone, climbing aboard.

When he arrived at the customs desk in Singapore's crowded terminal a man from Constabulary Central was waiting, politely asking if Captain Slinng might come along to clear up a bit of confusion. An official car was double-parked outside and he was handed into the back seat while the constable slid behind the wheel. In the back, Slinng found himself next to a man in his sixties with a full head of graying hair and a marvelous mahogany complexion.

"Captain Slinng, I'm Inspector Swee."

"Yes, of course."

The car moved through the tangle of traffic to exit at Upper Changi Road and the city highway. Slinng put his head back against a starched antimacassar, eyes half shut, and had a view of the constable's back, white cotton gloves at the correct steering-wheel position. The sun seemed very bright through the windshield and the shine of glass particularly painful to his eyes.

"I've tried to follow your course since you first arrived in the city," Swee began. "It hasn't been easy. Did you know you were identified twice by the same nurse at Keppel Road Hospital? Unusual." When Slinng didn't answer he went on. "The second time involved the shooting of a young Chinese girl. She claimed to have been kidnapped by unknown persons. And can you believe this? There in that same place were two of the Ah Kong recovering from a motorbike accident. All swear they never heard of you or each other. Much busy misinformation."

There was a pause as they continued on, and the glare on the windshield began to separate into vivid spots. He thought for a moment he was going to pass out.

"Are you ill?" The inspector unscrewed the top of a thermos, passing it over. "Try this cold tea?"

"Thank you . . ." He sipped, then rolled the cool container over his forehead. "I've been in the bush for the last few weeks—that sun . . ."

"I understand." They traveled on and when Slinng seemed recovered, Swee said, "I knew your father. Yes. My uncle worked as a cook at Raffles during the war years. He stole a few eggs and the Japanese tied him up in the Palm Garden and beat him for two days. You father cut him down, defied the Japanese and probably saved his life. Did you know that?"

"No . . . he never mentioned it."

"He was a brave man. He and Raffles belong to a time that is nearly gone. I just caught the end of it, and although we wouldn't want it back, it was a simpler period, decisions were easier to arrive at. Now it is difficult to get to the heart of any matter.

"When you arrived in Singapore I assumed it was to inquire into his death. I allowed you to stay out of respect for him. Now a thing has occurred that changes everything . . ."

"What is that?"

"One of my assistants, a Sergeant Wong, admits that he attacked you to protect his wife; that she had drowned your father. I can't tell you the anguish this causes. He was one of our brightest officers, the wife a respected person."

"She held him under scalding water with a toilet plunger!"

"Yes, yes . . . madness. Poor woman, terrible! What a tragedy! They have clever children."

"What happens now?"

"If you choose to pursue a full indictment, then you must stay over for the inquiry and testify."

"You don't recommend this?"

"It is of course for you to decide—but I must warn that you will leave yourself open for extradition to Sri Lanka. If you stay in Singapore it would be our duty then to inform ASEAN."

Well. There it was. It explained the privacy of the car and the inspector's personal attention. A deal. "If I don't appear against them, what about the Wongs?"

"She will plead guilty to a lesser offense and he will be allowed to resign. This is a pitiful matter. A family ruined, a young man's career finished."

And what about the old man's life? Is it any less valuable to him than a young man's? Who's to choose?

Swee answered for him. "May I drop you at Raffles? If you like we will see to your reservations for Hong Kong and have a car waiting to take you to Changi in the morning."

"You're very kind."

They rode in silence the rest of the way and when the car stopped at Raffles and Slinng opened the door to step out, Inspector Swee asked, "You don't remember me then?"

Slinng was puzzled. Another twist of the dragon's tail? "Have we met before?"

"I was the man who arrested you for cutting off old Raffles' head." He smiled.

Then Slinng remembered. He was the sergeant who had caught and taken him to his father, the beginning of his exile all those years ago. "No," he said, "I'm afraid I don't remember." And he did his best to smile back.

Slinng took a cab to the hospital and found Kim recovering. They sat in the sunny day room while he told her about Luke and his adventures. She was most interested in Luke's romance with the young Iban girl. "I can't believe that he would find an old-fashioned person like that to be attractive. All he talked of here was modern girls."

"There's something very appealing about an unspoiled people."

"I wouldn't call them unspoiled, I'd call them ignorant. They sit and do nothing but preen for tourists while the government and hard-working citizens must pay to subsidize their out-of-date ways."

"Well, I . . ."

"They should be brought into the modern world like the rest of us. It is not cheap to be modern and all should share the paying for it."

He changed the subject. "Are you anxious to get back to your job at Lloyd's?"

"Oh, no, I am going to return to schooling in the studying of a lawyer's profession."

"Really? That's exciting. What branch of law are you interested in?"

"The revenge branch. Since the police and politicians can't protect people against these gangs—triads—then maybe I can help ruin them by the law."

This was her only reference to her wounding and Slinng realized sadly that she was very bitter. Whatever had briefly been between them was gone. She blamed him for failing to protect her. For her, their relationship had been the old colonial one—the servant who faithfully serves the master expecting to be protected by him and, in the end, is disillusioned.

When Slinng got back to Raffles it was late and he was dead-tired. On his way to his room he found Groot alone in the dining room, eating as usual. "Larry! My God, boy, you look terrible! Down with the fever?"

"Something like that." Slinng sat down and rubbed his forehead.

"You don't drink enough, that's the problem." Groot filled a wineglass for him.

"I knew you'd have the answer."

"What's happened with the *Sulu* and all? The Colonel tells me you were out in Sarawak."

"I'll be reporting to him tomorrow before I fly out and he can give you the entire, morbid story." A thought suddenly occurred to Slinng. "Let me ask you something, Professor—it's very important to me. You know the history of the Brooke Rajahs, of course?"

"Of course."

"Was there, in this generation, a niece named Miri?"

Groot paused, fork poised at mouth, letting the gears grind. Then the walking (or sitting) encyclopedia had it. "Let's see—yes, several years ago on the anniversary of Sarawak's independence there was a special magazine section in the *Straits Times*. Pictures of the lot of them and I seem to remember there was a Miri among the current Brooke clan, a niece, yes."

"What did she look like?"

"An extraordinary beauty. That's why I remember. Remarkable blond hair."

"Thank you."

Slinng says good night and, pushing wearily up, continues on. Going through the deserted lobby, his mind is filled with her, remembering exactly how she looked, the very angles of her body, the halo of hair. Turning at the great staircase he puts his foot on the first step and stops, hearing a sound. A clicking of balls. Looking down the long corridor to the lit doorway of the billiard room, he catches a glimpse of someone playing. Someone familiar. He turns and walks slowly toward the light, not yet able to make out the figure. Then he is in the doorway and there she is, lovely body bent over the pool table, hair now cut in blond spiky tufts. Slinng is numb, finds it hard to hold back the tears, but he speaks very casually.

"We all thought you'd lost your head."

"No, just my hair—he fell in love with me." She went on playing.

"That must have been interesting."

"Yes, well, I always liked Tarzan pictures, but it didn't work out. I nagged him until he brought me back."

Slinng leans against the table, his head splitting. "Where do you go from here?"

"Why, to bed with you, I thought, for some civilized love." She makes the shot, sinks the eight ball in the side pocket.

"Let's go then," Slinng said aloud.

Another face looked up at him, smiling but wary. "I beg your pardon?"

He stepped back with an odd wave of the hand, seeing a stranger. "Sorry . . . sorry."

Turning, he went toward the broad staircase and his room. Behind him he could still hear the clicking of balls.

EPILOGUE

~~~~~~~~~~

ARROWJOY GRADUALLY RECOVERED and although he was left with a limp and a bit of a tremor, his speech returned fully. When he came back to Kapit he gathered the Iban men in from Rumah Bujana for a celebration. It was a wake, really, to honor the dead who had not returned down the Rajang. As their longboat slid up to the splintery dock he stood and waited, greeting each man solemnly as they came ashore. The headman, Salt, was there still grieving for his son, the Dreamer, and with the others walked with his head lowered as was the custom. They were dressed in their best Javanese sarongs in the traditional brown, black and white pattern. Many wore strings of tiger teeth, Salt a headdress of hornbill feathers.

At the site of the celebration, a grove of traveler's palms, gifts were presented: salt, rice, sticks of sugee, cooking oil, pigs, chickens, clothing and many thousands of ringgits. Arrowjoy explained that these gifts had been sent by the white dayung to honor the dead. Heads were nodded in approval. Despite the disaster of their expedition up the mountain— or because of it—the storytellers were now at work converting it into legend. Arrowjoy had already heard versions of the Great White Prav repeated with variations and embroidery. It would grow until its fame gradually wiped out the sorrow and the tribe would finally come to think of it as a victory. For it was true that their enemies the Tantu were gone. They had vanished.

The party was launched with palm wine and arak and accelerated to drunkenness and dancing, with the men leaping up to act out the bravery of the fallen. When they had worn themselves down there were professionals, Malay dancing girls, who with a crook of a finger suggested paradise. Then the food, lavish and heaped on: curries, edible worms, fried tapioca and dozens of kinds of fish. But best was the meat, hunks of it cooked over open coals and slathered with hot sauces. At the end

Arrowjoy presented his own special gift. As he showed it, explaining its significance, teeth were sucked and breath escaped in wonder.

When the men returned to Rumah Bujana, Salt called the tribe together: his wife, Pepper, the women and children and old. Arranging themselves in a circle, he stood at its center and with great ceremony spread out Arrowjoy's gift. It was a large square of common butcher's paper, wrinkled and spotted with dried blood. It had held the frozen meat eaten at the feast.

Written in grease pencil across the paper in bold letters was a name:

Hartog

About the Author

William Overgard (1926–1990) was a syndicated cartoonist, screenwriter, and the author of several books, including *Shanghai Tango* and *A Few Good Men.*